D1042211

# DEATH
# EX MACHINA

Also by Gary Corby

*The Pericles Commission*

*The Ionia Sanction*

*Sacred Games*

*The Marathon Conspiracy*

# DEATH EX MACHINA

Gary Corby

First published in the United States by
Soho Press, Inc.
853 Broadway
New York, NY 10003

Library of Congress Cataloging-in-Publication Data

Corby, Gary.
Death ex machina / Gary Corby.

1. Nicolaos (Fictitious character : Corby)—Fiction.
2. Diotima (Legendary character)—Fiction. 3. Private investigators—
Fiction. 4. Murder—Investigation—Fiction. 5. Athens (Greece)—Fiction.
6. Greece—History—Athenian supremacy, 479-431 B.C.—Fiction. I. Title.
PR9619.4.C665D43 2015 823'.92—dc23 2014042465

HC ISBN 978-1-61695-519-9
PB ISBN 978-1-61695-676-9
eISBN 978-1-61695-520-5

Interior design by Janine Agro, Soho Press, Inc.

Printed in the United States of America

10 9 8 7 6 5 4 3 2 1

For Gweneth Mary Corby
because every writer has a Mum

# ATHENS

IN THE TIME OF

NICO & DIOTIMA

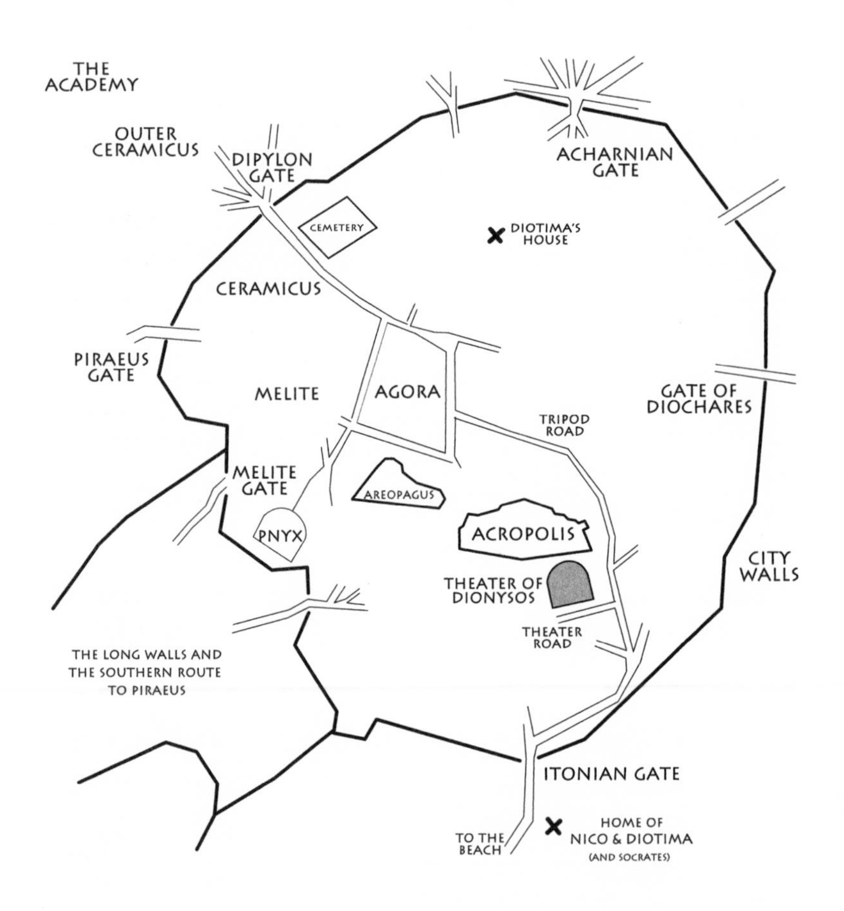

# THEATRICAL TERMS

MODERN THEATER COMES from the plays of classical Athens, including most of our theatrical terms. Many of the words haven't changed their meaning in 2,500 years. A chorus is still a chorus. An amphitheater is still an amphitheater. There's a certain magic in the idea that actors on stage today use the same words that you would have heard on stage in 458BC.

A few words have changed their meaning slightly. The wall at the back of the stage was called a *skene*. The latest innovation in Nico's time was to paint the skene to match the subject of the play. That's the origin of our words scene and scenery. In this book, Nico says skene to mean the wall, and scene to mean the action on stage.

In ancient Greek, the word orchestra means the place where the chorus stands. The classical Greek orchestra is the stage! To avoid confusion, Nico always uses the modern word stage where in his own tongue he would have said orchestra.

Greek plays were arranged in scenes, but they didn't have acts. Scenes were interspersed with songs sung by the chorus, who commented on the plot, rather like a narrator.

There is one technical term in this book written in Latin, which is an odd thing in a mystery of classical Athens, but that's how we know the term in modern English. I refer of course to the infamous plot technique, created by those dastardly Greeks, of *deus ex machina*.

# THE ACTORS

Every name in this book is a genuine one from the classical world. Some are still in use. To this day there are people named Nicolaos. It's also the origin of our Nicholas.

Other names you might already know because they belong to famous people, such as Socrates and Pericles.

But some names from thousands of years ago are unusual to our modern eyes. I hope you'll say each name however sounds happiest to you, and have fun reading the story.

For those who'd like a little more guidance, I've suggested a way to say each name in the character list. My suggestions do not match ancient pronunciation. They're how I think the names will sound best in an English sentence.

That's all you need to read the book!

**Characters with an asterisk by their name were real historical people.**

| | | |
|---|---|---|
| Nicolaos<br>NEE-CO-LAY-OS<br>(Nicholas) | Our protagonist | "How do you get a ghost out of a theater?" |
| Pericles*<br>PERRY-CLEEZ | A politician | "How in Hades should I know? That's your job." |
| Diotima*<br>DIO-TEEMA | A Priestess of Artemis<br>Wife of Nico | "There's no such thing as ghosts. Of course, there might be a *psyche* haunting the theater." |
| Socrates*<br>SOCK-RA-TEEZ | An irritant<br>Brother of Nico | "Have you ever wondered why dead bodies mummify?" |
| Sophocles*<br>SOFF-O-CLEEZ | A playwright<br>Author of *Sisyphus* | "That's the machine. We use it to lift actors into the air when they're playing gods." |
| Aeschylus*<br>AY-SHILL-US | A playwright | "Every writer in Athens is desperate to see his work at the Great Dionysia. It's a wonder there isn't a blood-bath every time the authors apply." |

| | | |
|---|---|---|
| Chorilos*<br>KORR-E-LOS | A playwright | "If only it were that simple." |
| Euripides*<br>YOU-RIP-ID-EEZ | A wannabe<br>Creepy and intense tragic fan | "My mother didn't send you, did she?" |
| Cleito*<br>CLY-TOE | Euripides's Mother | "You want to buy my onions?" |
| Lakon<br>LAY-KON | Lead actor (protagonist) of *Sisyphus* | "I'm not the monster you think I am." |
| Phellis<br>FELL-ISS | Second actor in *Sisyphus* | "It's not my fault. There's a slippery patch." |
| Romanos<br>ROM-AN-OS | Third actor in *Sisyphus* | "The fact is, if I'm to get ahead in my profession, then I must become a citizen." |
| Kebris<br>KEB-RIS | An old actor | "Death happens." |
| Kiron<br>KEE-RON | Stage manager | "You probably think I'm a tough boss." |
| Akamas<br>AK-AM-AS | Member of the stage crew | "If Thespis can be a ghost, and I saw a ghost, then it must be Thespis, right? That's logic." |
| Stephanos of Vitale<br>STEFF-AN-OS | Scene painter | "It's the clients in this town that drive me crazy. You wouldn't believe how many of them demand changes to perfectly good pictures." |
| Theokritos<br>THEO-KRIT-OS | High Priest of Dionysos | "Real men drink wine." |

| | | |
|---|---|---|
| Euboulides and Pheidestratos<br>YOU-BOL-EED-EEZ<br>FIE-DE-STRAT-OS | Two slaves of the Scythian Guard | "It don't normally take only a cup of wine to knock me down, master. Normally it's more like . . . uh . . . ten." |
| Melpon<br>MEL-PON | A doctor with a machine | "If you must throw up, do it outside." |
| Kordax<br>CORD-AX | Captain of *Salaminia* | "I've become addicted to speed. Do you know I've traveled faster than any man who's ever lived?" |
| Lysanias*<br>LIE-SAN-E-US | An elder statesman | "Is Athens in dire peril? Is our city on the verge of destruction?" |
| Pythax<br>PIE-THAX | Chief of the city guard of Athens<br>Father-in-law of Nicolaos | "Sisyphus had it coming to him." |
| Sophroniscus*<br>SOFF-RON-ISK-US | Father of Nicolaos | "Sometimes the best thing to do is accept a defeat and move on." |
| Phaenarete*<br>FAIN-A-RET-EE | Mother of Nicolaos<br>A midwife | "Your father is right, Nico." |
| Euterpe<br>YOU-TERP-E | Mother of Diotima | "I think you should thank me for choosing you such an interesting husband." |
| Habron*<br>HAB-RON | The Eponymous Archon<br>Also, he's the man in charge of the calendar | "What's the date today?" |
| The Basileus<br>BASS-IL-E-US<br>(origin of our word Basilica) | The city official in charge of religious affairs | "Gentlemen, this is a murder committed in the presence of the God." |

| | | |
|---|---|---|
| The Polemarch<br>POL-E-MARK | Official in charge of resident aliens in Athens | "That's it, then. We're doomed." |
| Andros<br>AND-ROSS | Assistant to the Polemarch | "Nobody ever reads government records. We just keep them." |
| Thodis<br>THOAD-ISS | Choregos (producer) of the play *Sisyphus* | "They tell me that protagonists are important people." |
| Maia<br>MAY-AH | A professional mourner | "*Euoi saboi! Euoi saboi!*" |
| Petros<br>PET-ROS | Husband of Maia | "Did you enjoy it?" |
| Sisyphus<br>SISSY-FUSS | King of Corinth Also, he pushes boulders uphill | A character in the play *Sisyphus* by Sophocles. |
| Thanatos<br>THAN-A-TOS | God of death | A character in the play *Sisyphus* by Sophocles. |
| Thespis*<br>THESP-ISS<br>As in, thespian | A ghost | The world's first actor. He's been dead for fifty years, but not even dead actors can resist an encore. |

## The Chorus

Assorted guardsmen, sailors, drunken revelers, actors, stage crew, and believe it or not, a Greek chorus!

# SCENE 1
# REHEARSAL FOR DEATH

IN MY TIME as an investigator I had received many difficult assignments, problems that were usually dangerous, often deadly, and sometimes downright impossible.

But no one before had ever asked me to arrest a ghost.

"You can't be serious, Pericles," I said.

"Of course I'm not," he replied. He sounded exasperated. "But unfortunately for both of us, the actors are completely serious."

"What actors?" I asked.

"The ghost is in the Theater of Dionysos," Pericles said. "The actors refuse to enter the theater until the ghost is gone."

"Oh," I said, and then, after I'd thought about it, "Oh dear."

The timing couldn't be worse, because the Great Dionysia was about to begin. The Dionysia was the largest and most important arts festival in the world. Thousands of people were flocking into Athens. They came from every corner of civilization: from the city states of Greece, from Egypt and Crete and Phoenicea and Sicily, from Ionia and Phrygia. All these people came to hear the choral performances and to see the plays: the comedies and the tragedies.

Most of all they came for the tragedies. Every city has fine singers. Every city has comics who can make you laugh. But only Athens, the greatest city in all the world, has tragedy.

"The producers have ordered the actors back to work," Pericles said. "The playwrights have begged them, even I have spoken to them, but the actors say they fear for their lives."

He wiped the sweat from his brow as he spoke. Pericles had hailed me in the middle of the agora, which at this time of the morning was always crowded. He had called me by my name, so loudly that every man, woman, and child in the marketplace had turned to look. Then Pericles had lifted the skirt of his ankle-length chiton and in full view of the people had run like a woman, leaping over jars of oil for sale and dodging around laden shoppers, all to speak with me. That alone told me how serious the situation was. Pericles prided himself on his statesman-like demeanor. It was part of the public image he courted as the most powerful man in Athens.

It was easy to see why Pericles was worried. If the actors refused to rehearse, they would put on poor performances. We would look like idiots before the rest of the civilized world. Or worse, the actors wouldn't be able to perform at all. The festival was in honor of the god Dionysos, who in addition to wine and parties was also the god of the harvest. If we failed to honor the God as was his due, then there was no telling what might happen to the crops. The people might starve if Dionysos sent us a poor year.

There was no doubt about it. The actors had to be induced to return to work.

Pericles said, "What I want you to do, Nicolaos, is make a show of investigating this ghost. Do whatever it is you do when you investigate a crime. Then do something—anything—to make the actors think you've captured the ghost."

"How do you get a ghost out of a theater?" I asked.

"How in Hades should I know?" Pericles said. "That's your job."

I couldn't recall placing a "Ghosts Expelled" sign outside my door.

"Surely there must be someone who can do this better than me," I said.

"You're the only agent in Athens, Nicolaos," Pericles said in persuasive tones. "The only one who'll investigate and then tell the people that the ghost is gone."

Which was true. Though there were plenty of thugs for hire, and mercenaries looking for work, I was the only man in Athens who took commissions to solve serious problems. I pointed out this commission aspect to Pericles.

"You may consider this a commission," Pericles said, through gritted teeth. He hated spending money.

The promise of pay put another complexion on it. When Pericles had waylaid me I had been on my way to see to my wife's property. My wife, Diotima, owned a house on the other side of the city, one in a sad state of disrepair. Repairs cost money. Money I didn't have.

I still didn't think I was the man for the job. Yet I reasoned it must be possible to remove a ghost, assuming such things even existed. Otherwise our public buildings would be full of them, considering how many centuries the city had stood.

Expelling a ghost might prove difficult, but it certainly wasn't dangerous, deadly, or downright impossible. I made an easy decision.

"Then I shall rid the theater of this ghost," I promised Pericles.

# SCENE 2
# THE PSYCHE OF THE GREAT DIONYSIA

THE CASE WAS urgent. I abandoned my plan to see to repairs and turned around. I had no idea about ghosts, but I knew someone who would. I went home to ask my wife.

I found Diotima in our courtyard. She reclined on a couch, with a bowl of olives and a glass of watered wine by her side. My little brother, Socrates, stood before her, reciting his lessons. Socrates had been expelled from school the year before, for the crime of asking too many questions. Ever since then, Diotima had been his teacher. The arrangement had worked surprisingly well.

I interrupted the lesson to deliver my news.

"There's no such thing as ghosts," Diotima said the moment I finished speaking. She paused, before she added thoughtfully, "Of course, there might be a *psyche* haunting the theater."

"Is there a difference, Diotima, between psyches and ghosts?" Socrates asked. He'd listened in, of course. I'd long ago given up any hope of keeping my fifteen-year-old brother out of my affairs.

"There's a big difference, Socrates," Diotima said. "Everybody has a *psyche*. It's your spirit, the part of you that descends to Hades when you die. Ghosts, on the other hand, are evil spirits that have never been people. The religion of the Persians has evil spirits that they call *daevas*. I think the Egyptians have evil spirits too. But we Hellenes don't credit such things."

"Then the actors might have seen a psyche?" Socrates said.

Diotima frowned. "I hope not. If a body hasn't been given

a proper burial then its psyche will linger on earth. It should never happen, but sometimes it does." She turned to me. "Nico, are there any dead bodies lying about the theater?"

"I like to think someone would have mentioned it if there were," I said. "If there's a body, we'll have to deal with it, but there's another possibility."

"What's that?" Diotima asked.

"That the actors are imagining things." I helped Diotima off the couch. "We'll have to go see for ourselves."

# SCENE 3
# THE GHOST OF THESPIS

SOCRATES TAGGED ALONG. There are few things harder to shake than a little brother.

Our house lies outside the city walls, to the southeast. The three of us entered the inner city through the Itonian Gate.

Two guards stood on duty, both of them bored, but too scared to slack off for fear their officer would check on them. They were *ephebes*, trainee recruits who were serving out their mandatory two years in the army, as must every young man from the moment he turns eighteen until he's twenty. I knew how bored they were because three years ago, I'd been one of them.

These two were local lads from our own deme. Their families lived only a few streets from our own. They knew us and waved us through with a pleasant word and an appreciative glance at Diotima.

Diotima wore a new chiton of linen that she'd dyed in bright party colors. When she'd appeared in it that morning, I'd pointed out that the Great Dionysia hadn't begun yet. Diotima had replied that it was close enough.

She wasn't the only one to have started early. Many of the travelers who passed through the gate were already in their best, brightest clothes. Complete strangers talked to one another, smiled and laughed at each others' jokes. Even the air we breathed was in a party mood. The one thing you are guaranteed to find at any gate in Athens is donkey droppings, yet on this day the aroma was fresh and pleasant. Diotima said it was because Gaia, who ruled the Earth, wished Dionysos well. I suggested it might have more to do with the frequent showers we'd been having. The rain kept down the dust. Diotima replied that was Gaia's way of arranging things.

We walked north up Tripod Road. Both sides were lined with three-legged braziers. They were the trophies given to previous winners at the Great Dionysia, each erected along this road, with a plaque, for the passersby to admire and for the victors to gloat. One of those trophies belonged to Pericles. He had been the *choregos*—the producer—of a winning play fourteen years ago. The truth is that Pericles had won because he'd hired Aeschylus to write the script. When you're Pericles, you can afford the very best. He was inordinately proud of that achievement. Every day since, Pericles had sent a slave to polish his trophy.

We turned left just before the Acropolis, onto a street that was well kept but that had seen recent heavy use. It was Theater Road, and right before us was the Theater of Dionysos. The Acropolis towered above, directly behind the theater.

A wooden wall painted in blues and reds blocked the view of the backstage. Men clustered at this wall. As we approached, we could hear them arguing with tired voices. The way they stood with shoulders bowed, I guessed they'd been at it for some time.

". . . and I tell you again, Sophocles, we're not going in there until the ghost is removed."

"I remind you once more, gentlemen, there are no such things as ghosts."

The man who didn't believe in ghosts was of middle age, with a long face that was well bearded. I thought he must buy his clothes from the same place as Pericles. Both of them were top-notch in respectable fashion. This man must be the one of the playwrights, or a choregos.

The argument broke off when Diotima, Socrates, and I stopped before them.

"Who are you?" one of the men asked. He was dressed in an *exomis*, typical clothing for an artisan. I guessed he must be a stagehand. I preferred an exomis myself because it left my arms and legs free to move.

"Nicolaos, son of Sophroniscus," I said. "Pericles asked me to look into this ghost."

The well-dressed man looked at me oddly.

"You're going to get rid of the ghost?" someone else asked. I would need to learn all their names before this was done. For now I thought of him as the one with the strong muscled arms.

"Yes," I said confidently.

"Who are they?" He pointed rudely at Diotima and Socrates.

"My brother and my assistant," I said. "This lady is an expert on ghosts."

Diotima looked startled. She said, "But Nico, there's no such thing as—ouch!"

I'd stamped on her foot.

"There's no such thing as a ghost Diotima can't find," I finished smoothly.

They looked doubtful.

"Well, I may as well get started," I said cheerfully. "Let's have a look at the haunted theater, shall we?"

"I'm not going in there, it's dangerous!" said the well-muscled man.

I'd wondered if the whole story might be an excuse to avoid work, but the man was genuinely scared. So, by the look of them, were the others. I said, "If you won't, who will?"

"I am Sophocles, son of Sophilos," the well-dressed man said.

"Are you a choregos, sir?" I asked.

Sophocles grimaced. "If I was, I would this moment be facing financial ruin. No, young man, I am the playwright, and if this problem is not solved then my only fear is utter professional disgrace before my fellow citizens."

He glared at the men about us.

"If these foolish men are too scared to enter the theater, I am not. Let us go."

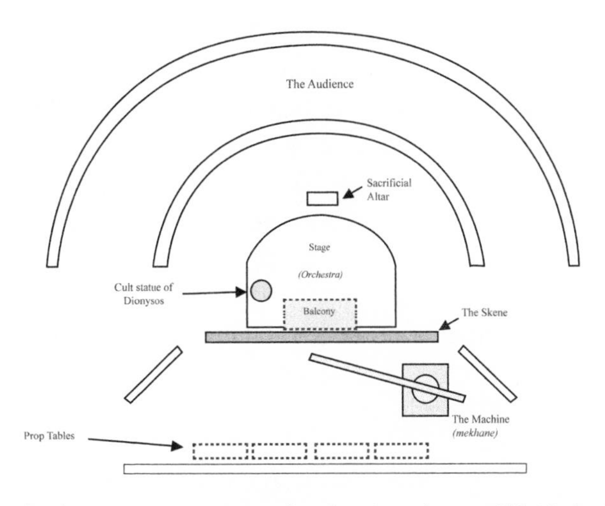


The backstage was open to the sky. Another wall hid the backstage area from the audience's view. The effect was a room with no roof and wide entrances to each side. The walls that were so gaudy on the outside were rough, unpainted and drab within. It seemed that theatrical illusion stopped at the surface.

One large item dominated the space.

"What is *that*?" I said, pointing.

"That's the machine," Sophocles said. "We use it to lift actors into the air when they're playing gods."

"Oh, of course."

I'd seen actors float off the ground during plays. They hung from a rope at the end of a wooden arm. I'd never given a thought to what must be happening behind the scenes. The machine looked much like the dockside cranes at the wharves at Piraeus. I said as much to Sophocles.

"Very similar," Sophocles agreed. "Ours is of more delicate construction. We need a longer arm to reach over the *skene*—that's the wall you see there that separates us from the stage—and ours has a thinner arm so it's less noticeable. Our machine only needs to lift a man."

"Sir, may I ask, how does the machine work?" Socrates asked. He stared at it in fascination.

Sophocles looked at the boy in surprise, then said, "Well, lad, three men hold the end with the short arm. They pull down and the long arm goes up. They push the short arm sideways and the long arm goes over the skene. It's very simple."

"Yes, sir, I see that," Socrates said. "But three men couldn't normally lift one man so high, could they?"

"No," Sophocles said.

"Then the machine must be doing something. How does it do that?"

Sophocles shrugged. "Who cares? It works. That's all a theater man needs to know."

"Thank you, sir," Socrates said politely.

Socrates walked over to inspect the machine more closely. I knew that would be the last we saw of him until he had worked out the machine to whatever satisfaction he required, or until someone physically dragged him away.

"Tell us about this ghost, Sophocles," Diotima said.

"I was startled when you said Pericles had sent you. He knows perfectly well there is no ghost."

I nodded. "His plan is not to try to convince the actors and crew that there is no ghost, but instead to fool them into thinking that the ghost has been removed. He thinks it would be easier than convincing people who believe in the ghost that there never was one."

"His idea is clever," Sophocles said.

I said, "Sophocles, what is it that's caused so much fear among the crew?"

Sophocles frowned and pursed his mouth. "There have been a few accidents, probably due to negligence among the men. That, and a little bad luck, and some over-active imaginations were enough to convince everyone that a malevolent spirit is haunting the Theater of Dionysos."

"I see." I didn't like the sound of that. Accidents and an over-active imagination are a normal part of life. But bad luck is sent by the Gods, and usually means something has offended them.

"Since we all agree that there's no ghost, what are we doing in here?" Sophocles asked.

"We're inspecting the entire theater, sir," I said. "So that we can report to the crew that we've found definite signs of the ghost and are taking steps to expel it. Then we'll go away, return with some seawater, some herbs, and a small sacrifice. Diotima will perform a ceremony—a genuine one so that the Gods are honored—and then we'll tell your actors and crew that the ghost is gone, cast out by . . . by . . ."

I wasn't sure who would cast out the ghost.

"By the power of the Lady Artemis, goddess of the hunt," Diotima finished. "She's the only goddess I'm qualified to officiate for."

Sophocles nodded his appreciation. "The Huntress is a fine choice for chasing an evil spirit." Then he frowned, in afterthought. "Should we not also sacrifice to Dionysos? It is his theater after all."

That was a good point.

"We'll need a priest of Dionysos," Diotima said.

"That will be no problem," said Sophocles. "The high priest of Dionysos is known to me."

Sophocles was clearly a man who moved in exalted circles. There was another important man who should be present, but I hadn't seen him. I asked, "Who is the choregos of your play, sir? Where is he?"

"His name is Thodis, of the deme Pallene. He returned to his home when it became clear that the actors could not be moved. Probably to weep in private."

Pallene was one of the most ancient demes, so old that it had once been its own city, until Athens grew to encompass it. It was a place of wealthy estate owners and old money. I could easily see how a man of Pallene would have the funds to back a tragedy in the Great Dionysia.

Diotima said, "You spoke of accidents."

"Things have gone wrong during rehearsals," Sophocles said. "But only since my play was given use of the theater. Before that, everything was running smoothly."

"I don't understand," I said.

"There are ten choral performances, five comedies, and three tragedies to be played, in that order. It's the custom that we take turns for use of the theater, to practice our work, in the order in which we appear."

"I see," I said.

"The tragedies occupy the final three days because they are the most important event," Sophocles said without the slightest hint of modesty. "By the drawing of lots my play is the final performance. I am therefore last to rehearse in the theater. There were problems from the moment we took possession. No one noticed at first because things always go wrong during rehearsals. Then the wave of little problems mounted until even the stage crew began to mutter. Each incident on its own was entirely trivial, or obvious bad luck."

"Could you list them, please?" I said.

"The first was the broom left lying at the stage entrance. Romanos tripped over it as he made an entrance."

"Romanos is?"

"Our third actor—the *tritagonist*. It was only a little thing, really, but it spoke of sloppiness on the part of the stagehands. Kiron—he's the stage manager—had harsh words for everyone who works backstage. They all denied dropping it."

"It doesn't seem like much," I said dubiously.

"That's what I just told you," Sophocles said in exasperation. "But then we all fell ill."

"Surely a ghost couldn't cause that."

"No, but the tainted water in the water bottles could."

Sophocles pointed to the back tables, where amongst all the stage kit was a row of ceramic water coolers and clay cups.

"We drink from those. The slave who sees to filling them must have collected bad water, because after a rehearsal a few days ago every one of us fell ill. Half of us had vomiting and diarrhoea. We couldn't work the next day, and it was a struggle the day after."

Bad water happens to every household from time to time. It only needs the house slave to fill the water bottles from the public fountain at an unlucky time.

"What else?" I asked.

"The broken props. We came in one morning to find that the masks had been torn."

Diotima had walked to the back wall. A row of tables was arrayed along it.

"These?" Diotima asked. She picked up a mask that lay on the prop tables.

Sophocles nodded. "Precisely. The actors wear them, to represent different characters. All our masks were damaged one night. We arrived to find them slashed."

"By a knife?"

"It looked more like claw marks to me. I thought some animal must have got at them. Perhaps a wild cat. I had to ask the choregos to pay for new masks. Fortunately the maskmaker was available. He'd finished all the masks for the festival. But he charged extra. *He* at least didn't think there was a ghost. Oh no. He thought we hadn't taken proper care of his work." Sophocles threw his arms up in frustration. "By this time the muttering among the men had turned to open talk. They are convinced it's the ghost of Thespis."

"Who's Thespis?"

"The first man ever to act on stage. He's long dead. My friend Aeschylus tells of seeing Thespis act when he was but a small boy. Aeschylus says Thespis was not only the first actor, but the best he's ever seen."

I knew Aeschylus. He was an old man about to retire. If he'd seen this Thespis as a small boy, then Thespis had indeed lived long ago. I pointed out the obvious, "If it's the ghost of Thespis, then why did he wait all this time to appear?"

Sophocles grimaced. "It's nonsense of course. I'm afraid it was me who put the idea of Thespis in their heads. Rehearsals haven't been going well. You can see why. To lighten the mood I made a half-hearted joke that Thespis would be furious with us if he saw the state of our play. Someone latched onto my comment and magnified it into an angry spirit. The worst was when one of the men saw the ghost."

"What?"

"Akamas. He's one of the stagehands. The one who was rude to you out back. He's also a troublemaker. He says he was in here late one night and saw the ghost. That was the over-active imagination I told you about. He turned up next morning babbling about a ghost in the theater."

I made a mental note to talk to this Akamas.

Sophocles went on, "That same morning, the railing on the balcony suddenly collapsed. No one was hurt, fortunately, but it was a close call for Lakon, who was standing on it at the time. That was the end of any chance of getting the players to play."

"Where's the balcony?" I asked.

Sophocles led us around the skene and onto the stage.

The balcony was directly above us, held up on four long wooden legs that had been painted white. It looked sturdy enough.

Sophocles pointed. "The actors stand there when they are playing a god. During the incident with the railing, Lakon leaned upon it, and the railing simply fell away. He almost went over with it, which would have been a disaster for the play. Lakon is our first actor, our *protagonist*. He's irreplaceable." He sighed. "I had harsh words for the carpenters. They fixed it at once, but what's the point if the actors won't play?"

"Must gods stand upon the balcony?" I asked. "Maybe you could avoid it."

Sophocles held his hands up in horror. "Don't even suggest it. Imagine if you were the goddess Athena, I mean *the real goddess*, and you looked down from Mount Olympos to see that someone in Athens was not only pretending to be you, but stood on the same level as ordinary mortals. How would you feel?"

I thought about it. "Not good," I said.

"Exactly. Our gods stand above the crowd, to avoid insulting the real ones."

"Does Athena appear in your play, Sophocles?" Diotima asked.

"No. I have Zeus, the king of the Gods, and Thanatos, the god of death."

"Death! What's the play about?" I asked. "Or shouldn't I ask?"

"Certainly you may ask. The title is *Sisyphus, King of Corinth*. The story is of that ancient king's fall from power due to his serious personality defects, and his subsequent terrible punishment in Hades."

"Doomed to push the boulder uphill, only to have it roll back down again, for all eternity," I said.

"Yes, that's how the play ends." Sophocles sighed. "The net result of all these problems is that, even if the actors and crew return to work at once, we still won't be ready in time for the Great Dionysia."

"Don't worry, Sophocles," I said. "We'll help you."

"So you will tell the men the ghost is gone?" Sophocles said.

I thought about the bottles of tainted water, the broken props, and the damaged balcony.

I said, "The problem is, I think the ghost might be real."

# SCENE 4
# THE MASK

"NO, I DON'T think there's an evil spirit haunting the theater," I said. "But I'm sure there's a mortal man of ill will. Someone's trying to wreck the play."

Diotima and I had left the theater, leaving behind Socrates, who was still prodding and poking the machine. We had stopped only long enough to tell the men waiting outside that we had detected clear signs of a malign presence (which was true), that we knew how to deal with it (which was also true), and that by the time we were finished there would be no ghost in the theater (take that one as you will).

"They all look like accidents, Nico. You can't prove otherwise," said my wife, who is the logical one in our partnership.

"Yes, but there've been too many to call it coincidence. The best explanation is sabotage," I told her. I'm the cynical, suspicious one.

Diotima bit her lip while she thought about it. "I was wondering the same thing," she admitted. "But I'm less certain than you are. Why would someone want to wreck the Dionysia?"

I had no idea.

I said, "Maybe he's merely an idiotic prankster. Do we necessarily have to know his motive? Or even find him? The job after all is to get the actors and crew back to work. We can expel the imaginary ghost without having to find the real culprit."

"But if you're right, the saboteur will try again," Diotima said.

"So we'll be on the lookout for him. We'll watch every rehearsal, check everything every morning. If he tries again, we'll catch him."

We had stopped on the corner of Theater Street and Tripod Road. The backstage of the theater was clearly visible from there, including the wide-open side entrance.

Diotima pointed and said, "Anyone could walk in there, any time they wanted. You can guard the theater all day, Nico, but your prankster could sneak in at night, no trouble."

That was true.

"I'll arrange for a watchman," I said.

"How?" she asked dubiously.

"I'll think of something. We have to stop him."

"You really think these are pranks then?" Diotima asked.

"A troublemaker, for sure."

"Sophocles called one of the stage crew a troublemaker," Diotima said.

"The one with the muscles. Akamas. We'll have to look into him."

"Then this is the perfect moment," Diotima said. "Because here he comes."

Which indeed he did. Akamas was walking down Theater Road, swinging his arms with a slight swagger.

I held up my hand as he passed and said, "Akamas, I'd like a word."

He stopped and stared at us. "Yeah? I got business to attend to."

I was surprised. "You do? But rehearsals are stopped until the ghost is gone."

"That don't stop me drinking. There's a decent tavern over there." He pointed to a place across the street.

It wasn't even lunchtime yet. The value of anything Akamas had to say was going rapidly downhill.

"Sophocles told us you saw the ghost."

"Yeah."

I waited. Akamas had nothing else to say.

"What happened?" I prompted.

"I saw the ghost. It was nighttime."

"What were you doing in the theater at night?" I asked.

He spat on the ground. "Kiron made me work late after everyone else had gone."

"Kiron's the stage manager?"

"Yeah. He said one of the actors had complained about the footing on the stage. Said it was too slippery. I had to grind it rougher. That was when I saw it."

"The ghost?"

"I was down on my hands and knees, scrubbing the stage floor with a stone, you know? I looked up, there it was."

"Standing in front of you?"

"No. On the balcony. Way above me. I don't know what made me look up that high. Maybe some movement."

"What did it look like?"

Akamas scratched his head. "It was getting dark, you know? With the festival so close they work until it's too dark to see. I saw the outline and I saw it was acting, but no sound was coming out."

This was interesting. "Acting how?" I asked.

Akamas shrugged. "I dunno. You know how actors move around. They exaggerate everything? It was like that. It was like there was an audience there and the ghost was acting to it."

"But no sound," I repeated.

"Totally silent," he agreed. "Until the whistle."

"Whistle?" I repeated.

"Yeah. The ghost kind of disappeared. Just faded away. Then from nowhere I heard this ghostly whistle."

"What were you doing while all this happened?" Diotima asked.

"I was . . . er . . ."

"Backing away?" I suggested. It was obvious Akamas had been terrified, but as a proper man he would never admit to it.

"Getting ready to attack the ghost if it came my way," Akamas said.

Diotima said, "Was the noise in front or behind you?"

"In front."

"So from where the ghost had been standing?"

"Maybe from behind the skene," Akamas said. "I dunno. It was dark."

"Anything else?" I asked.

"Sophocles said it was the ghost of Thespis."

That wasn't quite the way Sophocles had explained it. "Sophocles told me he made a joke about this Thespis."

Akamas shrugged. "Same thing. If Thespis can be a ghost, and I saw a ghost, then it must be Thespis, right? That's logic."

"I know you said it was getting dark, but did you see its face?"

"No. I told you it was acting. The ghost wore a mask."

"What mask?"

"The mask of comedy."

"IT'S A MAN for sure," I said, after Akamas had departed for the wine. We had extracted only one extra piece of information: that the well-muscled man had run away from the ghost.

"Let's go back to the theater for a moment. There's something I want to see." I led Diotima to the balcony on the stage. This was where the ghost had appeared.

I stared at the wall, saw what I expected to see, and walked behind the skene to backstage. Built into the skene was a small door, exactly where the balcony stood on the other side, and below the door a small ladder for access.

"This is how the actors exit the balcony, isn't it?" I asked Kiron the stage manager. He was still there, tidying up.

"Yes, it is," Kiron said. "The door is low so the audience can't see it."

"This is how our 'ghost' exited," I said to Diotima, after Kiron departed. "I'll bet he wore a black cloak. When he was done, he swirled the cloak over himself and crouched down. From the audience side, in the dark, it would look like he disappeared, just faded away. He opens the door, crawls through to backstage, and then he wanders off, whistling."

"Whistling because he's of a happy disposition?" Diotima asked.

"Or for the effect," I said. "It really would sound eerie, coming from out of sight, echoing around the empty theater."

Diotima nodded. "Your theory of a prankster sounds good, Nico."

"We'll stop him," I said. "We'll watch like hungry hawks."

# SCENE 5
# DRAMA THERAPY

THE DESTRUCTION OF the ghost went without a hitch. There was already a sacrificial altar installed at the theater, in front of the stage. The altar was made from quality marble. It was a permanent fixture of the theater that saw frequent use, because every day of the Great Dionysia begins and ends with a sacrifice.

The statue of the God was in his place for the festival. Before the Dionysia begins, the cult statue of Dionysos is taken from his nearby temple and settled on stage, so that Dionysos can observe the plays in his honor.

The High Priest of Dionysos was a middle-aged man named Theokritos, with a round belly and a bald patch. His affable looks belied his business-like approach to priestly affairs.

The first act of Theokritos the High Priest was to bow before the God. He then turned back to the altar, where Diotima stood waiting, with a goat on a tether.

The rest of us sat on the audience benches. All the actors of all the plays were present, both the comedies and the tragedies, and the singers of the choral performances, plus the *choregoi* and the three tragic playwrights for this Dionysia—Aeschylus, Sophocles, and another man named Chorilos. I had gathered them all, with help from Pericles, to make sure *everyone* saw the cleansing.

I myself sat beside my father-in-law, Pythax, who was chief of the Scythian Guard of Athens, but who was with us this day in his role as proud father. This was Diotima's first official ceremony since becoming a married woman. When Pythax had heard that his daughter would be performing before the combined artistic dignitaries of Athens, nothing could keep him away. He watched as closely as anyone, a slight smile on his lips.

Theokritos offered the blade to the goat. The goat stared at the sharp knife for a long moment, while everyone held their breath. Then the animal seemed to nod its head.

A collective sigh of relief swept across the audience.

The hand that held the blade swept across the goat's throat. Blood poured quickly into a bowl held by Diotima beneath the wound. Both she and the High Priest were spattered, but both were far too professional to flinch. The goat stood stock still for longer than I thought possible. Then its legs buckled. Diotima and the High Priest were ready. Diotima lowered the bowl as the sacrifice fell. Theokritos had his arms wrapped around the animal so that it came to earth gently.

"It was a good sacrifice," someone behind me said. "The victim went willingly."

Voices all about echoed the same sentiment. The sacrifice had been as perfect as could be. I breathed a silent thanks to Sophocles for recommending this priest. He was excellent.

Theokritos waved to his attendants. Three men hurried from amongst us to take the deceased goat, one at each end to carry the animal by the legs and another in the middle to take the weight. These three hurried out of the theater. They would take the animal to the Temple of Dionysos, a mere hundred paces to the southwest. A butcher and a hot brazier waited there, to cook the sacrifice.

The meat would be given to those poor of Athens who asked for it, to feed families whose children would not otherwise see meat this month.

The sacrifice to Dionysos was complete. Now it was Diotima's turn. Theokritos stood back.

Diotima placed the bowl of blood upon the altar. The bowl was full right to the brim. Some of the blood sloshed over the side as she set it down. It formed a small puddle upon the altar.

Diotima raised her arms. The sleeves of her chiton fell back to bunch at her shoulders and expose the skin. Her hands and wrists were red with blood. It trickled down her arms.

"Hear me, Lady Artemis of the Hunt, I am your priestess Diotima," she said. "Artemis, daughter of Zeus, who rejoices in the chase and the kill, who shoots the arrow from your golden bow. Hunt with me, Goddess, to cast from this place the malign influence that inhabits it."

Diotima lowered her arms. She picked up the bowl.

"Far-shooting Artemis, I hold the blood of sacrifice to your kinsman Dionysos, he whose place is profaned. Let this blood mark the boundary, Lady Artemis, swift Huntress, you whose father mighty Zeus gave permission to kill at your pleasure: let all within these bounds who oppose your kinsman Dionysos be your rightful prey."

At these words Diotima lowered the bowl and tipped it, ever so slightly. A thin stream of blood began to fall. At once Diotima began to walk around the entire theater, dribbling blood into the dust as she went. The entire audience followed behind, to see the deed done.

Diotima crossed the ground between stage and audience, then turned to walk down the side, pouring all the while. When the theater was at her back she turned again to walk parallel to the backstage area, before returning to the front, where she ended at the altar. The last of the blood dripped from the bowl at the moment the two ends of the red line met. The theater was bordered in blood.

Diotima put the bowl on the altar. She wiped the sweat from her eyes, inadvertently smearing blood across her brow.

Slaves hurried forward to take the bowl and, at her nod of permission, carried it away to be cleaned.

The ceremony was over. Men stood to mill about and talk. Diotima walked over to me and smiled.

"How did I do?" she asked.

"Excellent," I said. I wanted to kiss her, but it would have scandalized the old men about us. Not even Pythax would have approved. This was not the time to upset people.

Everyone had gathered in clusters to talk about the ceremony. They spoke to each other in a friendly, relaxed, confident tone that had been entirely absent in the theater yesterday.

Sophocles broke away from one of these groups and came across to speak to us. "The ceremony went well," he said.

I said, "No ghost in its right mind is going to wait for the Huntress to come calling."

Sophocles stroked his beard and smiled in satisfaction.

"I believe you are correct. Already the men ask when rehearsals can resume. I told them we begin at once. I must see to arrangements."

Sophocles hurried off.

Another man emerged from the largest group of chatterers. It was Theokritos, the High Priest of Dionysos.

"You did exceptionally well for such a young lady," he said to Diotima.

"Thank you, sir." Diotima fell into the demure pose she reserved for middle-aged men who thought they were smarter than she.

Theokritos wasn't fooled for an instant. "No need to play that game with me," he said. "I can see you know your business. Where have you served?" he asked, meaning, in which temples had Diotima served the Goddess, for it was obvious that Diotima was temple trained.

"The Temple of Artemis Agroptera here in Athens, and the Artemision at Ephesus," Diotima said.

"The Artemision!" Theokritos was impressed, as well he

might be. The Artemision was the most prestigious temple in the entire world.

Theokritos said, "The Temple of Dionysos could use a good priestess. We have places available. I don't suppose you'd consider switching allegiance?"

"Thank you sir, but I serve Artemis," Diotima said.

"Well, the Huntress gains where the god of wine loses," he said, cheerfully. "You'll let me know if you change your mind."

With those words and a nod, Theokritos gathered his slaves and departed.

Pythax had stood to the side. He had heard the words of Theokritos with pride for his daughter.

"Well done, lass," Pythax said, when Theokritos had left. To my surprise he gave Diotima a hug, in public. Pythax was not a demonstrative man, unless you counted the way his guards demonstrated their clubs whenever they caught a thief.

"It was a lucky thing the goat was so complacent," I said to Diotima.

"That would be due to the large amount of poppy juice I fed it this morning," Diotima said. "The goat didn't feel a thing."

The nature of the smoke rising not far to the southwest changed. An aroma of barbecue wafted across the theater. It reminded me of lunch and made me hungry. The other men thought the same. They quickly departed, in twos and threes, no doubt to their homes for an early bite. One of the last to leave, on his own, was a young man. I had noticed him before, when he sat at the back of the audience. He had watched the ritual with an expression that struck me as rather intense.

I pointed him out to Diotima and Pythax.

"Is there something wrong with him?" she asked.

"I don't think he's a member of the crew," I said. "I didn't see him speak to anyone else."

"It's a public theater," Diotima said. "Maybe he's interested."

"Maybe. But you and I know we have to be on the look out for a saboteur."

Diotima gave the back of the departing stranger another look. "We could chase him down?" she said.

Pythax snorted. "No you can't. He's a citizen, it's a free city, and he ain't committed a crime."

Those words from the city's senior law enforcer ended the question.

"Well, nothing can go wrong at today's rehearsal," Diotima said "We didn't announce the ritual until the last moment, a hundred people have been watching the stage, there hasn't been time for the saboteur to do any damage since, and the rehearsal is about to start."

Indeed it was. Men were already on the stage, preparing. Backstage, someone was shouting at the chorus to get in line.

In the time I had, I took a quick look at the God's statue. I had never before seen our city's statue of Dionysos up close. Our Dionysos was wooden, and very old. The God was sculpted in the stiff style of past generations. There were cracks where the wood had dried and shrunk. Those had been artfully hidden under recent paint. The eyes in particular looked very realistic. They were the eyes of a god who saw everything.

One thing the God saw, standing as he was at the far edge of the stage, was something that hadn't been there yesterday. Someone had painted words onto the rear wall, out of view of the audience but fully visible to everyone backstage. They were in large, unmissable letters of commanding red paint, and they said:

NO WHISTLING!

I entered the chaos of the preparations backstage to ask what it was for.

"I just put it up," said Akamas.

"Why?" I asked.

"You expelled the ghost, right?" he said.

"Right," I agreed. That, after all, was what Pericles had hired me to do; to convince everyone that the ghost had been sent away.

"Well, we don't want the ghost to come back, do we?" Akamas said.

I thought about trying to explain that there was no ghost, realized that was futile, and instead said, "No, of course not."

Akamas said knowingly, "Well then, there was whistling when I saw the ghost. So if no one whistles, it won't tempt the ghost to return, or bring back the bad luck with it. That's logic, right?"

It wasn't any logic that I recognized. But I could sense that all around me, the crew and actors were listening in on this conversation, waiting to see how I would react. If I told them to remove the sign, they might think the ghost could return.

It occurred to me that the signed command couldn't do any harm, and if it made the actors and crew feel more comfortable and safer in the theater then it was all to the good. So I said, "Excellent thinking, Akamas. Keep up the good work."

At that moment the chorus began, singing the opening song. I had to run across the stage to the audience seats. Sophocles shot me a look of reproach—he was directing from the front—but he was too polite to rebuke the man who had cleared the theater of ghosts.

Diotima and I had promised to keep an eye out for any recurrence of a saboteur. That was the excuse we used to settle down in the front row and enjoy the play.

# SCENE 6
# FALL FROM FAVOR

THE PLAY BEGAN in earnest. The chorus finished singing the opening song. They bowed in homage before the statue of the God. Even in a rehearsal this religious observance was required, lest the God be offended.

An elbow jabbed me. It was Pythax, who sat on my right. Diotima was on my left.

"What's happening?" Pythax whispered.

"We're sitting in an amphitheater watching a rehearsal," I said.

"Yeah. That's what I mean. What's it about?" He sounded embarrassed.

I suddenly realized that Pythax, who was from Scythia to the far north of Hellas, didn't know the great stories as we knew them.

"The play's about the legend of Sisyphus," I told him.

Pythax grunted. "The guy with the boulder. If that's all that happens it's going to be a bit boring, isn't it?"

"The boulder is the end of the story, Pythax. It starts with Sisyphus as king of Corinth. He's a bad king. He kills visitors to his city just for laughs. He tries to kill his brother. He seduces his own niece."

Pythax thought about that for a moment. "The man's an asshole," he concluded.

My father-in-law had clear views on the proper behavior for a man.

"Zeus feels the same way you do," I said. "Zeus sends

Thanatos, the god of death, to capture Sisyphus in chains and carry him off to Hades."

Pythax nodded approval. "Sisyphus has it coming to him."

"Right. Only Sisyphus asks Thanatos how the chains work, and Thanatos demonstrates the chains on himself."

Pythax looked at me as if I were insane. "You're joking, aren't you?" he said, then added loudly, "If one of my guardsmen screwed up an arrest that badly, I'd tear the skin off him."

Sophocles stood before the stage shouting directions as the actors acted and the chorus sang. He had stopped them several times to make them do parts again. Now he turned and shot Pythax and me a black look.

"If you can't be quiet, there are other places to chatter," he said. "We're under-rehearsed as it is, as you can plainly see. We'll be here all night at this rate." There was sweat on his brow, and it wasn't from the day's heat.

"I'm sorry, Sophocles," I said. "We'll be quiet."

Sophocles turned back to his actors. One of them tripped right at that moment. He sprawled hands first across the stage.

"Dear Gods, Phellis," Sophocles shouted. "Can't you stay upright?"

"It's not my fault, Sophocles," Phellis said. "There's a slippery patch."

That halted everything while both Sophocles and the stage manager came to inspect.

Sophocles rubbed his foot over a patch of the stage. He frowned. "So there is. How did that happen?"

Kiron yelled, "Akamas!"

Akamas emerged from behind the skene. "Yeah?"

Kiron put his hands on his hips and said angrily, "I ordered you to roughen the stage floor."

"I *did*," Akamas insisted.

"Then how come it's smooth and slippery?!" Kiron yelled.

"It's not *my* fault," Akamas bellowed.

I wondered if they might come to blows.

Another man walked to stand between the stage manager and his crewman. It was Romanos, the third actor, acting as a peacemaker. "There've been hundreds of men standing about here all morning, Sophocles," Romanos said. "Maybe one of them was planning to go to the gymnasium next, maybe he's got a leaky oil flask."

Sophocles shrugged. "We'll never know," he said.

The stage manager snorted his disgust and signaled to two slaves who stood to the side. "Bring sand," he ordered.

It must have been a common occurrence, because the slaves instantly shoveled beach sand from a small nearby heap into a bucket. They scattered it across the stage like a farmer feeding chickens.

Sophocles returned to his position at front of stage.

"Is the actor all right?" I asked.

"It was a lucky escape," Sophocles said. He frowned. "We only have three days before the Dionysia begins. The only actor who has his lines down is Romanos, and he's our third. In the state we're in now, it's going to be a disaster."

"Is there anything you can do, Sophocles?" Diotima asked.

"Extra rehearsals," Sophocles said. He sweated freely. "Also every morning and evening for the next three days I'll be sacrificing to Dionysos. A little divine intervention wouldn't hurt at this stage." He clapped his hands. "Onwards!" he announced to the actors.

Two men appeared, one from each side of the stage. The first wore a tragic mask and kingly robes threaded in gold. The second wore the mask of a supplicant and a bright formal chiton. The first I guessed must be Lakon, playing Sisyphus. The second must be Phellis. Beneath the masks and robes it was impossible to recognize them, though I had seen both actors only moments before. They must have changed clothes and masks in an instant. Each character announced who he was in his first lines—I had guessed correctly—and the play went on. Both actors stumbled over words from time to time and Sophocles had to prompt them.

"I wasn't joking about the chains, Pythax," I said quietly, as the actors declaimed their lines. "Wait and see what happens in the play. Sisyphus tricks the god of death into chaining himself. Thanatos escapes, eventually, and when he does he carries Sisyphus off to Hades. That's the first time he dies."

"The *first*?"

"Sisyphus talks the Queen of the Underworld into letting him come back to Earth. He says he has to arrange his own funeral."

"And she believed that, did she?"

"Apparently so. Then Sisyphus refuses to return to Hades. Eventually Zeus, the king of the Gods, gets tired of all the mistakes. That's when Sisyphus dies for the second time. Zeus personally carts Sisyphus off to Hades and arranges the boulder scheme."

The play went as I'd outlined to Pythax. Sisyphus the crafty king of Corinth managed to offend everyone. When Zeus had had enough, he sent Thanatos to collect the miscreant king.

The god of death was about to descend from Mount Olympus.

In the background, the long arm of the machine rose. It was painted to match the background. The rope that hung below had been painted sky blue; it was almost invisible in the daylight.

The God appeared above the skene, suspended from the machine. I gasped.

I'd expected Thanatos to be a shining, fearsome god, but Sophocles had done something else, something quite innovative. Sophocles had given the god of death the appearance of a corpse. The actor seemed to hang from a noose. His neck was slumped over at an odd angle. His body was flaccid.

I'd seen men hanged, and this was so like the real thing that I could have sworn a corpse had risen. Diotima grabbed my arm.

The dangling corpse crossed over the skene into the air above the stage.

The neck, which I could have sworn was snapped, suddenly jerked up. The eyes within the mask opened. They stared at us. First at Diotima and Pythax and me, for that was how he faced. Then the direction of his gaze lowered until he saw the playwright. He opened his mouth to speak.

"Sophocles, this harness hurts like Hades," the god of death complained. "There's something wrong with it."

"You only wear it for a few moments, Phellis," Sophocles said in patient, soothing tones. He was obviously used to dealing with actors. "You're a professional. You can do it."

For a moment there they'd had me completely fooled. The actors might be behind on their lines, but if this was to be the standard of the play, it might very well win the contest.

"It doesn't feel right, Sophocles," Phellis said. "I honestly think something's wrong with the harness."

"There's nothing wrong with it," the stage manager shouted. "I made that harness myself."

"I'm sorry, Kiron, but there is," Phellis shouted back. "The harness is pressing under my armpits, and it's not in the right position at my back. Look!"

Phellis twisted to show those of us on the ground what he meant.

At that moment, we all heard a loud snap.

The god of death hung in mid-air. Then he fell.

# SCENE 7
# BREAK A LEG

PHELLIS SCREAMED.

The bone had broken through the skin of his right leg. It poked out at an unsightly angle. He lay crumpled upon the stage where he had hit feet first. Phellis wanted to roll, but he couldn't because of the leg. He was reduced to rocking back and forth in agony.

"Hold him down!" the stage manager shouted. He'd heard the thud of the falling body and emerged from behind to see what had gone wrong.

Pythax, Diotima, and I rushed to the middle of the stage. Lakon stood there in shock.

Pythax used his immense strength to hold down Phellis.

I said, "Diotima, that poppy juice you fed to the goat, is there any left over?"

Diotima nodded. She ran to the backstage area to collect the bag she brought with her.

Sophocles stood over us. He had gone dead white.

The stage manager said, "I don't understand it. The harness was perfect." He sounded stricken.

Diotima returned with her pouch. From it she produced a flask that was half full. Phellis had reduced himself to sobbing. Diotima poured all the poppy juice she had into Phellis while the stage manager and I inspected the rope that dangled from the machine.

Kiron said, "There should be a metal ring. It goes through the loop of leather strap on the actor's harness."

Indeed there was no ring. Nor was it still attached to the harness. I said, "Where is it?"

One of the slaves pointed at the ground, a few paces from the stage. "Here it is!"

There lay a metal ring, of the sort you might see in a boat, through which lines could be run.

I picked it up. The metal on one side had broken away. The leather strap must have fallen through the gap. No wonder Phellis had fallen.

I held it up to show the stage manager.

"Let me see that." He snatched it from my hand, turned it this way and that. "This has been filed," he said.

"You're only saying that to avoid responsibility for your incompetence," said the third actor. He had joined us as we searched.

"That's not true, Romanos," said the stage manager angrily. "I checked everything personally."

Romanos snorted. "A likely story." He pointed at the machine. "Any one of us could have been up there when that thing snapped." Then he pointed at the shattered leg of Phellis. "That could have been me!"

I took back the ring. I held it this way and that, and stared at it closely. There were striations that, had I seen them on marble in my father's workshop, I would have said was the work of a hard metal file.

I said, "This is evidence."

"Evidence of what?" the stage manager demanded.

"I don't know yet."

Diotima had finished feeding poppy juice to Phellis. He lay quieter, but his terrible wound was still there.

Diotima asked, "Where's the nearest doctor?"

"I know of one," said Kiron. "There's a healer who lives in Collytus."

That was the deme directly south of us.

"They say he's very good," Kiron added.

He would need to be.

"Take us there," I said.

Kiron gave instructions to a slave, who nodded. That slave and another lifted Phellis, who rose from his stupor to scream again when his shattered leg was grabbed by thigh and calf. But there was nothing else the slave could have done. The leg couldn't be left to dangle while they carried him.

The slaves struggled to carry the actor to the nearby doctor, who people said was good. Phellis passed out on the way.

# SCENE 8
# THE HEALING MACHINE

"WILL HE LIVE?" I asked.

"How in Hades should I know?" the doctor said testily.

We had been admitted to the doctor at once. He kept a large house in a busy street. The house slave opened the door to my insistent knocking. The first thing we saw within were twelve children playing together in the open courtyard. Six boys and six girls of different sizes. They took no notice of strangers carrying a wounded man.

"The master's children," the slave explained without being asked. I wondered if the doctor sold fertility potions.

The slave showed us into the front room. When the doctor arrived—his name was Melpon—he shook his head over the broken leg and told us to follow him. The slaves carried Phellis into another room where, in the middle, squatted a large, ominous-looking wooden table. We laid Phellis there.

Melpon peered closely at the break. He even used his hands to gently pull away the torn skin. Merely watching him turned my stomach.

Melpon looked up at us. "Why isn't he screaming?" he said. "This man should be almost dead of the pain."

"We fed him some extract of poppy," Diotima told the doctor. "The same as I use on sacrifices."

Melpon shrugged. "Well, you're an untrained woman, but I suppose you know what you're saying. What matters is that we have to save this leg." Then he added harshly, "If we can."

The doctor seemed a stressed sort of person. I supposed it was from having to deal with sick people all the time.

"The leg is attached to a man," I pointed out.

He softened at my words. "It lies with the Gods," he said. "Sometimes you do everything you can, but the flesh-eating sickness gets them anyway. I hate it when that happens. I've learned the hard way not to hope too much. How did this happen?"

"He fell from the god machine. The one at the theater. This man is an actor."

"He used to be an actor. Now he's a cripple."

"You mean he won't be able to walk again?" Diotima asked.

"He'll be lucky if he keeps the leg," the doctor said. "If he does, he'll walk with a limp for the rest of his life. That's the best I can offer."

I was sure the harness had been sabotaged. Whoever had done it hadn't only damaged the play, he'd ruined Phellis's life.

The doctor bent over the unconscious Phellis. Diotima leaned over too.

Melpon glanced up at Diotima beside him. "You seem to be interested in medicine, young lady."

"Yes," Diotima said.

"Then I will show you something. Do you see here?" The doctor poked his finger inside Phellis's leg. Diotima didn't turn a hair; instead she watched with interest.

"The bone sheared away," the doctor said. "Like a stick that breaks when you push from both ends. I suppose he fell feet first."

"That's right," Diotima said. "How did you know?"

"The sharp end of the broken half pierced his skin. Here." He pointed just above the knee. "Once the bone had come through the skin it was like a knife ripping through soft fabric. That's why the wound's so long. It wasn't helped by the muscles pushing the bone along. The muscles are these bits here, here and here." The doctor pointed out these parts to Diotima, who leaned closer.

The doctor said, "Often when that happens the patient bleeds to death and there's nothing anyone can do. Your friend was lucky."

The doctor had an interesting idea of what constituted luck.

"So we put the bone back in place?" Diotima asked.

"Yes, and then we must hope it heals. But there's another problem that will stop us."

He touched various parts of the inside of the leg. Diotima leaned closer.

"These muscles contract," the doctor said. "They'll stop us from putting the broken bone back where it should go."

"Then we can't save him?" Diotima said.

"Yes we can, or I would have said so. You don't credit me with knowing my business. Take a good look at the table he's lying on. It's a healing machine. I had this specially constructed at enormous expense."

The doctor busied himself with the machinery about his bench. It was a wide table, longer than a man, upon six sturdy legs; two at each end and two in the middle. The surface was planed smooth and oiled, which hadn't prevented various dark stains of a depressing nature from seeping into the wood up and down the length of it. At the foot end of the healing machine were various ropes and chains. At the other end, above Phellis's head, was a barrel round which was wound rope. The purpose of all these things I could not guess.

Melpon stood at the foot end. He tied one of the thick ropes that hung there about the broken leg, now padded. He made sure this was tight. At the other end he tied more rope—I recognized it now as the sort found on ships—looped under Phellis's armpits and about his chest. This rope was wound about a barrel at the head end of the table.

"You," Melpon pointed at me. "See that wheel near the patient's head? Turn it on my command."

I positioned myself. Melpon stood by the leg. He held thread in his hands.

"Turn," he said.

I pulled on the wheel. It rotated the barrel, which wound the rope, which pulled the body of Phellis along the table.

The upper half, that is. His broken leg was tied to the other end.

Despite the poppy juice Phellis woke. His eyes rolled and he said, "What are you doing?"

Melpon said, "Harder."

"No!" Phellis shouted.

The broken leg of Phellis was being stretched. One of the slaves who had carried him gagged.

"If you must throw up, do it outside," Melpon ordered. He hadn't taken his eyes off the bones under his hands.

Phellis begged for mercy.

"Harder!" the doctor ordered me.

I had to hope the doctor knew what he was doing. I pulled as hard as I could.

The broken shard of leg aligned with its other half.

"Hold it there!"

Melpon pushed the broken ends together. Phellis sobbed. Melpon ignored his patient's moans.

Phellis fainted again.

Melpon said, "Thanks be to Apollo. At least now we can work in quiet."

He pushed the distended tendons back in place. This he did with care, taking time about it.

The doctor said, "As long as his leg isn't allowed to move, the two ends will stay joined. They might even heal, if he stays immobile for long enough, and if he's lucky."

"That's why you have the machine," I said.

"Yes."

The doctor pushed the flaps of torn skin back over the

wound. He took up a sewing needle and thread and then, to my astonishment, sewed the skin together as if he was a woman sewing clothes. Of all the sights I'd seen, this for some reason turned my stomach the most; even more than the shattered bone exposed.

Melpon gave the thread a final tug. Then he bandaged the lot.

Throughout this I strained at the wheel.

"Can I let go?" I asked.

"No!"

Melpon hurried to my end. He inspected the wheel. He placed a chock so that it could not turn. He took chains from the floor and anchored them to the wheel. He tested these with great care before he said, "Now you can let go."

I did, and the wheel didn't move. The chock and the chains held it in place. Melpon didn't have the most inspiring manner, but I had to admit he knew his business.

"The two ends of bone must remain close together," Melpon explained. "If they do, there's a chance they will heal back together. But for that to happen they *must* be held in place. Only the machine can do that."

"It's like an instrument of torture," I said, gazing at the ropes and pulleys.

"You're not the first person to suggest it," the doctor said. "Most of my patients say the same thing after they've been released."

"So this machine has worked before?" I said.

"Of course."

It was ironic that one machine had hurt Phellis so badly, and another was going to heal him. These machines seemed like strange things.

"How long must he stay there?" I asked. "A few days?"

"Oh, he'll have to stay for the next month," the doctor said, matter-of-fact. "The only way this man has any hope of walking again is if we keep him immobile. Sometimes the bones heal back together. Sometimes they don't." He shrugged. "As I said, it lies with the Gods, and the flesh-eating illness might still get him, and even if he does heal, I guarantee this leg will come out shorter than the other one. Of course, that's assuming he has the money to pay for the machine."

"What?" I said, confused. "What does money have to do with this?"

The doctor pointed to his convoluted stretching device. "While your man is in this machine, no one else can use it. This is the only one in Athens. If a rich man needs it, I'll have to swap them over."

To our combined looks of stunned contempt, the doctor held up his hands and said defensively, "Look, I'll keep Phellis in there as long as I can, but if someone else comes by with another broken leg—someone who can pay—then your friend's got a problem."

"You could build another machine," Diotima said coldly.

"Using what for money?" the doctor asked. "These things are expensive. After I've paid all my costs, I barely have enough to support my family. Lady, I don't have the money to build another."

I looked about the comfortable house in which we stood. The courtyard was spacious. But a doctor in a shabby, poor house wouldn't inspire confidence. His furnishings were modest, but he had a lot of children.

"You'll get the money," I said.

Diotima looked at me in surprise. She knew what I knew. We didn't have such wealth.

"Very well then," the doctor said. "Your friend stays in the machine if the money arrives. I'll expect to see you later."

# SCENE 9
# THE TRITAGONIST

"WHERE ARE WE going to find the money to help Phellis?" Diotima asked, as we returned to the theater. "We don't even have enough money to fix the house."

"Maybe Phellis is rich," I said. "Perhaps he doesn't need help."

Diotima laughed. "You said it yourself. He's an actor."

"Or maybe the choregos will provide it," I added. "After all, Phellis was injured while working for him."

"Maybe," Diotima said, in a tone that told me what she thought of that idea.

"Well we couldn't leave Phellis to be discarded in the street, could we?" I said.

"No, we couldn't, Nico, you're right," Diotima conceded. "Let's ask Sophocles what he thinks."

We arrived back at the theater in time for the end of an argument. The crew was still bickering over the failure of the god machine. Everyone stared malevolently at the stage manager.

They turned as we entered.

"How is he?" Sophocles asked at once.

I told them what the doctor had said of Phellis and his prognosis, that he would be a cripple for the rest of his life. If he lived.

The stage manager buried his head in his hands at these words. Sophocles merely nodded. Others of the crew mentioned the ghost.

"No ghost," I told them. I held up the metal ring, which I'd taken with me. "This is the ring that held the harness to the rope. It was tampered with."

"I *told* you," said Kiron.

I nodded. "Kiron said as much when the slave found the ring. I looked, and he's right. A segment of the ring snapped off when Phellis was in the air. But if you look carefully at the broken ends, you can see where they've been filed halfway through."

That news was greeted with silence and obvious skepticism by the entire crew.

"Ghosts don't use a metal file," I added.

Someone muttered something about the ghost being real, unlike fanciful stories of metal files.

A long pause ensued. Then Lakon asked, "Where do we go from here, Sophocles? I suppose we replace Phellis?"

"Yes," Sophocles said.

The crew exclaimed.

"You can't be serious," I said, astonished. "We have incontrovertible proof that someone is setting dangerous traps. One of you tripped over the broom—Romanos, wasn't it?—someone poisoned the water, someone made the floor slippery. Now Phellis is crippled. You can't continue until we catch whoever is doing this."

Lakon answered. He said, "This is the biggest show any of us will ever play. Would you turn away from the most important job of your life?"

"No, of course not," I said.

"Nor will I." Lakon paused, then added, "Besides, think of the shame to Athens if we behave like cowards. We *cannot* abandon."

Lakon spoke with the conviction of an actor who believed his lines. Even the crew seemed moved, who only moments ago had muttered about the ghost. Every man present had at one time or another stood in the line of battle for this city. Not one of them wanted to be called a coward by his fellow citizens. I saw several heads nod.

Sophocles saw his chance to strike. "Lakon is right," the playwright said. "Our duty to the God and to Athens is clear. We must recast. We can't win the contest—not now—no actor could learn the lines in the two days we have left—but we must try."

Lakon glanced at Romanos, with an expression of calculation. Then he said with authority, "I know casting is your decision, Sophocles, but I have a suggestion."

"Yes?" Sophocles said. "Speak up, Lakon. I'll hear any idea that gives us a chance."

"Then hear me now. You should cast Romanos as second actor. If you do, we can still win."

Every head turned to Romanos. The younger actor stared at Lakon in surprise. He said, "Me?"

"Why? How?" The stage manager asked the two questions the rest of us were thinking.

"Romanos knows the second actor's lines," Lakon said. "I heard him once when we were practicing."

"Is this true?" Sophocles asked.

Romanos said, "Lakon flatters me, but it's true that I know the second actor's part. If it will save the play, I'll do my best."

Sophocles shook his head. "I admire your willingness, Romanos, but that would only leave us with *two* actors forced to learn new lines in a hurry. You know your own lines so well, Romanos. I cannot credit you know the second actor's part as well."

"As it happens, Sophocles, yes I do."

Romanos began to speak the second actor's lines. He spoke quickly, but confidently, and he didn't stumble. In fact, it seemed to me that Romanos spoke the lines better than Phellis himself had during the rehearsal.

Sophocles looked impressed.

"I didn't know you had those lines so well. How do you come to have another actor's part?" the writer asked.

"Phellis spoke them. I have an excellent memory." Romanos made an attempt to look modest. He failed. Instead he looked confident.

Lakon said, "The third actor is easier to replace, is he not?"

We remained silent while Sophocles considered.

"Lakon's plan is a good one," Sophocles said after a long pause.

Heads nodded all about the theater.

Sophocles saw agreement. He said, "Then here is our plan. Romanos becomes the second actor. We replace his third actor role with a quick study. And if Dionysos grants us favor then we still have a chance. I must see Thodis the choregos for his approval—it's his money we're spending, after all—but he'll agree. Thodis no more wants to bring shame to Athens than do we. Perhaps he'll also know of a third actor we can hire on short notice."

Lakon snorted. "All the good ones have already been hired."

That made sense, even to me. Anyone not already cast in one of the tragedies or the comedies must have been judged second rate by experts. The glum looks of the stage manager and his crew told me they agreed.

"Does anyone know of a good actor who's free?" Sophocles asked the assembly.

Silence.

Then Romanos raised his hand, hesitantly.

"I might know of someone," Romanos said. "He's a good actor."

I could hear the "But" in his voice. So could everyone else.

"But?" Sophocles prompted.

"Well sir, he's never played in an Athenian theater." Romanos said it hesitantly.

Almost everyone looked dubious. I could understand their reaction. A man who had never worked the world's most important theater was hardly the man to walk into this crisis.

"What's his name? Do you vouch for him?" Sophocles asked.

"He's called Kebris. He's not protagonist material, sir," Romanos said. "Kebris spent his life as a touring player, going from town to town." He spoke almost apologetically. "I worked with him once. He's very quick to learn lines. Well, you have to be, on tour. You all know that. He's not the world's best actor, sir, but he's reliable."

Sophocles smiled ruefully. "My first actor chooses my second, and my second chooses my third. I'm fairly sure that's not the way things are usually done. Well, reliable is what we need around here. All right, as long as your friend can stand and deliver lines, he's in." He wiped the sweat from his brow. "Maybe we can survive this disaster after all."

# SCENE 10
# THIS IS BECOMING A HABIT

MEN SCATTERED IN all directions. The crew moved to repair the machine and also, at Kiron's stern command, to check everything in the theater all over again, to make sure all was in order. Akamas muttered darkly that he'd lost track of how many times they'd done that in the last few days, and yet still men were being hurt.

Sophocles and Romanos departed to interview the actor Romanos had recommended.

Diotima and I walked over to Kiron after he finished barking out orders. He stood there with hands on hips, glaring at the working buzzing about him.

I said, "Kiron? We need to know, did anything unusual happen when Phellis was attached to the machine?"

"Akamas does that job," Kiron said. He waved to the stagehand. Akamas sauntered over, wiping his grimy hands on his tunic. I was struck by what a large and strong-looking man he was. The cloth of his exomis bulged slightly over a belt made of rope. Akamas was a man who didn't miss meals. I repeated my question.

Akamas said, "I reach down the back of the actor's neck for the leather strip. I pull it up and clip on the rope. That's it. And before you suggest it, I didn't make any mistake with Phellis."

"So everything was the same as normal?"

"Yeah, just like any actor, except when Phellis goes on as Thanatos I got to put the noose around his neck."

I'd forgotten about the noose. "That's a good point. Wouldn't Thanatos choke to death on the noose?"

"Funnily enough, we thought of that," said Kiron. "The noose is loose. It looks like solid rope—it *is* solid rope—but the rope that makes up the noose doesn't go anywhere. See here . . ."

Kiron held up the noose for Diotima and me to inspect. The noose ended only a few hand lengths from its loop. Thin threads had been sewn and looped around the thicker rope. The threads had clearly been torn apart.

Kiron said, "The noose is attached to the rope of the machine with only this thin piece of sewing thread. We bind it carefully to make it look like one piece from afar."

"I see," said Diotima. "When Phellis fell, the sewing thread broke. That was all that held the noose in place. It fell with him. That's why he didn't strangle."

Kiron dismissed Akamas back to his work, then beckoned Diotima and me to follow him. "There's something you ought to see," he said.

We followed him to the wall that backed the stage. Kiron gestured at the scene on the skene. "What do you think of it?"

The skene had been painted to portray the city of Corinth. In the middle was an agora. Tiny figures were going about their business. Buildings surrounded the market. The buildings became smaller the further they were from the agora, so that it was like looking down on the city from a high place. Off to the side was the Acrocorinth, a high hill fort like our Acropolis. Everything was painted in bright, vibrant colors.

"Ah, it looks very nice," I said. I wasn't sure what Kiron expected of me.

"Look here." He pointed at one of the figures in the agora. "See this one?"

I peered closely. So did Diotima. The tiny figure wasn't

upright. It seemed to be flying across a brown line, or about to sprawl on the ground.

Diotima said, puzzled, "Is that a picture of someone tripping?"

"I think it is," Kiron said. "And see this?" He traced the thin brown line that I'd noticed. "There's a tiny dab of light yellow paint at the end of this line. I think it's supposed to be a broom."

A man tripping over a broom, like happened to Romanos.

"It has to be a coincidence," I said.

"That's what I thought. Then, after the incident of poisoned water, I looked again. I noticed this . . ."

Kiron's finger traced the outline of one of the stalls in the agora. It showed a typical wine vendor. Men stood about drinking from cups.

Amongst the crowd, one man was doubled over. He appeared to be vomiting.

"He wouldn't be the first man to throw up after drinking too much," I said.

"But painting it for decoration?" Diotima said in disbelief.

She clearly hadn't been to the same parties I had. Among my acquaintances were several with party-ware decorated with the figures of men who had drunk too much of the bounty of Dionysos. I recalled one particularly detailed decoration on a wine cup, of a slave girl holding up a bowl while a man vomited into it.

I made a mental note never to introduce my wife to that particular friend.

I said, "The point Kiron's making is that the figures in the skene painting seem to presage the accidents at the theater."

"Or maybe they were drawn in afterward?" Diotima suggested. She looked to Kiron. "Do you know? Were the figures there *before* the accidents?"

Kiron shrugged. "I didn't notice them until afterward. But then, I wouldn't, would I? As your husband says, they're not so remarkable on their own."

Diotima looked closely at the figure of the man throwing up. She shook her head "I can't tell if he was painted in later. Maybe an expert could tell."

"There's something else," Kiron said. He looked worried. "After you left with Phellis, while everyone around here was arguing, I had a close look at the skene. And . . ."

He pointed at a spot below the Acrocorinth. "Right here, see this building? It was always there, but I never noticed before how much it resembles a theater."

Diotima and I leaned forward. It did indeed look like a theater, and in the middle, on what would be the stage—

Diotima gasped.

I turned to Kiron.

"I'll swear it wasn't there before," he said. "I'll swear it."

In the middle of the theater upon the skene wall was the god machine. And falling from it was the tiny figure of a man.

"What do you think?" Kiron asked.

"I think we need to speak to the artist," I said. "Who painted your scenery?"

"Stephanos of Vitale. Everyone uses him."

"Vitale? Where's that?"

"Some place among the islands of the Cyclades, I think. He's a *metic*."

Athens is full of metics. Their numbers increase every year as people from poorer cities flood in to enjoy our wealth and success.

Kiron told us where to find this Stephanos. The artist lived in Outer Ceramicus. It was one of those places where rich and poor mingled together. We arrived at his home—a small artisan's house, neat and tidy—only to be told by the house slave that Stephanos wasn't in. He was painting a mural for a client at a house close to where my family lived . . . in the exact opposite direction, back past the theater.

As we walked all the way back I realized, too late, that I

should have sent a runner ahead to inquire if Stephanos was in. But then, knowing the way my luck ran, if I had sent the runner, he would have returned to say Stephanos was at home and I would have wasted my time waiting.

We finally found Stephanos at work in a house in the deme of Agryle. There was no trouble getting in to see him. The front door was wide open. Tradesmen streamed in and out with their tools and materials in hand.

I stopped one of the men, to ask him what was happening and where I might find the painter. It seemed the home owner was renovating. He'd moved his family elsewhere while his home was stripped to its bare beams and rebuilt from the ground up.

Inside, I paid close attention to what the workmen were doing. I counted no fewer than twenty of them. Carpenters cut away and replaced walls. One man was tearing up the treads of the stairs to replace the old wood. Stone workers laid new paving in the courtyard. Two thatchers stood in the courtyard and stared straight up, pointing at this or that as they discussed how they would replace the roof.

This was what I wanted to do to Diotima's house, but could never afford unless I did it myself. The mere sight of all the work involved depressed me. On my own it would take ten years, or maybe a hundred.

We followed the tradesman's directions to the only room that was complete: the master's bedroom, to the left off the courtyard. The room had that new wood smell that makes you want to breathe deep. But it was mixed with an aroma that was even sweeter. It smelled like honey.

A thin man of medium height stood with his back to us, bent over pans. He wore an exomis spattered with colors that ranged from faded pastel yellow to recent hits of vibrant red and blue. It could have been a bright party dress, except the paint was crusted hard.

This must be the artist.

"Stephanos of Vitale? My name is Nicolaos, son of Sophroniscus. I have a few questions to ask—"

"They'll have to wait. I'm working."

He hadn't even turned to speak to us.

Stephanos pulled a sponge from the small brazier over which he leaned. The brazier stood upon a tripod. A gentle fire lapped at the metal from an oil lamp placed beneath. A layer of something sticky coated the sponge in the artist's hand.

"What's that?" Diotima asked.

"Beeswax."

He began to wipe the sponge across the wall in broad, easy strokes. When the sponge ran out of wax he dipped it back in the brazier for more. He continued this way until the wall was coated top to bottom and side to side in a wax undercoat. Stephanos seemed to use a lot of beeswax. Were there really that many bees in Athens?

"I can't stop now that I've begun," he explained as he worked. "The wax undercoat needs to be soft for the next part. If you want to talk, go ahead, but I'll be concentrating on this."

He picked up a stylus, of the sort people use with a wax tablet. But instead of writing notes, the artist sketched the outlines of the mural to come. It was hard to see the scratchings against the translucent background, but I discerned large, robust figures and petite women.

"What are you drawing?" I asked.

"Satyrs ravishing maenads," he said without stopping.

"Interesting choice for a bedroom," I said.

He shrugged. "I'm just the hired help. You'd have to ask the owner's wife. *She* chose the subject."

"Hmm."

Stephanos completed the outline of an enormous half-man, half-beast, to which he added an anatomically correct phallus that was entirely rampant. Diotima leaned closer to inspect it.

"Not bad," she said.

"If you're thinking about redecorating," I told her, "you can forget it."

In a row along the floor were blocks of pigment: red, blue, yellow, green, and white. Stephanos picked up a block of white. He used a knife to scrape flakes into a second brazier.

"Now for the color," he said. Then added, "Was there something you wanted to ask me about?"

"Yes," I said. "We believe you painted the skene for the play *Sisyphus*, written by Sophocles."

"I do the skenes for all the plays," he said as he stirred the contents of the brazier. "Both the tragedies and the comedies."

Stephanos added some olive oil. He stirred the brew, then added more oil.

"How did you end up as everyone's skene painter?" I asked.

"I paint murals," he said. "One day—it must be almost fifteen years ago—how do the years pass so quickly? Anyway, I'd been hired by a citizen to do a mural for his courtyard. The client was an important man by the name of Aeschylus. He wanted a Battle of Marathon."

"I've seen that painting!" I said. I had been a visitor to the house of Aeschylus. "It's very good."

Stephanos said, "Thanks. Aeschylus watched me for most of the day while I worked, like you two are now, only he talked less. When I was done, he admired my work, and then he said, 'You know, something like that would look great in my next play.'" He shrugged again. "So I painted the skene like it was a mural. It was a huge hit with the audience. Aeschylus paid me double what he promised, then made me swear that I'd do it again the next year."

Stephanos stopped stirring.

"After that, well, everyone else wanted me to paint their skenes."

The flakes and the oil had melted into solution. He took the gooey mess to the wall. With the cup in his left hand and the palette knife in his right, he spread the white onto the warm beeswax. I could see the color embed itself into the wax.

"You see why this must be done before the undercoat cools," he said.

"What's in the pigment?" I asked.

"For white? You take strips of lead, as thin as you can make them, and lay them crossways in an open tray. Then you pour in vinegar and toss in a pile of goat droppings. Wait a few months, and you've got white pigment."

"You're kidding."

"I wish I was. Vinegar I can get from bad wine; the Gods know there's plenty of that in this city. Goat droppings are free for the taking from any street, but lead ingots cost a fortune."

"You don't sound entirely pleased with Athens," I said.

He shrugged. "It's the clients in this town that drive me crazy. You wouldn't believe how many of them are amateur artists. Always watching over my shoulder, demanding changes to perfectly good pictures."

He glared at me as if it were my fault.

"I've got a plan," he said. "When I've made enough money, I'll buy a nice farm on some island in the Cyclades and live simply and raise goats and chickens. Have you ever heard a goat complain about a painting?"

"No."

"There you are, then." He nodded sagely. "Goats are civilized."

As he spoke Stephanos continued to press and spread paint into his creation. The style was clearly the same as the skene at the theater.

"Stephanos, did you make any changes to the backdrop of *Sisyphus*?"

"I see you know nothing about painting. Every artist has to touch up some places."

"I mean, after you'd finished the skene, did you return to add anything extra?"

Though he was still painting, he turned his head to look at me. "That is a very odd question," he said.

"But an important one. We need an answer."

"I don't even know who you are or why you're here."

I decided not to enlighten him. Not until we had our answers.

"You drew all the scenes on the wall?" I said.

"Of course."

"Did anyone else paint any of it?"

"Are you suggesting I subcontract my work?" he said it angrily.

"No, not at all Stephanos. I merely don't know much about how artists work."

"Who decides what you draw?" Diotima asked.

"The paying client, obviously," Stephanos said. "Sophocles told me he wanted Corinth."

"Was that all that Sophocles said?" Diotima asked.

"Yes. I took it from there. I decided to draw the agora and the city as if looking down from a high mountain. Like the Gods were looking down on the action, you know?"

"Did you draw a man tripping in the agora?"

"How should I know?"

"You don't remember?"

"I draw hundreds of little background figures every month. I don't keep a list."

"What about a wine bar?" I asked. "Did you draw that?"

"Probably. Every agora has one."

That was true enough.

"What about someone throwing up?"

He laughed.

"What about a picture of the god machine and a man falling from it?"

"Look, who are you people?"

"We're investigating a series of sabotage attempts against the theater."

"It's nothing to do with me," he said.

"The last one resulted in a man having his leg destroyed. And mark this, Stephanos: every single booby trap that's hurt someone is drawn into the skene that *you* painted."

Stephanos had switched colors. He hesitated while he worked on a particularly tricky piece of blue clothing that a satyr was ripping off a maenad.

"I haven't hurt anyone," he said.

"Do you know a man named Phellis?" I said.

"One of the actors?"

"He's the one with the crippled leg," I said.

"Bad luck for him then."

"What about the stage manager?"

"Kiron? I know him well. I deal with him whenever I work at the theater. He's a good man."

"Do you have an apprentice by any chance?" Diotima asked. I thought it was an inspired question.

"No."

So much for inspiration.

"Did you alter the skene painting?"

"No." He sounded tense.

"Did you draw in the god machine?"

"No. I might have done those other figures you talked about. I can't remember."

I didn't know whether to believe him or not. I couldn't think of any way we could break his statement. Not unless we could find someone who'd seen him working on the skene in the last few days. I looked Diotima's way to see if she had any ideas. She silently shook her head.

Stephanos must have sensed the pressure was off. He put down the paint pot and began to flake another into the brazier.

He cleaned off the palette knife and the other tools. Seeing a few spots of white paint on his hand, he licked them off.

"Is that safe?" I asked.

"It's only lead. It can't hurt you."

"HE WAS TENSE when you questioned him about the wall," Diotima said when we were outside.

"Hardly surprising, since I'd just accused him of assault in a sacred area," I pointed out. "Most people would be a little put out."

"If anyone had seen him at the theater in the last few days surely they would have mentioned it," Diotima said.

"Maybe," I said doubtfully. It was amazing what people remembered only after you asked them. But there was another problem. "What possible motive would he have to foul the plays?"

"I don't know."

Diotima's point, though, applied to everyone. I said, "There's one thing we know for sure. *Someone* painted in the god machine and Phellis's accident."

"That's true," Diotima said.

"So your logic applies to everyone. Whoever did the paint job, why weren't they seen?"

"For the same reason nobody saw the booby traps being laid," Diotima said at once. "Someone sneaked in and did them at night."

"How good are you at painting in the dark?" I said.

"They used torches," Diotima said.

"And yet they escaped detection. Or else they did it in the glaring light of day."

"They'd have to be very confident," Diotima said. "People walk in and out of the theater all the time."

"Or maybe the pictures were there all the time."

We reached the deme boundary at Piraeus Way. As we

crossed the road I felt a few drops of water land on my head. I looked up. A drop landed in my eye. The sky had clouded over and it was about to rain, something that rarely happens in spring, but when it does it can turn into a late winter downpour.

Diotima had felt the drops too. She put out her hands to confirm. She said, "Nico . . . what about my house?"

Dear Gods. Diotima's house. She'd inherited the house from her birth father. We lived with my parents, because that was how things were done in Athens, but the house was part of her dowry.

The problem was, the house was in a state of disrepair. I'd been meaning to fix the roof for the past month, but it hadn't seemed urgent. Now I was going to have to do it in the rain.

We turned left, and passed through the agora. Those vendors who hadn't already left for the day were packing their stalls as quickly as they could. We dodged around the line of departing donkeys laden with goods. Only a few blocks later we came to Diotima's house.

It had been something of a puzzle what to do with that house. It was a grand place with a fine courtyard and large rooms, but city homes were a sink for wealth, not a source. We couldn't move in even if we wanted, because we couldn't afford to maintain and staff it, not on my income.

We'd tried renting it out to visiting trade delegations and wealthy merchants who were in Athens on extended stays. There were one or two men of influence in Athens who were well-disposed toward me, and they sent wealthy visitors my way. The rich tenants had complained constantly about every little thing, demanded extra slaves to serve them, and when it came time to settle the bill looked for every possible excuse to reduce the agreed amount. I'd decided that wealthy men got that way by never paying their bills. Also these men invariably left the place in a worse state than they found it. They would hold parties in our house but not replace the broken furniture. I knew for sure that one man who owned a merchant fleet in Rhodes had departed with our complete set of new kitchen knives.

Something had to be done. Somehow we had to make that house pay.

Achilles let us in. Not the hero of the Trojan War, but an old slave, crippled in the heels, who for his faithful service Diotima had promised to care for to the end of his days. There used to be two house slaves as well, but we'd sold them when we stopped renting the place. We simply couldn't afford to feed that many mouths.

"Master, mistress," Achilles said as he opened the door. Every time I talked to him, he seemed older. "It's good that you're here. What am I to do about the women's quarters?"

"You're not to do anything, Achilles," I said. If he tried to climb onto the roof, he would certainly die.

"I've placed pots where the worst of the leaks are," he said.

I walked into the central courtyard to inspect the damage. The courtyard itself was jumbled. The garden beds were full of weeds, the furniture looked the worse for wear. But there was nothing that couldn't survive some rain.

The hole in the inner wall where a drunk partygoer had punched his way through was under the cover of the eaves. The eaves themselves showed signs of wet rot setting in, and the coming rain would worsen that, but there was nothing to be done about it now.

The immediate problem was higher up. If I craned my neck, I could see where holes had developed in the thatching in numerous places. If the rain came down as hard as I thought it might, there'd soon be pools of water on the second storey floors. That wouldn't do.

I fetched the ladder from out back and carried it up to the women's quarters in the right wing. That was where I could see was the worst of the damage. Achilles followed after with the canvas of an old musty army tent that he struggled to hold. Diotima carried rope. It wouldn't be the best fix, but it would have to do for now.

I climbed up.

Things crawled all over me. I jerked back but they clung on. I waved my arms and they fell off. But there was one on my head.

"Ugh!"

"Nico! What is it?" Diotima called up. She sounded worried.

"Mice. The thatch is full of mice. They're crawling on me!"

Peals of laughter from below. So much for sympathy from a worried wife.

Then I felt something crawling up my leg.

"There's one under my chiton!"

More laughter. Now even our slave was laughing.

"Arrgh! Oh, dear Gods . . ." On the ladder, I bent over in excruciating pain. It hurt so much I thought I might faint.

"Nico! What's wrong?" Diotima called from below.

"It bit me."

"Where?" Now she sounded worried.

"I'm not going to say. But it hurts like Hades."

"Oh Nico, be careful." That part of me was essential to Diotima's life plans. "We'll have to get a cat," she called up.

"Two cats. One would die from overeating."

It was clear now what had caused the holes, and if we didn't do something about it, and soon, I'd have to replace the entire roof. Worse, mice can easily jump from one roof to another. Which meant I'd have to warn our neighbors. I could imagine how pleased they were going to be at the news. I just hoped they wouldn't decide to sue me.

The rain was heavy now. My body poked halfway through the roof. From the waist up I was above the house. Achilles passed up the canvas, which I spread as wide as I could to cover the worst of the holes. From where I stood I could see a second mouse nest. Terrific.

I lashed down the canvas and tied it tight. There'd still be drips, but damage to the floor was averted.

The moment I was down, Diotima knelt and stuck her head under my chiton to inspect the damage to my nether regions.

"That looks nasty," she said from underneath my clothing.

"If you say anything," I warned Achilles, who watched this with an amused smile, "I will . . . I will . . ." I couldn't think of anything bad enough.

Diotima emerged from my chiton.

"It needs a wash and definitely some ointment."

Some nice oily ointment sounded good.

"Your mother will know what to do."

"My mother!"

"She is a midwife after all, Nico."

"That means she knows how to treat *your* parts, dear wife, not mine. All it needs is a gentle rub, and, er—"

A massive thunderclap.

Achilles hurried to place more pots where leaks dripped.

Zeus, or Apollo, or Dionysos, or whichever god had caused this rain, it was like he had an Olympus-sized bucket and had turned it upside down over Athens.

I said as much to Diotima. She considered the downpour for a moment and said, "The amount of water that's coming down, I think it must be Poseidon."

"We could stay here for the night?" I suggested.

Diotima hesitated. "I'd rather not . . ."

This old house had some terrible memories for Diotima. That was the other reason we didn't live here.

"Then we run for home."

We ran.

It was immediately obvious that this was a bad idea. Diotima tripped over her chiton and landed face first in the mud. She was still wearing the bright Dionysiac festival chiton that she planned to wear throughout the festival. The material covered her arms to the wrists and her legs to the ankles, and that was her downfall. She picked herself up at once and I wiped her down. The rain helped by washing off a lot of the street muck.

Diotima lifted the skirt of her chiton. Together we splashed our way to the agora.

We were so saturated now that it didn't matter, but the rain was unpleasant enough that we wanted to get out of it.

As we hurried, we passed by people who also looked for shelter. Most of them did the same thing we did. We ran up the steps of the nearest stoa, the covered, colonnaded porticoes that surrounded the agora of Athens. This stoa was already crowded with people sheltering from the rain. We didn't let that stop us, we pushed our way in.

"This is the curse of Dionysos," an anonymous man amongst us said.

It had become surprisingly cold. The chilly wind didn't help. Other men, new arrivals, all soaked, tried to make their way under cover, but there was no more room and the men on the outer edge pushed away the latecomers. Diotima and I had wriggled our way to the middle where the mass of bodies created some warmth and our clothing began to steam. I put my arm around Diotima to make it clear she was my wife, so that no man thought to grope her. An Athenian would never take liberties with another man's wife—not if he wanted to live—but if there were any slave girls in this press of people then they were probably getting more attention than they wanted. Come to that though, no slave girl would risk the wrath of her mistress by tarrying under cover. She would run for home.

We stood like that for a long time. I thought about our farm. There was nothing I could do about the olive trees—either the fruit would drop too early in the wet or it wouldn't—but I hoped the slave we left to mind the farm would at least make sure the chickens were safely in the henhouse.

Another man raced across the agora, coming from the south, head down and hands raised in an ineffectual shield against the downpour.

He saw the crush under the stoa and that there was no more room but he shouted. “Make way!”

He didn’t stop to see if anyone made way. He ran in.

Men moved back because they had no choice.

The new arrival raised his head. It was Romanos.

He shook his hair, which was unnaturally long. Droplets sprayed the men beside him. That caused more complaints, though these were perfunctory since we were all damp anyway.

Romanos caught my eye. I waved to him, and motioned for him to join us. The actor pushed his way through with polite, muttered apologies.

“What are you doing out in this weather?” I asked him.

“I was at the theater,” he said. “I was rehearsing the new third actor in his lines.”

“Isn’t that Sophocles’s job?” Diotima asked.

Romanos shrugged. “Our director and playwright is a busy man, and it was I who recommended Kebris. I feel responsible. Besides, I know the lines better than anyone, even better than Sophocles, perhaps, since I’ve practiced their delivery.”

“How’s Kebris working out?”

“Very well indeed. I am confident.”

I could only admire his dedication. I said as much to him.

“I do what I can,” he said modestly. “And I got drenched for my effort. There’s no shelter at the theater. Kebris ran the other way to his home. I ran this way to mine.”

“You came to Athens to be an actor, didn’t you? You’re not from here.”

“I come from Phrygia. It’s a very rustic place. You wouldn’t know what it's like. You two grew up in Athens, the most sophisticated city in the world."

"Diotima and I have been to Ionia," I told him. Ionia is the province next to Phrygia and, though the city of Ephesus on the coast was the height of civilization, when you got into the back country it was endless farms and tiny villages.

"Then perhaps you do know what it's like," he said. "There's no work there for an actor. Most people barely know that plays exist. Or if they do, they think it's a child's game, not fit for adults."

"How did you discover acting, may I ask?" said Diotima.

"A mime came to our village one day. He danced out a story while his wife played the flute. The people in my village laughed and threw him a few coins, but I followed the whole story and was entranced. From that day on, all I wanted was to tell stories too."

"Acting seems a difficult profession," I said. "What do you do when you don't have work?"

"What do you do when *you* don't have work?" he countered.

It was a good point.

"So no plans to return to Phrygia?" I said.

Romanos laughed.

I tried to estimate the age of Romanos, but it wasn't easy. He was one of those men who could be an old-looking twenty-five or a young-looking thirty-five. There were lines of experience about his eyes, but I guessed that he'd had a hard life and he could have acquired those at an early age.

Romanos looked out from our shelter, into the pouring rain.

He said, "I would like to be a citizen of Athens one day."

That made sense to me. Who wouldn't want to be a citizen of Athens? Yet Phrygia was a long way away, and I couldn't imagine a man willing to abandon his homeland without a good reason.

I asked, "Would it help you?"

Romanos looked surprised. "Of course it would. Citizens get all the best parts."

"You're second actor now," I pointed out.

"Because Phellis had his accident." Romanos frowned. "And before that I was only third actor because Aeschylus and Chorilos had already snapped up the two best third actors who happen to be citizens."

"Sophocles seems to like you," Diotima said. "I heard him say Romanos is a good actor."

Romanos said in a harsh voice, "Romanos is the man Sophocles calls for when he's run out of other good options." Then he shrugged, an actor's expressive shrug of despair. He said, "The fact is, if I'm to get ahead in my profession, then I must become a citizen."

"My father became a citizen," Diotima said. "And he used to be a slave."

"He was? He did?" Romanos looked down at Diotima in some surprise. "How? How did he do it?"

"Through his enormous merit," I said. Because I was proud to be the son-in-law of Pythax, though some might call him a barbarian.

Romanos said, "Your father is that impressively large barbarian whom I saw with you, once or twice at the theater?"

"Yes."

"What did a barbarian do to deserve such elevation?"

"Have you noticed how little crime there is on the streets of Athens?" I asked.

Romanos thought about it. "Now that you mention it, Athens does seem safer than most cities."

"You have Pythax to thank for that," I said.

"Oh, I see."

Romanos questioned Diotima closely as to how Pythax had come by his citizenship. What the process had been and whether anyone had objected. It was an odd place for such a conversation, the three of us all facing each other, squeezed together, other men pressed against us in every direction. But the sound of the rain was loud in our ears; from where it bounced off the tile slate roof above our heads, I could barely hear the words of the men talking right next to us. Our conversation was essentially private.

Pythax had been made a citizen by acclamation of the *ecclesia*, the Assembly of the People of Athens. When Diotima explained this to Romanos, he looked despondent and said that no assembly of citizens would ever vote for him to join their number.

"Is that really so, Romanos?" I said. "You've been a great help to Sophocles. You've become instrumental in saving the Dionysia. If men see that you do great service to Athens, might they not think you also worthy of citizenship?"

He brightened. "Yes, I suppose that is possible. I wonder who might sponsor me for citizenship?" He went into a reverie, no doubt contemplating his future, and said little else.

THE MOON WAS high in the sky by the time the rain slackened and a few gaps in the clouds appeared. Men scattered from under cover like ants from a nest. It was very late when Diotima and I made it home, so late that my parents and even the slaves had gone to bed, leaving only one slave awake to open the door for us. This he did, grumpily pointing out how late it was, then he too shuffled off to his bed out the back.

Our clothes were a disaster. We dropped them on the floor by the door. It was too dark to do anything else. This left us naked, standing at the front of the house, with Socrates snoring not twenty paces away.

We tiptoed up to the women's quarters, where Diotima had a private bedroom. When Diotima had joined the family I'd built her a separate room so that she and my mother would have some privacy from each other.

We closed the door behind us.

"There's no point waking your mother for some ointment," Diotima said. "The rain will have cleaned the bite anyway . . . but perhaps some light massage."

"Good idea."

Diotima felt below.

"Nico, it's swollen from the bite."

"Diotima, that swelling is for a different reason."

She felt again.

"Oh, so it is."

She dragged me down onto the bed.

# SCENE 11
# CROWDED HOUSE

DIOTIMA AND I had barely slept, but for all that we felt refreshed. We ate a hearty breakfast, of yesterday's bread dipped in wine, lentils and eggs from our farm. The eggs were a luxury few could afford. The whole family was present: my father and mother and Socrates, who was still puzzling over the machine.

Socrates had reached the age where he ate everything he could grab, and then some. As he filled his bowl with third helpings he demanded that we tell him what had happened at the theater. Diotima brought him up to date.

Our father, Sophroniscus, listened to Diotima without comment. He had eaten sparingly of his bread and wine. I was happy to see he popped half an egg into his mouth, and then the other half.

My father had never become reconciled to my chosen profession—he had wanted me to follow in his footsteps—and yet it was my work that had brought the farm into the family, small though it was. It pleased me that he enjoyed its produce.

Thought of this raised another point to mind.

"Father, we have a problem," I said. "There are mice in Diotima's house."

"Find a cat," he said absently. I could tell he wasn't paying attention. In his mind he was probably planning his day's work.

"They're in the roof."

That made him look up. He knew what mice in the thatching meant.

I detailed the extent of the damage.

"We will have to sell the house," my father said.

I glanced at Diotima. She looked studiously down at her bowl.

"I'd rather not, sir," I said, somewhat hesitantly. Father had not been keen for me to marry Diotima in the first place. Having won that major battle and installed her in my life, I hesitated to antagonize my father over a lesser disagreement.

Sophroniscus put down his bowl. "Son, I know you like the place, but a house that doesn't pay, that we don't need, that's costing us money . . . it's a drain on the household finances. I'm sure you understand. That old house needs a lot of maintenance, doesn't it?"

"Yes, but—"

"I know you've tried to make it pay," he said. "The renting scheme was a good idea—"

"Yes, but—"

"But it hasn't worked out, has it?"

"No, but—"

"Sometimes the best thing to do is accept a defeat and move on. You've done well with this career of yours, I admit it. I'm proud of you."

Father was being reasonable. I hated that.

For so long as he lived, my father was responsible for our family, and I was a child in the eyes of the law. If he'd simply ordered me to sell the house, I could not have refused. But Father wasn't going to order me. Instead he was going to make me see reason.

My mother, Phaenarete, had listened to all this in silence. Phaenarete *never* questioned her husband in front of us. She had other ways of expressing her viewpoint, typically by failing to offer an opinion whenever Father said something of which she disapproved. Phaenarete's silence could be more devastating than other wives who threw plates. I hoped that she would keep a studious silence, or perhaps even say a few words in my support.

Now she crushed my hopes by saying, "Your father is right, Nico."

That ended it. We would have to sell the house.

# SCENE 12
# TIME PASSES

WE ALL THREE of us traipsed to the Theater of Dionysos. Socrates wanted to see the god machine.

We found the stage manager there, though it was still early in the morning. Other than him, the theater was deserted. I noticed at once that on the back wall, someone had added a line below the No Whistling sign. The addition was in a different hand. Now it said:

NO WHISTLING!
*and watch your feet—don't trip or fall*

I felt it was good advice, but hardly needed saying.

Or did it? Romanos had tripped over the dangerously placed broom. That could have broken his leg. Lakon had almost fallen from the sabotaged balcony. That could have ended with a broken limb, or a broken neck. Phellis had fallen heavily and now his leg was crippled.

"You back again?" the stage manager said when he saw us. He held an actor's mask in his hands.

"There's a criminal assault to avenge," I said.

He grunted. "I visited Phellis last night."

"How was he?"

"Tied up in that machine in the doctor's house, but he wasn't screaming. Doctor said the leg was as good as you could expect. He also said Phellis can never act again."

"I'm sorry."

"Yeah, me too. All right, I can't say I like having you amateurs behind the skene, but I guess I got no choice."

"You're here early," I said.

"It occurred to me nothing got put away properly last night," he said. "After all the rain I thought I better check the damage. Look at this." He swore as he held up the mask that had been in his hands. "Someone left it lying on the ground. It's ruined now."

It did indeed look the worse for wear: muddy, and the material was splotched.

The stage manager tossed the mask onto the bench beside him.

"Can I have a look?" Diotima said, and before the stage manager could object she picked it up.

"Here, you're a woman—"

"Yes, I'd noticed." Diotima spoke through the mask. There were eye holes to see through and a mouth through which to speak. She looked very strange to me with the rigid mask covering her face.

"Acting's not for women," the stage manager said. "That'd be immoral."

"Sir? Then who plays the women characters?" Socrates asked.

"The men do. That's moral. If a woman was on stage, all the men would be ogling her, right?"

"Of course," I said.

"Well, that isn't right, is it? Would you want *your* daughter on stage, and a horde of men eyeing her? Thinking about her because they want to . . . well, do you-know-what with her."

When he put it like that . . . "No, you're right," I said. "I definitely wouldn't want my daughter on stage, if I had one."

"Well then, there you are. Every woman is someone's daughter. The only proper thing to do is not allow the ladies on stage."

"It's ridiculous," Diotima said, in an irritated tone. "If women can be priestesses then they can be actresses, can't they? Priestesses perform in public and everything's fine."

"It's like this, young miss—"

"I am Diotima, the wife of Nicolaos."

"If you got up on stage, a lady who looks the way you do—" He looked her up and down, then said, "If you were up there, we'd have to beat back the audience with shovels." He shook his head. "It just wouldn't work out. No one would pay attention to the play."

THE CAST SPENT the next two days in intense work. And so did I. I didn't take my eyes off the actors, the stage or the backstage area for a moment while the crew were there. Of course I couldn't see all those things at once. I had to constantly run from the back to the front and then back again. I felt like a parent with twenty children. My constant movement irritated the actors and everyone who supported them, yet no one complained. They knew as well as I did that whoever was set to sabotage the play was still out there, waiting for an opportunity.

But I couldn't be there all night as well. I went to see Pythax, to beg the loan of two of the Scythian Guard. There are three hundred of these guards, all of them barbarian slaves, their job to patrol the streets and keep the peace. My father-in-law Pythax was their overseer.

Pythax was good to me, as he always is. He arranged for two of his men, Euboulides and Pheidestratos, to be detached to my service. I ordered them to protect the theater at night. I specifically wanted two guards so that they would keep each other awake. A man on his own can easily doze. They took the moonlight shift and I relieved them each dawn.

Throughout the rehearsals, Romanos was a workhorse. He was first at the theater every morning. He was last to leave. There was no task too small that he wouldn't lend a hand. There was no task so large that he was daunted. When anyone expressed doubt that the play could be ready on time, it was Romanos who encouraged them, or cajoled them, or did whatever was necessary to keep everyone at work. He had become friends with Akamas, which I suspected he had done with the assistance of some wineskins. The other stagehands took their cue from Akamas. They volunteered to work longer each day. *Sisyphus* was being carried by the sheer force of will of its second actor.

The new third actor, Kebris, proved to be a find. He was an old trouper, and looked it when his mask was off. He had thinning hair and deep lines in a face that seemed perpetually sad. But he picked up the lines with such speed that even Sophocles was pleased. "I've never known an actor to fall into a part so easily," he said.

The truth was that Romanos had worked extra time outside the rehearsals to get Kebris ready, which Diotima and I knew perfectly well because we'd met Romanos that rainy night, leaving the theater after working with Kebris. Diotima and I discussed Romanos in low whispers as we sat in the stalls, out of earshot of the cast and crew.

"He took your advice," I said to Diotima.

"What advice?" Diotima asked.

"Don't you remember? Under the stoa in all that rain. You advised him to become as indispensable to the Athenians as your father. Well, he's doing it. If he goes on like this, Sophocles will be *insisting* that they make Romanos a citizen," I said.

Diotima nodded. "He deserves it."

THE MORNING BEFORE the Great Dionysia wasn't a rehearsal day. Instead every single act—not only the play of Sophocles, but the other two tragedies as well, and the comedies, and the ten choral performances—*everyone* was due to arrive to set up their pieces. The Dionysia was held over five days. The people today would organize the logistics of moving their acts in and out in order.

Diotima and I arrived at the theater with Socrates in tow, just as Apollo's light peeked over the east. We found both guards slumped against the back wall, sound asleep and snoring.

I kicked them awake.

"Get up, you idiots. What do you think you're doing?"

They opened their eyes, but they were still sleepy. They stared up at me in confusion for a moment. Then their state of confusion turned to horror when they realized it was me staring down at them, and that they had fallen asleep.

They scrambled to their feet and stammered, "We're sorry, master, we don't know what happ—"

"Don't bother," I interrupted. "Pythax will hear of this."

They trembled. Pythax was a stern disciplinarian. One of the toughest men in Athens, he expected every man he commanded to be his equal in application to duty. I foresaw many long disciplinary marches for these two, in full armor, through the day and night without rest, so that they could learn how not to fall asleep.

I myself had once drilled with the Scythians, at the insistence of my future father-in-law, so that he could teach me how to stay alive in a street fight. The memory of Pythax's brutal training still haunted my nightmares, but I had never forgotten his lessons, and I hadn't been killed yet either.

"Come with me," I said. "We'll have to check every tiny thing backstage, to make sure nothing's been tampered with. And when the stage manager arrives, he'll have to check it all *again*, because he might spot something that we'd miss."

We did that, the two guards and Diotima and me. We picked up every prop and every mask. Not only the ones for *Sisyphus*, but the props and masks for the comedies and the other tragedies. I had to stop Euboulides and Pheidestratos from playing with the pig's bladders that the comedians used. They made a farting noise that the guardsmen thought was hilarious. I thought it was funny too, but Diotima didn't. Nor did I want the guards to be caught playing with the props when the actors and crew arrived, which would be at any moment.

I crawled across every part of the backstage floor in search of booby traps. There were none.

I stood up and dusted off my hands and knees.

"All right, that's about it. You two can think yourselves lucky nothing went wrong."

"What about that thing, sir?" Euboulides pointed at the machine.

We all stared at the mechanism, but none of us had any idea how it worked. There was a chock between two of the cogs, but it was easily visible and for all I knew it was supposed to be there.

"It looks all right to me," I said hesitantly. "We'll have to have Kiron check it before anyone uses it."

Socrates said, "Nico, the machine's not in rest position."

"What?" I said, startled. "That's impossible. Nobody's holding it."

Socrates pointed to the machine's arm. "It should rest level. But the arm's up and over the skene."

So it was.

I walked over to the mechanism. It looked the same as always. Yet the short end was pressed down as far as it could go.

I found the answer at the hinge. Someone had pressed down the short end lever and then pushed a chock into the hinge. I'd seen Melpon the doctor do the same thing, when he wanted to lock his healing machine in place. I understood what had happened here. The arm was up because it *couldn't* descend.

I turned to the guards. "How was it set last night?" I asked. Maybe the arm had been left this way by the actors.

The guards looked at each other, both waiting for the other to speak.

"The arm was level?" Euboulides guessed.

I sighed. "We'll check the stage."

We walked around the skene onto the stage and looked up. The arm of the god machine poked thoroughly over the skene and high above us.

Hanging from the arm was a man. Or rather, a god. Because whoever was up there was dressed as Thanatos, the god of death, slumped over exactly as he appeared when he made his entrance during the play.

Romanos, I thought, must be practicing his part. He had worked like a slave over the last two days to get everything right. I'd come to appreciate what a stickler Romanos was for getting things right.

I called up, "Are you practicing early, Romanos?"

Then I realized what a stupid question that was. There'd been no one working the machine when we walked in. It was impossible for Romanos to be up there.

At that moment the first of the actors and crew arrived to begin their day. They walked in from the audience end. Aeschylus and Sophocles walked in, and a gaggle of men followed. One of the men pointed and screamed. The body slowly rotated in the air.

"Get him down!"

A voice roared across the theater. It was Aeschylus.

"Get him down now!" Aeschylus shouted again.

Aeschylus had seen what I already knew: that Thanatos, the god of death, was dead.

SOME FOOL SHOUTED, "Is he still alive?"

Whoever was up there obviously wasn't, but there was the slimmest chance and we had to act on it.

I turned to Euboulides and Pheidestratos. "You two," I said.

"Get back there, pull the chock and let him down. Socrates, show them how."

Both guards sprinted backstage as if their lives depended on it. Which they might well. I couldn't remember the last time I'd been so angry at anyone. Their lax work had led to this death. Worse, the safety of the theater had been *my* responsibility. Pericles was going to blame *me* for this disaster.

A brief moment passed. From behind the wall I heard Socrates issuing instructions—a daunting prospect at any time—followed by swearing that was the guards. Then the arm above me made rapid up and down movements. The body jerked in the air like a dying fish as they tried to control the machine. I guessed one of them was pulling on the arm while the other tried to dislodge the chock. I spread my arms, ready to collect the body as it descended.

I heard a yell of triumph, followed by some anxious swearing and then a voice yelled, "Look out!"

The distraught call made me look their way. But nothing was happening there.

When I looked up again it was to see the underside of Romanos's feet, approaching rapidly.

The dead man fell on me.

# SCENE 13
# JUST HANGING AROUND

"ARE YOU ALL right, Nico?" Diotima asked.

"Never been better," I said. I'd fallen backward onto the hard stage. Now I found myself staring into the dead eyes of Romanos. He stared back. His eyes bulged slightly. His tongue poked between his teeth, disturbingly close to my face. His lips were blue. There was a stream of dried saliva coated on his chin.

"It's a good thing you broke his fall," Diotima said. "He might have been hurt."

I decided not to point out the illogic of that. Instead I rolled the corpse off me, then knelt. I wanted to apologize to Romanos, but it was too late for that.

I turned over the body. I looked at the noose tight about his neck. Romanos had been hanged, and now he was dead. There was no doubt about it.

I was struck—as I always was in these circumstances—by how still were the dead. The slight movements of the living were entirely absent, the chest as it breathes, the small involuntary twitches, things that go unnoticed until they're gone. Romanos was as flaccid and unremarkable as any corpse.

"I DON'T SUPPOSE it could be suicide?" Aeschylus said hopefully. "Men have hanged themselves before now."

"Not unless you know of a way to raise the lever at one end, chock the hinge in the middle, and get the noose around your neck at the other end."

"It does seem unlikely." Aeschylus rubbed his chin.

Diotima, Sophocles, Aeschylus and I stared down at the body.

"If it wasn't suicide, what happened here?" Sophocles demanded angrily. "Nicolaos, I thought you had guards posted. You said nothing could happen while they watched."

He was right. I had indeed said that. I had promised him the theater would be safe. I had said there would be no more "accidents." I had failed.

"Sophocles, I will see this put right," I said.

"Young man, *my actor is dead*. The play is in ruins. The Great Dionysia is probably at a halt. We are shamed before the whole world who have come to watch this debacle. Which of those things do you think you can *put right*?"

"We'll start with finding out how this happened," I said. I grabbed Euboulides and Pheidestratos by the arms and dragged them away from the others. Diotima joined us.

"All right, now tell me how you both managed to be sleeping on the job while one of the men we're supposed to be protecting was murdered."

They looked at each other. Already I could see the lies forming.

I said to them, "If you lie to me and I find out you lied, Pythax will be the least of your problems."

"We were drinking, master," Euboulides said at once.

I'd already guessed that.

"How?" I demanded. "Do you mean to tell me you left your post to get a drink?"

"No sir," said Pheidestratos. "We never left the theater. Honest. There was a woman with us."

I groaned. "This is getting worse."

"No sir, he means the woman came to us," Euboulides corrected. "She wanted to sell us a drink—"

"But we didn't have no money," Pheidestratos broke in. "On account of us being slaves. So she said, seeing as how we were only slaves, that she'd give us a cup for free."

"A strange woman offers you a drink, and you just take it, no questions asked?"

"Yes sir!" They said in unison.

"We're slaves, sir," Euboulides added helpfully.

If I'd been them, I would have drunk alcohol at someone else's expense too.

"It was cold in the middle of the night, master," Pheidestratos said. "We didn't think it would do any harm. One little drink to keep us warm."

Pheidestratos was begging for forgiveness. I could ignore that, but not the information that came with it.

"*One* drink?" I repeated.

"Yes, master."

"She didn't leave an amphora or a wineskin?"

"No, master."

"Do you both swear by Zeus and Athena that you each drank one normal cup?"

They both swore.

"Then we got tired, master."

"After just one cup?" I repeated.

"Yes, master." Euboulides frowned. He was the smart one. "It don't normally take only a cup to knock me down, master. Normally it's more like . . . uh . . . ten."

There was no way that a normal healthy man could be felled by one cup. Nor were these ordinary men. They were the Scythian Guard of Athens, under the care of Pythax, whose idea of light exercise was an all-day march in full armor. It was impossible that these men could have been knocked out by a single drink.

Diotima looked at me and I looked at her.

"A *pharmacis*," she said. "A witch woman."

I nodded. A *pharmacis* was a woman expert in herbs and medicines . . . and in poisons. How many *pharmacai* were there in Athens? A hundred? My mother would know. Pregnant women were among the biggest buyers of pharmacis medicines. There must be a pharmacis in every deme, two in the poorer demes where people couldn't afford a doctor, and would turn to their local pharmacis for help.

But why would a witch woman want to kill an actor?

"What did this woman look like?"

"Don't know, sir!"

"Why not?"

"She wore a cape, sir. One of the ones with a hood."

"Was she tall or short?"

"Kind of stooped, sir," Euboulides said.

There wasn't the slightest chance of identifying her, whoever she was.

"Come with me."

I returned to Sophocles and Aeschylus, and told them what we knew. Sophocles looked disgusted.

I grabbed an *ostrakon*—a broken shard of pottery—that lay on the ground amongst the seats of the theater. I scratched a message into it, then handed the ostrakon to Euboulides. I said, "Take this to Pericles."

Euboulides nodded. "Yes, sir." He left at a trot.

"What was the message?" Sophocles said.

"That we have a problem," I said. "My commission is with Pericles. He needs to know." I winced.

"You're worried?" Aeschylus asked.

"Sympathy for failure is not one of Pericles's strong points."

"It's not your fault," Aeschylus consoled me. "I'm sure Pericles will understand."

I wished I had his confidence.

A reply came back sooner than I expected, carried by a slave runner. He handed it to me.

PERICLES SAYS THIS TO NICOLAOS. I HAVE CALLED AN EMERGENCY COUNCIL TO DISCUSS THE CRISIS. WE MEET AT NOON AT MY HOUSE. THAT WILL GIVE MEN OUTSIDE THE CITY TIME TO ARRIVE. IT WILL ALSO GIVE ME TIME TO THINK WHAT WE ARE GOING TO SAY TO ALL THE DISTINGUISHED GUESTS FROM OTHER CITIES WHEN THEY LEARN OF THIS DEBACLE. SAME SUMMONS TO MEET IS GOING TO THE ARCHONS, TO THE CHOREGI, TO THE WRITERS, AND ALL OTHER SENIOR MEN OF THE DIONYSIA. INFORM EVERYONE AT THE THEATER WHO FITS THAT DESCRIPTION. PERICLES.

I silently handed the ostrakon to Aeschylus, who read it with raised eyebrows. He handed it to Sophocles, who handed it to Lakon, who handed it to Kiron. The ostrakon made its way around the producers, writers, and actors of every comedy and every tragedy.

"Thank you," I said to the messenger slave. "Tell Pericles we'll be there."

"Sir, I also have a message for you," said the slave.

"For me?" I said. "What does Pericles say?"

"My master Pericles says you are to arrive early, if you can manage to do that simple thing without tripping over your own feet, you incompetent moron."

The slave grinned as he said it.

I had little doubt that the slave had passed on the message exactly as Pericles had spoken it, but I was equally sure it was the slave's own special touch to repeat it in front of all these leading citizens.

Aeschylus broke the embarrassed silence. He squinted up at the sun. He said, "Noon. That gives us plenty of time before the meeting."

"I'll need it," I said.

"Oh?"

"I have to inform a family that they're bereaved. Where did Romanos live?" I asked, then added, "Does he have family here?"

"Not as far as I know," Kiron said. He turned to Sophocles, who shrugged.

"I hired him because he's a good actor, not because he's a friend," the playwright said. "I have no idea about his family." Sophocles turned to the man beside him. "Do you know, Lakon?"

"I'll need to think about that," Lakon said. He immediately struck a thoughtful pose, hands behind his back, chin sunk to his chest. After a few moments he said, "Yes, I do believe the poor fellow lived in Melite."

Melite was a deme to the west of Athens but within the city walls. It was a place of narrow lanes and crowded tenements. Finding the victim's home amongst them would be a nightmare.

I said, "I don't suppose you know where in Melite he lived?"

"I'm afraid you'll have to ask around. I said I knew the man, not that I socialized with him."

"You mentioned that before," Diotima said. "Was there some bad blood between you?"

Lakon turned to her. "Not at all, dear lady, but being a woman, you wouldn't understand."

I quickly stepped between Lakon and Diotima, in case Diotima decided to punch out our lead actor. I'd seen her hit before in anger and we needed Lakon to remain conscious. But Diotima showed creditable restraint.

"Why don't you try anyway," Diotima said, through gritted teeth. "Despite my obvious limitations."

"I am a citizen actor," Lakon said. "I do not act for money. That would be demeaning."

"What about Romanos?"

"He acted for money."

# Scene 14
# Descent into Melite

IT WAS ESSENTIAL we find the family of Romanos, if he had one, and if not, his home, so that we could search it. Someone, somewhere, had a reason to want Romanos dead. Someone, or some evidence, was going to have to tell us why.

Lakon had told us that Romanos lived in Melite, a deme directly west of the theater. I refused to have Socrates with us when we delivered bad news. He was the least tactful person I knew. I sent him home. As we walked away in the opposite direction, Diotima said, "If Lakon turns out to be the killer, I will personally offer my thanks to the Gods with a fine sacrifice." She was still angry about his attitude. In her sandals, Diotima kicked a loose stone on the path in anger. The stone went flying, and she spent the rest of the trip cursing her sore toe.

THERE ARE NO signs to mark the boundaries of the demes within Athens, but you always know when you've stepped from one into another because their characters are quite different. It was only a matter of crossing the southbound road to Piraeus to take us from influential Collytos into downmarket Melite.

Piraeus Way is one of the busiest thoroughfares in Athens: all the commercial traffic from the port to the agora is on that road. The east side is lined with expensive town houses. The west side is lined with houses too, less expensive ones. Diotima and I walked along one of the paths between them into the narrow byways of Melite.

Melite had been the home deme of Themistocles, the great General and traitor whom Diotima and I had met in Ionia. We thought of him as we passed by his old house. A hundred steps further on, we passed the small temple to Artemis that Themistocles had commissioned. It was in a sad state of disrepair; a chipped façade of faded paint and wooden columns with hairline fractures.

In the days of Themistocles he'd seen to it that Melite was the best decked out deme in Athens. Since then Melite had absorbed much of the influx of metics to the city. Several families crammed into buildings that had once housed only one. To make extra room, the men had extended rooms so that they overhung the street or encroached at ground level. Streets that had once been narrow but adequate had become almost impassably narrow and claustrophobic. This change had happened in my own lifetime.

More people meant more sewage. It all went into the open drains that ran down the middle of the street. Combined with the muddy walkways and the second storeys that loomed above, Melite had acquired its own unique aroma.

Diotima and I took care to walk the outer edge of these mean streets, because what floated down the center didn't bear thinking about.

Naked or ill-clothed children watched us from doorways. Some of them asked for money. A mother told them sternly not to bother the citizens passing by.

Diotima was having none of that. She stopped at the doorway where the mother had issued the rebuke. Diotima glanced at the mother, bent to talk to the snotty-nosed children. She held up three obol coins—half a drachma. It was a paltry sum, but the children's eyes went round as bowls.

"Do you know a man named Romanos?" Diotima asked them.

The children said nothing, but their eyes never left the coins.

"They don't, but I do," their mother spoke up. She was dressed in a chiton of some heavy material and had a weary air.

When the woman said nothing more, Diotima said, "We'd like to find his home."

The mother thought about it. Then she asked, "How do I know you'll pay the children when you're done?"

Diotima handed over the coins on the spot, one to each child. Each clutched the coin to their bosom as if it were their most prized possession.

Their mother said, "I suppose it can't hurt." She bent to the children and gave them instructions on where to take us. Having heard her words I could have gone straight there myself, but I wasn't going to deprive the children of their work.

The children led us deftly down the paths. I guessed the two older for seven and eight, a boy and a girl. The youngest was perhaps five and had to be stopped by his older siblings from playing with the muck in the drains.

They led us left, right, left to the center of the deme, where there was a square, a tiny one from which someone had swept the rubbish. Old women hawked their wares from faded wooden boxes: wilted vegetables, cheap pottery, and good luck amulets. No doubt the sellers weren't paying the vendor fees with which the city hit the stallholders in the official agora. This was some sort of unofficial agora that had sprung up, discreet enough that the archons probably didn't even know it existed.

On the opposite corner of the agora was a house, and it was before this that the children stopped. They looked up at us expectantly.

"This is the place?" Diotima asked.

They nodded.

"Thank you."

They turned to run home.

"Hey, kids!" I called.

They stopped.

"Here," I said. I handed each of them a full drachma piece. I used my body to block the transaction from idle sight.

"Now I want you to take these to your mother. You're to give them to her, and nobody but her. And you hide them, right now, you understand?"

I worried that in these parts, there were people who would beat a child for a drachma.

They nodded and three drachmae disappeared beneath three rag-thin tunics. The children might not say much, but they lived on these streets and they weren't stupid.

"All right. Run."

They ran.

"Melite's a lot poorer than it used to be," I said to Diotima when they were gone. "It wasn't like this when I was a child."

"I wouldn't know," Diotima said. "I wasn't allowed out of the house."

"I probably ran down every street in Athens," I said. "I remember when they were building most of these places."

We knocked on the door.

It was opened by a slim young woman.

"Yes?" She peered around the edge of the door, ready to slam it shut.

Her hair was ragged and shorn. The classic signs of bereavement.

I was taken aback.

"I'm sorry," Diotima said, equally nonplussed. "I see you're already in mourning."

"I am?" the young woman blinked at Diotima. The two women looked much the same age. But whereas Diotima was dark, this woman was light skinned with light brown hair.

She realized we were both staring at the top of her head.

"Oh, you mean my hair. It doesn't mean anything. I'm a professional mourner."

It was my turn to be surprised. Of course I'd seen

professional mourners in the street, but I'd never thought I'd meet one. In every case I'd seen them walking behind a cart upon which a dead person had been laid, on their way to the cemetery at Ceramicus. Mourners were hired by the family, to express their grief, which they did with loud wails, graphic tearing at their hair, and the rending of their clothes.

Until that moment it had never occurred to me that professional mourners must have normal lives, when they weren't walking behind dead people.

"Then you *haven't* heard," I said, relieved to have solved at least one tiny puzzle.

"Heard what?" she asked.

"That Romanos is dead," I told her.

The young woman raised her arms to the sky and screamed.

# SCENE 15
# WHOOPS

"WELL HOW WAS I supposed to know she was his sister?" I protested.

Diotima had spent considerable time listing my various defects: mental, moral, and social. She paid particular attention to my lack of tact.

"Nico, they're living in the same house. *Of course* she was a relative of some sort. I thought at first she must be his wife."

Diotima had had plenty of time to berate me. The woman—her name was Maia—had installed us in the visitor's room at the front while she went off to inform the rest of the house of the disaster. As she spread the word the wailing rose throughout, until it sounded like a house of madmen. But it wasn't; it was a house in genuine mourning.

A man entered the room. His hair was freshly cut and ragged.

He greeted us and said, "My name is Petros." Beneath the sadness his voice was pleasant. "I would offer you refreshments," he said politely, "but . . ." His voice trailed away.

"But a house in mourning doesn't serve refreshments," I finished for him.

"No. My wife didn't ask you for details."

"Your wife?"

"Maia. Romanos is my brother-in-law."

"I'm sorry."

"So are we all. I must ask you what happened, and even more urgent, where is my brother-in-law's body?"

"At the theater."

I told him, as succinctly as I could, what had happened.

At the word murder, Petros turned gray and staggered back until he leant against the wall. "Dear Gods, no," he whispered.

I said, "I'm sorry to have delivered such harsh news to your wife. But we had no idea Romanos had so much family in Athens. The people at the theater could tell us nothing, except for Lakon—"

"Lakon?"

"Another actor. He told us Romanos lived in Melite, but beyond that he too had no information."

"I see."

"Do you know Lakon? I suppose you must know other actors, your brother-in-law having been one."

"Everyone in this house is an actor. Even the children."

"Oh?"

"I must ask you to excuse me. My brother-in-law's body must be brought back here."

I nodded. Petros was right. Already the psyche of the murdered man would be loose from its body. Romanos's psyche needed to descend to Hades, but the psyche couldn't begin its journey until the rites had been performed. Until then it should stay close to its mortal remains. But in the theater, alone, a psyche could become lost. The last thing Athens needed was a real psyche haunting the Great Dionysia.

No, the sooner Petros got the body back here the better. They would place the body in the inner courtyard, with its feet facing the door. That would prevent the psyche from straying.

"Do you need help?" I asked. I wouldn't normally offer to help strangers move their dead, but I felt sympathy for these people.

"Thank you, but there are plenty of men in this house. Far too many men, in fact."

"Many men?" I said, surprised.

"And their families too," Petros said.

"Did you all come to Athens together?" Diotima asked.

"No. Romanos was here long before the rest of us. He is . . . was . . . an Athenian in all but name. He moved to Hellas as a young man, to make his fortune. Maia and I didn't leave Phrygia until after we married. The others drifted in over time. It's easier for folk from the same place to get along."

"One last question then. Do you know of anyone who might have wanted your brother-in-law dead?"

"No."

"Had he any enemies?"

"None that would murder," he said shortly. "And now I must go."

"WELL THAT WAS a waste of time," I said as we walked away.

"No it wasn't, Nico," Diotima said. "We told a family they were bereaved. Now they'll collect Romanos and he won't lie alone."

"We'll have to interview them again," I said. "But not until they've had a chance to calm down. The next question is, which persona did the killer intend to kill?"

Diotima looked at me oddly. "What do you mean, Nico?" Diotima said. "Nobody could have mistaken Romanos for someone else."

"No, but there were *three* men in the same body," I said. "There was Thanatos the character in the play—"

"You mean someone was trying to kill *the character*?" Diotima said. "What sort of a crazy person would do that?"

"Characters kill other characters," I said.

"Characters aren't real, Nico," Diotima said. "Real people kill other real people. They don't kill fictional people."

"Then why did the killer choose to kill Romanos as if he were Thanatos?" I said. "There are so many easier ways to kill a man than hanging from a god machine on a stage, in the dead of night, with two guards close by."

Diotima chewed at her lip while she thought about it. "The method does sound rather dramatic," she conceded. "Or it's a crazy person. Go on."

I said, "Then there's Romanos the actor. That's how he's best known to men in Athens. Was this a professional quarrel that turned violent? Then there's Romanos the metic who lives in a crowded house in Melite. Nobody at the amphitheater even knew he had a family in Athens, that's how secretive he was."

"Nico, you're talking about motive."

"All right. But which of those three men did the killer intend to strike down?"

# SCENE 16
# THE ACADEMY

IT'S A STRANGE case when you know who the body is, but aren't sure which man died. Was it Romanos the actor? Or the character he played? Or perhaps because of his life outside the theater?

Diotima's point that it came down to motive was true, but the three different identities of Romanos were so extreme that we felt we had to begin with this question: who was Romanos that someone would want to kill him?

Diotima pointed out that Phellis had fallen in exactly the same situation as we had found Romanos dead, and both men had been dressed as the god of death.

"It's almost as if the play was unlucky," Diotima said.

"Don't be ridiculous," I scoffed. "Whoever heard of an unlucky play?"

Diotima shrugged.

I said, "Besides, we know that Phellis was brought down by the saboteur."

"Do we?" she asked. "Is the saboteur the same person as the killer?"

It was my turn to shrug. "We'll have to find out."

"What do we make of the woman who drugged the guards?"

"I think they saw the killer."

"So do I. But it might have been a man."

"They said it was a woman."

"Nico, actors pretend to be women all the time."

Romanos might have walked to his place of execution, but

more likely he had been carried—perhaps they knocked him out first, or perhaps he was drunk—either way there would have to be at least two men; one at each end. This idea caused us to knock on the door of every house close to the theater, in the hope that someone had seen a body being carried down the street.

It turned out there had been at least seven. The people of Athens hadn't waited for the Great Dionysia to start before the dionysiac parties had begun. All across the city, symposia had raged through the night. Exhausted drunk men had been carried home by their slaves.

The heavy intermittent showers that had soaked Diotima and me had forced everyone to rush from place to place between spells of rain. Witnesses saw many incapacitated men on the street at the same time, and to an observer at night, there was no difference between a man who was dead drunk and a man who was dead.

It occurred to me that the perfect time to carry a body through the streets of Athens was on a party night.

Whatever, it meant there was no useful witness, and if someone *had* seen something, they would have been too tipsy themselves to be a reliable witness.

We abandoned the search and decided instead to question Sophocles. After all, he was the author of this tragedy.

Sophocles lived in the deme of Colonus, which lay to the northwest of the city. I sent a slave runner with a request to visit him, and received an immediate reply that Sophocles had gone to the local gymnasium to relieve the tension of the disaster, and that I was to see him there. His local gymnasium was the Academy.

I passed through the agora on my way to the Dipylon Gate, which was the closest exit to Colonus. In the agora all was chaos. Chaos was the agora's usual state, but today's chaos was different from the norm. Today, the market stalls had not been raised. Instead, slaves were hard at work hammering together long planks to make tables and benches for the party to come. Women strung chains of flowers between poles that the men had raised. Children carried baskets of flowers for the women or ran between the legs of the adults. Dogs followed their masters or ran with the children. People smiled as they worked, even the slaves. Men and women laughed and sang songs in praise of Dionysos, the god of wine and the harvest.

I followed the Panathenaic Way northwest from the agora and on through Ceramicus. This was the deme where the potters worked, and it showed in the large clods of clay dropped here and there, and the men working with their hands behind their wheels, in workshops that were open to the road. None of them looked up as I passed. Nor did the people here seem as interested in the Dionysia as other parts of the city. Perhaps it was because they were too busy making money.

These men were famous throughout the world, because only they knew how to paint their handiwork with red figures on a black background. The red figure pots of Athens were one of our biggest exports. A "ceramic" jar could command an outrageous price in places where the potters weren't as talented as ours.

Every second house had a serving hole cut into its front wall, with a wooden door that opened upward to form an awning for the women who served behind the counters. They hawked the wares that their husbands and sons had made in the workrooms. In Athens, every business is a family business. Even mine. Diotima was as much a part of my work as I was.

Ceramicus was also home to another place where business was booming: the city's cemetery. I passed it on the right, and reflected that soon Romanos would be cremated here.

The other side of Ceramicus backed onto the double portal of the Dipylon Gates, the widest way in and out of Athens. Despite this, there were so many people coming into Athens that I had to step back and wait for the tide to ebb.

I passed the time with one of the guards at the gate. He swore at the visitors and told them to hurry along, talking to me between the cuss words.

"Most of this is people coming for the party," he said to me.

"Then why are they all coming from outside?" I asked.

"They're camping outside the city walls." He spat on the ground, narrowly missing a tourist. The tourist scowled but took one look at the unhappy guard and decided to make nothing of it.

The guard said, "Have you seen what the inns are charging for a bed?" He spat again. "If it were me, I'd be sleeping on hard ground too, if I had to pay a week's wages for one night."

"And then a lot of them will stay for Dionysia."

I looked back at the crowd entering Athens. The sight of all those happy people made me nervous.

Outside the gates was the deme known as Outer Ceramicus, not as salubrious as Inner Ceramicus, but close enough that it did good business with passersby. Outer Ceramicus gave way to groves of olive trees, sacred to the goddess Athena, and orchards, all within a walled park. The fruit was free for the picking and I didn't hesitate.

I had arrived at the *akademia*—the Academy. The Academy housed the city's third, newest, and most glorious gymnasium. Many years before my time it had been a run-down hovel. Then a nearby stream had been diverted to irrigate the land, and now it had become an earthly vision of the Elysian Fields.

The path to the gymnasium was lined with statues, and fountains fed by the stream. Three of the statues had been made by my father. I stopped to admire them as I passed.

The gymnasium was a thing of beauty, one of the first buildings in Athens to be made of marble and painted in bright reds and blues and yellows to contrast with the fine green grass. In the morning, with the sun at my back, it shone.

The wide entrance opened into a quadrangle lined on all

sides with porticoes. Right away the sweet aroma of olive oil hit my nose, barely masking the musky odor of heavy sweat. Which was how the Academy always smelled, because every alcove in every portico about the inner courtyard was filled with naked men, fresh from exercise, all anointing themselves with oil.

Men looked up as I entered to see if I was someone they knew. This was a place where men came to socialize as much as to exercise. I wasn't a regular at the Academy; the habitués didn't recognize me and returned to their own affairs. I didn't see Sophocles, nor did he hail me. I would have to wander around to find him.

I couldn't walk straight across the sunlit inner yard because it was divided into training patches, each a shallow square pit filled with sand, five paces by five, where a man could exercise or two men could box, or wrestle, or practice the martial art called *pankration*. At this time of day the patches were all in use.

I didn't expect to see Sophocles among the trainees and so wasn't disappointed when I didn't find him. I did however see my best friend, Timodemus. He stood by one of the patches, where two men fought a practice bout. They traded blows while Timodemus watched them with a jaundiced eye and barked instructions.

Timodemus was one of the best pankration fighters alive, famous for his victories in competition against other cities. He had recently retired from active fighting and moved with his new wife to a house not far from here. Now every day he came to the Academy, where he commanded outrageous fees as a coach.

Timodemus saw me and waved. He shouted, "*Chaire* Nico! Greetings! Have you come for a practice round?"

I shook my head and called back, "I'm on business. Do you know where I can find Sophocles?"

Timo shrugged and returned his attention to his students. He probably didn't even know who Sophocles was. My friend had no interest in plays, or philosophy. But he was really good at hurting people.

I felt a tap on my shoulder. I turned to see a wiry old man, shorter than me, with a friendly expression and not much hair. I knew him. This was Lysanias, one of the elders of Athens, who had helped me on a previous case. He was also unbelievably good at throwing quoits.

He said, "I thought I heard you, young fellow. How are you? Have you come to practice your quoit throws?"

This was the way of the gymnasium. As soon as you walked in, everyone who knew you would stop to talk, would demand your attention, if only for a moment, would invite you to stay for half a day or the whole day.

I had to shake my head regretfully, because I liked Lysanias and would gladly have spent time with him. "I'm sorry, sir, I'm here on business. I'm looking for Sophocles."

"He's in the next courtyard," Lysanias said. "I saw him come in. I will show you to him. Then I will sit down with you and listen shamelessly to your conversation." He led me by the arm. As we walked he said, "I know you, Nicolaos. If it is you who has work, should I take this to mean Athens is in dire peril? Is our city on the verge of destruction?"

"Only our reputation for staging plays," I said. Somehow Lysanias had managed to miss what had happened, probably because he spent all his time in exercise. Though he was an old man, I would not want to face him in combat. I explained to Lysanias what had occurred, that the theater was polluted by murder, and that the Great Dionysia could not proceed unless the terrible crime was avenged.

Lysanias wasn't a man to worry about trifles, yet at my words he looked stern and said, "This is more serious than you seem to think, young man."

"I'm already aware how bad it is, sir."

"Are you? How many people come from abroad to see our plays?"

"Hundreds?" I guessed. "Perhaps thousands?"

"Certainly more than a thousand," Lysanias said. "Every bed in every inn is full. Private homes are renting out their spare rooms and people are camping outside the walls."

"Yes," I said. "The guards at the gate told me."

"Have you ever been to the home of a man who proved to be a buffoon?" Lysanias asked. The question seemed to come from nowhere.

"Why, yes, I have," I said, thinking of some of my father's friends. Every now and then he dragged me along to visit his cronies.

"And what did you think of those men?" Lysanias asked. "Did you think more, or less, of them?"

"Why, less," said. "No one respects a buffoon."

"Precisely. Now what of a man you visit, who proves to be a man of culture and dignity?"

"Then that would be someone I respect," I said.

"Yes," Lysanias said. "Now, young man, think of all these people who have come to Athens to be entertained by us, to see our plays, which are the best in the world. If we cannot show the plays because of murder, if everyone sees we cannot keep our own actors alive in our own city, if we must send all those people home having admitted we can't stage a play, then how will we appear to our visitors?"

"We'll look like buffoons," I said.

Lysanias nodded. "You understand. I will add this: that it is easier to attack an enemy whom you don't respect. But it is harder to feel animosity against someone who shows competence in all things."

"Surely, Lysanias, this cannot be a matter of war or peace," I said.

"The entertainment a man provides for his friends says as much about him as how he carries his spear," Lysanias said, and his voice became hard. I remembered that this was a man who'd carried his spear many times. He added, "The Great Dionysia tells the rest of the world how we wish them to see us. Our poets are as much a function of the state as our diplomats."

We had passed through to the second courtyard, where we found Sophocles lying face down in the shade, on the cool stone floor. A slave rubbed olive oil into his shoulders and back.

He looked up as we approached, and said, "Join me."

Lysanias said, "Hello, Sophocles. Don't mind if I do." He dropped his clothes and lay down beside Sophocles. His whole body was wiry and thin. A slave appeared with oil flask in hand. The slave began at once to massage the back of Lysanias and pour oil on his skin.

I hesitated. I wasn't used to enjoying the gymnasium with respectable old men. In fact, unlike most men I rarely visited the gym at all—somehow I never seemed to have the time—and when I did, it was usually to see my friend Timo, who would often be surrounded by young men our own age.

I knew the etiquette though. It would be rude if I stood, or merely sat beside them.

I pulled my chiton off over my head —it saved having to undo the shoulder knot—and handed the clothing to a slave, who placed it on the bench against the wall. I lay down on the other side of Sophocles.

Another slave appeared, also with a flask of oil. He commenced to massage my shoulders with oily hands. I tried to relax.

I said, "I came to see you, Sophocles, because I must learn about Romanos."

"He was a metic," Sophocles said, as if that explained everything.

"Yes, but what was he like?"

Sophocles considered the question.

"As a man, I really can't say," he said, after thinking about it. "Professionally, he was a good actor. I had used him before in minor roles. Certainly this play offered him a big chance and I must say he impressed me. It's unusual for a metic to have a major role in a Dionysia."

The slave began to massage my legs.

I said, "Did you socialize?"

"As I said, he was a metic."

It occurred to me that Sophocles preferred the company of his peers.

"What about Lakon?" I asked.

"Lakon's a citizen," Sophocles said. "And I've known him a very long time."

"Then how does he come to be an actor?" I asked.

"You have it the wrong way round," Sophocles said. "Most actors are citizens. The exceptions are the metics."

I asked, "In the play, with the original cast, was Phellis the only man to use the machine?"

"Both the first and second actors flew on the machine. Lakon played Zeus in a later scene."

"What about the third actor?"

"Third actors never play a god. They're not important enough."

"How does that work?" I asked. "Does importance matter?"

"Not the way you're thinking, but consider the scene casting," Sophocles said. "There's only one machine. There can never be two gods onstage at the same time."

"Oh, I see. Is there much squabbling over the parts?" I asked.

"Constantly," Sophocles said.

His tone alone was worth a day of explanation.

"You said you'd used Romanos previously?"

"Several years ago, when another actor failed me—the poor fellow had been beaten by brigands as he traveled the country roads—I needed a quick study. Someone suggested I look at Romanos. Well, I was desperate, I would have hired a donkey if it could speak the lines. But Romanos was everything the recommender had said."

"Then you knew Lakon first?"

"Citizen actors start when they're boys. They come up through the chorus. Throughout the year there are festivals and choral performances where we need children to sing. I and the other directors choose from among the sons of respectable citizens."

I knew that part all too well, because when I was a boy I had volunteered, but had never been chosen. I remembered standing nearby while someone told my father it was because I couldn't sing. My little brother Socrates had never been chosen because they said he was too ugly.

"Most of the boys are talentless, of course," Sophocles said, not knowing my own history. "Perhaps a quarter of the boys can sing passably well. We directors notice the ones who sing well. We choose the cream from throughout the year to fill the choruses for the Dionysia. Of the cream, a handful can also dance. From each year, perhaps one or two of the best will like the stage well enough that they stick with it when they grow to men."

I was astonished. "Do you mean to say you hired Lakon when he was a boy?"

"How old do I look?" Sophocles demanded. I'd insulted him. Lysanias tittered.

"Sorry, Sophocles, but I don't understand."

Sophocles rolled over so the slave could massage his front. He added, "That's something Lakon and I have in common. We both got our start in the chorus."

"You were an actor, Sophocles?" I said, surprised.

"I was passable, in my day," he allowed, in the tone of voice a man uses when what he means is that he's too modest to say he was the best.

Sophocles continued, "I was selected by Aeschylus to perform in the chorus. These days Aeschylus is my friend, but back then he was my director. Lakon too, when he was a boy, was selected by Aeschylus. By that stage I was a young man, serving as an elder member of the chorus. I remember standing in the same chorus line with Lakon."

"In a sense you grew up together," I said.

"No. Lakon returned with his parents to their home town, Rhamnus. He didn't play again until he returned to Athens more than a decade later, as a young but fully grown man. By then I had given up acting. A man can't be both an actor and the writer, and the writer is of more service to the state."

"He is?"

"Certainly he is," Sophocles said. "I'm surprised you even question it. Tell me, young man, why do *you* like tragedies?"

I didn't like tragedies. I'd always preferred the comedies. But this didn't seem the moment to mention it.

"Well," I said, desperately trying to think of something. "Tragedies are very . . . er . . . tragic—"

Lysanias laughed.

Sophocles frowned. "Of course you know the purpose of our plays—"

"To entertain people," I said at once. "That's why more people go to see the comedies than the traged . . ." I trailed off.

Sophocles stared at me openmouthed, and I suddenly realized I'd blundered.

"Er . . . that is . . ." I groped for the right words.

Lysanias was rolling on the floor, tears running down his face.

"I'm sorry, Sophocles," I said.

Sophocles sighed.

"Don't bother trying to talk yourself out of it," Sophocles said. "Now listen closely, young man. The whole point of tragedy is to teach people the difference between right and wrong." He glared at me.

"It is?"

"It is. In tragedy a great man makes a mistake. He does wrong when the Gods gave him the power to do right. Then we see his downfall: the consequences of his mistake. This teaches the people that right might not always be rewarded, but wrong is always punished. A tragic writer has the greatest responsibility to the people, because we are the teachers of morals. If we produced plays that praise bad behavior, then the people would copy the behavior of their onstage heroes and the state would collapse."

"I see."

"We must hope that as you grow older you acquire some taste for both the tragedies *and* the comedies. I despair when I look at the stuff that passes for comedy these days. How anyone could think it's funny to watch people hitting each other with pigs' bladders is beyond me."

Sophocles clearly didn't frequent the same circles I did.

"Tell me about the noose," I said.

Sophocles said, "It was my idea to hang the god of death. The noose is joined to the machine's rope on a stretch that is *longer* than the remaining rope to the actor's harness. The difference is only a hand's length, but it's enough."

Sophocles demonstrated with his hands.

"You see the effect?" Sophocles said, warming to his subject. "I thought, since it was impossible to hide the rope from which Thanatos hangs, I may as well make it work as a part of the play. The real remaining length of rope is painted blue to match the sky. The noose seems to be the only rope up there. To the audience they see the god of death appear as a hanged man."

"It was certainly realistic from where I sat during rehearsals," I said. "Everyone was terrified."

Sophocles beamed. "It's always nice to hear that an effect worked."

"Perhaps a little too well?" I suggested.

"That's not my fault."

I was frustrated. I'd hoped to learn something of Romanos. But other than that he was a good actor, which I already knew, I'd learned nothing. It seemed odd that the man should be such a cipher. He'd seemed perfectly open when Diotima and I had spoken to him in the rain. I said as much to Sophocles, who shrugged.

But Lysanias poked up his head from the massage and said, "Have you talked to his sponsor?"

"Who?" I said. "What sponsor?'

"Didn't you know? All metics are required to register with the state, and they must have a sponsor."

"I never knew," I admitted. It occurred to me, with some surprise, that except for Diotima, who had been a metic before we married, I too had never socialized with metics.

"Who was the sponsor of Romanos?"

"You must ask the Polemarch," Lysanias said.

"Did the Polemarch know Romanos?" I said.

"I doubt it. But the Polemarch is responsible for all metic affairs. If anyone would know who the sponsor of Romanos was, it'll be him. You probably need to do it anyway. The sponsor must be informed that his client is dead."

# SCENE 17
# THE POLEMARCH

IT SEEMS TO be a rule that every important official in Athens must have a long queue of men outside his office door. I had never been to see an archon who wasn't overwhelmingly busy. The Polemarch was no exception. The difference was, the men outside the Polemarch's door spoke with foreign, non-Athenian accents.

The Polemarch's office was an ancient building called the Epilyceum. It stood just beyond the official bounds of the agora. The Epilyceum showed several centuries of maintenance. The original wooden beams, so old that they'd turned deep black, poked out between the newer stone facade of later renovations.

It was a measure of how long you had to wait to see the Polemarch that supplicants had scratched game boards into the stone of the street outside. Even the game board scratchings were well worn from years of game pieces moving across them. Men were hunched over these boards. Others silently watched the traffic pass by, and many talked amongst themselves.

I listened carefully to the words of the other men, to place their accents. It isn't always possible, but you can take a guess at a man's home because most cities have slight differences in the way they say their words. At Diotima's suggestion I had recently begun to pay attention to such differences.

A handful of accents were northern, from Thebes perhaps. The people of the north spoke with an accent that approached barbaric, and sometimes used words common to the barbarian tribes to the north of Hellas.

The great majority spoke the Ionian dialect of the Aegean Islands. It was the same dialect that was spoken in Athens. There are a hundred of these islands. Common among them was the distinctive Ionian as it was spoken on the mainland and on the other side of the sea, in the region that is called Anatolia.

Listening to their conversation, I realized many of the men who waited with me had come to apply for permission to live in Athens.

So many men. Was it like this every day?

"Is there a Nicolaos, the son of Sophroniscus?" A voice called from the Polemarch's door. Not the Polemarch, but his assistant. He held a wax tablet and frowned.

"That's me," I said.

The Polemarch sat at a writing desk, on a chair of curved timber and a comfortable rounded back. The table and chair were both expensive pieces whose legs were shaped to resemble the legs and feet of a lion. I guessed they were both from the same carpenter, and that they were the personal property of the Polemarch, the more so because the wood was polished elm, which is very heavy and hard and far beyond the budget of the state. The Polemarch was a rich man to own such things.

"You're the man I received a note about," the Polemarch said as soon as I entered. His voice was a deep bass. "From Pericles. Something about a total disaster at the theater? He seems to blame you."

"A murder, sir."

"That sounds bad. Why did you do it?"

"I think you might misunderstand, sir. I'm the detective."

"Ah, I see. And there's a meeting this afternoon?"

"Yes, sir. At the home of Pericles."

"Well I have a lot of work to get through before then. What can I do for you?" he asked.

I said, "I hoped, sir, that before the meeting you could tell me something about metics. They must come to you, mustn't they, to live in Athens?"

"Yes. That's what that long line is outside. Any man from another city who wants to live in Athens must register with my office. As long as he pays his registration fee and names his patron, he's in."

"Are there any restrictions on the metics?"

"They may not own land. That is reserved for citizens. Metics pay slightly higher taxes, though the difference is nominal. I assume you know that a trial for the murder of a metic is heard in a lesser court than that for a citizen."

"No sir, I didn't."

"Well you do now. If one metic kills another, we're as likely to exile the murderer as execute him. It's so much less messy that way."

"What if a citizen murders a metic?" I asked.

"That's why these cases are always heard in a lower court. The citizen would be exiled for a period of years, or face a massive fine. If metic murders were heard in the highest court, it would mean a citizen could face death for killing a non-citizen. That wouldn't do at all."

"I see."

The Polemarch said, "I must warn you that it's very hard to obtain justice for a metic. Juries are not generally sympathetic."

I said, "Do you know who was the patron of a man named Romanos?"

The Polemarch asked, "Why do you care about this Romanos?"

"Because he's the dead man."

"That sounds like a good reason. Everything you want to know will be in the records." To my blank look he added, "We record the patron of every metic. If the metic does anything wrong, it will reflect on the patron."

"I see."

The Polemarch banged on his desk, which wobbled under the pounding despite its sturdiness. The Polemarch was a strong man. The door behind me opened. An assistant poked his head in.

"Yes sir?"

"A metic named Romanos," the Polemarch said. "Who's his patron?"

"It'll be in the records," the assistant said promptly.

"Yes, that's why I'm asking you," said the Polemarch. "Is there anything else?" the Polemarch asked me.

"No sir. Thank you for your time."

"Then go with Andros here. He'll give you everything we have on this Romanos."

Andros was a short, wiry man who liked to talk. He led me out of the building, out of the agora, and down the road. He talked every step of the way, about his job (tiring), about the price of poultry (too high), about the weather (too hot), about his children (unruly). It was a relief when we finally came to a nondescript building, a small warehouse on the main road in the unfashionable southern deme of Coele.

"This is where we keep the records," Andros said.

A slave stood guard outside, but otherwise there was nothing to indicate this was a government building.

"I've lived all my life in Athens," I said. "But I never knew this place was here."

"No reason why you should," Andros replied. "It's just a storehouse. The only people who come here are assistants to the Polemarch."

"Do the other archons have a store like this?"

"I suppose," Andros shrugged.

The slave opened the door for us.

The building was dark within. As my eyes adjusted I saw the reason why. Every wall had been covered in shelves of thin pinewood. The shelves covered every window. Upon them were heaped scrolls, some in cases, some lying loose, but most in pottery jars that lay sideways to offer the scrolls within. The horizontal shelving visibly strained under the weight.

I took one step inside, and almost fell over. My foot had kicked something.

There were more jars on the dirt floor. These were upright, but for the ones that had been knocked over. Like the scroll jars on the shelves, there poked out of them more papyrus than I'd ever seen in my life. To get from one end of the room to the other would be like climbing over a field of rocks.

There was a distinct musky odor. One that I knew all too well. A cowardly part of my anatomy shrank inward at the memory.

Something scuttled out of the jar I'd knocked over. More than one something. In the dark of the floor I couldn't see what it was.

Andros said, "Don't mind them. That's just the mice."

"Terrific."

"They seem to eat the old paper."

But for the scrolls, the jars, the shelves, and the mice, the room was empty. No one worked here. In the close, dusty air that made me want to sneeze, the lack of light, and the mice, I wouldn't want to work in here either. I'd be happy to get my scroll and get out.

"Thanks, Andros," I said. "Which jar has the Romanos scroll?"

"How should I know?" he said.

"What do you mean, you don't know?"

"I have no idea," he said cheerily. "We just dump all the paper in here."

"There must be *some* sort of order to all this, mustn't there?"

"No."

"Then how does anybody ever find what they're looking for?

"You weren't listening, Nicolaos. Nobody ever reads these records. We just keep them."

"The Polemarch said the records were consulted, whenever a metic committed a crime."

Andros laughed. "That's what every new Polemarch thinks. The elected officials only hold the office for a year. Either they don't stay long enough to learn the truth, or they get disillusioned. The ones who learn the truth don't admit in public that the system's broken. If they did, they'd have to do something about it."

"Then why keep the records?"

"In case someone needs to read one."

"But you just said no one ever reads them."

"Well, there's you," he said, reasonably enough.

I looked at the row upon row of scroll jars and the teeming piles of paper. I would have to read everything until I found the one page I wanted.

"This is going to take some time," I said. I mentally added days to the time it would take me to solve this case. Many days, unless I was lucky.

"I'll leave you to it then. Careful you don't drop that torch. We don't want a fire in here." Andros turned to go, then stopped and said, "I'll tell the slave out front to let you in whenever you want."

Andros left.

I stood there a long time, wondering how I was going to trawl through this disaster area and at the same time conduct an investigation. Then, in a flash of inspiration, the solution came to me. It was a brilliant solution.

I FOUND HIM still at the theater. He must have remained there the whole time. He seemed to be playing with sticks that he'd balanced over a stone. He looked up as I approached.

"Look at this, Nico. I think I've worked out how the machine lifts a man. It's all to do with how long the lever is on each side. You see here? When one side's longer than the other—"

"Socrates, I've got a job for you," I interrupted.

"What job?" he asked suspiciously.

"You like to read, don't you?"

"Sure."

"Good. Then you're going to love this."

I LEFT SOCRATES inside the records warehouse, volubly protesting, but with firm instructions not to come out until he had everything he could find on Romanos. I promised to send a slave with food and spare torches.

When I emerged from the records room for the second time, I blinked and stared at the sun. It was past time to see Pericles. Where I expected to have the skin torn off me.

## Scene 18
# CONFERENCE OF WAR

I LOST TRACK OF time while Pericles flailed me with his words. He could be cutting even on a good day, but now he was at his brutal worst. I had no choice but to stand there and take it.

Pericles paced back and forth in angry strides across the ground of his private courtyard in his private home. His anger was such that even his own slaves quailed in the shadows. He waved his arms as he described my numerous defects.

He ended with, "You idiot, Nico. I send you to quell one simple ghost, a job anyone could do, and we end up with a crippled actor and a dead one." He stopped his pacing to glare at me. "Are you the most incompetent private agent in Athens?"

"I'm the *only* private agent in Athens," I pointed out.

"Yes, well. Point made." Pericles resumed pacing.

I said, "I'll add, Pericles, that you commissioned me because you said I was the best man for the job."

"Apparently I was wrong," Pericles said, still pacing. But that statement brought him up short. He considered his own words, then said, in a tone of surprise, "But wait, I'm almost never wrong."

I stood silent while Pericles considered this paradox he had suddenly discovered.

A large group arrived while Pericles stood in agitated thought. The new arrivals were the senior men involved in the Great Dionysia that was due to start next day: the archons who ran the city, plus all the producers and the writers and the protagonists of each of the plays.

Pericles had called a council of war, and the highest citizens had obeyed. It spoke volumes about the influence that Pericles wielded in the city that he thought nothing of summoning fellow citizens, that even the archons who were senior to Pericles in rank came at his call. It was nothing to do with his official position, which was an elected *strategos*, a General of the Army. Strategos was a position of great power, but there were nine other men with exactly the same title and no one treated the other nine with such deference. The power of Pericles lay in his voice, which was an instrument of the Gods, and in the charisma he exuded as easily as he breathed. I often forgot how easily others fell under his spell. I seemed to be the only man in Athens who wasn't impressed.

There were more than twenty men in the courtyard and not enough places to sit. Though he was a wealthy man, Pericles hated spending money on anything, even on his own comfort. *Especially* on his own comfort. Pericles liked the best of everything, but not much of it. His courtyard was barely larger than that of a normal man. As the least important man present I stood. So did the lead actors and several of the others. Pericles ensured that Aeschylus sat in a seat of honor, and beside him the archons. These were the three executives responsible for the running of the city: the Eponymous Archon, the Basileus, and the Polemarch. I'd had cause to deal with all three offices in the past, but there'd been a recent election and these men were all new to their jobs. The final man arrived at that moment: the High Priest of Dionysos, the man with whom Diotima had first expelled the ghost. He looked slightly out of breath.

Pericles brought the archons up to date with what had happened. The three nodded grimly.

Throughout this Pericles couldn't hide his irritation with the situation.

These powerful visitors stared at Pericles with some

astonishment. Pericles had a reputation for being the calmest, most dignified, and certainly the most decorous man in Athens. They had never before seen him so upset. I, on the other hand, was used to it. I usually saw Pericles in his private office, when a crisis was at hand and events had turned against us. At those times he could be the most demanding man in the world. He had no tolerance for anyone whose service to the city was less than perfect.

Pericles continued the meeting with a question.

"Who is the victim?" he asked.

"Romanos of Phrygia," Sophocles said. "I'm the author of this tragedy. May the Gods forgive me. Romanos was *deuteragonist* of my play."

"The dead man's not a citizen then?"

"No, he's a metic."

"What do we know about him?"

"Very little," I said. "The only man who knew him at all was Lakon."

Lakon gestured in an elegant movement that reminded me of someone, but I couldn't say whom.

"Hardly that," Lakon said. "I knew Romanos. Of course I did. But there isn't much I can tell you. One doesn't like to move in such circles." Lakon pronounced every word perfectly and yet oddly rounded. His voice was rich and flowed like honey, as full of pleasant timbre and as precisely controlled as Pericles's own. I thought it quite remarkable.

"What circles?" someone at the back of the courtyard asked.

"Metics," Lakon said. He gave the word just enough stress to show what he thought of metics. "Romanos was merely a professional colleague. Even then, I'm not quite sure what he was doing in a Dionysia play." Lakon cast a sidelong glance at Sophocles, as if to say the playwright had been slumming when he invited Romanos onto the cast.

Sophocles turned a dangerous red.

"I don't think I know you?" Pericles said to Lakon. I knew what Pericles was thinking. I could imagine the effect if that voice spoke before the People's Assembly. If Pericles had a competitor for best orator in Athens, he wanted to know about it before they faced each other in debate.

"You don't recognize me, yet you have seen me many times," Lakon replied with a superior air. "I am the protagonist, the lead actor of this play."

"Oh, I see. Nice to meet you," said Pericles dismissively, and with an audible trace of relief. He had once said to me that no one in their right mind would ever vote for an actor. That Lakon had trod the stage automatically meant he had no future in politics.

Pericles said to the assembly at large, "Is there anyone in Athens to avenge the murdered man?"

"His family," I said. "He has a sister and brother-in-law here. But they of course are also metics."

Several grunts of dismissal sounded around the room. Everyone knew a metic had little chance of avenging a murder in Athens.

Pericles said, "Are there any other questions?"

The Eponymous Archon had only one. He said, "How quickly can you get the play restarted?"

Everyone present stared at the Eponymous Archon in astonishment.

"We can't," Sophocles said.

"What? Don't you have a replacement actor? Surely you do."

Sophocles said, "The problem is it would be impious to continue."

"Even so I must insist the festival carries on," said the Eponymous Archon. He sounded angry. "It's a question of national pride."

"Didn't you hear what Sophocles said?" asked the Basileus.

He was the archon in charge of religious affairs. "Did you not hear that the God's statue was placed on the stage, facing the crime? Gentlemen, this is a murder committed *in the presence of the God*. On his most sacred ground—the theater—right before his most sacred festival, the Great Dionysia."

Everyone glumly contemplated his words.

"The god Dionysos must be furious at what's happened. Can you imagine the bad luck that would descend on the city if we continued as if nothing had happened? I'm sure the High Priest of Dionysos agrees with me."

All eyes turned to the High Priest Theokritos. He nodded unhappily. "It's true."

"What would it take to appease the God?" the Eponymous Archon asked.

"Perhaps a major sacrifice?" the High Priest suggested. "Like the Eponymous Archon, I too am most reluctant to abandon the Dionysia, or even delay it for an instant."

"Your reluctance is understandable, my friend," said the Basileus. "But we all know impiety is a major crime, the biggest there is."

Theokritos sighed. "Yes. I know what you're about to say."

"The Great Dionysia must be suspended," said the Basileus.

In the shocked silence that followed, the Eponymous Archon asked, "What would it take, then, to restart the festival?"

"Punishment of the killer, of course," the Basileus said.

"What's the penalty for impiety?" someone asked.

"Death by stoning," Theokritos said. That meant the murderer would be taken to a nearby quarry, where he would be tied to a stake, and the people of Athens would take turns throwing rocks at him until he was dead.

"All right then," said the Eponymous Archon. "Let's execute the murderer and get on with the festival."

"There's only one little detail," Aeschylus pointed out. "We don't know who did it."

My stomach lurched.

"Whose job is that?" the Eponymous Archon asked.

"Er, that would be me. Sir," I said.

The most powerful city official in Athens turned to stare at me. "I didn't catch your name. You are?"

"Nicolaos, son of Sophroniscus," I said.

"I've heard of you," the Eponymous Archon said. He didn't say if what he'd heard was good or bad. Instead he went on, "This is a disaster on so many levels, I barely know where to begin."

I hoped he didn't mean me.

"Murder is always a disaster," I said.

The Eponymous Archon stared at me in surprise. "Murder? That's nothing. Young man, a dead actor is the *least* of our problems."

"It is?"

He pointed to the door, beyond which lay all of Athens. "Have you any idea how many leading dignitaries from other cities are out there? How many wealthy merchants? Dear Gods, we even have a contingent from the Great King of Persia visiting. If word gets out that we can't hold a play without it going wrong, we'll be the laughing stock of the civilized world."

"We need to think about this," the Basileus said.

"We have to *do something*," Aeschylus said. "Can you imagine what the other cities will say?"

"Can you imagine the jokes they'll tell?" a comedy writer said sadly. "And I won't be able to use a single one of them."

"Why don't we cancel the festival?" the Polemarch suggested.

The reaction to the Polemarch's suggestion could not have been more horrified had he suggested we eat live babies. When he saw the expressions on our faces he said, "What's wrong?"

"You're not an arts man, I can see," Aeschylus said. "Stop the Great Dionysia? It's unthinkable."

"You're not a religious man either," the Basileus added. "What would the God think if we canceled his most important festival? The final ceremony is the parade through the city, followed by the crowning of Dionysos. How do you think the god of the harvest will feel if he isn't crowned this year? Do you want to think about the consequences for the food supply?"

Heads nodded at the words of the Basileus. If the God was displeased, we could expect a pitiful crop. It would mean hunger for the city.

"Nor are you a diplomat," Pericles added. "Did you not hear the words of our Archon, that hundreds of representatives from the most important cities in the world are in Athens right now? They will watch and wait with interest to see how we handle this crisis."

"And then there are the Athenian people," the comic writer said. "They're expecting a party."

The Polemarch threw up his hands in surrender. "All right, it's only an idea. Let me know when you have a better one."

Pericles said, "Gentlemen, Aeschylus is right when he says we must act. If we don't, our esteemed foreign visitors will soon see a genuine Athenian riot. Could we proceed with the Dionysia, but without the play by Sophocles?"

A man whom I'd not seen before stood beside Sophocles, older, with short, dark hair and a pained expression. Sophocles turned to him now and said, "You've been quiet, Thodis. What do you think? It's your play and your investment."

So this was Thodis the choregos, the man who backed the play with his money. He had been strangely absent during the troubles. If my money had been at such risk I would have been present every day.

Thodis looked about the assembled company with wide eyes. "We must certainly do as Pericles suggests," he said. I had rarely seen a man appear so out of place as Thodis did.

"That idea's not a starter in any case," said the Basileus, and the High Priest nodded. "The crime of impiety is against the God. Whether *Sisyphus* opens is of no moment to cleansing the theater. You want to cleanse the impiety? It has to be vengeance. There's no faster way."

Sophocles said, "What say then we postpone the Dionysia? Tell the people the plays will resume after the murderer is caught."

"How long will that take?" someone asked.

Every eye turned back to me. I was the junior man in this company, by a long way. I felt my face go red.

"I don't know," I said. "A day? Ten days? Maybe a month?"

"Days?" the Eponymous Archon spluttered, as if I were a handyman who'd just delivered too high a quote. "Can't you hurry it along?"

I forbore from pointing out that I hadn't even started.

"You can't delay that long in any case," the Basileus said. He seemed to take a morose pleasure in destroying every suggestion. He said, "The crowning of Dionysos is scheduled for the fourteenth of Elaphebolion. It's a particularly lucky date. If we pushed the crowning ceremony back to an unluckier date—not something that I'd advise in any case—then the festival of Rhea that comes straight after would be delayed by the same amount. It gets worse. Even if you don't mind offending Rhea, the mother of the Gods, the rites of Pandia come straight after that, and *those* are in honor of Zeus. The Spring rites for the king of the Gods would land right at the end of the month. You all know what that means."

The unluckiest day in the calendar. No one in their right mind would schedule anything important to happen then. Every man present contemplated the effect of offending *three* gods.

"That's it, then," the Polemarch summarized. "We're doomed."

Pericles said, "The situation is this: we can't cancel the show because it's a sacred festival. Nor can we continue the play until the murder is avenged, and if we don't do something we'll look incompetent before the whole world. We must complete to schedule because the season is so busy for sacred rites."

Everyone agreed.

"Then there's only one solution," Pericles said with an air of calm logic. "We must suspend the calendar until the murder is solved."

"Suspend?" I said, confused. From the perplexed looks around the room I wasn't the only one.

Pericles said, "The calendar doesn't move forward until the crime is solved to the satisfaction of the Gods. That solves every objection."

"Except for one. You can't stop time, Pericles!" I said.

"You're right, I can't," Pericles said. "But *he* can." Pericles pointed to the Eponymous Archon.

The Archon nodded unhappily. "I don't like it, but if I have to, I will."

"But sir, you can't stop time either," I said.

"Yes I can. Do you understand the meaning of my title?" he said.

"Eponymous Archon? It means *the leader who gives his name*."

"Gives his name to what?" the Eponymous Archon persisted.

"To the year," I replied promptly. Everyone knew that. This year would be known forever as the Year of Habron, because Habron was the personal name of this year's Eponymous Archon. Then it struck me. "Sir . . . Habron . . . you *own* the calendar."

Habron the Eponymous Archon nodded. "We take our calendar months from divine Selene, who controls the movement of the moon. We take our years from Apollo, who drives the Sun about the Earth. Why Selene and Apollo can't coordinate themselves better I don't know; but the two of them *never* match up at the end of the year." The Archon shrugged. "Maybe they just don't get on. But for whatever reason, it means that at the end of every year, whoever holds the office of Eponymous Archon must add a few extra days to our calendar, to catch us up with Apollo." He thought about it, then nodded. "Yes, I see what Pericles is getting at. I can add the extra days *now*, and not at the end of the year. Then when you've caught this murderer and the plays resume, it will still be . . . what's the date today?" asked the man in charge of the calendar.

"It's the ninth day of the month of Elaphebolion," Sophocles said.

"Thank you," the Eponymous Archon said. "When the Great Dionysia resumes, it will still be the ninth of Elaphebolion, and it will be as if none of this ever happened. Yes. The more I think about it, the more I like this plan of Pericles'."

Smiles all round, from everyone except me. I said, "But sirs, what if I can't catch the kill—"

"Good, that's settled then," Pericles interrupted. "Eponymous Archon, would you like to make the announcement to the people?"

Habron the Eponymous Archon hesitated.

"Would you like me to make the announcement?" Pericles offered. There was no hint of modesty in his voice.

Habron accepted. His relief was evident.

"I have an idea how we might get away with it," Pericles said. He outlined his plan. Heads nodded once more.

When it was clear that he had agreement, Pericles turned to one of his assistants.

"Call for an emergency meeting of the People of Athens," he said. "Right away. Every citizen to meet at the theater."

# SCENE 19
# THE SPEECH

PERICLES STEPPED ONTO the stage, where most of the citizens of Athens had gathered. It was late afternoon, the perfect time to catch men between work and home. The word had gone out that there was to be an important announcement.

Diotima and I hid behind the skene, out of sight, where we could peek our heads around the corner. I wanted to see everyone's reaction to what Pericles had to say. The archons had followed Pericles into public view. They stood to one side of him. In fact, they looked remarkably like a chorus to Pericles's protagonist.

Pericles didn't shout for attention. That would have been undignified. He stood patiently until everyone noticed that the most powerful man in Athens awaited their pleasure. The people fell silent more quickly and effectively than if someone had bellowed at them.

"People of Athens!"

Pericles's voice was smoother than music. People listened because they wanted to hear more.

"People of Athens, today a murder has been committed within this theater in which we sit. That is bad enough, but the crime was in full view of the god Dionysos himself. This is impiety of the highest order."

Pericles paused to let the people think about that. The bright ones saw the implications immediately. A low murmur swept across the crowd.

"As long as the city does nothing, this crime reflects on us all. Dionysos will turn his face from us."

Lakon emerged onstage. He carried a white cloth of some delicate material. This he placed reverently over the head of Dionysos, to obscure the God's view.

Lakon stepped back from the statue and bowed like a supplicant. The movement was as smooth and elegant as might be expected of a professional actor. Yet the audience had no way of knowing who he was, for Lakon had assumed the mask that the victim had worn, the mask that had covered his face when his corpse hung from the machine.

To the audience it looked as if Thanatos, the god of death—or perhaps it was the murdered man—had returned from the grave to cover the eyes of the God whose most sacred festival had been polluted. I was privy to Pericles's plan, yet even I felt a shiver run down my back.

Pericles hadn't even turned to watch. Instead he spoke as commentary to the action, "The impiety must be avenged. The Great Dionysia is suspended from this moment, to resume on the same day when the murderer is brought to justice. Citizens of Athens, when I say the same day, I mean the same date as well. On that day, the cover will be removed and the Great Dionysia will continue."

In the tense atmosphere the audience thought about the meaning of Pericles's words. It slowly dawned on them that he had just suspended the calendar. There were murmurs.

Pericles smiled and said in a jocular tone, "In the meantime, we must not forget the God. For this is the time to honor him. We will not allow crime to rule our lives. A public feast will be held in honor of Dionysos, a dionysiac feast, in the agora. The feast will be held five days hence, to give my staff time to prepare. It will be my gift to the people of Athens."

Pericles managed not to wince as he said this. A public feast was going to cost him a fortune. He was one of the few men in

Athens who could afford it, but I'd never known a man tighter with his money. I took some satisfaction in knowing how much Pericles was going to hate this.

There were murmurs of appreciation from all around the theater. Cheers erupted in several places. They merged into one large cheer for Pericles across the entire theater, as people realized he had promised them a free feast. Their minds had glossed over the news that the Dionysia would be delayed.

This was the effect Pericles had predicted when he outlined his plan, as we stood in his courtyard. Somehow Pericles had managed to turn this crisis into an opportunity to promote himself to the people. I wondered if he'd known this would happen when he first suggested his plan.

The speech had been brilliant. Pericles had announced a crisis, had unflinchingly delivered the bad news it implied, had shown the people a solution, and then given them a party to keep their minds occupied while someone else sorted out the details. I could already see some of the women in the audience discussing what they should wear to the public feasts, while the men were probably thinking about the free wine.

Pericles held up his hand. People realized he had more to say, and they fell silent.

"And now I say to you, go from this place of worship to Dionysos. Continue his celebration in the agora. When we meet here again the stain will be washed from the city and all will be well."

Pericles had once advised me to avoid acting at all costs, because, he said, "No one in their right mind would vote for an actor." Pericles may have avoided acting, but he had all the talent needed for a theatrical career.

As he walked past me, Pericles said out of the corner of his mouth, "That's my part done. Now it's up to you, Nicolaos. Don't fail us."

# Scene 20
# Writers' Conference

As the assembly broke up Diotima and I went straight to Thodis. This was our chance to find out what he knew.

"Thodis? Could we speak to you for a moment?"

Thodis looked at me as if I was some spirit raised from the earth.

He said, "You were at the meeting, but I don't recognize you."

That surprised me. Had Thodis paid no attention?

"Nicolaos, son of Sophroniscus, and this is my wife," I said. "I'm the investigator on this case."

"Then you are the one to blame for all the troubles," he said.

"I think that would be whoever harmed Phellis and killed Romanos," Diotima said to him.

Thodis looked at Diotima for a moment, plainly considered not answering her, then said, "But your husband failed to prevent it."

That was an interesting way of assigning blame, but Thodis was right. I *had* failed to protect his investment.

I said, "I wanted to ask you, sir, what's your interest in the theater?"

"I'm paying for the play written by Sophocles. I pay for every mask, every prop, every actor."

"And yet, sir, you never seem to attend the theater. We've been there almost constantly for six days, and we haven't seen you there even once. It seems strange behavior for a man who loves the theater, if you don't mind me saying so."

"I see." He considered my words. "I must disillusion you. I have no interest in the theater whatsoever."

"Then why—"

"Why am I spending such large sums on something I care nothing about?" He flicked away a fly that buzzed about his face. "I was advised by my friends to do so. My father died recently—"

"I'm sorry."

"I'm not. I found it rather convenient actually. You see, I planned a career in politics, but my father wouldn't permit it."

"I know that song," I muttered.

"You too?" he said sympathetically.

"Let's say I had a similar problem."

"Did you have to wait for your father to die?" he asked.

"No, I talked him round."

"Then you were lucky," he said sourly. "My father was most unreasonable. He insisted I learn to manage our estates. Then he died. As you see I am a man of middle age, yet only now can I begin my true career."

"Why begin with a play?" Diotima asked.

"My plan is to become the first man in Athens," said Thodis modestly. "To that end I have studied the career of Pericles most closely. When Pericles entered public life, the first thing he did was provide a play. He was a choregos."

That was true. Pericles had funded the play called *The Persians* written by Aeschylus. It was one reason the two were such good friends.

Thodis said, "I reason that if I do what Pericles did, then it follows that I must eventually attain the same position."

Thodis was fooling himself. He was no Pericles.

"Thus I spent a substantial part of my inheritance on a play to entertain the people. I'm pleased to say that if my father returned from Hades to see what I'm doing, he'd probably have apoplexy and die again."

I said, "When you said you had no interested in the theater, you really meant it."

"Yes. My friends advised me that with Aeschylus retiring, Sophocles is the coming man. As Pericles linked his name to Aeschylus, so I should link mine to Sophocles."

"I see. Then disaster struck. Is this why you're avoiding the theater?" I asked.

"Yes. I must dissociate myself from the disaster. Don't take this personally, but I can hardly afford to have my name linked to someone like you."

"What about the actors in your play?" Diotima asked.

"What do you mean?" he asked.

"There's someone who needs your help: Phellis, the actor whose leg was smashed."

Diotima explained that Melpon the doctor was demanding payment for his use of the healing machine. "Phellis is an actor, he hasn't enough money to pay the doctor to save his leg."

When she was finished, Thodis said, "I will think upon it, and I will take advice from my friends. I must say this is hardly my problem."

"He was injured working on your play."

"He was hired for the duration of the play, was he not?"

"Well, yes," Diotima said.

"If you hired an artisan to paint your house, and a third party came along and injured the painter as he worked, you wouldn't be responsible, would you?"

"Well, no," Diotima admitted.

"I feel sure the actor's correct course of action would be to sue the man who injured him."

"That would be the man who also killed Romanos."

"Then perhaps you should catch him?" Thodis suggested. "Then you could put your request to the correct source."

I asked, "Is there anyone you do want to associate with?"

He puffed out his cheeks. "Well, naturally I've entertained Sophocles."

"Naturally," I said.

"My friends suggested I should also entertain the lead actor. What do they call themselves? Protagonists, yes, that's right. They tell me that protagonists are important people."

"I like to think so," I said.

"Lakon proved to be an entertaining companion, a most charming man. Sophocles less so. He seemed a trifle uncomfortable. All he wanted to talk about was plays and writing."

"Sad."

"I thought so. There was no such difficulty with Lakon. He's a man I could introduce to my friends with no risk of embarrassment."

I made a mental note to discover who these friends were, so I could avoid them.

Thodis was still speaking. "In fact, I invited Lakon to dine with me on more than one occasion. He has a collection of amusing stories that he tells very well. My other guests were in stitches of laughter. He and his friend Romanos are valuable companions—"

"WHAT!" Diotima and I roared simultaneously, so loudly that Thodis staggered backward. He looked ready to run.

"I'm sorry, Thodis," Diotima said quickly. "You startled us with your last comment."

"And you startled me with yours!"

"Thodis, did you say Romanos was a friend of Lakon?" I asked carefully.

Thodis blinked in surprise. "Lakon arrived at one of my symposia arm in arm with Romanos. Of course to receive a guest of a guest is a time-honored tradition. This is how one enlarges one's circle of connections. I had no objection. I'm not sure why you ask."

"I ask because I was given to understand that Lakon never

socialized with Romanos. You heard Lakon say so himself, at the noon meeting."

"If he did, I missed it. I was . . . ah . . . preoccupied."

Thodis meant he hadn't followed events during the meeting. I said, "I distinctly heard Lakon say he didn't socialize with Romanos."

"Then you must have misheard, or misunderstood."

"WHAT DO YOU think?" I asked Diotima as Thodis strode off.

"He's not going to help Phellis," she said.

"No. It looks like we'll have to catch the killer and make him pay."

"But Nico, what if we can't do it in time to save Phellis?"

"Banks lend money. Maybe we could get an interim loan to cover the costs?"

"A loan where the only surety is our promise to capture a killer? Does your banker do deals like that?"

"Maybe not," I said, rubbing my chin. "All right then, what do you think of Thodis as a murderer?"

Diotima said, "Thodis is the last man on earth who would want to ruin his own play."

"Or at least, he should be," I said. "I agree."

"Logically we should cross him off the list of suspects," Diotima said.

"Right."

"Then why do I feel like he should be top of the list?" Diotima said.

"Me too," I said. "We'll have to keep him in mind."

"He might have something to hide," Diotima said. "He has a connection to Romanos that we didn't know about."

"Maybe," I said, though I felt dubious about her theory. "Thodis admitted he knew Romanos without being asked. That looks innocent. The more important news is that

Lakon lied when he said he never saw Romanos outside the theater."

Diotima's brow furrowed. "Why would he lie about that?"

"Good question. We'll have to find out."

Most of the men backstage had disappeared as quickly as they could, but three remained: Sophocles, Aeschylus, and Chorilos. The three tragic writers for this year's competition were in earnest conversation.

Diotima and I decided to interrupt.

"Excuse me, sirs," I said. "We have some urgent questions."

"Hello, Nicolaos. Yes?" Aeschylus said. He and I had become friends during a previous case. The difference in our ages was almost fifty years, yet we got on well. He also had a high regard for Diotima.

"It's about casting," I said. "How do you do it?"

"The Eponymous Archon selects who will be the writers, who will be the choregoi, and who can be cast for protagonists," said Aeschylus.

"Not you, Aeschylus?" Diotima said, surprised. "I thought you simply volunteered your services for the year and then chose your actors."

All three men laughed.

"If only it were that simple," said Chorilos. "Take me, for example. I applied to the Archon's office six months ago. I was one of thirty men. We were all applying for only three slots in the schedule."

Aeschylus added, "Every writer in Athens is desperate to see his work at the Great Dionysia. It's a wonder there isn't a bloodbath every time the authors apply."

"How does the Archon choose?" Diotima asked.

"Exactly the way any sane person would," Chorilos said. "The Archon chooses the most popular writers first." Chorilos glanced at his two colleagues. "I said before that I was one among thirty for three positions, but that wasn't quite accurate.

We all knew that Aeschylus and Sophocles had applied this year. That meant the other thirty had to fight for *one* slot."

"Is that fair?" I asked. "Shouldn't everyone have a chance?"

"Would you like to be the Archon who rejected Sophocles?" Aeschylus asked.

"I understand," I said. What Chorilos had said was clearly true. Sophocles accepted the tribute deadpan. He knew his own worth and saw no point in denying it.

"The protagonists are declared using the same system," Chorilos continued. "For protagonists the Archon declares a pool of suitable actors. The protagonists must not only be skilled, but men of the highest character, because they'll be called upon to portray the great heroes of Athens to young men and impressionable children."

Sophocles and Aeschylus nodded.

Aeschylus said, "The writer is paired with a choregos, who funds the play. The choregos and the writer between them choose a protagonist from among the available pool."

"That's how you chose Lakon?" Diotima asked Sophocles.

"Yes," said the playwright. "The trick is to match the actor's personal style with the play's main character. Lakon has a fine reputation, and like all great tragic actors, he has a flair for portraying powerful men with a fatal flaw. I felt he'd be good for *Sisyphus*."

"I see," I said. "Sophocles, at the meeting in Pericles's courtyard you seemed upset at one point."

"I did?" He raised an eyebrow. "I was probably thinking of poor Romanos."

"This seemed more specific," I said. "It was when Lakon questioned why Romanos was a member of the cast."

"Oh, that," Sophocles said. "Yes, his words did annoy me."

"Why?"

"Because it was Lakon who recommended Romanos for third actor. The protagonist must come from the Archon's list. The deuteragonist and the tritagonist are at the discretion of the management. After he'd been cast, Lakon had brought Romanos to my attention. It's quite usual for the protagonist to propose men he likes to work with. I was under no obligation to pay attention, but I had worked with Romanos before and knew him to be reliable." Sophocles paused. "I must say I had no idea Romanos would prove to be so outstanding."

"Yes, he was," I agreed.

"I underestimated him," Sophocles admitted. "If he'd lived, and if he hadn't been a metic, he would have made a fine protagonist one day."

"Would you have proposed him for citizenship, Sophocles?" Diotima asked.

"It crossed my mind," Sophocles said. "But of course that would have depended on the outcome of the play."

The sky had darkened as we spoke, and Diotima and I had exhausted our questions. The three tragedians made their way into the night.

There was no point in pursuing the investigation into the evening. Everyone involved had departed for home, or for dinner at the homes of their friends. None would agree to see us. Our only option was to go home and worry about how we were going to solve this crime.

It was going to be deeply embarrassing if we failed. All of Athens would know that it was I who had failed them, and not only brought shame to the city before visiting dignitaries, but, even worse, would deprive the people of the best party of the year.

# Scene 21

## ~~A New Day Dawns~~

## The Previous Day Dawns Again

APOLLO'S RAYS WOKE us as the God peeked over the horizon. It was still the ninth of Elaphebolion, and it promised to be a long day.

"Halting the calendar is very convenient," my father said over breakfast. "I'm contracted to a client to deliver a new piece on the first of next month. If you could delay finding this killer, I could get in an extra ten days of polishing." No sculpture could ever be smooth enough to suit him.

"That might not be convenient for the rest of the city, Father," I said.

"Oh well. Did Pericles mention whether we'd all stop aging while the calendar is stopped?"

"I'm afraid not," Diotima said.

"A pity." He ate another egg.

"Let's list our suspects," Diotima said. "Lakon has to be first."

"Lying about his friendship with Romanos looks dubious," I agreed. "What about the family of Romanos? His sister, Maia, her husband, Petros, or someone else in that crowded house. Any one might have hated him for some reason."

"How would we ever find out?" Diotima asked. "They're metics," she added, forgetting that she too had been a metic, though she'd lived her entire life in Athens. "Foreigners to the city aren't about to open up to us."

"We'll have to think of something," I said. "Who else?"

"A crazy person," Diotima said.

"We can't go back to that theory," I complained.

"But it's consistent with what happened," Diotima argued. "Remember, there's been not only the murder of Romanos but all the disasters during rehearsals, and they *weren't* directed at the murder victim."

"There was the broom he tripped over," I pointed out.

Diotima snorted contemptuously. "That hardly rates with Phellis's leg, or with Lakon almost falling off the balcony."

"The broom was the first attempt, though, if what we're told is true," I said. "It makes sense it would be the mildest attack."

"Like an escalation of hostilities?" Diotima said.

"Right. Each failed attempt to stop the play resulted in a stronger attack."

"The only problem is, I don't believe it. You still haven't answered why anyone would want to stop the most popular festival in Athens."

"Which brings us back to the crazy person," I groaned.

"Yes," said Diotima happily. "I like that theory."

"Maybe there's someone else with a motive we don't know about?" I said. "I can't get past the fact that there are three different victims. The actor, the play, and the man."

There were so many unanswered questions, it was hard to know where to start.

Socrates had listened with close attention as Diotima and I discussed the different theories we might follow. (I had allowed him out of the records room for sleep and occasional meals.)

Now Socrates said, "Nico, I've been thinking . . . the machine behind the stage, it lifts a man. With the lever, men can move something that they couldn't lift on their own."

"Yes. So?" I said impatiently.

"How did Romanos get into the air?"

"What do you mean?" I asked. "The killer used the crane, of course."

Socrates said, "Then the killer must have put the noose

around Romanos's neck, then walked backstage to work the machine?"

"Yes."

"What was Romanos doing while his murderer went backstage to kill him?" Socrates asked.

"Er . . ." I didn't have a good answer for that one. He would hardly have waited politely.

Diotima said, "Socrates has a point. Romanos must have been unconscious. Or perhaps he was already dead?"

"The body looked like a hanged man," I said. "Blue face, tongue poking out."

"Nico, you said the guards were drugged," Socrates pointed out.

"They were. You think Romanos was drugged too? Maybe." I didn't like the way Socrates was finding answers that I hadn't thought of.

"Maybe I can think of something else to help?" Socrates offered enthusiastically. He was obviously trying to avoid going back to the records room.

"Go inspect that machine again," I said, to get him out of the way. No one was using it, and he could hardly do any damage. "But once you're done, it's back to the records."

"Where will you be?" Socrates asked.

"Interviewing a suspect," I said.

"Have you given thought to selling the other house?" my father asked abruptly.

That brought me down to earth.

"No, Father, I haven't," I said. "I've been busy, and it is the time of the Dionysia after all."

"Not while the calendar is halted," Sophroniscus pointed out. "There's no point trying to delay the inevitable, Nico."

"No, Father."

"Give it some thought," he said. "If you're having trouble, I might be able to find a buyer among my friends."

He meant to help, but what it sounded like was a threat. Diotima had kept studiously quiet every time my father mentioned her house. I felt it was time to point out that the property wasn't my father's to dispense.

"It's *because* the house is part of her dowry that I am concerned," he said, when I'd made my point. "You're a husband now, Nico—"

"Yes, sir, I'd noticed."

"You have responsibilities," my father went on. "First and foremost is to support your wife. You're doing that. Second is to make sure her wealth remains secure. Preferably it should earn some income. That city house is the bulk of Diotima's dowry, son. You have to make it work for her."

"Yes, sir. We tried to rent it—"

"And the residents trashed the place, then disappeared to their own cities before you could sue them. Yes, I know. But son, it's still a problem, because while you dither, your wife's dowry is *going down in value*."

When he put it like that, it didn't sound good. It did seem like I was being careless with my wife's property.

"You are allowing your wife's property to go to rack and ruin," my father twisted the knife in a well-meaning way.

"Yes, sir, I'll see to it."

Breakfast was over. The slaves were clearing the bowls.

Diotima picked up the small leather pouch that she always took with her when she went outdoors. It contained only a few useful day-to-day items: a clean linen cloth, a handful of coins for emergency purchases, and a priestess knife sharp enough to slit any throat. Diotima jumped to her feet and hung the pouch over her shoulder by its long leather strap.

There was a great deal to do, but first, there was one absolute essential. We had to attend a funeral.

# SCENE 22
# THE FUNERAL

DIOTIMA AND I went to the house in Melite to pay our respects before the ceremony began.

Funerals are always conducted in the early dawn or in the late evening, so that Apollo the sun god is not forced to look down upon a corpse. The family of Romanos had opted for the dawn. The season was spring but the air was chilly, with the recent unseasonable rain and the breeze. We wrapped our arms about ourselves and shivered slightly.

"I'm looking forward to this," Diotima said as we walked through the twisty streets of Melite.

"You're looking forward to a *funeral*?"

"Nico, these people are professional mourners. Nobody knows more than they do about how to run a good funeral. I can't wait to see how the experts do it."

There was a considerable crowd outside when we arrived, and much murmuring. After Diotima's words it was quickly clear to me that they weren't friends of the family, but curious onlookers. They, too, wanted to see how the experts did it.

Within, the noise was unbearable. All the women of the house, and there were a lot of them, moaned and tugged at their shorn hair and sobbed loudly. The men beat at their breasts or looked grave and despondent.

Romanos lay in the courtyard. His body was carefully positioned so that his feet pointed at the front door. That was the necessary precaution, to ensure the dead man's psyche didn't escape to haunt the house before the body could be cremated.

Romanos had been dressed in his best clothes, then wrapped in his burial shroud. A white linen cloth was wrapped over his head and tied beneath his jaw, to keep his mouth closed. The coin had already been placed under his tongue. His *psyche* would carry the coin with him on his way to Hades. When he came to the river Acheron, he would pay Charon the Ferryman the coin to carry him across.

Romanos would not have been pleased by the attendance. The only actor from the cast was Kebris, the substitute third actor. He kept to himself in a corner of the room. Neither Lakon nor any of the stage crew had come to see him their colleague. Sophocles was leaving as we arrived. He nodded grimly to me and I to him. It was obvious he didn't intend to stay for the funeral, but that wasn't necessary to maintain the proprieties. He had done the right thing by coming to see his theatrical colleague.

Petros was chief among the mourners, as was proper. He greeted us as we entered.

"Thank you for coming," he said.

"How are you coping?" I asked him.

"I must carry the spear of vengeance," Petros said sadly. "I don't know if I can."

The spear of vengeance is always carried at the funeral of a murder victim, by the victim's closest relative. It meant the carrier assumed the responsibility to pursue the killer. Once the spear of vengeance had been held, the carrier had not only a moral and ethical duty to avenge the deceased, but also an obligation enforceable by law.

"I've carried that spear myself," Diotima spoke up.

"You have?" Petros looked at her in surprise

"For my father. It's not easy, but if I can do it, so can you."

Petros turned to me, puzzled, because it was inconceivable that a woman would carry the spear if there was a man to do it for her.

"It was before we were married," I explained. I didn't bother to add that though I'd been at that funeral, there was no force on earth that could have wrested that spear from my love's hands.

Petros nodded his understanding. "Ah. Then what would you advise me? I must carry the spear, as is only right and proper, but what do I do then?"

I said, "Petros, you're obliged to prosecute your brother-in-law's killer. That's the law."

"Yes."

"But the law doesn't say you have to do all the work yourself. Let Diotima and me find the killer. Then you can prosecute him."

Petros wrinkled his brow. "You would do this for a metic? Why?"

"I liked your brother-in-law," I said, thinking of the time we sheltered together out of the rain.

"I see." He thought about it for a moment. "I have no way to pay you."

"I'm under commission to cleanse the impiety in any case. You may as well take advantage of it."

"That would not be honorable," Petros said.

"I'm making the offer," I said. "And please don't be offended, Petros, but a man with all your problems can't afford to be too worried about niceties. Think of it as my Dionysiac gift to you."

"Then I accept."

Diotima and I left the house. Petros had left a bowl of seawater outside the door, as custom demands. We washed our hands then, lacking a towel, dried them on each other's chitons.

We stood outside, waiting for the procession to begin.

The family didn't leave the spectators waiting. Petros and the other men of the house emerged, holding between them a board on which lay the body of Romanos. The women and children followed. They had rubbed soot and dirt into their faces and hair. Every one of them had short, ragged hair, as befits a mourner. But of course, professional mourners *always* wore their hair ragged.

Petros separated himself from the bearers. I saw that he carried a spear in his right hand. Diotima and I knew that he was nervous, but no one could have told from his manner, which was calm and somber. His eyes met mine for an instant, and he nodded.

In every funeral I'd ever seen, the body was placed on a cart, to be taken to the city's official cemetery in Ceramicus. But there was no cart to be seen. Instead, the six grim-faced men who carried Romanos turned as one to face north. Petros spoke a word and they simultaneously lifted the board to their shoulders.

Petros spoke another word, and the bearers began to walk in time. A young lady among the mourners carried a flute. Another held a lyre. They raised their instruments and began to play the *epicedium*, the funeral song in praise of the deceased, a slow, sad song in the Lydian mode.

The bearers walked with identical manner: heads down, shoulders bowed as if under the weight of the world. Their steps dragged in the dust. They might have been marching to their own funerals. They said not a word.

Petros stepped in behind the men who carried the body. Maia was by his side. Petros raised his arm, so that everyone could see the spear of vengeance.

The other members of the household filed in behind them. They began the customary sobbing and cries of despair. The rest of us—friends, neighbors, and the simply curious—took our places behind the family. Diotima and I were careful to place ourselves directly behind the official mourners, so that we could watch.

The funeral procession marched north at a slow pace. Most families would carry their dead along the main roads, to garner the most attention. Instead, the professional mourners wended their way through all the minor streets, a long, unwieldy path. It seemed an odd decision, if only because it forced everyone who followed to squeeze together. But the choice of route had an interesting effect. People who weren't used to funerals passing down their street poked their heads out of windows to see what was happening. Many of these were interested enough to join the line, to watch the show. The tail of followers became longer and longer, and the more it lengthened, the more interesting the event became and the more joined.

By the time we arrived at Ceramicus, there were many hundreds of onlookers. The long line passed through the gates of the cemetery.

Ceramicus has been the official burial ground of Athens since time immemorial. I didn't know how many of my ancestors lay in the ground beneath my feet, but the line must have stretched back to the time of King Theseus and beyond. I knew that one day I, too, would lie here.

The bearers stopped by a funeral pyre that had been freshly built. They placed the board that carried Romanos upon the exact center, then stepped back, rubbing their sore arms.

Beside the body, upon the pyre, the women laid out three changes of clothing, which was the maximum that the law allowed. They returned with sweet cakes, which they placed beside his hands, for Romanos to eat on his journey to the underworld. Normally a family would send a loved one to Hades with some decent jewelry or fine belongings, but here there was nothing, until Maia approached.

Maia held the only extra grave goods that the family intended to offer. In her right hand she carried the mask of tragedy, in her left the mask of comedy. She laid the masks reverently beside her brother.

Petros took up a burning torch, one made of rags wrapped

around a pole, the whole dipped in olive oil. He walked about the pyre, touching the torch to every part.

As the flames rose, one of the men cast scented oil from an amphora that he held under his left arm. He held a scoop in his right hand, from which he flung droplets across the entire funeral pyre as he walked about. The oil sizzled everywhere it fell and a pleasantly sweet smell enwrapped everyone who watched.

The fire had built remarkably quickly. Sometimes, if a fire hadn't been stacked properly, the flames would exhaust before the body had been fully consumed, leaving the relatives with a gruesome problem and the guests with an unpleasant sight. There were no mistakes here though. I guessed the family of Romanos had used something to make sure the fire burned to the last bit of fuel. Nor was the pyre overstocked, another mistake that happened when nervous relatives overdid it, which would force the onlookers to step back from a conflagration. The pyre for Romanos was exactly hot enough, and exactly small enough for the mourners to stand respectfully close.

Romanos disappeared from sight behind the hot red flames.

Maia let out an ear-piercing scream that had my ears ringing. She collapsed to the ground. At first I thought she'd fainted. I made a step forward to assist her, as did several other men in the crowd, before I saw her twist on the ground and I realized it was part of her official mourning. She pushed her hands through the dirt and smeared them across her face and breasts.

Diotima had been right. This was the funeral to end all funerals, a mixture of elegance and drama. After this show, everyone, even the richest citizens, would be scrambling to match it.

The crowd slowly drifted away. As they walked, people talked to each other about what a fine funeral it had been. Diotima and I stayed to the very end.

Petros put his arm around Maia. She sagged against him,

whether from exhaustion or sorrow I couldn't tell, but if the shaking of her shoulders was any indication then she was quietly sobbing.

When only the family remained I went to Petros, to repeat our condolences and express our appreciation of the spectacle.

"You must know a lot about funerals," I said.

"We've had lots of practice," he said. His face and hands were smeared with the soot of the fire. When it had cooled sufficiently, the women would scoop the ashes into a funerary jar of alabaster, which would be erected somewhere on the grounds.

"How did you get into mourning?"

Petros grimaced. "We're actors, most of us. In Phrygia there wasn't much work. We came to Athens because we heard there were lots of plays staged here. When we arrived, we discovered we weren't the only ones to have thought of that. "

"Oh. I suppose it's hard for a metic to get acting work."

"Very much so."

This talk reminded me of something I'd heard Romanos say, something that didn't fit now that I'd met his talented family.

"There's something that surprised me, Petros," I said.

"Yes?" he said.

"We were there when Phellis had his fall."

"A terrible accident," Petros said at once.

"It certainly was." I shuddered, remembering the sight of his leg. Which reminded me that we still had to find some money to pay the doctor. "When we returned to the theater, Sophocles asked for recommendations to replace Phellis. Romanos convinced Sophocles that the best course of action was for him to take the second actor's job and to hire a new third actor. It proved a very sensible suggestion, if I may say so."

"Yes?" Petros said politely. He was waiting to see where this went, perhaps a little bored, or distracted by the solemn occasion.

I said, "It's just that when Sophocles asked for

recommendations for a new third actor, it was Romanos who named Kebris."

"*Romanos* recommended the replacement?" Petros looked genuinely surprised.

"You didn't know?"

"No." Petros sounded troubled. "He told me that Sophocles hired a new third actor. He didn't say it was his idea."

"Would you have taken the job if it was offered?"

"Do I look like an idiot? Of course I would have taken it in an instant."

"Yet your own brother-in-law never mentioned you. Can you explain that?"

"I cannot." Petros paused. "Unless he was worried about this . . ." Petros tugged his shorn hair. "But it should be irrelevant."

"I noticed Romanos wore his hair unusually long."

"When he started getting acting jobs, my brother-in-law swore he'd never do professional mourning again. He wouldn't even help us when we were a man short. He swore he'd never attend another funeral." Petros looked over at the remains of the funeral pyre. "Well, he got that wrong."

"Er . . . quite."

Diotima said, "How does this explain his hair?"

"Romanos grew his hair long to tell the world that he didn't need to mourn for money. It's the fashion among actors who have regular work," Petros said. He sounded sad.

I realized the opposite was also true. That an actor with ragged hair was telling the world that he needed the extra work. Which must surely tell against him when he applied for a part. Which would force him to do more mourning. This acting seemed a hard business.

Petros must have read my thoughts. He said, "A man has to eat. And feed his wife. And his children if he has any." He sounded defensive.

I said, "I understand, Petros."

"It takes a certain skill to pretend you mourn the death of someone you've never met."

"I'm sure it does."

"It's an acting skill," he insisted.

"Yes."

I felt sorry for Petros and all the others in his house. I thought they must have a difficult time explaining to their children what they did for a living, and why their hair was always shorn and ragged. I wondered if the other children taunted them in the street. But then I knew the answer. Of course they did.

"What will you do now?" I asked.

"We might have to leave Athens."

"Why?"

"The landlord's heard that Romanos is dead. He says we are bad luck. He wants us to leave his house."

I winced. The landlord was right. A dead body on the premises, particularly a murdered one, depressed property values, and people didn't forget that sort of thing. It reminded me that we would have the same problem when I put Diotima's house up for sale, something that I still hoped to avoid. There'd been a murder there too, years before. It would reduce the price we could get for the place.

Petros sighed. "I suppose it's for the best. It's not like we're getting work here."

I made a snap decision.

"Petros, I might know of a house for you," I said.

"What's this?" he said, surprised.

I looked at Diotima.

My wife knew what I was thinking. She nodded. "Whatever you say, Nico."

I said to Petros, "We own a house that's available for rent."

"You do? You, personally?"

"Yes."

"How much would you charge?"

"It's free," I told him.

Petros blinked. "This is impossible."

"I am offering you the use of our house, which stands empty this moment. You can move in this afternoon if you like."

"Why would you do this for us?" he asked suspiciously.

"It's, uh, not in very good condition." I admitted.

I explained about the mice, the rats, the roof, the puddles when it rained, the holes in the walls, the broken furniture. I hoped that with tenants in, I could delay the day when we would have to sell. The Phrygians would at least prevent the place from falling apart further.

I finished with, "So you see, this is no bargain. I am offering you the use of our house, at zero rent, but you'll have to do some work to make it habitable."

I could see Petros visibly relax once he understood what was in it for me.

"I see," he said. Petros rubbed his chin while he thought.

"I accept, of course. We'll never get a better offer."

"Petros, will your family be all right?" Diotima asked, concerned. "Nico didn't exaggerate when he described the house."

"Do not worry for us. I think you will find that we Phrygians are very inventive people."

INVESTIGATION IS AS much about finding inconsistencies in the witnesses as it is about finding clues on the ground. The funeral had provided our first real break in the case.

As we left the cemetery I said, "Did you hear what I heard?"

Diotima nodded. "Romanos didn't recommend his own family for the third actor role."

"Even though they're desperate for work," I added.

"And he lied to Petros about it."

Romanos had not only failed to recommend his own family for the third actor's job, he had actively recommended someone else, and then avoided telling Petros what he had done.

There was another possibility. I said, "Either that, or Petros lied to us when he implied Romanos lied to him."

"That's convoluted," Diotima said. "Why would Petros do such a thing?"

"I don't know."

Up until now, Romanos had seemed a perfectly ordinary man, if you didn't count the fact that he was dead. Now suddenly the dead man was exposed in what looked like a piece of chicanery, for no reason I could think of.

"Why would Romanos turn against his family?" I asked. "They seem happy to me."

"Should we challenge Petros about this?" Diotima asked.

I considered the idea. "No, I have a better idea. Let's ask *him*." I pointed down the road, to the distantly retreating back of Kebris. He had been the only other theater person who had stayed for the funeral. We ran to catch up with him.

I said, "Kebris? We haven't spoken before, but we're the investigators looking into the death of Romanos."

"Yes, I recognized you at the funeral," he said.

I'd seen before, when he first joined the cast, that Kebris was an old trouper. Now he looked like an old and very tired trouper. I looked about for a place to sit and saw a roadside tavern, a small one of the sort run by poor families. They had bashed a hole in their front wall through which to serve drinks to people who stood in the street. They had even placed a few stools and a table under a ramshackle awning. Diotima and I led Kebris to the table and I bought us all wine. It wasn't particularly good wine, but it was wet and it refreshed our informant.

"This must all be difficult for you," I said to him as he drank.

"Death happens," he said. "I've seen enough of it. Would that I could see no more."

"You've had another loss?" I intuited.

"My wife of forty years," he said.

The pain in his eyes was there to see.

"She died last year. Such a pretty young thing when I met her. She was a farmer's daughter. But she was willing to go on the road with a man like me, who could offer her nothing but constant travel and hard work and life in a tent. I promised her when I had enough money that I'd retire. We could live in one place and never have to travel again. Well, I did, and the next year she was dead."

"I'm sorry."

He sighed. "As I said, death happens."

"So you were at a loose end when they asked you to join the company. I guess it took your mind off things."

He shrugged.

"I admired the way you attacked the part," Diotima told. "They said you learned it faster than anyone could believe possible."

"That was sheer good luck. Or bad luck, rather. But the fact is, I already knew the lines."

It took a moment for that to sink in. Then, "Say that again?"

"Romanos taught me the lines."

"That was after Phellis had his fall," I said, and waited for him to agree with my correction.

"No, it was before."

"Are you *sure*?" I asked.

"Of course I'm sure!" Kebris looked at me as if I were an idiot. He knew the difference between one day and another.

The old actor said, "I was having dinner with Romanos one night. We were friends, you see. We had toured together. After my wife died he made a point of visiting me often. I appreciated that. After he won the part in *Sisyphus* he was very excited. He said he felt this was his big chance."

I nodded. "It was. But then it all went horribly wrong. How did he come to ask you to learn his part?"

"One night, after rehearsals had begun, he suddenly asked me. When I asked why, he said it was in case anything happened to him."

"He used those exact words?"

"Yes."

"Didn't you ask what he meant?"

"Obviously I pressed him about it. It sounded to me like he had an enemy he feared."

"Did he say whom?" Diotima asked.

"No, and when I pressed him he simply shrugged."

It occurred to me that old, out-of-work actors probably didn't eat well. I went back to the hole in the wall, and returned with a bowl of lentils and bread. It was the only food the woman behind the counter offered, served from a pot that rested on hot stones.

Kebris accepted the bowl as his due. As he ate, he said, "There's another reason one actor might ask another to pick up his part. If he knows he'll be taking on another role soon."

"He'd only just got this one," I pointed out.

"You are right."

"Could Romanos have been planning to supplant Phellis?" Diotima asked.

Kebris smiled. "Actors do connive against each other. You wouldn't believe some of the things I've seen in my years," he said. "But I cannot think it of my friend. Besides, it is the choregos and the writer together who select a replacement." He shook his head. "Not the outgoing actor."

"But Lakon recommended Romanos for the second's role," Diotima said. "He was quite forceful about it."

"Then Romanos suggested me," Kebris added. "Or so I'm told. I'll always be in his debt for that. To finish my career in a Great Dionysia is more than I ever hoped for."

"Is there any other reason an actor might pass on his part?" Diotima asked Kebris.

He looked slightly uncomfortable and said, "Well, if an actor's planning to skip town and he has a conscience, then he makes sure there'll be someone to replace him."

Kebris finished the last of his wine. "But I'm sure that can't be the case with Romanos."

"No," I said politely.

"It can only be what I thought at first. That my friend expected an attack. Or perhaps he was more superstitious than I realized, and that he feared the ghost."

As we left the grounds, Diotima frowned. "We have so little to work with, yet in a way we have too much. We know that someone was sabotaging Sophocles's play. We don't have a shred of evidence as to who it might be."

"Right."

"We know that Romanos was worried about something."

"Yes."

"We know that ended with Phellis taking a bad fall."

"That's presuming whoever booby trapped the machine on Phellis pulled the other tricks."

"It does seem logical, doesn't it? That might have been enough to halt the plays, except that Romanos worked like a slave to make the second actor's role his own and to train the replacement third actor. It looked like the Great Dionysia was back on."

"And then Romanos died," I said. "There's a lot to do. Where do we go next?"

She said, "Someone else lied to us, too. Lakon. Let's go find out why."

# SCENE 23
# THE PROTAGONIST

LAKON LIVED IN one of the fashionable streets north of the agora. His home was a narrow fronted building adjoined to the neighboring homes. The street in front was swept clean, which must have been the work of his slaves. Where some people placed a bust of Hermes outside their door, to wish good luck to travelers, Lakon had placed a bust of Dionysos.

We knocked on the door and were admitted by a polite house slave of older years. He took one look at Diotima and led us straight to the courtyard and brought us wine without even asking. Had I been alone, I would have been taken to the *andron* at the front of the house, but with a lady present the inner courtyard was the correct place for visitors. Lakon's slaves knew their manners.

The dining couches on which we sat were old and probably cheap, but well cared for, and there weren't any stains that I could see on the cushions. Vines had been trained up the columns that surrounded the open yard. The paved areas were swept. There weren't any cobwebs in the corners.

Lakon was a man who cared about appearances. I was willing to bet there were no mice in his roof.

Lakon joined us after a respectable time had passed. He was wearing a large blousy chiton of soft fabric, with no belt to tie it in. It was the sort of thing a man might wear in the comfort of his own home: man shaped, but on the verge of effeminacy.

Lakon greeted us with politeness and a raised eyebrow.

"Welcome though you are, I confess I wasn't expecting you," he said.

I said, "We were at the funeral of Romanos and we thought of you. In fact, we wondered why you weren't also there."

Lakon waved his arm in that airy manner of his. "As I told you, we weren't that close."

I said, "We've come across some information that appears to be a—how shall I put this?—a paradox."

"Yes?" He waited. There was no concern in his voice.

I said, "We understand that you dined with Thodis, the choregos of your play."

"So I did," Lakon said. "Perhaps even more than once. Is that a crime? Perhaps you should bring me before the courts. Though come to that, isn't it punishment enough that I've had to eat his ill-prepared feasts and endure whole evenings of his tedious conversation?"

"I was under the impression you enjoyed his company," I said. "Thodis says so."

Lakon laughed.

"Not that cultureless oaf. It was all I could do to prevent myself from falling comatose in the middle of his dreary conversation."

"Then why—"

"Why did I flatter such a contemptuous man?" Lakon said. "It's simple. I'm an actor. Actors are entirely dependent for their parts on men with no taste but lots of money." Lakon leaned forward in his chair, the better to make his point. He seemed genuinely absorbed in the subject.

"You see, all plays—all of them, every single one—are funded by wealthy men. Most of these men have no idea about theater. Some know just enough to sound knowledgeable before their friends, and some, a mere handful, really do understand our art. Your friend Pericles is among the truly cognoscente, by the way."

Of course he was, I thought sourly. Was there any subject on which Pericles wasn't an expert?

"But all of these rich men," Lakon went on, "every one of them thinks they can run a play better than the experts. Every one of them thinks they can write better than the writers and act better than the actors. They're used to running large estates, you see. They tell their workers what to do, and the workers do it, and by next summer there's a harvest. The rich think the theater works the same way. They think they need merely order 'write a successful play' and a successful play will be written to order."

Lakon was passionately involved in his art, that was clear. He spoke quickly. I felt for the first time I was hearing his honest voice, and not a façade.

Lakon said, "In particular, every choregos thinks he can cast better than the writer." He smiled. "Well, that's hardly a surprise, is it? *Everyone* thinks they can cast better than the writer."

I nodded, and so did Diotima.

Lakon saw that we followed his argument. He went on, "Writers must satisfy their choregos if they wish their works to be seen by an audience. So when a wealthy choregos suggests to a writer that Lakon would be the ideal protagonist for his play, the writer will simply agree, and hire me. Hence, I make myself agreeable to every man who might conceivably become a choregos."

"Isn't that cheating?" Diotima said.

"Young lady, I am telling you the deepest secret of the theatrical business," Lakon said. "One toadies to the men with the money, and from that small beginning, all things follow."

"But what if there's a better, more deserving actor?" Diotima asked.

"What does it mean to be more deserving?" Lakon waved his arm with a nonchalant air. "Be assured that if I was *too* bad, the writer would protest. I don't have to be the best actor," Lakon said. "I merely need to be good enough that the writer doesn't find me objectionable." He paused, to drink deep from his wine cup. Then he continued. "As it happens, I work very hard at my art. I love it. I flatter myself that I really am one of the best in Athens . . . not that that means anything when it comes to casting; I just explained to you why influence beats talent any day. I shall point out, too, that the typical audience member neither knows nor cares who is behind the mask."

"Surely that can't be true, Lakon," Diotima said. "Don't they respect you for your art?"

"How many actors do you see each day at the agora?" Lakon shot back.

"Why, I don't see any," Diotima said, puzzled.

"My dear lady, that is utter tosh," Lakon chided my wife. "You've seen many actors without their masks. You go to the agora to socialize, don't you? So do actors. Once we have our street clothes on, we are as other men. You pass us in the street and you never know it."

"Oh, I see," she said. "Without the mask, you are . . . er . . ."

"Nothing?" Lakon suggested with a gentle smile.

"An everyday person, just like the rest of us," Diotima corrected.

I said, "If I could ask a personal question, don't you find all this demeaning? Isn't it hard to ingratiate yourself to lesser men?"

Lakon nodded. "Yes, but if I want to reach the top of my field, I hardly have a choice, do I? Fortunately, I used to play comedy before I turned my talents to tragedy. I had no trouble amusing the boors that Thodis invited to his symposia. I steal mercilessly from the great comedies: an amusing anecdote, a little bit of business, some subtle flattery, and before you know it I have a roomful of wealthy men who think that Lakon the actor is a fine fellow. As to my feelings on the subject, I merely pretend I am in a play."

I said, "Thodis seemed less taken with Sophocles."

"Sophocles is a man of integrity." Lakon shook his head in dismay. "That trait will get him nowhere if he's not careful."

"What about Romanos?" I asked.

"I'd rather not talk about him."

"We'd rather you did. Our information is that Romanos attended at least one of the symposia with you."

Lakon assumed exactly the same pose that actors do on stage when their character is thinking deeply. "Now that you mention it, I believe I did see him there. Perhaps he was following the same ploy as me."

"Our information is that *you* brought Romanos along as your guest," Diotima said.

"Who told you that?" he said with annoyance. "No, wait, I don't have to guess. It was that idiot Thodis, wasn't it?"

We sat silent.

Lakon sighed. "Well, he didn't know any better."

"So you admit you lied. Tell me, Lakon, how did Romanos die?" Diotima asked.

Lakon looked at her oddly. "I think we may conclude," he said carefully, "that someone didn't like him very much."

"Would that include you?"

"Certainly it would. But if you want to blame someone for his death, you are looking at the wrong man."

I said, "Under the circumstances, you would have to prove that."

"Then consider this. Even if I had a motive, I would have to be insane to kill Romanos right now. This is the biggest moment of my career. I am protagonist for Sophocles! If I was planning to kill Romanos, I would wait until *after* the play."

His logic was excellent.

Lakon added, "And I *certainly* would not have sabotaged this play. From my point of view that's just as bad as the murder." He paused, then added, "I'm assuming the saboteur is the same man who killed Romanos."

"It seems logical," I admitted.

"There you are, then. It can't be me."

I said, "The problem is, Lakon, that you're caught out in a lie. You told us that you never socialized with metics. You told us point blank that you didn't know Romanos outside the theater."

"Compared to all the disasters that have occurred, it's not a very big lie, is it?" Lakon said.

"It's big enough. The fact is, you said you barely knew him, and now it seems you go to parties together."

"Who cares?"

"The jury will care."

He looked alarmed. "What jury?"

"Lakon, have you any idea how easy it is to be convicted of murder in this city?" I said. "I myself was once falsely convicted on evidence much weaker than we have against you."

"You were?" Lakon said, surprised. "How did you survive?"

"With enormous difficulty," I said grimly. "And a lot of luck."

"Nicolaos speaks the truth," Diotima spoke up. "Think about it, Lakon. You and the victim were rival actors. It's not exactly a profession noted for its easy relationships, is it? Romanos died in a place you know intimately. He died on a machine that only actors know how to use. And of all the suspects, you're the only one caught out in a lie. What lie did you tell? That you didn't know the victim outside the theater." Diotima let him think about that for a moment. "Any normal, suspicious jury will assume you lied to distance yourself from the crime," she said.

Lakon surely knew, and so did we, that Athenians plotted as easily as they breathed. Of course they would magnify his small lie into something more sinister.

"Not everyone would believe you," he said weakly.

"Not everyone has to," Diotima said. "We only need a majority of jurors. Enough of them would go our way." She added mercilessly, "If we gave this brief to Pericles, by the time he finished prosecuting you, there'd be only one performance left for you, Lakon: chained to a stake and waiting to be stoned."

"*Pericles?*" Lakon said, openly aghast. Pericles had never, ever lost a court case.

"He's the one who commissioned me," I said. "He's the one who'll prosecute."

Lakon was doomed, and he knew it. He stood up, paced back and forth, holding his head in despair. Diotima and I remained silent while he built up his angst. Before long, Lakon began to tear at his hair.

Then he turned to us abruptly. "I didn't want to tell you this," he said. "I truly didn't." He appeared deeply distraught, but with Lakon you never knew if it was acting or genuine emotion.

"Tell us what?" Diotima said.

"That Romanos was blackmailing me."

# SCENE 24
# FRIENDS MAKE THE WORST ENEMIES

"IT'S TRUE, I *did* take him with me as a companion to parties."

Now that the truth was out, Lakon had settled down. He called for more wine, drank off his first and second cups in about three gulps, then held out his cup for a third. This he clutched in both hands sitting far forward

"But I only took him to the parties of influential men," he added quickly. "Never to meet my friends. I would never be so cruel to my friends."

"Was Romanos blackmailing you for money?"

"No, for influence." Lakon sighed. "I recommended Romanos for third actor in the play. I suppose Sophocles told you that already."

We nodded.

"It was part of the hold he had over me. I found it impossible to disengage myself from him. Every success I had, every major part I landed, there was Romanos insisting that I recommend him for a role."

"So you recommended him for tritagonist," Diotima said.

"He insisted on deuteragonist!" Lakon said.

"What happened?"

"Sophocles wouldn't have it. He already had Phellis earmarked for second actor. I didn't dare insist too strongly. As it was, Sophocles looked at me a little oddly when I pressed the case for Romanos. It's not normal, you see, for an actor to take an active interest in casting a rival."

"How did Romanos take that news?"

"He was angry. I pointed out that I had done everything he had asked. I could not be blamed for failure. He threatened me with exposure anyway."

"That's why you pressed again, after Phellis was injured," Diotima said.

"Yes. Romanos gave me a look, as you carried away Phellis. I knew what he expected of me." Lakon knocked back the last of his third cup of wine. The slave who stood behind him filled the cup for the fourth time. At the rate he was going, Lakon would be drunk before the interview ended.

I said, "Did Romanos tell you *in advance* that he wanted you to recommend him that second time?"

"I resent that!" Lakon said at once in instant and unmistakable anger. He sat up straighter. "I had no knowledge that Phellis would fall. I had nothing to do with it. What's more, I don't think Romanos did either."

"Oh?"

"If I had any evidence that Romanos arranged that accident, don't you think I would have exposed him at once? It would have solved all my problems."

It would indeed. It occurred to me though, by the same logic, that Lakon had the perfect reason to kill Romanos.

"Besides which," Lakon added, almost as an afterthought, "I would never hurt a fellow actor."

"What did Romanos have over you?"

"My dear fellow, you hardly expect me to tell you that. We all have peccadilloes in our past."

"Your peccadillo is one we'll be hearing about."

"No you won't." He said it with surprising firmness. "Even if it means my death, you'll not hear it from my lips."

I could hear the genuine emotion in his voice, and this time, for a change, I had a feeling that Lakon wasn't acting.

"The hold Romanos had over you was that strong?" I said.

"It was," he said sadly. "Believe me or not, as you will. If you wish, I will swear by Zeus, by Athena, and by Dionysos whom I hold dear that I did not kill Romanos."

THERE WAS NOTHING more we could do. No threat would cajole Lakon into revealing his secret. Lakon himself shut the door behind us as we departed.

"What do you think?" I asked Diotima as we walked.

"I think we need that secret," Diotima said. "What sort of secret would a man be willing to die to protect?" she pondered.

"The sort of crime that merits death, would be my first guess," I said.

"Then how come no one noticed it?" she said.

I had no answer to that.

"Maybe it was an unhappy love affair? Maybe he was torn apart from his true love, and they decided that if they couldn't live together than they would die together. But then at the last moment, after she'd taken poison—"

I laughed. "What sort of idiots kill themselves merely because they can't get married? Any couple with half a brain would simply run away."

"We didn't," she pointed out.

"We were ready to!" I said.

Diotima had to concede that was true. When we had first met, during a moment of crisis, I had asked Diotima if she would run away with me, and she had said yes. Luckily circumstances had saved us the trip.

I said, "Anyway, that doesn't explain his reticence now."

"All right then, maybe he accidentally killed his own father?"

"I doubt it."

"In that case he avenged himself against his father's murderer, who as it turned out was his mother and her lover. He slaughtered them with an axe."

"You've been watching too many tragedies."

"Well so have you."

Try as we might, we couldn't think of a circumstance that would cause a man to be ready to face death today for something that had patently occurred many years before.

"Maybe he's merely sensitive about something embarrassing?" Diotima suggested at last.

"Lakon doesn't strike me as the sensitive sort," I said.

"I'm not so sure, Nico," said my wife. "That shallow actor's manner he puts on might be to cover a delicate and insecure nature."

I snorted amusement. "Yeah, right."

"All right then," she said crossly. "I'm the one coming up with all the ideas. Why don't *you* think of something?"

"I already have."

As we'd walked I'd led Diotima in a direction she didn't normally like to go.

"What are we doing *here*?" she said in distaste.

"Borrowing a boat."

I knocked on the door of Pericles's home.

Pericles and Diotima had never been friends. There was enough history among the three of us to explain the antipathy, but after three years it showed no signs of abating. I thought it odd because Diotima and Pericles were beyond doubt the two smartest people I knew.

Pericles frowned when he saw Diotima, but was too polite to throw out a lady. Instead we sat in his courtyard and discussed the case. I told him what we had learned. I finished with, "And so, Pericles, I want to borrow a boat."

"Why?" asked Pericles.

"Why?" asked Diotima, at exactly the same time.

The two of them looked at each other, startled.

I said, "Because as far as we know, Lakon has led a blameless life, if you don't count the possibility that he killed Romanos.

If there was any stain on him during his time as an actor then Sophocles wouldn't have had him in the play."

"Certainly not," Pericles said. "Sophocles is a solid citizen. What's your point?"

"That any dark secret Lakon carries is probably a *family* secret," I said. "Something beyond Athens."

"That's really quite clever," Diotima murmured.

"It was Diotima's list of great tragedies that made me think of it," I said modestly.

"I see," Pericles said. "What is his family's deme?"

"Rhamnus. It's about as far away as you can get and still be within Attica."

Attica was the region of Hellas controlled by Athens. It was a big area. Pericles saw my point. Now I showed him the solution.

"As it happens, Rhamnus is on the coast. That's why I want the boat."

"How fast a boat do you want?" he asked.

"How quickly do you want the case solved?" I countered. "If we have to go overland you can add at least three days for travel alone. Maybe four if there are brigands."

Pericles said nothing.

"Give me *Salaminia*," I said simply.

It was a measure of how far I had come that I dared ask for the fastest warship in the world. *Salaminia* had once carried me to distant Ionia on an urgent mission, and got me there on a single overnight stop. I knew her qualities. She could certainly get me to Rhamnus and back in a day, if we found what we were looking for quickly. Two days at the outside.

It was also a measure of how far I'd come that Pericles merely grunted.

He held out his hand and a slave instantly filled it with an ostrakon—a broken pottery shard. Pericles sent so many messages every day that he had a slave dedicated to doing nothing but collecting broken pottery.

"Take this message to her captain," he said, scratching words into the ostrakon. "I assume you leave at first light tomorrow?"

"Yes."

*Salaminia* was ready on a moment's notice, but there was nothing to be gained by departing for Rhamnus at once. The ship would only have to lie overnight in a port along the way.

Pericles handed me the order that gave me control of *Salaminia*. "This had better be worth it."

"We have another problem, Pericles," I said.

He frowned. "Yes?"

I explained about the problem with paying for Phellis's treatment. "He was injured through no fault of his own," I finished.

"This is a duty for the play's choregos," Pericles said.

"He denies it."

"I hope you're not suggesting that I should be paying for this?" Now Pericles sounded truly upset.

"No."

"Good. Because I'm already funding the public feast."

"How's that going?"

"I've ordered my estate manager to strip my lands of everything edible. Even so, I have buyers at every farm within cart distance of Athens. You wouldn't believe what this is costing me," he said, and he shuddered. "I said it before about *Salaminia*, but I'll say it again about the public feast. Nicolaos, this had better be worth it."

# SCENE 25
# A SUDDEN REVELATION

WE DECIDED TO make best use of our time before we left for Rhamnus by investigating Socrates's theory: that one man acting alone could not have murdered Romanos; not unless the victim was drugged. I pointed out, also, that we'd yet to inspect the scene of the crime, as we would with any normal murder.

Diotima snorted and said, "Good luck with that. How many people have trampled over the theater?"

Socrates was already there, looking closely at the machine. So were Kiron and Akamas. They were hanging around, Kiron said, because in the absence of a running festival they had nothing better to do.

"Excellent, I'm glad to see you," I said. "You can help us with an important point about how the machine works in *Sisyphus*—"

"Don't say that name!" Akamas almost shouted. He looked about suspiciously, before saying in a more normal voice, "You mean The Corinthian Play."

"The what?" I asked.

"The Corinthian Play," Akamas repeated.

"That's what all the crew are calling it now," Kiron said in exasperation. "On account of *Sisyphus* being set in Corinth." Kiron shrugged as expressively as one of his actors. "They've reached the point that they think even saying the name of the accursed play will bring back the Ghost of Thespis and all the bad luck."

I'd never heard anything so ridiculous in my life, but there was no point in arguing about it. Instead, we got on with our work.

We used Akamas to stand where Romanos must have stood, or lain, when the long arm of the machine rose during the murder. Kiron fitted Akamas with the harness and attached the rope. I took hold of the short arm backstage and tried to move it.

By heaving with all my might, I could raise Akamas into the air, but I was unsteady. Akamas was heavier than Romanos, but not so much that it would make a big difference, especially considering that the killer must have worked in the dark. The short arm I held was heavily weighted at the end, to balance the longer arm over the skene, but it wasn't enough to make my job simple. It was easy to see why during plays they used two men. When I said as much, Kiron nodded.

"That's why we use three," he said. "Two men to hold the actor steady, so there are no mistakes. The third man to direct the arm sideways." He paused, then added, "Plus me, of course. I have to make sure those idiots don't let go of the arm."

"Does that happen?" Diotima asked.

The stage manager turned to her. "Only once per idiot. If a man lets go of the machine while the actor's in the air, I beat him senseless to remind him not to do it again, and then I fire him."

"That seems a little harsh."

"You wouldn't think so if you were the actor." He rubbed his sweaty face with a thick cloth. "Look, you probably think I'm a tough boss—"

Diotima and I said nothing.

"But you know what my job is? It's to make sure nothing goes wrong. Nobody notices when everything goes right, but when something goes wrong, it's always the stage manager's fault." He wiped his brow again.

Socrates tugged on my clothing. "Nico? There's the other

problem for the killer." He pointed to the spot in the mechanism where the killer had placed a chock, to keep the long arm in the air. Socrates went on, "You can't both raise someone and chock the machine."

I tried. I wasn't a large man, but I was a strong one. My strength came from helping my father heave blocks of stone, from the training that Pythax had given me, and from my chosen profession. It would be an unusual killer who was stronger than me, and yet I didn't dare let go with either hand or Akamas would have crashed to the ground. My attempts to do so caused several anguished screams from Akamas, who suffered this experiment hanging in the air. Even half-drunk, he knew enough to be terrified with me at the controls.

I tried to reach from the end of the machine arm to the center where it pivoted. The distance I had to reach was simply too great. All this supposed that Romanos was waiting quietly to be hanged, or else was unconscious.

Socrates had made his point.

"What if the killer added more weight to the end of the short arm?" I said.

"That might work," Kiron said, "But see here . . ." He demonstrated the end of the short arm. "There are no rope marks, no peg holes, no nothing."

"The killer wrapped rags around the arm and then tied on weights?" Socrates suggested. "That would work."

"Getting a little complex here, aren't we, lad?" Kiron said.

Indeed we were. It seemed an extravagant way to kill someone. We needed a simpler explanation.

We abandoned the machine for the moment and turned to the next item: the search for any other clues.

It went as badly as Diotima had predicted. The plays this year included an axe murder (that was Aeschylus's contribution), various stabbings (Chorilos), and scenes of torture and incest (thank you, Sophocles). The comedies were barely any better. The props for all these evil deeds were scattered across the area behind the skene.

"Dear Gods," I said, "I never realized how violent these plays are."

Diotima held a stylus and a wax tablet on which she'd listed everything that would have been a clue at a normal crime scene, including all the potential murder weapons lying about. It was a long list.

Diotima chewed her lip and stared at the list. "I've been imprisoned in dungeons that were safer than this place," she said.

I nodded. I was beginning to understand why Akamas and the other theater crew lived in such fear of bad luck.

"Does your list of murder weapons include the machine?" I asked.

Diotima looked up at the machine that loomed above us. "Thanks. I forgot that one." She added another line.

I noticed that the prop knives and swords were sharp enough for battle, the cudgels were properly weighted to smash a skull, the axe propped in the corner was good enough to chop down a tree, or to chop down Agamemnon in his bath.

I queried Kiron about the lethal array. "Why don't you blunt them?"

He looked at me as if I were insane. "Every man in the audience is a serving soldier or a veteran."

"Yes, of course. All citizens are. So?"

"So to any man who's ever stood in the line, a blunt sword will look like a blunt sword. They know what a sharp sword looks like in the hand of a man who's coming at them. They've seen it often enough."

"Oh. I see what you mean."

"If we send the actors on stage with swords and spears too blunt to hurt a fly, the audience couldn't miss it. They'd complain later. Or they'd boo the actor, which would be even worse." The stage manager threw his hands in the air.

"You have no idea what lengths we go to, to get these details right."

"Even in the plays set long ago?" Diotima asked.

"*Especially* in the plays set long ago. If we get something wrong in those, every man, woman, and child will be backstage to tell us we got it wrong. Historical accuracy is very important."

"Doesn't anything ever go wrong, with all this stuff lying about?"

Kiron and Akamas both laughed.

"You better believe it. There was one time we had a man in the air—he was playing Zeus—the takeoff was as bad as you could get and he slammed into the skene and the entire wall fell over."

"What did you do?"

"Luckily we had Romanos with us that day. He played it for a comedy. He was on stage doing his lines about tragic death as the entire skene fell slowly forward, revealing us backstage crew and a man in the air swinging like a dying fish. Quick as lightning, Romanos grabbed someone's walking stick from the audience, then he chased us around the stage, whacking us with the stick while he repeated lines from some comedy he once played. This was in Pella, in Macedon. Those barbarians wouldn't know fine art if it hit them." Kiron hawked and spat in the dust. "The Macedonians laughed until they fell off their seats, and then they paid us extra 'cause it was so funny."

"Romanos saved us that day," said Akamas.

"Romanos was a good actor, I'll say that for him," said Kiron. He sighed. "We'll miss him. Who would murder a man like that? I can't believe it was one of our own."

"That's what the evidence says," Diotima pointed out. She was unsympathetic. "I'm sorry, Kiron, but it's one of your colleagues who's causing all the trouble."

"I've said this before," I told Kiron. "There are three possible victims: the man, the actor, and the character in the play. If

Romanos the actor is the victim, then almost certainly his killer belongs to the theater."

"You forgot another reason to kill Romanos," said the stage manager.

I sighed. Everybody thinks they can be a detective.

"What reason?" I asked him.

"Creepy fans. Men who want to be best friends with the actors."

"Does that happen?" Diotima asked.

The stage manager laughed. "Yes. Have you noticed how elegant actors are? Men get drawn to that. When I say these fans want to be best friends, I mean they want to be *really close* friends, if you get my meaning."

"Oh. I see."

"Mostly they're older men, but not always. You can spot them straight away. They linger about and try to look like they belong, but you can tell they're nervous as all Hades and when they get up the nerve to approach an actor—it's always the protagonist—they hold some love offering."

"Was there anyone like that yesterday?" I asked.

"Several."

"Anyone in particular?" I asked.

"No." Then Kiron thought again and said, "Wait, what about the strange kid?"

"What strange kid?" Diotima and I said simultaneously.

Kiron looked from one to the other of us. "There's a kid hangs about the theater like a bad smell. Stares at everything like he's never seen it before, even though I know he's watching almost every day. There's something weird about this guy. He's kind of intense."

"Does he go backstage?"

"Not since I caught him once and told him to bugger off."

Creepy, intense, and at the scene of the crime. That sounded like a killer to me.

"Why didn't you tell us this before?" I complained.

"Was I supposed to?" He looked insulted. "That happened long ago. When I said he hung around here, I didn't mean only recently."

Diotima said, "I think I know who you mean. When we expelled the ghost, we saw someone in the audience who didn't seem to quite belong." Diotima described the man she'd spotted that day. "Was that him?"

"Yeah, that's the kid," the stage manager said.

It was the man Diotima had pointed out to Pythax and me. I remembered what he looked like. When the stage manager had said "kid," what he'd meant was someone my own age. It made me wonder what the stage manager thought of me.

"Was he here today?" I asked. "Maybe we can catch him when he comes."

"Well that's a funny thing," said Kiron. "I haven't seen him since the murder."

Diotima and I shared a glance.

I said to Kiron, "I think we might need to talk to him. Does this 'kid' have a name?"

"Yeah, I heard someone talk to him, once. What was it?" The stage manager scratched his head. "I dunno. I can't remember."

"Do you know *anything* about him?" Diotima asked.

"Well, his mother sells vegetables in the agora. Woman has a voice like the Furies on a bad day."

"How do you know that?"

"She came here once, looking for her son. You should have heard what she had to say to the poor fellow. Apparently he was supposed to be moving boxes of vegetables instead of watching us work. Every man present could hear what she said, and it wasn't pretty." He paused. "Mind you, with her projection, if she'd been a man she could have had a career on stage."

# SCENE 26
# THE VEGETABLE WOMAN

DIOTIMA AND I went to the agora in search of a woman stall holder who had a voice like the Furies on a bad day.

Unfortunately, that description fit many of those who worked behind the stalls. Haggling with agora shoppers every day wasn't the kind of job that led to gentle feelings. The fishwives were the worst. They used language that would make a soldier blush. I wondered why. Was it their husbands? Was it all that salt?

Next for rudeness after the fishwives came the farmwives. I supposed it was all the dirt.

There's no official rule, but people who sold the same things tended to cluster in the same parts of the agora. I wasn't quite sure how this arrangement had come about, but like so many things it was traditional and thus no one questioned it. One area in the northwest held all the bronzeware stalls. The smell of fish came from another in the southwest, close to the road that leads to Piraeus port town. The east side serviced the many people who passed by along the Panathenaic Way. That was where the sellers of fashionable cloth and the wine sellers and the people selling ready food set themselves. They made a small fortune at inflated prices. Toward the center, behind the fashionable vendors, were the unfashionable vegetables.

Patches of dark clouds had been threatening all day. Now there was a sudden clap of thunder and it poured down, as it had the night before Romanos died. Everyone ran for the cover of roofs and awnings. With all the stalls up there were plenty of sunshades, under which people squeezed.

There was general agreement on the unseasonable weather: Dionysos had deserted us.

"He punishes us for the death at the theater," someone said.

Luckily no one had recognized me as the man supposed to find the killer to placate the God. If they did, they'd probably blame me for not having solved the crime yet.

"If it's to be like this throughout spring my crops will be ruined," a farmer said. "My family will starve."

"We'll *all* starve," said an optimist.

The storm dripped to a sudden end, to be followed by a burst of sun that did nothing but turn the puddles into muggy steam. It had been the worst spring of my remembrance. Everyone in the agora returned to business as usual.

Diotima and I walked along the two rows of vegetables, now somewhat damp. I imagined anyone who bought the produce now would see it rot faster than it usually did.

In the way of Athens it was mostly the women who managed the stalls while their men worked the fields. There were few men to check. It didn't take us long to see that the man we were looking for wasn't there. This reduced us to walking along the rows of vegetable merchants one more time, stopping to talk to each woman who looked old enough to have a grown son.

"Excuse me, do you have a son who likes going to the theater?"

This got us nowhere in the investigation, but a long way in invective.

I had lost hope by the time we came to the second to last woman in the last row, who said, "That'll be my good-for-nothing troublemaker son Euripides. What's he done this time?"

Hope returned, and also interest. Did this Euripides have a reputation as a troublemaker?

I told her the truth. I said, "As far as we know, your son has done nothing."

She snorted. "That'd be right. He's a lazy bugger."

I wondered how someone could be both a troublemaker and lazy.

I said, "We merely want to speak with him. May I ask your name, ma'am?"

"Cleito."

Cleito was larger than life, in the sense that there was twice as much of her in every direction as you would find on any normal woman.

"Why did you say, what's he done this time?" Diotima asked carefully.

Cleito scowled at Diotima. "Well, it'll be because he's the son of that other good-for-nothing lazy troublemaker, my husband Mnesarchus."

Cleito was angry about something. She shook her cleaver at us, decided against severing our limbs, and instead with a force that could have penetrated armor brought the blade down against an innocent, unsuspecting onion. The onion was stripped of its extra stalk. She tossed the stalk into one of the puddles at her feet and the onion in the basket, ready for sale.

"You want to buy onions?" she asked with a breath that indicated she'd been sampling her wares. "I got some good garlic too," she added.

"No thank—" I began, until Diotima jabbed me with an elbow. "Er, that is, we've been looking forward to some good onions," I corrected myself. "Diotima *loves* to cook onions, don't you dear?"

"I certainly do," Diotima agreed. "As much as you love to eat them, dear husband."

I loathed onions. When I'd been in the army, onion and cheese was all they fed us on route marches. The mere smell of onions reminded me of sore feet, cramped calf muscles, and given what usually happened during a forced march, having the runs in both meanings of the word.

If there was any food I never wanted to see again, it was onions.

"How many do you want?" Cleito demanded. "A basket?"

"That would be lovely."

Cleito looked around, expecting something that she couldn't see. "Where's your slave to carry them?" she asked.

"We don't have a slave."

She looked from one to the other of us, astonished. "None? You can't afford a single slave? How poor can you get?"

We weren't that poor. I just didn't like having a slave follow me around everywhere. In my line of business it didn't work.

She said, "In that case you gotta carry this."

She heaved up the basket with her massive biceps and practically threw it at me. I staggered under the weight.

Diotima paid Cleito the coins. It was a lot of coins, but at least we had enough onions to last us the rest of our lives, plus some useful information.

"Cleito, you haven't told us where we can find your son?" Diotima said.

"Where he always is, if he isn't mooning about in that theater."

"Yes?"

"At home avoiding as much work as possible."

"Where's home?" Diotima asked patiently. Getting information from the vegetable woman was like pulling thorns from your feet. Painful. And slow.

"Phyla," said Cleito. "Our farm is in the deme of Phyla." She told us where to find their farm, then waved her cleaver at us again. "And if you see the lazy good-for-nothing, tell him his mother expects him to come here to do some real work."

---

THE DEME OF Phyla is well to the northeast of the city. It's true farmland out there, where the success or failure of the harvest decided all our futures for the next year. It was, in short, exactly the sort of place where the god Dionysos would make us suffer if he was offended by the murder at his shrine.

We knocked on the door of the farmhouse. We heard footsteps behind. They grew louder, then stopped. There was a fumbling with the bolt, before the door opened a crack and two worried eyes stared out at us.

"Oh, I thought you might be my mother," he said. "Or the murderers."

"Are you Euripides, son of Mnesarchus?" I asked.

"I'm Euripides, son of Cleito, more to the point," he said.

I knew what he meant. I said as much.

He was suddenly concerned.

"My mother didn't send you, did she?"

"Your mother did mention something about doing useful work, but we'll tell her we couldn't find you."

His shoulders relaxed. "Thanks. You're theater people, aren't you? I saw you there."

"That's what we came to ask you about."

"The theater? I spend all my spare time there. I'm going to be a writer."

"I see." My tone must have told him how difficult I found that to believe.

Euripides sniffed. "I'm sure you've heard men say that a hundred times."

I hadn't. Normal men talked about sport and women.

"Well, I'm different," Euripides said. "I study the theater like other men study war."

I knew only two writers: Aeschylus and Sophocles. Neither of them was anything like Euripides. Aeschylus was a hard man, a veteran soldier who had survived the worst fighting of the Persian Wars. Sophocles was the very image of an Athenian gentleman, one of the rulers of the world. This Euripides was a weedy weakling who hid from his mother. To look at him up close, I realized Euripides and I must be almost exactly the same age.

"When did you complete your army time?" I asked, because every man must serve in the army from the year he turns eighteen until his twentieth birthday.

"Three years ago," he said. "Why do you ask?"

"I was in then too. I don't remember you."

Euripides shrugged. "We're in different tribes."

That was true enough. Army units are arranged according to the ten tribes of Athens. Euripides and I could have been on the same route marches and not known it. Yet I was struck by how different our physiques and our situations were. Somehow in the last three years I had progressed without even noticing it. I was a married man with a fine woman and an important job, and a few successes to my name, while Euripides, it seemed to me, was no different to the boy I had been on that first chilly morning when we all stood in line as raw recruits. I understood now why the stage manager had called Euripides a kid.

"I've studied every play, memorized every speech," Euripides said. He was back on the only subject he cared about. His voice rose with excitement. "I know who played what parts in every play that anyone remembers." He paused. "I guess you like that sort of thing too."

"No."

"Every proper man wants to be a writer," Euripides added, as if there must be something wrong with me.

"What about women?" Diotima asked.

Euripides turned to Diotima. So far he'd ignored her. "Women can't write," he said. "Everybody knows that."

"Oh, I see," Diotima said in a chill voice. I grabbed her right hand to make sure our witness lived long enough to tell us something useful.

"Did I hear you say that you saw the murderers?" I said, not because I thought he meant it, but to distract Diotima.

"I saw them. I was there," Euripides said. "I saw them kill him."

"What? When? How?" I demanded.

"It was late at night. I . . ." He hesitated. "You won't tell anyone about this, will you?"

"Of course not," I lied.

He looked relieved.

"Well, the thing is, I like to act out plays at the theater of Dionysos."

"Without performing a sacrifice first?" Diotima said, shocked.

"Well, no," Euripides admitted.

"That's against the law," Diotima pointed out. "The theater is a temple."

"Yes, that's why I do it late at night, when it's dark," he said. He looked from one to the other of us. "I've done it before; I knew I wouldn't get caught."

"Did you know I'd posted guards there?" I asked.

His eyes widened. "I didn't see them."

Either he was completely naïve, or a great actor.

"All right. Go on."

"With all the actors gone for the day and everyone at parties, I was inspired to go to the theater. I wanted to block out what I would do—stage movements, that sort of thing, you know what I mean—if in case I was asked to present at the Great Dionysia."

He had about as much chance of that as I had.

"In the dark?" Diotima asked the practical question.

"Well if I did it in daylight, people would notice, wouldn't they?" Euripides said.

That was true enough.

"I walked in from the audience end. It's easier that way."

He meant he was less likely to be seen.

"Right away I saw them, the murderers—"

"Them?" I interrupted. "More than one?"

"Yes."

"How many?"

"I didn't count."

I wanted to demand why not. But Euripides wasn't the man to notice details. He was too immersed in his own world.

"Are you sure it wasn't the guards you saw?" I said.

"Not unless the guards killed the actor."

Our witness must have sensed my annoyance. He said, "There was a whole group. They walked about the stage. The machine arm was already over the stage. They must have moved it before I arrived."

"If it was dark, how did you see this?"

"They carried small torches."

"What did they look like?" Diotima asked at once.

"They wore capes with hoods."

I swore.

Euripides said, "They all looked the same, and they moved about in the dark."

"Take a guess at their number," I ordered.

Euripides thought about it. "Ten?" he guessed. "More than five. Less than fifteen."

I had to hide my shock at the number of killers.

Diotima remained calm. She said, "Very well. Let's go from the start. You arrived at the theater. What happened then?"

"I sat down to enjoy the show." To our horrified looks he said, "Well, I didn't know they were about to kill him!"

"So you watched while they hanged that poor man," Diotima said in contempt.

"I told you I didn't know," Euripides sounded very unhappy indeed. "I thought they were . . . well . . . playing around in the theater, like I do. Especially with those identical capes and hoods. They looked more like a chorus than anything."

"Hmm." I could understand how someone might make that mistake. "Go on."

"There was a man in amongst them who wasn't wearing the cape and hood."

"Was he standing?" I asked. "Did they carry him?"

"Standing, but it seemed like they propped him up."

"Go on."

"They put the rope on him, and the noose around his neck, like I'd seen the players do during the rehearsals. They fussed about him. I thought they were putting the harness on, honest."

"But they weren't."

"No, I realize now they were tying the noose tightly to the holding rope. Three men went behind the skene. Then the machine rose."

Exactly as Socrates had predicted.

"It all seemed . . . well . . . very dramatic." Euripides shrugged. "He hung limp. Just like in the play. That was the other reason I didn't realize what was happening: there was no struggle. Hanged men struggle, don't they?"

"Yes."

"Well, this one didn't."

Romanos must already have been unconscious.

"What happened then?"

"They filed off. They walked straight past me!"

"Why didn't they see you?" I asked.

"I . . . uh . . . that is . . ." He gulped.

"You hid?" I helped him out.

"There wasn't anywhere to hide. I got down on all fours and crawled away between the wooden benches."

"You saw the killers, yet you didn't challenge them? You ran away?" Diotima said. Her tone told us what she thought of that.

"There were more of them than me," Euripides said.

"So what?" Diotima said. "A coward might turn away. A brave man would have turned to face the danger."

"Hmm." Euripides looked startled, then he stared at Diotima in a rather odd way. He reached for a scrap of papyrus. He wrote something on it.

As he scribbled Euripides tried to excuse his behavior. "When I saw those killers in the dark, I realized that I had a moral obligation to survive. I owe it to my future fans, you see. I have a sacred debt to art to avoid my own death."

I tried to ignore his rudeness in writing with his head down as he spoke to us.

Diotima snorted. "That's nonsense. Death is a debt we must all pay," she said.

"That's not bad either." Euripides kept scribbling.

"What are you doing?" Diotima asked.

"Writing down what you just said. I might have a use for it some time."

"I thought you just said women couldn't write?"

"Why didn't you tell anyone that you were a witness?" I demanded.

Euripides finished writing Diotima's words. He looked up. "You just said it: I'm a witness. How long do you think I'd survive when word got out? Even if I lived, I can't afford to be banned from the theater for the rest of my life. I have my plays to consider."

"You haven't written any," I pointed out.

"Yes I have!" Euripides practically shouted in his excitement. "I've written twenty-seven so far." Euripides flung open the chest beside him. There, lying in bundles tied with cord, was more papyrus than I'd ever seen outside a state office. It must have cost his mother a small fortune. No wonder she was cranky.

"You've submitted these plays to the archon," I guessed. I recalled Chorilos's description of desperate men applying to have their plays shown.

Euripides said, "For some reason, whenever I present myself to demand a place in the Great Dionysia, they throw me out."

"I can't imagine why."

"Yes, it's ridiculous, isn't it?" Euripides threw his arms up in despair and disgust. "The whole system's rigged to favor the writers people like best."

"But isn't that the idea?"

"Not at the expense of better writers. People like Aeschylus get a chance every time they ask for one, while people like me must struggle."

"Life is hard, Euripides, then you die." I waited, but Euripides didn't move.

"Aren't you going to write that down?" I asked him.

"No."

THAT ROMANOS HAD been killed by a cabal of midnight assassins was not news Pericles was going to welcome. He wanted a simple murder. He wasn't going to get one. At first this case had looked like a series of pranks that had gone horribly wrong. It had turned into something deeper and much more complex.

Of course, that was assuming Euripides had told us the truth. Perhaps he had made up his dramatic scene of midnight murder—he was certainly capable of it—but the moment Euripides had opened his mouth I'd dispensed with any idea of him being a ruthless killer. He'd pressed the manuscript of one of his plays on us as we left. I'd refused to take it, but Diotima, who was more polite, or maybe more desperate for evidence, had taken it with a thin smile.

"This changes everything." Diotima said, echoing my thoughts. "A whole group of killers. Nico, what do you think?"

"It looks nasty," I said. "What sort of people would remorselessly slaughter an actor?"

"Theater critics?" Diotima suggested.

"Besides them."

Every city has men of malformed spirit, who are never happy with anything that someone else produces. They talk loudly to their friends in the audience. They go over every scene in detail and point out every mistake with malicious, sad-voiced glee. But I couldn't imagine such people being willing to face the consequences of their words, let alone face a man and kill him.

No, whoever had done this was, above all else, competent.

"We must list every *group* of suspects," I said.

"There aren't any," Diotima pointed out.

"What about the Phrygians?" I said.

"Maia and Petros?" Diotima said. "Why would they want to kill her brother?"

"You know as well as I do most murderers are family members. Plus there's a whole bunch of Phrygians in that house. What other suspects form a group?"

"Thodis and his friends," Diotima countered.

"Why?" I asked. "He has no reason."

"Nor do the Phrygians," Diotima said, "But that didn't stop you condemning them. How about someone with a motive then?"

"Lakon," I said at once.

"There's only one of him."

"That is rather inconvenient," I said. "How about Lakon and a group of disaffected actors? If Romanos can blackmail one actor, he can blackmail lots of them."

Diotima scoffed. "How many actors with dark secrets do you think there are in this city?" she asked.

"Your turn to think of something better then."

"Your idea of actors does raise another possibility," Diotima said. "How about Kiron and the stage crew?"

That idea had its attractive points. It meant the murderers were *certain* to know how to use the murder weapon.

"I think we need more evidence," I said.

Diotima nodded glumly.

# SCENE 27
## *SALAMINIA*

DIOTIMA AND I woke in the false dawn, before Apollo rose in the East. I had ordered one of my father's slaves to stay awake all night, with strict instructions to wake me the moment the dimmest light appeared in the sky.

When the time came, the slave took his revenge by kicking me hard. I couldn't blame him. I told him to go to bed, and gave him permission to sleep through the morning.

Then I woke Socrates in turn, and told him to hitch the family's donkey to our cart. On my own I would have walked, but I didn't want Diotima to walk the whole way to Piraeus in the semidarkness.

Socrates rubbed his eyes and didn't protest too much. He knew only something very interesting indeed could cause me to get up so early. While Socrates hitched the donkey I went up to the women's quarters and gently shook Diotima awake. She looked beautiful in the starlight. But she shivered as soon as she was up. I wrapped a warm blanket around her.

The air was chill and brisk in our nostrils. The three of us made our way down streets that were empty but for slaves going about their masters' business, and the on-duty troops of the Scythian Guard who patrolled in pairs. Several of the guardsmen recognized us and saluted as we passed; they knew Diotima for the daughter of their chief, and me for his son-in-law, and I had spent enough time in the Scythian barracks that the men knew me by sight. I returned their salutes rather awkwardly, because no one had ever saluted me in my life. The highest rank I had ever attained in the army was common soldier—as low as you can get and still carry a spear.

We drove the cart through the Piraean Gate, which marks the beginning of the road to Piraeus. We couldn't see the land to either side of us, because the road is protected on both sides by tall, wooden walls, their purpose to make sure Athens can never be cut off from her fleet. The Athenian fleet is the lifeblood of our city. The Long Walls meant that the city, the port, and the road between were one large fortification.

The effect of the walls on that lonely morning was that it felt like driving down an enormously long corridor. Especially when our squeaky cartwheels echoed to make the sound of our passing unnaturally loud. I wondered that we didn't wake half the city.

As we drove, Socrates said, "Nico, I've been thinking."

"Yes?" I said warily.

"Well, you said maybe the killer wasn't killing Romanos, but the character he played."

"Maybe. It's a theory," I said.

"I was wondering, does a character in a play know when he's dead?"

"Do you mean the actor?" I said.

"I mean the character in the play."

"Is this some sort of a weird joke?" I asked. I'd learned to ignore the strange things that Socrates said, but this was beyond even his norm.

"No, Nico, I mean it," Socrates said. "After all, everyone knows when they're dead."

"Nobody knows when they're dead, Socrates," I said.

"Then how come when people die they go to Hades and remember who they are?" he shot back.

He had me there.

"All right, but that's real people," I said to him. "Fictional people are obviously different. For a start, they don't exist."

I felt this was over-explaining the obvious. But for Socrates, sometimes that was necessary.

"What happens to Sisyphus, when he dies in Sophocles's play?" Socrates asked.

"He goes to Hades."

"There you are, then!" he said triumphantly. "Sisyphus is a character but he knows he's dead. Maybe we're all just characters in someone else's play, but we don't know it."

"Don't be ridiculous, Socrates," I said.

Dotted along the way, here and there by the roadside, were heaped piles of building stone. Workmen had already begun to replace the wooden walls with solid stone ones, higher than the original wood, impenetrable, and spread further apart. It was a massive project that would take years to complete. Forty stadia is a long way.

I had once asked Pericles why we were going to so much effort to replace something we already had. Pericles had replied rather acerbically that it was all my fault. On a previous case I had accidentally destroyed the gates at the other end. The city leaders had realized that if enough force was applied then it was possible to break through the wooden walls. Stone was therefore required. Pericles seemed to blame me for the high cost of the rebuild, which I thought rather unfair.

The gates at the Piraeus port town were opening as we arrived. We passed through with a wave to the guards.

Piraeus has three bays. The largest is to the right as you enter the town. The docks there are reserved for commercial shipping, merchant boats, Athenian shipping lines, and cargo carriers from foreign lands. The Emporium, the corn exchange and the warehouses are directly opposite the commercial docks.

Socrates guided the cart left just before we reached the first of the warehouses. The road led us across Piraeus, past the smallest and meanest of the docks: old, gray wharves that seemed like they'd collapse if you set a foot on them. It was from here that the fishing boats worked. The smell of old fish was pungent.

The road beside the fisher wharves was deeply rutted. It had been worn by the many carts that were loaded every morning with the catch that fed the city. The jolting rattled our teeth.

The fish carts were already lined up, waiting for the boats to return laden with food. The fishwives stood about, all of them looking old before their years, waiting for their menfolk to return. They stared at us as we passed. We were unwelcome visitors to the only domain these poor people could ever call their own.

Diotima leaned close and whispered, "I wouldn't be one of those women for anything."

I could only nod agreement. Even slaves had easier lives than fisher folk.

The road passed on to the Naval Dockyards, the third and final bay at Piraeus. Athens has almost three hundred triremes in the fleet, but only twenty or thirty were anchored in the bay. All the rest were out on missions.

I raised my hand against the rising sun to see the reserve fleet of Athens. Each boat was a low, long, thin silhouette on the water. On each boat, a few men walked, looking like stick figures, back and forth across the decks, picking up and putting away, getting ready for the day.

Only one trireme was tied up at the naval dock, and this one was moored at the stern. It was *Salaminia* and she waited for us. She shone in the sun. In fact, she gleamed so much in reflected morning sunlight that we had to shield our eyes as we approached.

The moment they saw us I heard shouted orders. "Out oars!"

Long oars appeared on both sides, which was possible because *Salaminia* was rear end to the dock. They were poised to go. All they needed was us.

I jumped off the cart and handed down Diotima.

"Can't I come too?" Socrates said.

"No," I said firmly, to stop him getting any ideas about jumping aboard. "Keep searching the records room."

Socrates looked unconvinced and unhappy.

I left him that way. Diotima and I walked up the gangplank. Diotima went first. A sailor grabbed her hand to lead her over the edge and onto the deck. I followed without assistance. The moment I stepped off the gangplank, the *trierarch* called, "Pull!"

The starboard and portside rowing chiefs echoed his command. The *aulos* player began a high-pitched tune on his pipes and the singer beside him began a rhythmic song. The oarsmen bent their backs to the first laborious pull, the helmsman turned his tiller, and *Salaminia*, the fastest boat in the world, began to move. The gangplank fell into the water and would have been left behind had it not been tied on with a rope. The sailor who'd helped Diotima hauled it up as the ship gathered speed.

The trierarch walked over to me. "Good morning—*kalimera*—I believe our destination is Rhamnus?"

I nodded. To my surprise I saw that it was the same trierarch who had commanded *Salaminia* the last time I'd been on board.

"I know you!" I said.

"Yes. Kordax of the deme Oa at your service. The last time you were with us I was a complete beginner. I'm pleased to say I've learned something since then."

That had been three years ago. I said, "What are you doing still here?" Then, realizing that sounded rude, I added quickly, "I mean, I thought trierarchs only held the post for a year."

The captains of the Athenian Navy win their position by supplying the boat. A wealthy man funds a warship for a year, and in return he gets to call himself *trierarch*, which means captain. Most men are happy to pass on the command and the cost at the end of their year. To see the same man three years later was extraordinary.

Kordax smiled. "I discovered I liked it. I volunteered to serve another two terms." Then he lost his smile. "This will have to be my last year though. The cost has almost bankrupted me."

I wasn't surprised.

"What will you do then?" I asked.

"The problem is I've become addicted to speed. I love it. Do you know I've traveled faster than any man who's ever lived?"

"How so?" I said, confused.

"*Salaminia* is the fastest machine ever built. Therefore the men who travel on her have traveled faster than any man alive."

"I see."

"Last year we had a mission to carry dispatches to Egypt. On the return journey we were blown by strong winds." Kordax gestured to the mast and its squared crosspiece. "The men wanted to shelter but I ordered sails up. Then Poseidon threw everything he had at us. Not much rain, but squalls and following waves. The helmsman said we must broach, but I took the tiller with him and we held fast and got soaked to the skin.

"The men said I was mad. They said the mast must crack. But it held and we surfed those waves until the wind died. All the old sailors agreed it was the fastest any boat has ever sailed." He laughed. "I love that feeling of speed across the water."

Three years had changed him. The last time we'd met, Kordax had told me he was only doing this for the glory, that he strutted the deck while the helmsman made all the important decisions. Now he had the faraway look of a sailorman in his eyes. Kordax was a deeply sunburned man who confidently overrode his helmsman in a squall. Somewhere along the line this gentleman of Athens had turned into a man who could command a major ship of the line.

"You're going to miss it," I said.

"Yes, but I have a plan," he said. "When I retire out I'll start my own shipping line."

"Cargo boats?" I said.

He gave a moue of distaste but nodded. "They're slow, but they make the money," he said. "The real fun will be the passenger ship."

"What's that?"

"I've studied everything there is to know about how *Salaminia* is put together. I'll build a quarter-size version and hire her out to men who need to go somewhere fast. I'll command her personally."

"Is there money in that?"

He shrugged. "Who cares? As long as I get to fly across the sea, that's all that matters. But yes, think of all those merchants who want to beat each other to a deal on some remote island. One of them will pay me to get there first."

I noticed that Kordax's idea of "nearly bankrupt" meant he could only afford a small shipping line. I couldn't even afford a horse.

Diotima had listened in on the conversation—she kept well away from the sailors—and now she asked, "Captain, we were told that the machine used at the theater is like the ones used for boats. Is that true?"

"I know nothing about the theater," Kordax said.

Diotima described the god machine, at which Kordax nodded and said yes, it sounded much like the dockside cranes used to lift heavy cargo.

"What I wanted to ask is this," Diotima said. "Is it possible for a man to handle the rope at the arm end and work the machine at the same time?"

Kordax was plainly puzzled by the question. "Why would you want to do that?" he asked.

Diotima described the difficulty that Socrates had discovered, of using a crane to hang someone single-handed.

"Ah, I see your problem." Kordax called over the steersman. He explained the situation and together the two sailormen discussed lines and pulleys and weights and bending and belaying and all manner of nautical terms, until I felt myself going cross-eyed. I think even Diotima lost track of what they were saying.

Kordax and the steersman were clearly enjoying themselves.

There were animated hand movements to describe various arcane rigs that might be employed, exotic devices that might be fashioned to overcome obstacles, tricks of cordage that made the eyes water. When they were finished they turned to us with a definitive, unanimous answer.

"It's impossible," Kordax said.

"I had a feeling you might say that," Diotima muttered. "This complicates our problem."

"You say they have this machine in a theater, lady?" the steersman asked.

"They use the god machine all the time," Diotima said.

"They should put us sailormen in charge of their effects," the steersman said. "We could do a much better job."

Kordax had promised speed and he was true to his word. We stepped off onto the primitive wharf at Rhamnus that afternoon.

"Thank you," I said.

Kordax shrugged. "That was too simple. Give us a harder problem."

Behind him, three rows of exhausted men were slumped over their oars. The lips of the aulos player were puffed up red and the singer clutched a sore throat.

"Try this then." I handed him a small bag of coins. "See if the men can drink their way through these coins tonight."

I was pleased with the trip and feeling generous, as I could afford to be since the coins belonged to Pericles.

Kordax hefted the bag. The men at his back grinned.

"We wait for you?" Kordax asked.

"Yes. Our business here will be done by tomorrow." Either we would find the family of Lakon or we wouldn't. Either way it would be quick, but the second option worried me. I'd hate to have to go back to Pericles to report that after all this trouble, we hadn't found a thing.

# Scene 28
# THE SKELETON IN THE FAMILY CLOSET

Diotima and I walked uphill to the agora. Our mission was to find someone who might know something about the family of Lakon.

Rhamnus was an interesting place. It was larger than a town, smaller than a city. The buildings were rustic, yet there was a city wall. The voices about us spoke in an accent closer to that of Thebes than Athens. Not like Lakon at all, who spoke with one of the most cultured Athenian voices I had ever heard.

"I wonder how often people from here travel to Athens?" Diotima said.

"Not often, is my guess."

"Yet when he was a boy, Lakon was in the chorus," she said.

"Probably his parents took him to see the Dionysia. We can ask them, if we can find them."

The agora was quiet, for the time of day. There were two taverns along its border. At one of these, a group of eight old men sat under the shade of an awning.

"Good afternoon," I said to them, and smiled. They smiled back. They barely had thirty teeth between them.

"Sirs, I would like to buy you a drink." I waved to the inn-keeper, who had been watching me warily from within. I held up eight fingers.

He nodded. A moment later, a scowling slave appeared with eight clay cups which he set upon the table in front of the old men. The slave sloshed in wine from a small amphora. Almost as much hit the tabletop as went in the cups.

I paid the slave the going rate for tavern wine in Athens. He didn't move, nor did he say anything. In the lengthening silence I realized what had happened; the innkeeper had taken the opportunity to sell me his most expensive wine.

I added coins until he had twice what I'd originally paid him. That was enough to make the slave go away.

The old men raised their glasses to me. "May Zeus honor you, young man," one of them said in a croaky voice. Then they drank deep.

I said, as they drank, "Sirs, my wife and I are looking for a family. I don't know if you've heard of them. I can't even tell you much about them."

They looked at each other warily, then down at the drinks I'd just bought them. One of the old men said, "Well young man, I wouldn't normally go telling a stranger about a local family—you can't be too careful, what with the trouble that drifts into town these days. But seeing as you got your young woman with you"—he leered at Diotima—"I can tell you're right enough."

"Thanks."

"So who you looking for?"

I said, "There used to be a boy who lived here, perhaps thirty years ago. A boy by the name of Lakon. We're looking for his people."

They nodded knowingly. One of the men sighed. The man who had thanked me smacked his lips and said, "Ah yes."

Diotima and I shared a triumphant look. This was progress. "You know him?"

"Everyone in Rhamnus knows of him! Talk of the town, he was. First lad from these parts ever to get in the Dionysia. In the chorus, he was."

"Yes! That's him!" I cried, excited.

"Then the tragedy struck."

"What tragedy?"

"People were still talking about it years later. You'll be wanting the mother, I suppose?"

"Is she still alive?" I said, startled.

"Certain sure she is, unless Hades took her since yester morn. Delivered her vegetables like I always do, every third day. I used to grow 'em. Now my son does that. Back ain't what it used to be, you know."

"Please, where do we find her?" Diotima asked.

"It's Agne you want. Fine lady she is. In course, she has to mush up her vegetables, on account she don't have many teeth," explained a man with five. He pointed. "Go up that road and turn left at the place where Davo's farm used to be."

"Where did Davo's farm used to be?" I asked, reasonably enough.

"Just up there." He pointed along the road once more.

"That place burnt down, Patro," another of the men said. "Thirty, forty years ago."

"Did it?" Patro looked confused. "I could have sworn I was there yesterday."

WE WALKED WEST into rough farmland. It had taken another round of drinks, but in the end we received perfect instructions.

Our way took us to an old, small farmhouse that was run down, but neat. At least, it was neat on the outside on the ground floor. The ground outside the door was swept. The bare walls were clean until about halfway up. The top half of everything was filthy and covered in cobwebs. The small barn beside the house was the same: beautifully neat on the bottom, a mess on the top. It was as if someone had taken two different buildings and stuck them together.

There was none of the activity you always see about a farm. There wasn't a single animal we could see except for a few scrawny chickens. The fields about the farm were overgrown with weeds.

Diotima and I looked at each other. I wondered if we were about to find a house full of corpses.

I knocked on the door.

We heard soft footsteps on the dirt floor within. The door opened just a crack and the pretty eyes of a girl peeped out.

"Yes?"

This couldn't be the mother of Lakon. The girl was barely older than twenty, if that.

I said, "We're looking for a lady named Agne. Does she live here?"

"What do you want?" Her voice dripped suspicion.

"To ask some questions. That's all. The men in the agora told us where to come."

The girl looked to Diotima, then back to me.

"What men?" she said.

"Old men. At the tavern."

"Describe them," she ordered.

She was doing her best to defend her house. She didn't realize I could easily push my way in. I hoped no serious enemy ever came here.

I described the old men, down to the number of teeth each had.

The girl nodded. "That's Patro and his friends. He wouldn't have sent you here if he thought you were trouble."

She stepped back. The door opened.

She was holding a pot with a long handle in her right hand. She'd been prepared to hit me with it.

"I'll see if my owner is in." The girl went up the stairs.

This girl was a slave? She spoke primly, like a daughter in a fine mansion, but everything in this house spoke of poverty. The light that shone through the windows served only to expose a room with nothing in it. Not even dust. Just two old chairs and a table.

"My mistress will see you," the girl said. "You'll have to come up the stairs. Agne's not been well of late."

Agne hadn't been well for the last twenty years, if the sight of her was anything to go by. She was old, with but a few gray hairs left on a head that was otherwise bald. She was thin as a stick, and she was propped up in a bed that was more termites than wood. Two blankets covered her, but weren't long enough to reach her feet, which were swollen.

"Agne?" I said. "My name is Nicolaos. This is my wife, Diotima."

Agne looked at me with uncomprehending eyes.

Diotima greeted Agne as she might a senior priestess. She took over the conversation. "Lady Agne, we would like to ask you about your son."

Agne brightened. "My son!"

"Yes."

"My son was in the Great Dionysia."

"Yes, we know," Diotima said patiently. "We'd like to ask about what happened after."

Out of sight of her owner, the slave girl was jumping from one foot to the other in anxiety.

"We came home," Agne said. She sounded sad.

"But your son returned to Athens," Diotima said.

"Did he?" Agne asked, as if this was news. She suddenly sat up and smiled. On her ancient, ravaged face the effect was disturbingly skull-like. "I must have forgotten. Did he send you?" she asked, excited. "Is my son coming home?"

"Is there a reason why he might not?" Diotima countered. "Is there something that keeps him away?"

Agne was confused. "I . . . I don't think I can remember," she said. Agne looked to the slave girl, who turned away her head.

Diotima said, "What we want to know, Agne, is whether anything happened here in Rhamnus? Anything that might not reflect well on Lakon?"

Agne groaned. "No, that was a mistake. He didn't mean it."

"Mean what?" Diotima asked.

"There was so much blood."

She began to cry.

"Agne, about your son—"

A sudden change came over Agne. She looked blankly at Diotima. "Who?" she asked.

Diotima tried for a long time, but it was no use. Agne had forgotten that she'd ever had a son. The pressure of the questioning had driven her back into whatever world she inhabited in her mind.

We had come on a fool's errand. This poor old lady's wits were completely addled. Even if she told us something that seemed to make sense, we could never trust it.

I was angry, deeply angry, with Lakon, for allowing his mother to live in such squalor. It was none of my business, but I intended to tear strips off him when I returned to Athens. I would shame Lakon in public if I had to, until he took proper care of his parent.

SO MUCH EFFORT, so much travel, and it had all been for nothing. I wondered how I was going to explain this to Pericles.

"What's your name?" Diotima asked the slave girl, after we had taken our leave of Agne. We spoke in the downstairs room. The girl hadn't offered us refreshments. We understood why.

"Lysine," she said.

"You look after this place all on your own?"

"Yes."

That was why everywhere was neat and tidy, up to the point that she could reach.

"Aren't you tempted to run away?" I asked.

I shouldn't have said that to a slave, but it was patently obvious that Lysine could walk any time she wanted.

Lysine looked horrified. "And leave Agne to die? I couldn't do that. Besides, I never want to leave here."

I found that hard to believe. This was the most squalid farm I had ever seen.

I said, "What could be worse than looking after a demented old lady on your own?"

"My father sold me to a brothel when I was a child."

"Oh."

Lysine shrugged. "He needed the money. A few years later I ran away. The owner caught me and beat me black and blue. When I was healed I tried again. The owner chased me to this place. I was hiding in the barn when he found me. He swore he was going to kill me. Then this crazy old lady with a broom appeared and threatened him. It was Agne. She wouldn't let him take me. She hit him with the broom until he gave in. She paid him coins, and he went away."

"That was good of her."

Lysine shrugged again. "She was old even then. I think she realized that soon she'd need someone to look after her. I didn't mind."

"This is outrageous," I said. "I promise you, Lysine. I'll make Lakon shoulder his share of the responsibility for Agne if it's the last thing I do."

"That's impossible," Lysine said softly.

"Why?"

"Shh! I can't tell you here." Lysine looked about. "I'll show you."

Lysine led us outside. She walked past the barn, going out the back. Lysine walked through the backyard, past the rotted posts that had once held up a fence railing. She took us another hundred paces, to a low hill that overlooked the sea far away.

Sculpted stones jutted out from the ground. On each was engraved a picture and some words. Lysine pushed away the weeds to reveal the closest one.

"Here it is," she said. "This is the grave of Lakon."

# SCENE 29
# ALL IS NOT AS IT SEEMS

"SOMETIMES SHE THINKS he's still alive," Lysine said. "In her lucid moments she knows he isn't. She's happiest when her mind is gone."

We sat upon the large stones that were scattered amongst the weeds of the field. It was uncomfortable, but Lysine insisted we talk far from the farmhouse.

"How did Lakon die?" Diotima asked.

I could tell from her tone of voice that Diotima had as much trouble believing this as I did. Yet there was no doubt about it, we had seen a funeral stele engraved with the name Lakon. Beside it was the gravestone of his father. This was the family plot, overgrown with weeds. There was even a bush growing out that must have been there for years.

"It happened long before I got here," Lysine said. "Agne doesn't like to talk about it. They tell me it was after Lakon died that she lost her mind. But everyone else in Rhamnus, they talk about it all the time. And—this is the terrible thing—they say that Lakon killed his own father with an axe. They say he slit his own throat."

There was only one problem with Lysine's statement. Lakon was alive and well in Athens.

"Are you *sure* he died?" I asked.

Lysine looked at me as if I'd asked a stupid question. "Didn't I just say the tragedy was before I arrived? This happened decades ago. I don't even know if I was born then."

I had to concede that was a fair point.

Lysine said, "Look, if you want to know what happened you'll have to ask someone who was there. Ask any of the old men. Ask Patro."

"Are there any other men in the family?" Diotima asked. She was still searching for a way out of this paradox.

"None." She waved her arms to encompass the entire property. "Look at this place. Does it look like there's been a man here for decades?"

Diotima and I both shook our heads.

Lysine said, "One day there was Agne, her husband, and her son. The next day the son killed the father and then suicided."

"You're the true mistress here, aren't you?" Diotima said.

"No," Lysine said firmly. "That is Agne. I merely help her."

"What will you do?" Diotima asked gently.

"I'll look after her until she dies," Lysine said. "The old men from these parts bring us food. It's not much, but we get by. I have to grind up Agne's food and feed it to her. But we get by."

"And then?"

"I don't know." She looked about her, worried. "Last year Agne said I'm to be free, not a slave. She went to the local archon and declared it and everything. The archon said yes. Agne said to the archon that when she dies I'm to have her farm. I never want to leave here. But I don't know anything about farms. Maybe some man who wants a farm will marry me," she said. "We could grow food and maybe even have animals and we wouldn't have to be hungry."

Any man who married this girl would get something more valuable than a farm. I hoped for her sake that she could find a good man who wouldn't misuse her.

"There's the rest of the world," Diotima said. She pointed to the sea beyond Rhamnus, to the island of Eboea on the other side, clearly visible.

Lysine shivered. "No. It's terrible out there. Terrible."

---

WE THANKED LYSINE profusely. She had given us more than we had any right to expect. We declined the offer to say farewell to Agne; it was too uncomfortable, knowing what we did.

We returned to the agora at Rhamnus as fast as we could. Patro and his friends were exactly where we'd left them. I had the impression they never moved.

I said, "Patro? You were right, what happened at Agne's farm was a terrible tragedy."

Patro smacked his lips. "That it was."

"What happened, exactly? May I ask?" I could afford to put it nicely. If Patro didn't tell me, someone else would.

Patro was silent for a long time before he answered. "It was that Dionysia that did for them. They went there for a holiday. They wanted to show their son some city culture, do you see? Young Lakon got chosen for a chorus and when they returned to Rhamnus they were full of it. Proud parents, you know?"

We nodded.

"Young Lakon never forgot. He talked all the time about how when he was older he'd return to Athens and be an actor. His dad let him talk. That was his big mistake." Patro paused, remembering. "Ten years later Lakon wasn't a boy any longer. He was a young man who declared he was off to Athens to be an actor. His dad said no. Who'd look after the farm if Lakon didn't? Acting was all very well for boys, but it was no job for a proper man." Patro spread his hands, as if in apology. "Well, the father had the right of it, didn't he? But he shouldn't have let Lakon grow with such an obsession, you know?"

"I know."

I'd had my own problems with a father who didn't like my choice of profession. But I'd been lucky, my father was a reasonable man.

"Did Lakon run away?" Diotima asked.

I already knew the answer to that. I shook my head. "It

wouldn't do him any good. The father could go to Athens and drag his son home. The courts would support the father. No, Diotima, while his father lived, Lakon was a legal child . . ."

My voice trailed off as I realized the implications of what I'd said. "Oh no."

Patro nodded. "That's what happened. I reckon in a fit of madness Lakon decided to become his own master. He took an axe to his dad, in their own house. A single blow to the chest. I saw it. The axe went deep. Only the Gods know how much hatred there must have been in that boy. He must have come to his senses then, realized the enormity of what he'd done. I heard tell from the slaves who saw it. He walked outside, and the next thing they hear is a gurgling scream. When they went out, Lakon had sliced his own throat."

"Whom the Gods would destroy, they first make mad," Diotima whispered.

"You got the right of it, young lady."

Agne had seen this happen. No wonder her wits were gone.

Patro wiped away a tear. I carefully didn't notice that he was crying. Patro said, "That Dionysia destroyed their lives."

I said, "Patro, I know this is going to sound strange, but is there any chance that the man you buried wasn't Lakon?"

Patro did me the honor of not telling me I was crazy. Instead, he shook his head. "I knew Lakon, boy and man. It was me who put the torch to the funeral pyre. I saw them lying side by side. Him and his dad. It was Lakon I torched. I remember it like it was yesterday."

## SCENE 30
# THE LAKON IDENTITY

"IF LAKON IS dead, then who is the man back in Athens?" Diotima said.

It was a good question. But I had no answer for my wife.

We spent the entire trip home talking about it. In the end we could come to only one conclusion.

From *Salaminia* we went straight to the home of Lakon. I banged on the door, hard. When the slave opened it, I pushed my way in. Lakon was sitting in his courtyard. I stopped in front of him. Diotima stood behind me with arms crossed and looking angry.

Lakon stared up in surprise. I said, "I'm going to tell you a story. You don't have to confirm or deny it. Frankly, I don't care what you say."

Lakon put down the scroll he was reading. "I'm listening, and I'm not admitting to anything."

I stood over him as I spoke.

"Many years ago, there was a talented young metic actor who belonged to a touring company. We don't know his name, nor where he came from. But we do know his company stopped at a small city called Rhamnus. It's just the sort of place where a small, struggling touring company would play."

Lakon said nothing.

"This young actor, while he was at Rhamnus, heard the tragic story of a local lad. The lad's name was Lakon. When he was a boy, Lakon had gone to the Great Dionysia and played in the chorus. When he grew to be a man Lakon killed his father and slit his own throat, all because the father wouldn't let the son be an actor."

I paused. But Lakon made no reaction. His face was studiously blank.

I said, "The people of Rhamnus still talk about the tragedy to this day. Certainly they must have been talking about it when our young actor, the protagonist of our story, played there so many years ago."

Lakon said nothing.

I said, "Our protagonist probably drank at one of the local taverns after his performance. Actors like to drink, don't they?"

Lakon nodded.

"What more natural thing than to tell every visiting actor about the boy who once played in the chorus, and then slaughtered his own father?"

Lakon said nothing.

"So our talented young actor had an idea. He would go to Athens and say his name was Lakon. Nobody in Athens would question his identity," I said. "Everyone knew that Lakon of Rhamnus had served in the chorus as a young lad. What could be more natural than that he return in adulthood to take up acting? It was no different to what Sophocles himself had done. The fake Lakon was entirely safe, he had made himself a citizen of Athens with a fine career . . . until Romanos discovered him."

"He would be found out," Lakon said quietly.

"Would he?" I asked. "Rhamnus is about as far away as you can get and still be a deme in Attica. What were the odds that someone from that distant town would come to Athens? If he did, would he even notice that there was an actor in Athens named Lakon? Nobody notices the actor beneath the mask! And if by bad luck a townsman did learn of this Lakon, they would probably assume it was someone else of the same name. He certainly wouldn't connect a famous Athenian actor with a young man who he knew for sure died two decades ago."

Lakon said nothing.

"How did Romanos find out? Probably the same way *you* did. Romanos had served in touring companies. The stage manager told us so. However he heard, Romanos connected you with the story."

I paused.

"You can imagine his surprise when he found, as I did, that the man he thought he knew had died twenty years ago; that the man he did know was a thief."

Lakon said, "I stole nothing from that unfortunate young man."

"You stole his name!"

"And you stole his citizenship," Diotima added.

"It's all very well for you to talk," Lakon snorted. He pointed at Diotima. "*You* married into citizenship. A man can't do that."

"What I did is legal," Diotima said. "What you did isn't."

"Is it not?" Lakon raised an eyebrow. "Show me the law that says I can't name myself anything I like."

He had me stumped on that. As far as I knew there was no law about changing your name.

"You're a fraud," Diotima said. I was relieved that she had a ready answer. "You let everyone believe you were something that you're not. You accepted the benefits of citizenship." She let that sink in, then added, "The fact is, Lakon, or whoever you are, if this goes to court, even if they don't find you guilty you'll be finished as a citizen of Athens. You'll be run out of town, exiled forever."

Lakon blanched.

"Please don't," he whispered. "I'll do anything. Anything."

"Including kill Romanos?" I asked.

"I don't deny I'm relieved to see him dead. You have no idea what a burden he was for me. But I didn't kill him."

"Can you prove that?"

"No."

His first honest answer. He'd said it defiantly.

"All right then, Lakon—I suppose we'll have to keep calling you that—tell us everything you know. And I mean *everything*."

"If I could think of anything that would exonerate me, don't you think I'd mention it?" he said angrily. "I know full well how bad my position looks."

I had nothing to say.

Diotima tapped her foot. "Well?"

"All right, yes, it's as you say," Lakon said miserably. "Romanos came to me several years ago. He accused me of . . . ah . . . pretense."

"You mean fraud," Diotima said.

"Romanos was more polite. For my silence he required me to promote his career."

"Was he polite about that too?"

"Rather forceful. He pointed out that since I'd won my position by foul means, that I could help him do the same."

"What did Romanos want you to do?"

"Oh, introduce him to men of influence, such as that ghastly choregos, Thodis."

"Anyone else?"

"Almost everyone who was anyone. He was particularly interested in men of a commercial nature. I presume their money was the attraction." Lakon waved his hand airily. He was regaining confidence. "And now I have told you everything."

Diotima and I turned without a word and made for the door.

"Wait!"

Diotima and I both stopped.

Lakon said, "What are you going to do about my . . . ah . . . indiscretion?"

"I don't know," I said coldly. "We haven't decided yet."

# SCENE 31
# THE HAND OF SABAZIOS

SINCE WE WERE in the area we decided to see how Petros, Maia, and the other Phrygians were settling into Diotima's house. I wanted to make sure they hadn't done any damage.

Diotima's birth father had lived in one of the more salubrious demes to the north of the agora. The people there had gone to some trouble to prettify the street for the Dionysia. Chains of flowers hung along the walls. The hermae—the busts of Hermes placed outside every door to bring good luck to those who passed—were scrubbed clean. A few keen home owners had even washed their front walls and swept the road beyond their doors.

Diotima's house was presentable on the outside, which was a relief. What was disconcerting was the amount of loud bashing emanating from inside. I instantly had thoughts of the last tenants, who had trashed the place and then run off to their home cities. Diotima and I shared a worried look. I flung open the door and walked in unannounced, the better to catch them at whatever they were doing.

"Nicolaos!"

Petros stood in the courtyard. He was dusty and sweaty, wearing nothing but a loin cloth.

"We weren't expecting you," he said.

I walked in, with Diotima right behind.

"What's happening?" I said.

Three men behind Petros were crowded about the wall, the one the previous tenants had damaged.

"We're only doing a few small renovations," Petros said.

At that moment the courtyard's back wall crashed to the ground. One of the men shouted in triumph. They stepped back. I saw then that they'd torn down the smashed surface that the rich man had kicked in.

Another man walked over. He carried pine panels that were pristine and straight. One of the first three checked the peg holes in the uprights. He declared them good for reuse and they proceeded to hammer in the new panels.

Yet another man was bent over a pot which he stirred, brushes beside him. He was ready to repaint the repairs.

"I hope you like the color." Petros pointed. Diotima and I turned to see they had already repainted the rest of the courtyard walls, in a pastel blue with a red key pattern on the top and bottom. "It's not fancy," Petros apologized.

"It's lovely," Diotima said. "Do you know, the place looks quite different."

Yes, it did. Every bit of damage from the previous tenants had been fixed. The destroyed furniture had disappeared, to be mysteriously replaced by newly built tables and chairs.

"Where did you get the timber for this?" I asked.

"Oh, odds and ends, from carpenters who didn't need it," Petros said with a straight face, as two men walked past carrying a thick beam of naval quality. That beam had probably been intended for the keel of a trireme. On the other hand, it would be the perfect structural support for the wall in the kitchen, the one where the second storey above had begun to sag.

"We metics have to be quite resourceful," Petros added.

"So I see."

I wondered if I could be charged with theft. But no, of course I couldn't. I hadn't asked the Phrygians to steal all this material.

Or had I? I'd said to Petros that the house was rent-free as long as they maintained it. Perhaps the Phrygians had interpreted my terms with a wink and a nod. Which I certainly hadn't intended.

Then I wondered if I should order Petros to put it all back. But if I did that, they would have to *tear it out of Diotima's house*.

They had done such a good job. It was far better than I could have done.

If I pretended not to have seen what I'd seen, would that make me complicit in their theft? At the very least I would be in their debt, and like it nor not, these people were suspects.

It occurred to me that Petros was smarter than he looked.

"Would you like to see the roof?" Petros asked.

"Will I have to close my eyes while I see it?" I asked.

He laughed.

The stairs up to the women's quarters didn't creak. The treads had been replaced with new boards of thick pine. The Phrygians must have worked non-stop to have done so much so quickly.

Petros opened the door. It swung quietly. Someone had oiled the hinges.

The women's quarters looked like a village had camped there. Where the rooms had once housed four women, now there were nine separate spaces set out on the floor with bed rolls around each.

"I hadn't quite appreciated how many of you there were," I said.

"Nine families," Petros said briefly. "I thought you knew."

In the middle was the ladder I had climbed. It reached up into the thatching. Though there were no visible feet upon it, yet the ladder wobbled from time to time.

Petros peered up. "How are you two doing up there?" he called.

"It's gonna take a while, Petros," an invisible voice called back from above the thatch. "Whoever looked after this place was an idiot."

Petros turned bright red. "Merely our banter," he explained.

"I'm sure," I said, still looking up. "Is that new thatch?" I asked. Because it didn't look the same as it had the other day.

"Thatch is hard to come by," Petros said.

I could imagine. The thatch's previous owners would probably notice their roof was missing.

"What happened to the mice?" Diotima asked.

"We have lots of pets," Petros said. "Some of them eat rats and mice."

There was more swearing from above.

"Does he know how to fix the roof?" I asked.

"Melidoros is the man up there. He worked as a builder, back in Phrygia. Here in Athens, he is a common laborer for hire."

"Not all of you are actors then," Diotima said.

"Most are. A few of us are builders, one is a painter. We all work as mourners."

"Was it that bad in Phrygia?" Diotima asked.

"No, it's not," Petros said honestly. "The Persians rule there. It is a place of great stability. It's not a good place for anyone who wants to . . . to . . ."

He struggled for the words.

"To change things?" I suggested. "To change your life?"

"Yes, precisely! We wanted more. You understand."

I did. Athens was the place where things changed. Diotima and I had been to Ionia, which was ruled by the Persians. The Persians loved stability and order above all things; not the sort of place for a man who wants to improve his lot. Likewise the Spartans loathed change more than anything, and the other Hellene cities clung to tradition.

We walked downstairs as we talked. Diotima was interested in everything about the Phrygians. She asked several questions about their customs, as might a guest. She seemed to have forgotten that she was the mistress of this house. I was pleased to see that Diotima was more relaxed in her house than she had ever been since her birth father died.

We returned to the courtyard, to inspect the back of the house. Standing in one corner was a stone plinth, and upon the plinth was a statue of a hand. It was like a normal bust, but where a bust shows a head, usually of a god, this was a statue of a hand. I'd never seen anything like it. Maia stood beside it.

"What is it?" I asked, before Diotima could get in the same question.

"It is the Hand of Sabazios," Maia said lovingly. I could hear the reverence in her tone.

"What happened to the rest of him?" I asked.

"Sabazios is our god," Maia said.

"I thought you worshipped our gods," I said.

"No," Maia said shortly.

"I've seen a thousand busts of someone's head, never of someone's hand," Diotima added.

The Hand had been covered with white dust from all the nearby carpentry. Maia wiped the Hand clean with a piece of linen. The Hand of Sabazios was right-handed. The thumb, index and middle fingers pointed straight up at the sky. The other fingers were folded in to his palm.

"It is the sign of his benediction," Maia said. "Sabazios blesses us, and so we are fruitful in the harvest and in all other things."

"Sabazios is Dionysos then," Diotima said. "He is also the god of the harvest."

"We would say Dionysos is Sabazios," Maia pointed out. "But it all comes to the same thing."

"Yes, of course," said Diotima politely. "I myself am a priestess of Artemis. Artemis of the Hunt is our goddess in Athens; yet Artemis as she is worshipped at Brauron is a goddess of young womanhood; and the Artemis at Ephesus where I once served is a goddess of fertility. Different aspects, but they're all the one goddess. Of course your Sabazios and our Dionysos can be the one god."

"You served at the Artemision at Ephesus?" Maia said, amazed. Ephesus wasn't all that far from Phrygia.

"Briefly, but yes," Diotima said.

Maia and Petros glanced at each other. There was communication in that look, the communication between a couple that no one else can read. But I knew they had reached some conclusion because Petros said, "You have been very good to us, Nicolaos and Diotima."

"You're welcome."

"We would like to invite you to one of our services," Petros said.

I didn't have to ask what Diotima thought of that idea. She was always ready to learn something new.

"Thank you, we'd love to come," I said.

As we spoke there was an odd smell wafting in from the backyard.

"Are you making bread out back?" I asked. Because the smell reminded me of bread, but was somehow different.

"Not bread," said Petros. "Come see."

Like most large houses, beyond the courtyard was an open space surrounded by back wall. On one side was the kitchen, on the other was the midden, and in between was a space to park your cart, with a back gate that opened onto a narrow lane.

In that middle space, where I expected the cart, was an enormous wooden vat filled with liquid. Standing over it was a man with dark ringleted hair and a black, bushy beard. He stirred the contents with a stick so large that he had to hold it in both hands. The smell out here was strong. I hoped the neighbors didn't complain.

"It's a drink we make," Maia said. "It's called beer. Try some."

Petros handed me a piece of straw. It was dry and quite stiff, as old straw is.

I looked at it blankly. What was I supposed to do with a straw?

"Dip the other end of the straw in the vat," Petros said. "Put your lips on the top end and suck through it."

"Suck through a piece of old straw?" I said.

"Like this." He took a straw of his own and demonstrated. With one end in the liquid and his lips on the other. He sucked and his cheeks made a funny shape. Petros seemed to enjoy this.

I had worried that these Phrygians could be violent. It had never occurred to me that they might be insane.

I put the straw in the vat and stuck my mouth on the other end. I was sure that nothing much could come through that tiny hole, so I sucked hard.

Liquid spurted into my mouth, lots of it. I tried to swallow by reflex. I couldn't, there was too much in my mouth. I clamped my mouth tight shut to spare myself the indignity of the beer coming back out my mouth.

The beer squirted out of my nostrils.

"Perhaps a bit more gently?" Petros suggested, as I coughed and snorted.

I sucked again, this time determined to get it right.

A trickle of the drink flowed into my mouth. I sucked cautiously harder. The beer shot into my mouth and I had to swallow. The taste was like nothing I'd ever experienced. It wasn't wine, but it wasn't water. One thing was immediately obvious: this beer was alcoholic. It was stronger than the watered wine that Hellenes drink. I knew that Egyptians drank beer, but I'd never put any thought to what it might be like.

I asked, "What sort of grapes do you use to make this?"

"Not grapes," said the man stirring the vat.

To my blank look Maia added, "Beer is made from barley."

I couldn't imagine how anyone crushed barley to get enough

juice to make anything. But obviously someone had managed, because here was the beer to prove it.

Maia handed a straw to Diotima. She managed to drink from it more elegantly than I had.

I dipped the straw back in and drank more of the strange liquid, then offered my considered opinion: "It's awful. Don't you have any wine?"

Maia laughed. "Beer is the sacred drink of Sabazios, just as wine is sacred to Dionysos. In the land we come from, the men prefer beer."

"Weird."

The man with the stick smiled but said nothing. He was young and quite good looking. I wondered what had made him move to Athens.

AS WE LEFT the house, Diotima and I were approached by a man. He'd been waiting in the street.

"Nicolaos! Nicolaos, I must speak to you." His expression was grave.

"Yes, Theophrastus, what is it?" I asked. For Theophrastus was a neighbor; he owned the house beside Diotima's. I thought he was about to complain about the mice in the roof.

"It's these new tenants of yours."

"What's wrong, Theophrastus? Are they making too much noise?"

"No, they are very quiet, except when they make repairs, and they have apologized for that. They are much quieter than your previous tenants."

I was not surprised. The diplomats and wealthy merchants who had previously rented our house had held loud and frequent parties.

"Do they cause trouble in the street?" I asked. "Do they steal things?"

"By no means. They keep to themselves."

"Then I don't understand the problem, Theophrastus."

"They're *metics*," he said. He glanced left and right, to make sure no one was listening.

"Yes, I know," I said. "But you just agreed they're not causing trouble."

"They bring down the tone of the street," Theophrastus said. "All the neighbors agree. Everyone says your other tenants were much better."

I blinked. "Let me see if I understand," I said. "You would rather have neighbors who hold constant, loud parties, who urinate on your walls when they're drunk, and who let their house fall into disrepair, but who are wealthy and from good families?"

"Yes! Precisely! I knew you'd understand, Nicolaos," he said in relief. "They're not even Hellenes. They're from Phrygia. I asked and they told me so. If you could tell them to leave—"

"I'm afraid I can't do that."

It was his turn to blink. "You can't?"

"I made an agreement with them."

"Agreements can be changed."

"There's a contract," I said. I made a mental note to make a contract with Petros as soon as possible. "The actors have kept their end of the bargain. More than kept it. You see, Theophrastus, it's out of my hands." I held up my hands so he could see they were empty.

Theophrastus was taken aback. "This is very inconvenient, Nicolaos."

"I'm sorry."

"Does the contract allow you to evict them for bad behavior?"

"Did we not just agree that they are well behaved?"

Theophrastus rubbed his chin. "I'm sure I and a few of the other men in the street could testify to antisocial goings-on. If it came to court, that is. A jury would believe anything of non-Hellenes."

"I'm sorry, Theophrastus," I repeated.

"Think of the street's reputation, Nicolaos."

"I shall give it every consideration, Theophrastus."

THE MOMENT WE were out of the street and out of earshot, I said, "Diotima, I have an idea."

"What?" she asked.

I told her my thought. When I finished explaining she bit her lip and said, "Well, it's easy enough to check."

"Yes, let's go."

We found Euboulides and Pheidestratos, the guards who had failed their duty at the theater, outside the barracks of the Scythian Guard. They stood at attention in the middle of the combat training square, in the heat of day.

Diotima and I walked up to them.

"Good morning, sir, and you too, Lady Diotima," they said in unison.

"How long have you two been standing here?" I asked.

"What day is it, sir?" Euboulides asked.

"The ninth," I said automatically. Then I realized it had been the ninth for three days in a row. I corrected myself.

"Then we've been here three days, master."

"What, without moving?" I asked, incredulous.

"Chief Pythax mentioned something about tearing the skin off of us while we were still alive if we moved, sir. On account of us failing our duty. He said it would learn us not to doze. We gotta stand here till he says we can go. The other guards brung us water."

"What if you have to piss?" I asked.

"Look down, master," Euboulides said.

I did. I was standing in a wet spot. I took one step to the right.

Now that they mentioned it, I could smell a certain aroma wafting from their presence. The two Scythians hadn't washed in a couple of days. Their skin must have been unbearable in itchy sweat.

To confirm it, Pheidestratos lifted his arm to scratch his armpit, and the smell increased.

"I'll speak to my father about this," Diotima promised.

Euboulides and Pheidestratos looked horrified. "Don't do that, mistress. This is our just punishment for failing you."

I said, "I think you can earn forgiveness if you can answer a question."

"Sir?"

"That drink the woman gave you . . . was it wine?"

"No, master," Euboulides said. "It was beer."

As I thought. I shot a triumphant look at Diotima. But that left another question.

"How would two men of the lowest possible class know about an exotic drink like beer?"

"Everybody knows about beer, sir," Euboulides said. "There's people who sell it for a small coin."

Pheidestratos added, "I heard tell that in Egypt, even the slaves get to drink beer." He looked wistful.

WE HEADED BACK toward home, but took a detour past the records warehouse, to see if Socrates had made any progress. The slave-guard out front nodded his acquaintance. I slipped him a drachma, purely because I thought he had the most boring job in Athens.

I tapped on the door but didn't open it. It was smelly in there. I called out, "Socrates? How are you doing?"

A small voice replied through the door. "I'm doing all right, Nico. I haven't found anything about Romanos yet. Nico? When can I come out—"

"I'll send more food," I said firmly.

Then as an afterthought, I opened the door a crack and poked my head in.

Socrates had cleared a space around the door. He sat in the clear space with a scroll jar beside him, its contents spilled out onto the floor.

Diotima followed me in. She wrinkled her nose and said, "Phew."

"What are you doing?" I asked Socrates, because he seemed to have spent all his time making space.

"First I'm rearranging all the scroll jars by age," Socrates said. "I pick up one at random, then bring it to this place near the door. I empty out the scrolls, clear away the dead mouse bodies . . . Nico, have you ever wondered why bodies mummify? While I was sitting here scraping away the dead mice I wondered about it. I was thinking—"

"Try not to think so much, Socrates," I said. "Go on about the records."

"Oh," he said, crestfallen. "Well, it seems all the scrolls in the same jar are from the same year."

"That makes sense."

"So I only have to read one scroll to know which year it's for."

"Good."

"It saves a lot of time," Socrates said. "The only problem is, I don't know the order of the years."

"Why wouldn't you?" I asked, confused, then realized the answer to my own question. In Athens, every year is given the name of the Eponymous Archon who served at the time. This year was the Year of Habron. When I had begun my first case, three years ago, it had been the Year of Conon. Everyone knew who had served in what order, but of course a child wouldn't.

"How did you know which order the archons go?" I asked.

"Oh, I go out on the street and ask passersby," Socrates said.

"Don't they ask why you want to know?" Diotima said.

"Sure," Socrates said. "I tell them."

Terrific. The way rumors spread in this city, that meant all of Athens knew I was searching for information about metics. So much for a discreet investigation.

Socrates went on, "When I know what year a jar belongs to, I put it on the floor. The oldest on the left." He stood up and pointed to a dismal pile against the left wall. "The newest on the right." Socrates indicated a much larger collection against the right hand wall. "And all the other years in between, in order."

Socrates was only a fraction of the way into his task, but already from the number of jars in each pile left to right I could see how the influx of migrants had grown. It was more than a steady rise. If the size of the records was anything to go by, then each year there were almost twice as many migrants as the year before. No wonder the metics were becoming noticeable.

I wondered if anyone else had worked this out. But of course they had. The Polemarch must know, for one.

"It's a funny thing though," Socrates said. "None of the records are older than twenty-one years ago."

"That's because the Persians sacked Athens during the wars," I said. "They destroyed everything."

"Oh yeah," he said. "Why didn't I think of that?"

Socrates hadn't thought of it because he hadn't lived through it. He'd always known Athens as a wealthy city. I was born a few months after the Persians were defeated—my childhood had been spent in streets where the entire city was being rebuilt, bit by bit.

"Listen, Socrates," I said, "I also want you to find everything you can about Petros and Maia. They arrived after Romanos, so their records will be in a different jar."

"Oh, I can tell you about them," Socrates said.

"You can?" I said amazed.

"I saw their papers in passing," Socrates said. "They're

somewhere over there . . ." He gestured vaguely to the right side. "I can't remember which pile though."

"You didn't keep hold of their records?" I said, annoyed.

"You didn't ask me until now, did you?" Socrates pointed out, not unreasonably.

"Can you remember what it said?" I asked.

"Of course," he said confidently.

"Good. Who is their citizen sponsor?"

"He's from the deme of Bate," Socrates said. "Someone named Theokritos."

# SCENE 32
# THE HIGH PRIEST

I HAD TO GO to Sophocles next morning, to ask where I might find his friend Theokritos, the High Priest of Dionysos.

Sophocles smiled and said, "Where do you think you'd find a priest of Dionysos? At a winery of course."

Theokritos's estate lay to the north, along the route to Decelea, which meant that his land was as inland as you can get and still be in Attica.

It took me most of the morning to walk there, and I knew I would spend most of the afternoon walking back home. Not for the first time I wished for a good horse, but alas, our family wasn't rich enough to afford one. At least the road was a major route, wide enough that two carts could pass each other unhindered. It made travel faster.

The estate of Theokritos, when I arrived, was a revelation. I had never imagined that any farm could be so immaculate, so well-ordered. The *horos* stones that marked the border of his land were painted fresh white, and every one bore the name Theokritos in clear letters, which was how I knew I'd come to the right place. The orchards were extensive. Some slave with a scythe had walked over all of it, cutting back long grasses and weeds. It gave the property a look as manicured as any well-born lady.

The grapevines stood at attention, like soldiers in their ranks. The arms of their vines were strung out to either side. The posture of the plants was so reminiscent of the standard army maneuver—the one in which every man holds out his arms to evenly space the lines—that I instantly thought of Theokritos's grapevines as being like an army in phalanx. The plants were old and gnarled, grizzled veterans who'd seen one war too many.

There were so many rows of plants that I couldn't count them. Slaves walked back and forth along the rows. They stopped at each plant and poked their fingers in each one. I stopped one of the slaves and asked him what they were doing.

"Inspecting the vines for pests, sir," the man replied, as if it were obvious.

Theokritos had set his slaves to personally grooming each one of the thousands of vines on his land. At the theater I had thought of Theokritos as a jovial fellow. On his home ground he appeared to be a nitpicking sort of man.

I asked the slave where I might find his master. He pointed me to a large wooden shed in the distance.

The shed held a vast array of amphorae. They were stacked up high along every wall and each was tightly plugged. I had no doubt they all held wine.

Theokritos had his back to me when I entered. He was intently watching what was happening in the middle of the room, where there was a very wide vat. The vat held grapes, the tops of which I could see over the edge. A wooden device above the vat was lowering an enormous stone upon a flat, circular board. The board looked made to exactly fit the space into which it was being lowered. Men with long poles stood about the edge. Some of the partially crushed fruit tried to escape over the sides and they were scraping it back into the mix.

The wooden slats around the sides bulged under the pressure.

I recognized the vat and the machine. I had used a much smaller version on my own tiny farm.

Theokritos turned to me as I walked in. He was puzzled for

a moment, then said, “Greetings. You are Nicolaos, aren’t you? The agent.”

“Yes.”

“I remember your wife well. She did good work during the theater ceremony. Pity about that actor.”

I said, “Yes. I’m sorry to bother you, Theokritos. I can see you’re busy. But I need to ask you some questions.” Then, because I was truly impressed, I added, “That’s a huge press.”

Theokritos looked at me questioningly. “You know about wine making?” he asked. “You recognize a wine press. Are you a vintner?”

I said, “No, but I make some olive oil.”

I explained to Theokritos that I owned a small plot on which we grew olives and kept chickens. Each year I borrowed Pericles’s press to turn the olives into oil, which we sold in the agora. It was a very small business indeed. I ended with the words that I was fascinated by his winery.

“These are the early pickings,” he said. “We always do a small pressing at the start of the harvest, to see how the fruit is coming along. I find the flavor of early pressed wine quite distinctive.”

That vat was a *small* pressing?

Theokritos spoke about how the press worked. He talked with all the animation of an enthusiast. Sophocles had told me that the High Priest of Dionysos was an expert vintner. He would get no arguments from me; I was convinced.

When he was finished, Theokritos moved on to the rest of the operation. The High Priest of Dionysos took me by the arm and led me out to view his estates. I might have been an honored guest, not a troublesome agent.

Theokritos took me to the highest point of his land, from which we could see all the rest. It was an impressive sight. He spoke knowledgeably about soil, sunlight, and rain. He enumerated the dangers of too much rain or too little. He discussed drainage and how to collect fruit, and of the overwhelming importance that the slaves not bruise it. He showed me the proper way to handle large loads of fruit.

I paid close attention to the words of Theokritos. I thought to myself I would like to have a place like this one day.

There was even a small temple. It stood upon the hill to which Theokritos had led me. I boggled at this. Theokritos was the only man I knew who kept a temple on his land. It didn't look new either. I asked him about this.

"My father was High Priest before me," Theokritos explained. "He thought a temple to the god of wine would be perfect overlooking a fine vineyard. I find myself agreeing with him."

His enthusiasm for every aspect of wine making was infectious. I found myself imagining what it would be like to be a wine maker. But a man who can't afford a horse definitely can't afford a winery.

By this time Theokritos had led me back into the shed, where he ordered a slave to break out a small amphora of one of each wine he kept stored. Theokritos had the slave pour a cup from each. He then practically ordered me to relax on one of his couches and to drink his wine, one cup after the next, to appreciate the different flavors.

As we drank I said, "Theokritos, I must ask you some questions."

"Certainly."

"I understand that you are the patron of some metics," I said.

"Yes, I am," he agreed readily enough.

"How did that come about?" I asked.

"From my association with the theater," Theokritos said. "I am, as you know, devoted to Dionysos. Not only in wine, but in *all* his aspects. The theater is very dear to me. I've been a supporter ever since I assumed the position of High Priest."

"When was that?" I asked.

"When I was a young man. I inherited the title at an early age, as I did these estates."

"I see."

"Some years ago, I was approached by one of the actors—Romanos, in fact, the one who died. He told me his family wanted to come to Athens. They would need a patron. He asked would I oblige."

"So you did," I said.

"I asked a lot of questions first! I needed to know that they were not wanted criminals, that they were people of good character, that I would not regret my generosity in becoming their patron."

"Of course."

"I also reserved the right to withdraw after I'd interviewed them. As it happened, they seemed fine people and I was happy to lend my support. I haven't had cause to regret it. No one's complained to me about the Phrygians."

"You're on good terms with them then," I said.

"I haven't spoken to them since," Theokritos said.

"You haven't?"

"There's no reason why I should," he said. "Sponsorship isn't a sign of friendship, young man. It merely means that a responsible member of the community has checked out the applicants and found them worthy of a place in Athenian society."

He poured me another cup of wine, then took another for himself, both in generous proportions. I was beginning to understand where Theokritos's pot belly came from.

"I wonder that Romanos didn't ask his own patron to support his relatives," I said, as I sipped the wine. It was superb.

"I believe the patron had died," Theokritos said.

"I have another request for you, Theokritos," I said. "Before Romanos was killed there was the actor whose leg was broken. His name is Phellis."

"Yes? I hope he's recovering."

"That's the problem," I said. I explained the situation, as I had before to Thodis and Pericles.

When I finished, Theokritos gave me what had become the standard reply. "Surely this is a problem for the play's choregos," he said.

"I put the question to Thodis first," I said. "He denies any responsibility for the play's actors."

Theokritos scowled. "The more I hear of this Thodis, the less I like him. His part in the conference at Pericles's home was hardly praiseworthy."

I said nothing.

Theokritos put the tips of his finger together and leaned back in his dining couch. "I suppose it might be argued that the actor was injured in the course of service to the god Dionysos. To that end he might be supported on a temporary basis from temple funds."

"That would be most generous, sir," I said gratefully.

"But I'm afraid it's impossible," he finished.

"Oh. Why?" I asked. For a moment I'd thought Theokritos would save Phellis.

"Young man, if the temple supports Phellis, who I agree is more than worthy, then by this time tomorrow every actor in Athens will have stubbed his toe and will be claiming compensation out of the temple's treasury."

"Oh. Of course."

Theokritos was right. No Athenian in his right mind would pass up the chance for free money.

"The worship of Dionysos is too important to let this pass," Theokritos said. "A way must be found." He paused, then said, "What is the name of this doctor?"

"Melpon."

Theokritos scribbled the name on an ostrakon. "I will speak to him," he said. "Perhaps something can be arranged. If nothing else I can approach the other winemakers. If everyone contributes then all things become possible."

"Would they help?"

"Wine is the sacred drink of Dionysos. Did you know it's almost impossible to make wine without sacrificing to the God at every step? It's in their interests to keep the God happy. There's an association of vintners. As High Priest of Dionysos I have the honor to be their leader. They love wine and the god of wine as much as I do. If I suggest to my fellow vintners that Phellis was injured in the service of Dionysos I feel sure they will come to the party. It might be as simple as offering this Melpon a few amphorae of wine from each of our vineyards. A treasure in itself."

"Thank you, sir. If it's anything like what we've been drinking, he'll jump at the chance," I said. "Your excellent wine has washed out the taste of that other drink."

"What's this?" he said.

I told Theokritos of the strange drink of the Phrygians.

Theokritos looked as if he'd swallowed something particularly vile.

"Beer. Revolting stuff. It'll never catch on in Athens."

"They seem to like it in Phrygia," I pointed out.

"Yes, well. It's good enough for barbarians, I dare say." Theokritos looked put out. "Real men drink wine," he said.

I DIDN'T HAVE to walk back home. By the time we had finished talking I'd drunk so much of Theokritos's wine that I couldn't have made it. Theokritos insisted I take his personal cart, and a slave to drive it. It was only when we were halfway back, and I'd sobered up sufficiently to notice, that I saw that Theokritos had ordered his slaves to replug the small amphorae from which we'd been drinking and load them on the back. They were his gift to me.

My head began to pound, as it always did after I'd drunk

too much. Every time this happened, I swore I'd never drink again.

To get my mind off my pounding head, I asked the driver about Theokritos. It's not normally the done thing to question a slave about his owner, but I wanted to know.

"The master is a great man," the slave said without hesitation.

"From the look of the estate, I thought he might be very demanding," I said.

"He is," the slave agreed. "He demands perfection. But he rewards our diligence. You saw the temple on his lands?"

"Yes."

"Twice every month the master sacrifices at that temple, always the finest lamb. When he does, he insists that we all eat the meat of the sacrifice, even we slaves. Have you ever heard of a master who *insists* that his slaves eat meat? He *says* it's because a well fed slave can work harder, but *I think* it's because he's a humane man. Once I even saw him take a good portion to my daughter, when it was her birthday. He gave it to her with his own hands. He told her it was a birthday gift from the God."

"You have a daughter?" I said, amazed. It is rare for a slave to be permitted to have children.

"I have a wife!" he said proudly. "We have *three* children."

He could not have been happier.

The cart deposited me at my home, by which time I felt slightly better but no doubt looked the worse for wear.

Diotima greeted me at the doorstep with news that I really didn't want to hear.

"You have a message from Pericles," she said. "He wants to see you."

She frowned at me, at the cart, and at the wine amphorae that the slave gently deposited on the ground beside the door. He gave me a friendly wave and drove off home to his family.

I knew Diotima wasn't pleased at the state I was in, but she said nothing, but for a single suggestion. "Perhaps you might like to get rid of the stale wine smell before you go?"

"DO YOU KNOW what date it is today?" Pericles asked, the moment I arrived at his house.

"It's the ninth of Elaphebolion," I said instantly. He hadn't offered me a drink, but if he had, I would have declined.

Pericles said angrily, "If you don't get a move on, it's going to be the ninth of Elaphebolion for the rest of our lives."

"I'm doing my best," I told him. "These things take time."

"Has it occurred to you, Nicolaos, that you don't have to find the actual murderer of Romanos?"

"What?" I said. No such thing had occurred to me at all. "I don't understand, Pericles."

"It's simple. We need a solution. If this death had happened anywhere else, no one would care. But it happened in the Theater of Dionysos. The purpose of your investigation is to clear the theater of the *miasma* of desecration. The only reason we have this problem is the ritual pollution."

"The theater is considered a temple to Dionysos," I said. "Therefore any crime committed within is desecration. Yes, Pericles, I know this."

"Just as your original assignment was to purge the theater of a ghost—even though we all knew perfectly well you would do no such thing—so your assignment now is to purge the theater of the taint of murder."

"Which we do by finding the murderer," I said.

"Except that it isn't necessary to find the killer in order to clear the theater," Pericles said smoothly. "We must consider the practicalities here, Nicolaos. If the Great Dionysia can't proceed it will be a disaster for Athens."

"What are you suggesting here, Pericles?" I said.

"Only that to earn your commission you need merely follow

the forms to demonstrate good faith in finding a criminal. Any criminal will do."

"Do you have someone in mind?" I asked him.

"If you feel that a death is necessary to expurgate the miasma, then another metic would be your best choice," Pericles said. "What about one of the Phrygians?" he suggested.

"But I don't know that they did it!"

"Is that a problem?" Pericles asked. "The Polemarch himself has told you that if the killer is a citizen, then the penalty for murdering a metic would be a fine, or at most exile for a few years."

"There's also the charge of impiety," I pointed out.

"Yes, that would certainly lead to a death sentence," Pericles conceded.

I must have displayed my horror, because Pericles said, "Listen, Nico, we must consider which is the greater disaster for Athens: a failed festival, with all its international repercussions, or the death of one man who wasn't even a citizen. The good of Athens may demand a curtailed investigation. I think you can see that."

The problem was, I did see that.

But I also saw that I couldn't abandon the victim. For if Pericles, and Lysanias, and Sophocles, and everyone else was right when they said that our plays were as important to Athens as a diplomatic mission, then Romanos had died in the service of Athens as surely as any soldier who fell in battle.

I couldn't *not* find justice for Romanos, even if he had been a conniving blackmailer.

And as for framing another metic, because it was convenient . . .

"I can't do that, Pericles."

"Then you had better bring me a better solution. Quickly. The public feast is set for two days hence. I want this fixed by then."

# SCENE 33
# THE STRANGE TENANT

I RETURNED HOME WANTING to rant to my wife about my difficult boss. Instead I walked in to find my mother-in-law paying a social call.

Diotima and her mother, Euterpe, lay on dining couches in the courtyard. From the various empty small food bowls dotted about, I deduced the visit had been going for some time. My own mother, Phaenarete, had absented herself. The house slave told me as I entered that she had been called away on an urgent delivery, by which he meant a baby. Whether this was strictly true I didn't know. Phaenarete and Euterpe rarely got on, though they had worked at opposite ends of the same business.

My father, unsurprisingly, was shut away in his workshop. It was his natural place, but in any case it would never occur to him to entertain visiting ladies.

That left me to join the ladies and be polite, when what I really wanted to do was shout in frustration. Luckily it seemed the visit was nearing an end. Euterpe had come to hear the latest on the investigation.

"All of Athens is talking about it," she told me excitedly. I took this to mean *she* was talking about it.

As I sat, Diotima was winding down from a minor tirade that women were not permitted to act.

"I know what you mean, dear," Euterpe said. "I'm sure you would have made a fine actress. I myself was excellent."

"But you don't know how to act," Diotima said to her mother. "You've never acted in your life."

Euterpe looked at her daughter in some surprise. "I don't know what you're talking about, dear. A courtesan has to please her clients, does she not? Well let me tell you, if there's anything that a woman of my former profession is an expert at, it's making a man feel he's special, even when he isn't. Also that he has the biggest dong since Heracles. Every man thinks he's hung like Heracles. You wouldn't believe how much acting ability that requires with the average man."

Diotima stared at her mother openmouthed in shock.

Euterpe didn't seem to notice. She added enthusiastically, "I'm especially good at faking orgasms. Would you like to see one?"

"Thanks anyway, Mother."

Euterpe shrugged. "The fact is, my daughter, if it's ability to fool men that you're looking for, then I'm one of the best actresses in Athens."

As Euterpe stood to depart, she added, almost absent-mindedly, "Not that there's any need to, now that I'm married to your new father."

"Of course not, Mother," Diotima agreed primly, as she escorted her mother to the door. "You and Pythax have married for love."

Euterpe looked surprised for a moment, then said, "Why, that's so, dear, but it helps that when it comes to sex, there isn't much to choose between your new father and Heracles."

I heard the door open and shut, and Euterpe's departing merry laughter.

THAT NIGHT, AFTER dinner, Diotima read the manuscript that Euripides had given us. I don't think she intended to, but she always read everything within reach, and she did it out of habit.

When she was finished she put down the scroll and said, "I hate to have to say it, but his writing is very good."

"You mean that dysfunctional little creep really can write?"

"I'm afraid so," Diotima said. She rolled the scroll backward from the end. She looked down at the words printed there in Euripides's crabbed hand. "His stories are great, his characters are fantastic, his phrases are . . ." She groped for the right word. "Divine." She frowned. "But there's something odd. In every story, he progresses the plot very well. The tension builds. I was desperate to find out what would happen next, and then, every time, right before the climax, a god descends from the machine and wraps up everything. It leaves you dissatisfied with the story." Diotima looked up at me. "It's like he doesn't care how his story ends."

I shrugged. "If he thinks a god from the machine is going to solve the problems of we mortals, then more fool him."

Diotima said, "Do you think he's involved, Nico?"

"He's weird enough," I said. "But a killer? I don't know. Not many killers write plays."

Diotima put down the scroll. She hesitated, then said, "Nico, I've been thinking."

"Yes?"

"We've caught Romanos out on one fabrication already, or we think we have," she said.

I nodded. "Romanos didn't recommend one of his own family for the third actor role, and then didn't tell them what he'd done. It might not technically be a lie, but I follow you."

Diotima looked unhappy and said, "Plus he was a blackmailer."

"It doesn't exactly instill sympathy for our victim," I agreed.

Diotima said, "I wonder, is there anything else Romanos might have lied about?"

"Do you have something in mind?" I asked. I took her idea seriously, but I had nothing to suggest.

She gave an uncertain shrug, which was unlike her. "I've been thinking over everything I ever heard him say," she said.

Knowing Diotima's memory, she could probably quote his every conversation verbatim.

She went on, "It's only an idea, but that night, when we three sheltered from the rain . . ."

She hesitated.

"Yes?"

"Romanos said he was on his way home."

"He probably was."

"Yes, Nico, but Melite is almost due west of the Theater of Dionysos. We met him in the agora, which is almost due north."

Romanos had lied. Diotima was right.

Diotima hammered home the point. "He can't have gone to the agora to shop on his way home," she said. "It was late at night."

"Right."

"And he can't have been out for a pleasant stroll on the way. It was pouring rain. He would want to take the fastest route."

"What a silly, trivial thing to lie about," I said.

Diotima nodded. "All he had to say was that he was on his way to a party, or to visit a friend, and we would have been none the wiser."

I said, "Keep in mind that at that stage, we didn't know where he lived, and had no reason to care."

"I thought so too. So maybe he wasn't lying."

"What?" I said, perplexed. "You just proved to me that he did."

"It's what you said a moment ago, Nico. A lie for no reason makes no sense. Maybe he really was on his way home, but not to Melite."

Diotima's idea hit me then. Perhaps Romanos had a second home. One that his family didn't know about.

"This is a lot to build on one small slip of the tongue," I cautioned her.

"Yes, I know. That's why I was hesitant to mention it, but . . ." she trailed off.

I finished it for her. "Either Romanos lied for no reason, or he told the truth and has a second home. You're right, Diotima. I just don't know how to prove it."

"We'll have to look for a house."

"How? They don't normally come with names inscribed in the walls."

Something else occurred to me. "The Polemarch told me that metics aren't allowed to own houses in Athens."

Diotima nodded. "That's true. In the days before she married Pythax, my mother had to have my birth father keep our home in his name."

"We're looking for a rental home then."

That turned the task from impossible into merely very difficult.

"It can't be too far away," Diotima said. "Romanos was running through the rain to get home."

"It can't be outside the city walls!" I said in sudden revelation. "When we saw him, the gates had already been shut for the night."

"We know it's north of the agora, because that's the direction he was headed," Diotima added.

What had seemed impossible suddenly looked doable.

"Anything else?" Diotima asked.

"The city is full to overflowing with visitors," I said.

"So?"

"I wonder if the landlord knows that his tenant is dead?" I said. "If he does, he'll be the only man in Athens with a room to rent. He could make a killing."

IT TOOK A day of door-knocking, but we found the place by pretending to be visitors to Athens for the Dionysia. We were directed from house to house, at each one asking if there was a room that might be available, even if a local currently rented it.

Romanos had rented a room in the upper storey of a house owned by a man who needed some extra cash. When we told him that his tenant was dead, his shoulders slumped.

"I needed that money," he said. "I got kids and not enough work."

"You can rent it to the Dionysia crowd," I said. "There are hundreds of people camped outside the walls, maybe thousands. I'll bet there's a family out there that would pay you plenty."

He brightened. "Say, that's a good idea. Thanks."

"You're welcome. Do you mind if we take a look at the room?"

"No way," he said at once.

"Why not?"

"Well, it's not your room for a start."

"We only want to look at the things Romanos kept there," Diotima said.

"His things don't belong to you either," he pointed out.

Of all the landlords in Athens, Romanos had to rent a room from the only honest one. Remembering the landlord's comment about needing money, I said, "What if we were to *buy* those things from you?"

That put a different complexion on it. I could see the thoughts running through the landlord's mind. I decided to help him out.

I said, "If a tenant doesn't pay his rent, or if he never returns, the landlord's entitled to sell whatever belongings remain, to pay for back rent. Right?"

"That's the law," the landlord agreed.

"Well I'm pretty sure Romanos won't be returning," I said. "So he owes you rent, right?"

"That's true."

"I'm offering to buy the things that you'd be allowed to sell anyway," I said. "That's logical, isn't it?"

The honest landlord decided it was logical. We agreed a price that made me wince. I made a mental note to add it to the bill I sent Pericles.

The landlord showed us up to collect our new belongings. He didn't even stay to watch what we took.

Diotima and I pulled on a rough wooden door that opened into a rough wooden room. There was a bed, a table, a chair, and a chest. It wasn't the sort of place you invited friends to for a sophisticated symposium.

"I wonder what Romanos was doing here?" Diotima asked.

"Maybe he wanted the privacy," I said, thinking of the crowded house the Phrygians inhabited.

We had bought everything inside the room that wasn't furniture. So far, that came to nothing, but for some ceramic cups and plates on the table and an old lamp that smelt of rancid oil. A single small, shuttered window looked out over the street. The shutter squeaked when we opened it.

"It's dismal," Diotima said.

"Yes," I said. "But if I was a bachelor in a house full of families, I wouldn't mind somewhere like this where I could get away from everyone else."

"It must be a man thing then, because I wouldn't," Diotima said. She looked at me quizzically. "*You* don't have a place like this hidden somewhere, do you Nico?"

"No," I said. I'd spent long enough trying to get Diotima into my home. I wasn't about to escape now that I'd finally succeeded.

We continued the search. There were a chamber pot pushed under the bed. Diotima found it. It was half full. The contents sloshed over her hand when she pulled it out.

"Gaah!" She pushed it back under. The contents sloshed again. She wiped her hand on her chiton.

"Careful with that!" I said. "We own the wee in that pot. It cost us a small fortune."

"You're welcome to it then," she said.

"Is there anything else under the bed?"

"Cobwebs and small spiders."

"We own those too."

The chest proved more fruitful. It was the sort of chest that officers took with them on campaign, worn enough to have been through several wars.

"Why would an actor own a campaign chest?" I said.

"Oh Nico, isn't it obvious?' Diotima said. "He was an actor. This is his touring chest. It's what he took with him when he joined a company that was traveling from town to town."

Diotima was right. It was obvious.

Sitting on top of all the clothes were several masks. One was a comedy mask, the face distorted into grotesque features. The other two were tragedy masks, one for a man, one for a woman's role.

Diotima pulled out these masks. She held them up to the light and said, "I wonder . . ."

She placed them on her lap.

Beneath the masks were clothes.

We pulled them out, one by one. Each was recognizable as a stage costume. The top costume was obviously for kingly roles, with its elegant gold patterns. The next one down was a regulation generic costume that would do for many characters. Under that, the bright, gaudy, flamboyant costume of a comic.

Diotima said, "Oh, yes, Romanos did do some comedy, didn't he?"

"He was a working actor," I replied. "He probably did whatever he got paid to do."

After we'd pulled out the clothing we found wax tablets and some papyrus. Diotima snatched at these. We spread them out on the table and, when we ran out of room, across the floor as well. Diotima and I crouched down, side by side, to read.

We only needed to read a bit to know what we were looking at. Here were the documents that proved the real Lakon had died. In our hands was a copy of the young man's funeral stele; a statement of the tragic events, as related by a local and written down by Romanos; and a statement from the head man of the deme of Rhamnus that Lakon was deceased.

We had everything we needed to prove that Romanos was blackmailing the Lakon we knew.

"If we'd found this room first, we wouldn't have had to travel all the way to Rhamnus," I moaned.

"What's done is done," Diotima said. "It's easy to see why he kept this away from his family. He didn't want them to know he was a blackmailer." Then she added, "There's more on the wax tablets."

So there was. Facts and figures, notes about the cost of barley, lists of wine vendors who sold in the agora, and frequent references to beer.

Diotima turned the tablets this way and that, as if she could somehow find more evidence. "He cares about beer so much that he's written down everything he knows about it. It doesn't make sense."

"Yes it does," I said. "These are business notes. I'd say that Romanos was planning to sell beer."

# SCENE 34
# THE RITES OF SABAZIOS

THERE WAS PLENTY of opportunity to ask about the beer, because this was the night of the ceremony Petros and Maia had invited us to attend. Petros had given us instructions to meet them at the Diochares Gate, which is in the eastern wall. I took this to mean the rites of Sabazios were to be conducted outside the city. Many Hellene rites were conducted in the forests too, so there was nothing remarkable in that.

Going east was a good choice. To the south one came quickly to Piraeus, the beach at Phaleron, and a lot of people. To the north were the landed estates, whose owners would not take kindly to strangers damaging their orchards—I could only imagine what Theokritos would say to anyone who trampled his grapevines. West of Athens was the major thoroughfare to the rest of Hellas, with many small towns and cities.

Thus any Athenian who wanted privacy for his devotions went to the forests and glades in the east. The followers of Sabazios were no different.

The Sabazians were already congregated when we arrived. We were greeted with warm, friendly words, even from those we didn't know. I apologized, because I thought we must be late, but they said they were waiting for several more families, though I noted there were no children. There were perhaps a hundred and fifty or two hundred of them, which surprised me. That was many times the number who lived in Diotima's house. What surprised me more was that some of the men and women who greeted us spoke with Athenian accents.

"Sabazios has more devotees in Athens than those of us from Phrygia," Petros said, when I asked him about it. "Every year our numbers grow."

A few hundred followers wasn't much to speak of in Athens, which is the largest city in Hellas. There were other barbarian religions with much greater appeal, particularly the deities from Egypt. Even so, the crowd that had assembled was respectable.

A small group joined us, more greetings were exchanged, and we set off along one of the paths that lead into the forests. Everyone seemed to know where they were going.

We stopped at a glade, after a pleasant, cool walk. People sat down on the comfortable grass. Everything was prepared when we arrived. The vat of beer that we had last seen at Diotima's house was in the middle of the clearing. I wondered how they had carried it here. Then I noticed the grass growing up about the edges. This vat had been here for some time. The Sabazians had *two* vats. They needed only transport the beer in standard amphorae.

And transport it they had. Because the vat was full to the brim. Torches had been set up all around the edge of the glade. Their light was more than enough to show the drink.

The light somehow shone particularly brightly upon the Hand of Sabazios. It practically glowed, no doubt because the bronze of which it was made had been polished to perfection. The hand was raised high for all to see; the column on which it stood had no other function.

"Other than the Hand, I see no altar," Diotima said to Petros. "Isn't there to be a sacrifice?"

"There will indeed be," Petros said, smiling. "But not the sort you're thinking of."

Among the men who had walked with us were several who carried musical instruments: more drums than Hellenes would use, plus long flutes. They began to play. The music was strongly rhythmic.

People around us got to their feet and formed a line.

"What do we do now?" I asked.

"Now?" Petros said. "Now we dance."

I stood. Diotima put out her hand and I pulled her to her feet. We joined the line of dancers.

It was like the *komos* dance that we Hellenes perform in moments of victory, only whereas we would have held on to the partner in front, the Sabazians danced freely, whirling and gyrating as they wished, as long as they followed the leader. I was embarrassed to join in at first. Then I realized no one was taking the least notice of me, and I copied the other dancers. The music was so strong that it was almost impossible *not* to move in time to the drums. Diotima got into the spirit of it at once. She whirled and twirled with the best of them.

The circle of the dance began by tracing the edge of the glade. On each cycle we moved closer to the center. On the next pass a woman stood by the line. She was passing out straws. Each dancer stopped just long enough to grab a straw before moving on. When my turn came I saw that the woman with the straws was Maia. She smiled at me. To Diotima she shouted a greeting above the loud music.

The dancing was thirsty work, but they had a cure for that. The line had compressed tight now, but elongated into an oval. At one end the vat became the turning post. As Diotima and I approached I saw every head before us dip down in turn and every straw go into the drink. The dancers sucked as much beer as they could before the dance took them away once more.

I held up the straw and shouted to Petros, who was two ahead of me in the line, "You know, this stuff could grow on you."

Petros laughed.

I don't know how long we danced to that incredible, mesmeric music. Maybe it was half the night. I do know that by the time I thought to notice, the vat was less than half full. How much beer had we each drunk? At that moment I was too happy to care. The compressed line meant we were rubbing against each other. Between Petros and me was a woman with red hair and ample breasts. She rubbed them against me and laughed and looked mischievously into my eyes every time she whirled.

I worried about Diotima seeing this, then I notice that *she* was doing the same thing, not only to me, but to the man in line behind her. Diotima was usually the most prim and decorous woman in Athens. What was my wife thinking?

I was about to put a stop to it when the music suddenly ceased. Everybody collapsed in a heap where they were. I should have been exhausted, but I was too excited by the drink and the dance. Because we'd been following the line, the panting devotees formed a circle about the vat and the Hand of Sabazios. We all lay back in the cool, reviving grass.

A different music started up, this one of castanets and tambourines. At first there was only the music, then a woman appeared from the darkness beyond the Hand of Sabazios. She danced into view. I thought at first the music came from her, because she held something in each hand. Then I thought they were sticks she held, because they were long and thin. Then one of them moved, and I realized the woman held live snakes.

I hadn't recognized the woman at first. Firstly because the snakes grabbed one's attention, secondly because the lady wore nothing but a skirt. Her breasts bounced in time to the wild dance. It took some while before I thought to look up at her face. When I did, I got a shock.

I said, "Petros, is that your wife?"

"Did I not mention that? Maia is a priestess of Sabazios. Here in Athens, she is *the* priestess of our god. There is no other like her."

There certainly wasn't.

Maia, now completely naked, danced within the circle. She held the writhing vipers high above her head, one in each hand. In her frenzy she chanted the same words over and over, "*Euoi saboi! Euoi saboi!*" Maia was caught up in religious ecstasy. I wondered if she even knew where she was.

The audience chanted in time to the beat, "Euoi saboi! Euoi saboi!" They were totally caught up in the moment.

One of the snakes bent over and bit Maia solidly on the arm.

I clutched Petros's arm. "Petros, the vipers have bitten Maia!"

"Their fangs have been pulled," he said calmly. "They cannot harm her."

Maia barely noticed. I saw when she came close that her eyes were almost rolled up. She gyrated in a way that had the attention of every man in the clearing, and probably half the women too.

Somehow Maia found Petros. She bent over him, her breasts swaying and with a wild snake to each side of him. I had to lean back to avoid a viper in my face.

Petros knew what she wanted. He got to his feet and joined her in the dance. That lasted until Maia wrapped her arms around Petros, still gyrating. At some point while I'd been watching her, he had shed his clothes. It was obvious he was enjoying the attention. Maia pulled Petros down on top of her.

All about us, the followers of Sabazios were doing the same thing. We were surrounded by heaving bodies and cries of ecstasy.

There were men who went to symposia for the flute girls, or for the girls who euphemistically called themselves flute girls. I was not one of them. For one thing, Diotima had proven a very passionate woman; for another, my best and only real friend Timodemus was besotted with his own wife. When we visited each others' homes we'd even been known to take our wives along with us.

I wondered what to do.

Diotima solved the problem for me. She stared at me as if she'd never seen me before. She licked her red lips and I knew she was tasting the last drops of the beer. Then she threw herself at me and ripped off my clothes.

DIOTIMA AND I awoke in each other's arms and, almost, the arms of the couples all around us. We looked into each other's eyes, at close range. We were both thinking about what had happened.

I said, "Whatever they put in this beer, we need to get some of it into our wine."

Diotima shifted closer, to avoid the couple behind. They too were waking to the dawn.

"I'm not so sure, Nico. If they did, people would never get any work done."

The feel of her warm breasts against my chest elicited the usual response. Diotima felt it happening.

"Again?" she murmured.

"How many times is that?"

"I lost count."

"One more for good luck." I was ready and raring to go. I positioned myself beside her.

"Did you enjoy it?" a voice behind me asked.

It was Petros.

"Yes, we did, thank you very much," I said from the prone position.

I stood up. Diotima hurriedly pulled clothes about her.

I added, "But Petros, the Sabazians will have to stop these rites."

Petros looked surprised. "I don't understand. Don't Athenian men indulge in orgies all the time?"

"Yes, but not with our wives! That would be immoral. Seriously, Petros, if the Athenians find out you followers of Sabazios behave like this, you're going to be in big trouble."

"This we know. It's why we perform our rites outside the city, where none will notice. Also, in the grove we have more room to . . . er . . . spread."

All about us, entwined bodies were waking up.

"I can see what you mean," I said. Then, recollecting why we'd come, I said, "Did Romanos participate in these rites?"

"Of course he did." Petros looked puzzled.

"And Romanos knew the effect of beer on happy, cavorting people," I said.

"It's not the beer that causes the orgy," Maia said. She had walked over to us as we spoke to her husband. "It is the spirit of Sabazios. He is the god of the harvest. He makes all things fruitful. When Sabazios enters into you, then you too become fruitful." Maia shrugged. "Some people resist the God. For others, they find it difficult to let the god come to them, even when they are willing. For such people, beer is the sacred drink that opens the door to the God."

"Your brother must have known this about the beer," Diotima said.

"Yes," Maia agreed.

"Then why was he planning to sell it?" I asked.

"Sell it? You must be confused," Petros said. "We have no such plan."

"I'm relieved to hear it," I said.

"No, we're planning to give it away," Petros went on. "To everyone in Athens."

Maia smiled the smile of a religious fanatic who knew everything she did was for a divine cause. "Isn't it wonderful? We will spread the sacred word of Sabazios. With free beer!"

# SCENE 35
# PROFESSIONAL INDISCRETIONS

THEOKRITOS, THE HIGH Priest of Dionysos, looked askance at Diotima. "You, a priestess of Artemis, partook in the orgiastic rites of this barbarian god Sabazios?"

Diotima looked at me. I looked at her. We both wondered how to explain what had happened.

"It seemed like a good idea at the time," Diotima offered.

"These people don't drink wine," Theokritos said. "They drink *beer*!"

"Yes."

*"This must be stopped!"* Theokritos thundered.

Diotima and I had washed in the Ilissos River on our way home, where we stayed only long enough to change clothes. They were covered in various bodily fluids. The washing slave looked disgusted as we handed them to her and asked us what we'd been doing.

We went straight to see the High Priest of Dionysos. Diotima insisted. The Sabazian rites might have been fun—I certainly thought so—but having experienced them, it was obvious to us both that they were in direct opposition to Dionysos. At any other time of the year that might have been acceptable, but to invoke a rival god at the height of the Dionysia was perilously close to sacrilege. The high priest had to be informed.

Theokritos muttered, "I see Dionysos demands more of me."

"I know it's a problem, Theokritos," I said. "But is it really so bad?"

"Of course it is!" Theokritos almost shouted. He made a visible effort to calm down. "I know you're a man after my own heart, Nicolaos. That was obvious from our last meeting. Do you not see that if beer becomes popular among the ignorant, it must inevitably lead to a loss of worshippers for Dionysos?"

I rubbed my chin and thought about it. "I see what you mean. But what can you do?" I asked. "Forgive me, Theokritos, but there's no law against handing out free beer."

"There is against importuning the Gods of Athens!"

That was true. The impiety laws in Athens were very strong indeed. I for one wouldn't want to be on the wrong side of them. Indeed that was the crime which we'd been hired to solve, not the murder.

Diotima said, "But if the Sabazians distribute their beer without proselytizing their god, then they haven't broken any laws, have they sir?"

"That's not the point!" Theokritos went red in the face. "This drinking of beer in the time of Dionysos defies every ethic; it passes every boundary of common decency."

"Yes, I know. Nevertheless sir, if you went to the courts and argued before a jury that free beer was a crime, I fear you might lose."

Theokritos took visible steps to calm himself. He wiped his brow and took a cup of wine. "I believe you're right, Nicolaos. Yet steps must be taken."

"I hope you won't do anything rash, sir," I said, slightly alarmed.

"I will do all that is good in the eyes of Dionysos."

# SCENE 36
# THE FEAST

DIOTIMA AND I talked through the rest of the day. We were too exhausted to do much else. The last days had been more than intense. More to the point, we felt as if we'd learned everything there was to learn in the time we had left. Pericles's feast was due to begin that evening. Failure beckoned, unless we could solve the crime with what we had.

We considered every possible combination of killers, but no matter which we tried, there always seemed to be an objection that was hard to remove, or worse, no proof good enough for a court.

In the end, as the sun began to set, we resigned ourselves to the inevitable. Diotima put on her special party chiton, though she said she hardly felt in the mood. Together we set off for the agora, certain to be last to arrive at the biggest party of the year.

Where stalls normally stood, slaves had erected long rows of trestle tables. Barbecue pits had been hastily dug about the periphery. Beside the pits, temporary altars had been erected so that the meat could be blessed before it was cooked, and beside the altars, priests stood ready and waiting to perform the blessings. Chief among these was Theokritos, the High Priest of Dionysos, which was no surprise since the festivities were in honor of his god.

Women slaves carried in basket after basket of fruit: olives and quince and apples—more baskets than I could count—hundreds of them, all decked in flowers.

The fishermen had been cleared of all their stock. There

was a traffic jam of fisher carts waiting to offload their catch at special fires along the west side of the agora.

Musicians played at every corner. They played upon aulos pipes and lyres and drums. As soon as you passed by one group you came upon the next, so that the entire agora was bathed in music. The sights and sounds were enough to lift our hearts, at least enough to enjoy the night's show.

The Altar of the Twelve Gods stands at the center of the agora. Diotima and I pushed our way through, the better to see everything. The Altar too had been wreathed about in flowers.

I led Diotima by the hand to the statues of the Ten Heroes, each of whom lends his name to one of the ten tribes. The Ten Heroes are spread out in a line, each hero in such a noble pose that I'm sure his own mother wouldn't have recognized him: Ægeus, Erechtheus, Pandion, Oeneus, Leos, Acamas, Cecrops, and Hippothoon; then there was Ajax, who fought at Troy, and finally Antiochus, the son of Heracles, to whose tribe my own family belonged.

Some wag had tied giant wooden dildoes to each of them. The heroes didn't seem too upset about it.

Phalluses are charms of the greatest good luck. Phalluses had been hung from poles all about, made of wood or clay or carved in stone. They were various models, but all of them of a shape and size to please even Diotima's mother.

People wore good luck amulets with models of phalluses dangling upon their chests. A troop of small boys walked past. Each carried a giant phallus made of light wood.

Diotima watched these pass and said, "I wonder if Theokritos would appreciate it if I pointed out the correspondence between the phalluses in the agora and the rites of Sabazios in the glade?"

"I wouldn't mention it if I were you," I said. I took her hand. "Come with me behind the Ten Heroes."

"Why?" she said suspiciously. But then she followed me behind the statuary. I showed her, scratched deep into the buttocks of Antiochus, just below the cloak line, a large N.

"I did that when I was a boy," I said proudly.

"Congratulations," she said. My wife seemed strangely disinterested.

We weren't the only ones arriving late. People streamed in from all directions, all of us looking forward to a free meal of the best Athens had to offer.

I took pleasure in the knowledge that Pericles was paying for the feast. This magnificent display of public benefaction must be killing him.

The thought took me in search of the man himself. We found him upon the steps of the Painted Stoa, where he could be seen by all the merrymakers, and from whence he could direct the festivities. From time to time he called out instructions to the slaves who served.

Diotima and I climbed the steps to join him.

Pericles stood and watched while the entire year's produce from his estates went down the mouths of his fellow citizens. He smiled benignly, with that serene composure for which he was famous, and waved when the people cheered him.

As he smiled and waved, out of the corner of his mouth he muttered, "I want you to know that this party has cost me a fortune, and then some."

Pericles said it as if it was my fault.

"I actually had to *borrow* to fund it."

"Is that bad?" I asked.

"When every drachma I borrowed is being poured down someone's gullet and will be excreted by this time tomorrow? Of course it is. This had better be worth it, Nicolaos. Are you making progress?"

"None whatsoever, Pericles," I said, for the pure joy of seeing his reaction.

We left him before he could reply. Diotima and I plunged back into the crowd.

I was whacked on the head from behind. It wasn't a hard hit, but it was unexpected and the more painful for that.

"Ouch!"

I turned at once to see that the weapon was a giant phallus, one made of light pine. It was carried by a small boy. He grinned up at me.

The boy rested the phallus on the ground beside him. The phallus was taller than he was.

"Now you're going to have good luck!" the small boy said.

It was the children from Melite, the ones who had led us to the home of Romanos. They hadn't said a word before. I had thought they must be mute.

"How come you talk to us now?" I asked.

"We've been eating lots of food!" the boy said proudly, and his sisters nodded. "Our mother bought us some with the money you gave us."

"What about your father?"

"He's dead." The boy shrugged, but I could see him struggling not to cry. "After we came here he got a disease and then he died."

"I see."

It happened. The orphans of citizens were cared for—the archons saw to that—but the same wasn't true of metics. They could look after themselves. Or they could go away. In a city that struggled to feed its own children, there was nothing left over to feed someone else's offspring.

Diotima asked, "Where were you before you came here?"

"Some other city. I don't remember it. Our mother said we were poor there. Father brought us here to get rich."

And now he was dead. I remembered the mother of these children. She had insisted they maintain standards, even while they starved.

I crouched down to their level and said, "Listen, do you know I owe you again?"

"Why?"

"You just gave me good luck, didn't you? That's very valuable. Here you go."

I gave the boy every coin I had. It wasn't much.

"Now you take these straight to your mother, all right?"

"Yes sir."

"And make sure you stuff yourselves full tonight!" I smiled.

They ran off.

Diotima leant over and kissed me on the cheek.

"Diotima!" I said shocked.

"You're a good man, Nico," Diotima said.

"I'm a foolish one. I can't support that family. All I'm doing is prolonging their agony."

The party was in full swing. People were sitting at the long benches to eat. We grabbed food from the stalls. Then I elbowed room at one of the benches for Diotima and myself. We'd seen Pythax and Euterpe on the other side of the agora, but it was too hard to get across in the press.

The conversation at our bench was all about the festival and the plays to come. Then one man said, "Hey, have you heard about the psyche?"

"What psyche?" I asked.

"The psyche at the theater. They say the psyche of Thespis is haunting the place. They say he's really angry."

"I'm not surprised, with the quality of plays we get these days," said a critic. "Someone pass me that ox meat?"

"I heard they tried to expel the psyche, but they failed," a woman said. She appeared to be the wife of the first man. She clutched a piece of lamb in one hand and an onion in the other. "It was the ghost that came back and killed the actor."

"Shoddy work on the expelling rite, if you ask me," said the critic.

"Excuse me, it was an *excellent* rite," said Diotima, deeply offended.

"How would you know, lady?" the man scoffed.

Diotima was angry now. "Because *I'm the one who—*"

I jabbed her with my elbow. Diotima glared at me but wisely said nothing more.

The critic said, "Well I say we can expect more of this sort of thing if the plays don't improve. Psyches haunting theaters."

I was amazed that people were still talking about the ghost. People would believe anything.

"Are you sure there's a psyche at all?" I said.

"Of course there's a psyche. They tried to expel it, didn't they?"

"Well, yes," I admitted.

"They wouldn't try to expel something that wasn't there, would they?"

Heads nodded up and down the bench.

"You don't think there might be some other cause?" I inserted into the conversation.

"Like what?" someone asked.

"Oh, I don't know. Maybe some insane person is hanging about the theater."

They all laughed. They thought a ghost was a better idea. Cups were upended and wine was drunk.

A voice spoke from behind us. "Hey, can I join you?"

Diotima and I turned to see the honest landlord. He stood at our backs, holding a bowl of hot food in one hand and a cup of wine in the other. His breath blew over me. This wasn't his first cup of wine, but he was steady on his feet.

Beside him juggling four bowls was a woman who was obviously his wife, and three small children who in the crowd held on to their mother's chiton as if their lives depended on it.

Diotima grabbed some of the bowls to help. I made room to one side and they squeezed in. The landlord said, "I saw you sitting here. I wanted to thank you for letting me know about Romanos, and your great idea."

"What idea?" I asked.

"You said I should get some of the Dionysia crowd to rent my room. Would you believe there's a whole family living in there? They were camping outside the city, you know. They wanted to escape the heavy rain we've been having. They're paying me well above rate to get under cover."

"I'm pleased for you."

He put a chunk of meat in his mouth and talked around it as he chewed. "Still and all, it's a pity about Romanos. He seemed a nice guy."

"Er . . . yes."

"You never know when you're gonna go, do you?"

"I guess not."

"Goes to show how important is to enjoy your time. A man needs to enjoy his time, doesn't he, Dora?"

Dora looked up from feeding their children. She said, "Yes, dear."

"That's why we rent our spare room," he confided. "It means I don't have to work so much. Landlording is easy."

"I should imagine," I said. The honest landlord was also a talkative one when he was in his cups. I desperately cast about for some question that might end the dialogue.

"Especially when the renter is someone as quiet as Romanos," I said.

"Don't know about that," the landlord said, to my surprise. "He came and went at odd times. Not many visitors though, I'll say that for him."

It had never occurred to me that Romanos might have had visitors to his secret room.

I asked, "Did he by any chance have visitors on the night he died?"

The honest landlord spat the gristly part of his meat onto the ground. "Nah. He was off to a party somewhere else. I wouldn't let a renter have a party on my property."

I thought about my own experience renting Diotima's house, and could only agree with him.

The landlord was still speaking. "So Romanos went out. Late at night it was, after all the rain. Saw him run into some friends. They were happy to see him. Isn't that right, Dora?"

Dora looked about and said, "Yes, that's right, dear. I saw them. Hugs all round."

At these words Diotima's eyes lit up.

"Can you describe his friends?" Diotima asked.

"Tipsy," said Dora. "They were carrying wineskins. One of them passed his skin to Romanos. Poor fellow."

Everyone at the table had been listening in. The tale of men with wineskins had inspired the revelers. There were cries of, "More drink! More drink!"

A man with an amphora under each arm came over to fill cups.

"Would you like some beer?"

I looked up to see the man with the amphorae. I knew him. "Petros, what are you doing here?" Unfortunately I had a fair idea.

He smiled. "Did we not tell you that we want to show Athens what beer is like?"

"Here? Now? Is that a good idea?"

"Why not? No one has to drink the beer if they don't like it. We merely offer. The Athenians might decide beer isn't so bad after all." Petros grinned. He was a happy man. "Already many Athenians have drunk our beer and called for more."

"Does Pericles know you're doing this?" I asked, worried.

"You think a metic ever gets to speak to Pericles?" he said. "If Pericles can donate food and drink to the people, so can we."

"Petros, I have to tell you, if what happened at the clearing last night happens here, it's not going to be good." I had visions of the people of Athens descending into one enormous orgy. What would the children say?

Petros shrugged. "Our beer maker Marinos says it will be fine."

It wasn't the most reassuring answer, but it was too late to do anything about it. Half of Athens was already drinking beer. In fact, if the rapidly increasing merriment was anything to go by then the Athenians had drunk an awful lot of beer, and an equal amount of wine.

The landlord put down his cup and wiped his lips with the back of his hand. "Say, this beer is pretty good. Do you have more?"

"Desecration! Abomination!" A voice shouted above the crowd, so loud that everyone heard it. The shouting came from the other side of the festivities, close to where Pythax and Euterpe sat. The speaker was Theokritos. I had a feeling he'd just discovered beer on the premises.

Theokritos mounted the steps of the Painted Stoa, beside a startled Pericles. Whether he knew what was coming, or simply didn't want to be associated with anything controversial, I don't know, but Pericles quickly disappeared from view.

Theokritos stood with his arms raised. Behind him stood the assembled vintners of Athens, with their arms crossed and stern expressions.

"People of Athens!" Theokritos spoke. "I remind you that this is the festival of the Great Dionysia. Today we worship the god of the harvest, Dionysos, who is also the god of the theater and of wine. Wine is his sacred drink. We praise the God when we drink it. We dishonor him when we drink anything else. It has come to my attention that there are people here drinking beer. This is a sin against the God. Think what you are doing. This is his festival. Beer is impious! Spurn it!"

Theokritos wrested a cup of beer from a nearby drinker.

"Here now!" the drinker objected loudly.

The High Priest poured the offending liquid into the dust.

The man whose drink he'd destroyed stood up suddenly and punched the High Priest. Theokritos fell. The other vintners moved to defend their leader.

The beer drinker's friends stood up to defend their friend. They'd probably been drinking beer too.

That was enough to start the riot.

Fists flew. Strong men cursed. Women called for help and threw food.

So far the fight was limited to the men about the High Priest. The problem with Athenians is, they're always ready to lend a helping hand. The bystanders weren't moving away from the trouble; they were moving toward it, to break it up or more likely to take sides, either for beer or for wine.

There was plenty of that already. Even from my distance I could hear the debate as the punches flew.

"Beer!"

Whack.

"Wine!"

Thump.

I jumped onto the plinth of a statue, the better to see what was going on. It was the statue of Hephaestus. I apologized to the god of artisans but didn't let go of his arm. I didn't know where my parents were. I could see Pythax on the other side. He had placed Euterpe on top of the table where they'd been sitting and now he was defending the position. Several other men had followed his example. Euterpe looked like a beleaguered heroine out of the ancient tales. I had a feeling she was enjoying every moment. Three rioters tried to overwhelm Pythax. Euterpe smashed a jug of beer down on the head of one of them. That evened the odds and Pythax disposed of the other two.

This had to be stopped. Quelling riots was a job for the

Scythian Guard. The problem was that Pythax was completely cut off in the dead center of the riot. Somehow he had to get out of there and take command.

"What are your orders, sir?"

It was a voice from below. I looked down to see the faces of the men of the Scythian Guard. A whole squad of them. They looked up at me expectantly.

"Sir? Your orders?"

Me? They were asking *me* for orders?

Then it occurred to me that their chief was my father-in-law. In family-oriented Athens, where every business is a family business, that made me practically his lieutenant. The men had seen Pythax chew me out on more than one occasion for various faults, and probably sniggered behind my back. That didn't make me lesser in their eyes, it made me a junior officer. The Scythians were always deferential to Diotima when she passed them in the street. Most of all, Pythax had given me his men in ones and twos for my own work. They knew me.

"Sir? What are your orders?"

The guard sounded worried. I knew him by name. Eusebius. We would nod to each other whenever I visited Pythax at the Scythian barracks.

I had to say something.

I'd never run a battle in my life. I had no idea what to do. I cast about, wondering what someone with experience would say.

What about Pericles? He was a General. What orders would Pericles give in this situation?

No, scrap that. I couldn't even begin to imagine what Pericles would do.

I felt the first stirrings of panic in my guts. Dear Gods, how did Pythax cope with this every day?

Pythax! Yes, there was a man I could hope to emulate. What would Pythax do?

I'd once seen Pythax quell a riot by hitting a troublemaker so hard he flew into a wall. But it was too late for that. The riot was well and truly underway. Besides, I couldn't hit that hard.

Had I ever seen Pythax deal with a mob?

"The ropes!" I said. "Where are the ropes?"

"At the barracks, sir."

"Bring them all! And wake up the other shift. I want every guardsman here."

Eusebius pointed to two men. They didn't need more instructions. They took off up the Panathenaic Way as if Hades was on their tail.

I breathed easier. I had once seen the Scythians deal with a mob by using long ropes strung out to make barriers. They had herded a rioting mob away from a trouble point and then got them into single file to deal with them one by one.

"Here's the plan," I said. "We'll use the ropes to pull rioters away from the center of the agora. We'll pick them out in manageable groups by flinging the longest rope over their heads and pulling on both ends."

They looked dubious.

"We don't have enough rope for all that, sir," Eusebius said.

"Yes, I know. We'll use the narrow streets that run off the major roads. We'll use them like corridors," I said. "To split the mob. The more we can separate them, the less they'll fight. We'll station men at the other ends. The rioters will have no choice but to keep moving along because we'll be feeding more citizens in."

I felt proud of myself for already having thought of that. For once the narrow backstreets of Athens would turn out to be useful. I did a quick calculation. With three hundred men we could run two corridors side by side, with enough men left over to intervene if things got ugly.

The men looked happier.

"Like pushing sheep through a run," Eusebius said.

"Precisely."

"What if they argue, sir?"

"Then knock the bastards out."

"Yes sir!" Eusebius said happily.

That was a command any Scythian could understand. But I was betting there wouldn't be many who argued. The people of Athens were too used to following the lawful commands of their guardian slaves, as long as we could calm the people down long enough to listen.

The two runners returned with the rope plus every spare man who'd been off duty, more than a hundred men in double file. They quickly created a rope cordon that led away from the agora.

"You need any help?"

I turned. It was Akamas, the well-muscled stage crewman.

"Stand there." I pointed. "Hit anyone who tries to turn back to the agora."

"Can do," Akamas said.

The Scythian at the front flung the rope over the heads of the nearest people, then pulled them in toward the cordon. Those Scythians not involved in the cordon stood alongside, with their unstrung bows in hand. Several times an Athenian sought to break through the barrier or continued fighting. Every time two Scythians leapt to the trouble spot and dealt with it. As each group was pushed into the cordon the Scythians at the front flung the first rope again. It was like net fishing for people.

Under the urging of the guard the crowd flowed away from the trouble, into the narrow side streets of the city, from whence they dispersed, most of them carrying as much food as they could from the free stalls.

Eventually we came to the core of the troublemakers. Euboulides and Pheidestratos, the two guards who had fallen asleep at the theater, were stationed alongside the cordon.

"You two! Do you want to redeem yourselves?"

They both stood at attention. "Yes, sir!"

"Then come with me."

I left the Scythians to their work. The remainder of the crowd were the serious rioters. I ignored them and instead jumped onto the long benches. I ran along these with Euboulides and Pheidestratos at my heels. Euterpe and the other women had taken refuge on the heights. I knocked one matron over into a fish pie in my haste, but didn't stop to apologize.

The route brought us to where the vintners of Athens were brawling with the Phrygians and the dedicated beer drinkers.

The two Scythians and I reached them only moments after Pythax got there. Between the four of us, we made short work of anyone who still felt like fighting.

When it was over, I said to the man who stood defiant amongst the vintners, "Theokritos, High Priest of Dionysos, I charge you with crimes against Athens."

Theokritos raised an eyebrow above a black eye. "For inciting a riot?" he asked.

"No. For murder."

# SCENE 37
# THE FALSE TRIAL

"YOU HAD BETTER have a good reason for this," said the Eponymous Archon.

"I do, sir," I said.

We were assembled once more in the courtyard of Pericles, everyone who had been there for the first meeting, plus Diotima, and Petros and Maia of the Phrygians.

The Eponymous Archon crossed his arms and stared at me in obvious anger. "You do realize, don't you, that Theokritos is one of the most respected men in Athens? This charge is grotesque."

I said, "I promise you that Theokritos is responsible for the death of Romanos."

I turned to face the assembled personages, none of whom were smiling. Though this wasn't a trial, it felt very much like one to me. I was all too aware that I had to defend my position here, or I might be the one who ended up facing the jurors.

I said, "Let me explain. The problem all along was to decide which of the three versions of Romanos was the victim. Was it Romanos the professional actor, or Romanos the metic with an extended family in Athens? Then there was the character Romanos played, Thanatos, the god of death."

I paused to let them consider that, then added, "Initially it seemed the last option was best, that the killer had been out to murder Death."

The Eponymous Archon snorted derision at that.

I said, "Yes sir, yet ridiculous as it sounds, Romanos died

dressed as Thanatos, in a manner identical to the entrance of Thanatos in the play. We kept our eye out for someone so disconnected from reality that he thought killing fictional characters was a sane way to behave."

"Was there such a man?" Pericles asked.

"There was one suspect who might fit the description," I said. "A fanatical theater fan. But he proved innocent. The evidence he gave corresponded exactly with what we'd deduced not long before we met him: that Romanos must have been killed by more than one man."

I explained the logic that one man alone could not have used the machine, that it must have been a group. I didn't mention that it was Socrates who had deduced it.

I added, "One insane killer was believable, but no one could credit a whole group of them."

Everyone nodded in agreement. Athens had its fair share of crazy people, but that would be stretching it even for us.

"This took us back to the first motive," I said. "That Romanos had been killed because of his work as an actor. Here we had more luck. We discovered that Romanos the actor was prepared to do anything to claw his way to the top of his profession. Romanos was blackmailing Lakon."

"Here now!" Lakon objected. "Surely we don't need to go into that."

"But I'm intrigued," said the Basileus. He was obviously a gossip. "What did Romanos have against Lakon?"

Lakon looked into my eyes, imploringly.

"It was a . . . er . . . personal peccadillo," I said. "One that might reflect on the first actor's popularity with theatergoers." It was technically true, while at the same time being a complete lie. Yet Lakon didn't deserve to have his life destroyed.

Every man in the room contemplated Lakon with varying expressions of interest and intrigue. I could almost see the speculation running riot in their heads.

To quell it I said, "Gentlemen, we all have one or two little peccadilloes in our past, do we not? Ones that we'd rather our friends and acquaintances didn't know about?"

Every man present older than thirty nodded.

I said, "Imagine how much harder such things must be for an actor, who relies on his good name for work."

"Then it should be Lakon who murdered Romanos," Sophocles said.

Lakon turned bright red with anger.

"This is a lie!" he shouted.

I shook my head.

"Your idea is very natural, Sophocles," I said. "But there's an objection to Lakon killing Romanos: why would he choose the moment that did himself the greatest possible harm? Lakon would have been better off waiting until after the Dionysia was over. Lakon himself pointed this out, and he was right."

"Sometimes men act too soon," Aeschylus said. "Or they act against their own interests. We all know the old saying, whom the Gods would destroy, they first cloud their minds and muddy their senses, so that their mistakes betray them."

I said, "Aeschylus is correct that Lakon *might* have decided to murder Romanos. But we know that he didn't, because of the evidence of the theater fan, the rather intense fellow I mentioned before. I can produce him for court. He was there that night. He saw a group kill Romanos, not a single actor. What group could that possibly be?"

There were expressions of bewilderment among my audience.

I said, "That brings us to the final version of Romanos: the private man. The most obvious candidate for a group of killers was the family of Romanos: the Phrygians."

Everyone turned to stare at Petros and Maia, who stood side by side in a corner of the courtyard. They glanced at each other in open-mouthed surprise, then they said as one, "That's not true!" Maia added, "I loved my brother."

I ignored that and said to the assembly, "The Phrygians would certainly be convenient. Metics never get a fair trial, do they?"

"But what of a motive?" asked the Polemarch, whose job was to manage the affairs of metics. He was also a fair-minded man.

"The Phrygians are followers of Sabazios, who is a rival god to Dionysos," I told them. "Maia and Petros and the other Phrygians had long been planning to hijack the Dionysia to promote their own faith . . . and their own drink." I paused, then added, "We all know what that led to."

There were growls of unhappiness from around the room, particularly from Pericles, whose party it was that had been destroyed.

I said, "Of course Romanos must have known of his family's plan to spread the word of Sabazios by distributing beer. But the same grasping ambition that caused him to blackmail Lakon then surfaced against his own sister. Romanos decided to make beer and sell it, like we do wine."

"What's this?" Petros and Maia exclaimed.

I had no choice but to tell Maia of her brother's plan to turn beer into a money-making venture. She didn't believe me until I produced his notes, and told her of the hideaway he kept secret. I finished by saying, as gently as I could, "No doubt he did it to promote his own interests to become a citizen."

Maia was visibly shaken.

"Then the case is simple," said the Eponymous Archon. "The Phrygians, having learned that one of their number was set to betray them, killed the man before he could do so. Nothing could be simpler." The city's highest official spoke with obvious relief. "Any jury would convict them on that evidence."

"Yes, sir, but the jury would be wrong," I said. "The Phrygians had no idea what Romanos was planning. You need only look at Maia and Petros here to see how surprised and devastated they are by this news."

"That's not evidence," the archon scoffed. "They could be acting."

"They could be," I agreed. "But it's definitely evidence that the Phrygians invited my wife and me to attend their . . . er . . . religious observances."

"So they're a religious people," said the Basileus.

"You could say that, sir," I said with feeling. "The point is they made no attempt to hide their beer. If you had killed a man for such a reason, you would hide your motive, would you not? The fact that they went ahead and gave away the beer at the festival shows that they didn't think they had anything to hide."

"Who else, then?" the Basileus challenged.

I said, "Theokritos the High Priest of Dionysos is a popular man. The workers at his vineyards would do anything for him."

I paused, then added. "Theokritos also leads the association of vintners."

"Surely you are not about to accuse all of our winemakers!" the Eponymous Archon said.

Athens would still need her winemakers after this was over. I said, "I merely point out the economic motive, sir. Theokritos himself was moved by his religious devotion. Anyone who's spoken to him can tell you he is devoted to Dionysos."

"That's fairly normal for a high priest, don't you think?" the Eponymous Archon said sarcastically.

"Yes, sir. But the point is Theokritos had a ready-made group of followers, if he chose to use it." I quickly drew breath before he could argue again and carried on. "Then there is Thodis, the choregos, who also has a group: the friends who advised him to get into the theatrical business."

Thodis scowled angrily but remained silent. No doubt he would speak after he'd taken advice from his friends.

"What of Lakon?" Aeschylus asked.

I said, "Lakon *might* have been able to persuade his fellow actors to join him in revenge on Romanos, particularly if they knew it had been Romanos who was sabotaging them. The family of Phellis might happily have joined in."

That completed the list of possible murderous conspiracies. Everybody whom I'd mentioned was glaring at me.

"Which of these groups, then?" I asked. "Or more to the point, which of their leaders? Theokritos, Thodis, Petros, or Lakon?

"None of them make any sense," Sophocles said. "You forget, Nicolaos, that my play was sabotaged right from the start. Thodis would not wish to destroy the play; he paid for it! Lakon would not damage his biggest role. The High Priest of Dionysos would sooner die than harm the Great Dionysia, and I dare say the metics desperately needed the income Romanos brought in."

"Yes, that confused me too, sir," I said. "But there was another possibility: Romanos himself. Romanos yearned above all else to become a citizen of Athens. We know this because he said so, to Diotima and me, under a rain-soaked stoa. He questioned Diotima closely as to how her father Pythax had achieved his citizenship."

"Through his vast merit," Aeschylus said. "I know Pythax and I would be proud to stand beside him in the line as a fellow citizen."

"I said the same thing," I said ruefully. "I didn't know then that Romanos had already reached the same conclusion. How many men are gifted with an opportunity to display their talents in the way that makes a whole city admire them? It's not a question of merit, it's a question of a crisis occurring that brings you to the fore, or being in the right place at the right time."

"Yes, I concede this difficulty," Aeschylus said. "These things are as the Gods ordain."

"Sometimes the Gods get assistance. Romanos decided to

make his own crisis. One that would bring his talents to the attention of every man in Athens."

I paused, then said, "It was Romanos who sabotaged the play."

Silence, for a long moment. I wondered if the audience would believe it.

"Romanos *manufactured* the crisis?" said Sophocles, aghast. "But . . . but . . . he helped to solve it. He was *instrumental* in saving us."

"Yes, precisely!" I said. "Because of that, we suddenly noticed a man we had always taken for granted. Romanos even said to me that Romanos is the man Sophocles calls for when he's run out of other good options."

"I see." Sophocles looked ashen. "I helped bring on this crisis by taking a man of talent for granted."

"I'm afraid so. He was probably inspired by the skene painting. It contained enough incidental disasters to make the situation look spooky. He complained to the stage manager to force Akamas to work back late one night, then appeared wearing a mask to create the rumor of a ghost. He laid the first trap for himself, to allay suspicion: he tripped over a broom. There was no danger, not for a man who has played comic falls on stage. The next two incidents were far more serious: the balcony attempt and the fall of Phellis."

I could see people puzzling through the idea. A few looked convinced.

I said, "Lakon is extraordinarily lucky that Sophocles refused to hire Romanos as second actor. If he had, it would have been Lakon, rather than Phellis, who had the near-fatal accident. Romanos, you see, had to step into a higher role to save the day."

Lakon paled at my words. He understood that what I described was possible.

"Not only that," I continued, "Romanos had to save not

only the play—actors step into emergency roles quite often—but Romanos had to be seen to save a major festival. And not just any festival, but the Great Dionysia, which all the world attends."

"This seems a big stretch," Aeschylus said. "What possible good could come of this?"

"Imagine if Romanos had not died. Imagine if the Dionysia had proceeded. We all remarked how Romanos worked like a slave to recover the festival. You yourself, Sophocles, said that Romanos had been instrumental."

Sophocles said. "That is true. I was wondering how I might reward him for his good work."

"Had he lived, and had you asked him, he would have asked you to sponsor him for citizenship."

Sophocles frowned. "Such a thing is highly uncertain, and extremely rare. How could Romanos have thought I could deliver on such a request?"

"You underrate yourself, Sophocles. The people respect you. Everyone knows you are the obvious successor to Aeschylus." I turned to Aeschylus. "You said, sir, that you would be proud to stand beside Pythax. How would you feel about a metic who almost single-handedly dragged the Great Dionysia back from the brink of disaster?"

"I would support him for citizenship," said the master playwright. "Of course I would."

I turned back to Sophocles. "You see? If you and Aeschylus made the request, especially with Aeschylus retiring, how could the citizen body deny you? The People's Assembly would declare Romanos a citizen by acclamation."

"I see the logic of your words." Sophocles's voice wavered. He was deeply upset. "Yet still I'm astounded. How could he have taken us all in?"

"Because he was a great actor."

Sophocles nodded. "That he was."

"There is this to remember about Romanos: that he was a curious mix of a great man who would work his heart out for the theater, but who was utterly amoral when it came to his own ambitions. The stage manager told of us of an incident years ago, when Romanos saved a play by brilliant improvisation after the skene collapsed. This was the same man who blackmailed without hesitation. He was prepared to cripple Phellis and bring the Dionysia to the brink of disaster. Then he drove himself to save the play he almost destroyed.

"Kebris told us that Romanos began to teach him the third actor's lines even before the crisis had begun. That seems extraordinary."

All eyes turned to Kebris.

"Because my friend feared for his life," Kebris said angrily. "I don't believe your fantasy for a moment. Romanos said he wanted me to know his lines in case something happened to him."

"Yes, Kebris," I said. "I don't doubt you for a moment. But Romanos didn't teach you the lines because he thought something might happen to him. He taught them because he *knew* something was about to happen to Phellis."

I paused to let that sink in. I could see the thoughts rearrange themselves in people's minds. Then I said, "Romanos prepared for his own promotion in advance. Why? So that when the crisis came he would be the hero who saved the show."

There was a pause, before Lakon said admiringly, "That's really very clever."

I said, "This means the murder of Romanos is disconnected from the disasters at the theater. It opens up the field to every suspect."

"But it doesn't explain why Theokritos would want to kill him," Pericles said. Like the Eponymous Archon, Pericles wasn't happy with my choice of murderer.

"I've eliminated the need for a theatrical motive," I said. "Let me explain the real starting point of this disaster."

I said, "Lakon had introduced Romanos, at his insistence, to many of the most prominent men in Athens. Lakon even told us that Romanos had specifically asked to meet men of the merchant class. Lakon assumed it was so Romanos could promote himself in search of a choregos, as Lakon himself had successfully done with Thodis. In fact, Romanos's notes make it clear that he talked to the merchants about his plan to sell beer. He was probably looking for backers or partners.

"It probably never occurred to Romanos that anyone would be upset. Romanos wasn't one to consider propriety when self-interest was at stake. Such men often fail to understand the reactions of others.

"Inevitably word of his plan reached the winemakers, and Theokritos. After all, they moved in the same merchant circle. Or perhaps Romanos was foolish enough to approach Theokritos directly. Either way, it was a disaster. The wine growers saw competition. But Theokritos saw something much worse. He saw sacrilege."

The Eponymous Archon scoffed. "Theokritos couldn't have done all this on his own. Who helped him? Answer me that!"

"His estate workers," I said at once. It was the simple, easy answer. "And *possibly* some fellow winemakers." Then I hastily added, "The trusting winemakers of course would have been led astray by their high priest."

I could already see it would be politically impossible to get a conviction if it meant wiping out our vintners. I had offered the archons a way to punish the leader alone.

Pericles's slaves had supplied refreshments all round and my mouth was dry. I stopped to pick up a cup of watered wine.

"The final proof is in the manner of Romanos's death. A landlord saw Romanos step outside his private room to run into a party of friends. They hailed him. Perhaps they even called up to him in his room to join them. In either case, Romanos was pleased to see them.

"Right away we know these were not Phrygians. Romanos would have been disconcerted to say the least if his family saw him stepping out of the room he kept hidden from them. There certainly would not have been hugs all round."

"That seems reasonable," said Sophocles.

"We also can guess they were waiting for Romanos to appear," I said. "*There were heavy showers that night.*" I paused, to let them think about it. Then I went on, "Parties don't walk the streets when there's a good chance of getting saturated. That's when they sit indoors, under cover. The chances are miniscule that a party of acquaintances could accidentally happen upon Romanos, as he leaves his private room, on a night of sudden, heavy rains. No, the odds are overwhelming that Romanos had met his murderers."

"It's possible," Aeschylus said.

I said, "The landlord's wife saw someone pass Romanos a wineskin. That wine was probably drugged."

"Total speculation," Theokritos said.

I turned to Theokritos. "Sophocles said it just a few moments ago. The High Priest would sooner die than harm the Great Dionysia. In *your* mind, it wasn't an impious act to kill Romanos. The killing was a sacrifice you made to Dionysos, *in his own temple*, of a man who planned to commit sin against the God."

Men looked askance at the High Priest. He stood there and said nothing.

No one wanted to think of such a popular man as a murderer, but that he would kill to protect his god, that they could comprehend. I felt the audience suddenly shift my way, and my inner relief was enormous. It was like a battlefield defeat turned to unexpected victory.

I waited. So did everyone else.

Theokritos thought for a very long time. He stood, arms crossed, as he looked to each person present, one after the other. He reserved most of his attention for the senior men who would decide his fate.

After that long time he said, "Very well, it was as Nicolaos says. In every detail. What of it? I killed a metic who by your own evidence was a blackmailer, who was ready to not only commit impiety, but was going to undermine the wine industry at the same time. He even betrayed his own people." Theokritos paused, then said, "He's dead. Does anyone care?"

I sucked in my breath. Theokritos had admitted the crime and then dared us to do something about it.

Everyone waited for someone else to speak. The reluctance was palpable.

"We must consider this," said the Eponymous Archon eventually. "Perhaps we were mistaken in declaring a crime."

"What?" I was shocked.

"We must consider, young man, what is in the best interests of Athens," the archon said.

"Who would be the judges, if this went to court?" someone asked.

"We three archons," said the Polemarch. "Me, the Eponymous Archon, and the Basileus. Normally it would go to one of the six lesser archons who hear trials, but for a high priest who is charged with murder, it could be nothing less than the senior archons, and a jury of not less than five hundred and one members."

We all knew what that meant. A show trial. When the jury was large the winner was whoever could entertain the jurors the best. Theokritos was an amiable, well-liked man. There was every chance he could walk away.

"We must keep in mind the likely sentence," the Polemarch said. "For the death of a metic, a citizen could expect exile or an enormous fine. No worse, unless there are aggravating circumstances."

"But what about the charge of impiety?" I said. "That's the crime I was commissioned to solve."

"Who decides whether impiety has been committed against a god?" the Eponymous Archon asked me.

I said, "Normally it would be the senior priest of the relevant temple . . . oh." I saw the point. Theokritos need only argue that as the resident expert on what pleased Dionysos, if he said it was all right to slaughter Romanos in the theater, then it was.

"Surely there must be a way around this," Diotima said.

"There is," said the Basileus. "I'm the archon in charge of religious affairs. I could determine that impiety has occurred that displeases the Gods."

"Well?" she demanded.

"There's a problem with that," Pericles answered for the Basileus. Pericles had never liked Diotima. "Have you forgotten the thousands of important visitors in Athens this moment? If we put our own high priest for Dionysos on trial on the first day of the Dionysia, in front of the whole world, we will look like complete idiots."

"Apparently we are," I pointed out.

"Yes, but we don't want the rest of the world finding out," Pericles said. "The Great Dionysia is as important to our diplomacy as any trade negotiation. We can't put Theokritos on trial. It would be a diplomatic disaster."

There was a difficult silence.

"He's right," someone said from the back of the room.

"Perhaps a significant donation, in lieu of a fine?" Theokritos suggested. "Something equal in size to the sum a court might have levied?"

Heads slowly nodded, albeit reluctantly, but they nodded.

Maia suppressed a sob.

"That would be satisfactory," said the Eponymous Archon. Then he asked, "Now can we get on with the Dionysia?"

IT HAD ALL been for nothing. We stumbled from Pericles's house into the street.

Someone put a hand on my shoulder. I turned to see the Polemarch.

"I know how you feel, Nicolaos," the Polemarch said. "I warned you before, it is very hard to obtain justice for a metic."

"I understand," I said. The Polemarch was a good man, trapped by circumstances.

He said, "The fine that Theokritos is paying is the same as a court would have ordered. It comes to the same thing."

"Yes." There was no point arguing.

It wasn't fair. Not only was Theokritos going to get away with it, but when he donated to the temple it would enhance his reputation.

Diotima and I stood forlornly in the street outside Pericles's house. We were joined by Petros and Maia, Kiron and Lakon.

The Polemarch departed, to be replaced by Aeschylus and Sophocles. Both men looked very unhappy.

"The decision is a bad one," Aeschylus said at once. He was a stickler for proper behavior. "But, Nico, the word of the archons in this matter is law. I want you to know, you did a good job."

"I would refuse to proceed," Sophocles apologized. "Except that honor requires otherwise."

"Can you go on?" I asked.

"*Sisyphus* will be a disaster," Sophocles admitted. "At this stage all that matters is we do our best. Kiron told you how Romanos once carried on when the stage fell in on them. That's what honor is to an actor." He turned to Petros. "I can offer you condolences and the place of second actor, if you wish to accept. You will be well compensated from my own funds. It's the best I can do."

"I accept," said Petros.

Aeschylus and Sophocles departed.

The others who had been present passed us by without

a word. Theokritos gave me a good long stare, but he said nothing. Petros took a step toward the departing murderer. Kiron, Lakon, and I held him back.

Maia said, "I know my brother was prepared to leave us, but he was still my brother."

"It is hard," Kiron said to Maia. "I can make sure the other theater people know what happened but . . ." He shrugged. "It will mean nothing. Theokritos is a powerful man."

"If it's any consolation, this is manifestly unfair," Lakon said to the Phrygians. "I can say that, and *I* was one of his victims."

"Thank you," Petros said.

"I may not be a good man," Lakon said. "But I'm not a bad one either."

I made a decision. It was an idea inspired by something Socrates had said a few days ago.

I said, "Would you be willing to embarrass Theokritos?"

"Yes."

"All right, this is what we're going to do."

I explained my plan to Diotima, to Petros and Kiron, and to a somewhat reluctant Lakon.

When I finished, heads nodded.

"SOCRATES, I HAVE a job for you," I said. I'd found him at home, reading.

Socrates said, cautiously, "Another? The last one wasn't much fun, Nico."

"I think you'll prefer this one. Do you remember a few days ago, you talked about characters not knowing they're in a play?"

"Yes?" He looked at me oddly.

"We're about to do something like that. You understand how the god machine works, don't you?"

"I think so."

"I need a machine." I explained what I wanted.

Socrates said excitedly, "Sure, Nico! I can design that." Then he looked worried. "But Nico, who's going to build it?"

"Leave that to me."

"CAPTAIN KORDAX!"

"Nico! What are you doing here?" I had found him on *Salaminia*, inevitably. I had the impression Kordax never willingly stepped ashore. The captain was stripped bare but for a loincloth, as he and his men crouched over some detail of his boat. He stood up and wiped his hands.

"Captain, last time we spoke, you said, 'Give us a harder problem.'"

"So I did. Yes?"

"Well, here it is . . ."

"HELLO, MOTHER."

"Diotima? What are you doing here?" Euterpe was plainly astonished. Diotima never visited her mother if she could avoid it. But my wife had insisted that this request must come from her and not me.

"Mother," Diotima said through gritted teeth, "we were wondering if—maybe, don't feel as if you need to—that you might like to help us with a job we have in mind." Diotima paused, then added, hopefully, "You don't have to if you don't want to—"

"I accept," Euterpe said without hesitation.

"You haven't asked what the job is yet," Diotima pointed out.

"Do I need to? Whatever it is, dear, if you two are involved, it's bound to be intriguing. I think you should thank me for choosing you such an interesting husband."

"I chose him."

"You're going to love this, Mother-in-Law," I said, before that could turn into a fight. Then I explained.

I was right. Euterpe loved it.

# SCENE 38
# DEUS EX MACHINA

IT WAS THE twelfth of Elaphebolion.

The final day of the Great Dionysia had arrived. The people had been assured by the archons that the impiety had been cleansed. Theokritos had stood beside them as they spoke. The hypocrisy had been enough to make me gag, though in truth it would have looked strange if the High Priest of Dionysos had *not* been present for that announcement.

The Dionysia had proceeded, and it had been as fine as any in recent memory. The choral performances had been well received, and the comedies had everyone laughing and repeating the best jokes.

The greatest excitement had been the day before, when Aeschylus had put on his final play, the last Aeschylus original that anyone would ever see. The theater had been packed to overflowing and beyond. Aeschylus had outdone himself. The chorus in his play had been made up to look like the Furies, with real snakes writhing in their hair. The effect had been so overwhelming that when the Furies rushed onstage one heavily pregnant young woman in the audience had screamed and gone instantly into labor.

It might have ended in disaster had not my own mother been nearby. Four men carried the woman away, even as Phaenarete tended to the rapidly arriving babe. Phaenarete reported later that night that mother and child were both doing well.

Now on the final day it was the turn of the ill-fated

*Sisyphus*, or as I was supposed to call it these days, The Corinthian Play. Many people had turned up for what everyone knew was going to be a disaster. They had probably come to enjoy the wreck.

All about the amphitheater, people shifted on their backsides and tried to pretend that no one could see them doing it. The anticipation of the play wasn't enough to overcome the discomfort of the cold stone seats or, in the cheaper rows at the back, the temporary wooden benches.

I wished I could have gone to the very back, where the poorest people had to stand. But that would have been unthinkable. This was the Great Dionysia, the greatest arts festival of the greatest city in all the world, and a citizen of Athens has standards to maintain, whether he likes it or not.

So instead I sat on the hard stone bench beside Pythax. I noticed with some surprise that Pythax was developing a paunch. On this festival day he wore a formal chiton dyed in bright reds and greens and blues. I had to assume this was his wife's idea, because Pythax was a man whose workday clothing was the leather armor of his guards. After work he invariably chose the sort of plain, simple chiton that was favored by the most conservative of citizens.

Yet throughout the Dionysia he had worn colored ribbons hung from his belt, and the bright chiton covered him from neck to ankles and wrist to wrist. A flowery Dionysiac wreath sat askew atop his meaty brow. The overall effect was to make him look like a giant walking flower. The only reason he didn't appear out of place was that the rest of us looked like walking flowers too.

I pushed back the circlet of blossoms upon my own head, sat up straighter and looked about the audience to see what had become of Diotima. I found her in the stalls reserved for women, where she sat toward the front. She caught my eye—she'd been searching for me as I had her. We waved nervously at each other. We had a lot to be nervous about, but didn't dare show it.

An elbow jabbed me so hard that I almost fell into the stranger to my left. Pythax wanted my attention.

"Here, lad," he whispered. He reached under the material of his chiton and pulled out a bag. This he offered to me. The bag dripped red.

So that was the reason for his sudden paunch. Pythax had smuggled a wineskin into the theater.

I whispered back, "I knew I'd married into a good family." I took the wineskin from him and squeezed the contents for a good mouthful. I handed it back to Pythax so he could do the same.

The play began. The chorus walked on, singing the opening song. They stopped before the city's statue of the god Dionysos, to whom they bowed in homage.

The play went as planned, with fewer stumbles than might have been feared. Sisyphus the crafty king of Corinth managed to offend everyone. When Zeus had had enough, he sent Thanatos to collect the miscreant king.

The audience was hushed. The god of death was about to descend from Mount Olympus.

In the background, the long arm of the crane rose. It was painted to match the background. The mechanism by which the God would descend was quite difficult to see, even if you knew it was there.

As the arm rose, the rope that was attached to it also rose. It was like a giant fishing rod. Only at the end wasn't a lure, but an actor. Any moment now we'd see him appear over the top of the scenery.

The God appeared, suspended from the machine. It was Thanatos, as Sophocles had designed him. His neck was slumped over, his body flaccid.

Everyone gasped at the realism.

Then the head of Petros, who played for his brother-in-law, suddenly perked up. He spoke.

THANATOS

I, Thanatos, god of death,
Bringer of doom to mortal man,
Have been sent by mighty Zeus
to bring to justice King Sisyphus of Corinth,
whose crimes of murder and
worst of all, impiety,
have infuriated vengeful Zeus.
Hades awaits this miscreant king with open arms.
I bear these chains of oh dear Gods what in Hades is that . . .

Someone behind me said loudly, "That doesn't rhyme."

Sophocles almost jumped up, but I pulled him back down. The playwright scowled angrily and said, "Those words aren't in the play. I hope that fool isn't about to improvise."

Petros on the god machine pointed over and above and, rather strangely, *behind* the audience.

Everyone seated in the audience looked behind them.

Every man, woman, and child in the theater gasped at the same moment.

Descending from atop the Acropolis, two hundred paces behind the audience, and a hundred above their heads, was a figure swathed in bright light.

The figure was walking through the air.

As she approached—for it was definitely a she—the reason for the aura became apparent. The lady was dressed in gold: gold helmet, gold shield, and in her right hand she held a spear tipped in gold.

It could be none other than Athena the goddess of War. Athena, the patroness of our city, for her home was atop the

Acropolis, and it was from the Acropolis that she descended through the air.

The name Athena was whispered here and there amongst the audience, until it became louder and everyone was speaking it. Such a thing had not happened since the days of King Theseus. The more fearful stood and ran away in the opposite direction. Most stayed to see what was about to happen.

The Goddess stopped in mid-air before the people of Athens. She spoke these words:

ATHENA

Do not seek to flee, mortals,
For you are fleeing one who is not an enemy,
But gracious to all who inhabit Athens.
I, Athena Pallas, have come to you,
Entreated in this course by my father's son, Dionysos,
God of the harvest and of the theater,
For he does not think it fit to come into your sight,
When impiety has been committed against him.
The god of the theater sends me to tell you this:
That there is one among you who has murdered
Within his sacred precinct.

The audience looked at one another. They all knew of the impiety that the Goddess meant. The murder of Romanos had been sacrilege because of where it took place. But the people had been told the impiety had been cleansed. Here was a goddess who begged to differ.

Athena raised her bright spear high. Its golden tip flashed in the sunlight.

ATHENA

*Raises her spear.*
See this spear? It is my spear of war,

Destroyer of men,
But today I carry not a weapon of war, but the spear of vengeance.

Every man and woman knew what that meant. If Athena declared her spear to be one of vengeance, it meant someone was about to suffer for the crime.

The chattering became loud.

ATHENA

*Points spear at a member of the audience.*
You it was, who murdered Romanos,
You desecrated this holy place.
You of all mortals should have known better,
You, Theokritos,
High Priest of my brother Dionysos.

Gasps from across the theater. Every eye turned to Theokritos, who as High Priest sat in a position of honor in the front row. It made him visible to everyone. Theokritos was already standing, like everyone else in the theater. Now he jumped up upon his seat.

THEOKRITOS

*Shakes his fist.*
That's not true!
I deny your charge.
You can't prove a thing.

ATHENA

*Ignoring his interruption.*
Let all Athens hear this.
You it was, Theokritos, who lured the actor to his death.
You ordered your men to wait

Outside the secret room he rented.
They met him with false cheer.

A LANDLORD

*Jumps up from among the audience.*

Hey, that's true!
I was the landlord of Romanos.
A group of men *did* meet Romanos outside my house.
I saw it with my own eyes.

The people of Athens looked to the man who had suddenly spoken. They saw that he was a man just like them. More than that, he was known as the most honest landlord in Athens.

This ordinary, honest man had confirmed the words of the lady who floated in the air above them. They were all thinking the same thing: how could she have known about a secret room?

ATHENA

These men fed Romanos a drugged drink.
They led him to the theater and there,
While the actor was comatose,
They hanged him upon the god machine.
A double impiety.

Gasps from many across the theater. Someone in the audience called out, "The Goddess will make it right!"

ATHENA

I have had a chat with Sabazios,
The Phrygian god has agreed
That the making of beer will cease
And in return
The children of Sabazios will go unmolested
In my city of Athens.

There were groans from the crowd at this news. Many in Athens had acquired a taste for beer.

At that moment Maia leapt to the stage, from where she spoke with perfect projection, so that all of Athens heard her.

MAIA, A PRIESTESS OF SABAZIOS

I am Maia, a priestess of Sabazios,
I have heard the Goddess.
The Phrygians shall no longer make beer.

The point had been made. There was imbalance in the world. The Gods were putting it right. There had been impiety, committed by mortal men, led by Theokritos. Now it was only a question of who were these other men. Was the Goddess about to reveal them? Of course she was. She was a goddess. She knew everything.

A WINEMAKER

*Jumps to his feet in fear.*
It's true!
I confess!
Theokritos said we must stop the beer!
Theokritos said we should do it!

THEOKRITOS

You idiot!

Theokritos bolted. Not through the audience; he wouldn't have gotten ten steps. Theokritos turned and ran across the stage. As he passed by, Lakon put out his foot in an exaggerated motion that, had it occurred in a comedy, would have had the crowd laughing.

Theokritos sprawled.

The stagehands fell upon Theokritos. So did Petros, in the

guise of Thanatos, and in his hands were the chains intended in the play for Sisyphus. When the men rose, Theokritos was in the stage chains. They were strong enough to hold one fat priest.

*Exit Theokritos, chained, led away by Thanatos.*

The winemakers who had joined Theokritos were rapidly making their confessions, before anyone could charge them with anything. Every man of them pointed at Theokritos who had told them, in his role as High Priest, that what they were doing was divinely inspired.

The murder of a metic hardly warranted a fine and exile. But the crime of impiety was invariably fatal. Theokritos was on his way to Hades.

The Goddess spoke one last time.

ATHENA

The Gods are always late, but in the end they are just.

With those words the Goddess turned and walked through the air back to the Acropolis.

The chorus had stood silent upon the stage. Now they sang.

CHORUS

Those who have a troubled house
Should place their trust in the Gods.
For in the end, the good shall get what they deserve,
But the bad by nature can never fare well.

# SCENE 39
# A HAPPY ENDING!

SOPHOCLES, AESCHYLUS, AND I joined the actors and crew backstage. Pericles and the archons were explaining what had just happened to the visiting dignitaries. I wondered what lies they were making up. The archons would be furious with me. I consoled myself with the knowledge that they would only be in power for a year. They had that long to make my life miserable.

Sophocles was not entirely pleased with me either. I and the others had hijacked his play. But, since he was expecting total disaster anyway, he conceded that not much had been lost. Mostly he was impressed by our staging.

"How did you get the actor to walk through the air?" Sophocles asked. "I might have a use for that effect."

"You'll have to ask Captain Kordax," I told him. "He and his men strung the lines overnight. The lines were painted blue of course. He and his men were atop the Acropolis, controlling the machine. The machine was designed by . . . er . . . I must admit it was Socrates."

"He seems a bright lad."

Two women entered. One of them was Diotima.

"How did I do?" Euterpe asked breathlessly. She took off her mask to reveal that the goddess Athena was in fact my mother-in-law.

Sophocles turned to me. "A woman?" he said, shocked. "You allowed a woman to act?"

"She did a good job," I pointed out. "She fooled everyone."

Sophocles considered that. "It's true," he admitted. "Even I was taken in for a moment." He said to Euterpe, "I must say, madam, that had you been a man you might have made a fine actor."

Euterpe glowed with the praise. She said, "Did you really like it? I can also do a fake orgasm—"

"Thank you, Mother," said Diotima firmly.

"Congratulations, young man," Aeschylus said to me. "You've joined the ranks of theater people."

"I didn't do a thing," I said. "I only arranged for everyone else to play their parts."

"Yes," Aeschylus clapped me on the back. "That's what a choregos does, you know. By the way, who wrote those lines?"

"A fellow named Euripides."

Aeschylus looked blank. "Who?"

"A wannabe," Sophocles explained. "You might have seen him around. He's a little weird. You know the type."

"Ah," Aeschylus said, and nodded. Apparently he did know the type.

"What happens to Theokritos?" Petros asked.

"Trial for impiety," Aeschylus said. "Followed by death. He can't avoid it now. Not with every man, woman, and child in Athens present at the confession of the winemakers."

"What of them?"

"They'll get off," I said. "Nobody wants to run out of wine. The vintners did it to kill the competition. But Theokritos led them into it because he's a religious fanatic." I turned a hard look to Maia. "That's not a good idea around here."

Maia looked solemn and said, "I understand you, Nicolaos. Sabazios will no longer attempt to convert the Athenians."

# SCENE 40
# DENOUEMENT

I SURVIVED THE WRATH of the archons better than I hoped. Which was to say, they didn't actually draw their daggers and knife me where I stood. But if words had edges then I would have died a thousand times. Pericles admitted to me later, as the people brought down the decorations and prepared to resume normal, post-Dionysia life, that it had been easy to placate the official visitors.

"They enjoyed your show," Pericles told me. "Several of them asked if we could do the same again next year."

That left Pericles happy. He was satisfied as long as nothing disturbed his grand strategy. What he had in mind I didn't know, but whatever it was, the psyche of the Great Dionysia hadn't interrupted his plans.

There were only two last points to see to. I went to talk with Lakon.

I FOUND HIM in his courtyard, where he quietly celebrated a triumph. Not of the theater, but of his personal survival. Lakon invited me to sit and offered me wine. I accepted both and got to the point.

"Lakon, you're not a murderer, but you're guilty of the crime of fraud. You've lived off the name of the real Lakon for decades, and never given his family a thing in return."

He sipped his wine and said, "I could hardly do that, could I?" He leaned back in his dining couch. It was clear he felt comfortable now that the crisis was over.

I said, "I didn't reveal your secret to the others, when I accused Theokritos."

"I will be forever grateful, believe me." Lakon sounded sincere. I believed him.

"There's to be no official trial for you, Lakon, so I must be your judge," I said. "My judgment is this: that there is restitution to be made. I sentence you to play the part of Lakon to his mother. That poor old lady is in a terrible state. Her mind is gone. When she sees her son returned, she'll be overjoyed. You will make her last days restful. You will be the most dutiful son a mother ever had."

"I see." Lakon toyed with his wine cup. "You know, I'm not the monster you think I am."

"Prove it."

"I will."

"And another thing. There's a girl there named Lysine. She will inherit the family's farm."

"Fine. I don't want it."

"You will treat her like a cherished sister. You will spend whatever it costs to fix up the place. You will give her slaves to work the farm. If she wants to marry, you will dower her. You will scrupulously check over her choice of husband like a brother should."

He held up his hands in defeat. "I've got the idea. You'll have no cause for complaint."

I had better not. Or Lakon the Actor would be exposed as a fraud to his admiring fans. I hadn't voiced the threat, but I didn't need to with Lakon.

LAKON'S HOUSE LAY not far from Diotima's. It was only natural that I should stop by, to see how the Phrygians were getting on.

The house was in pristine perfect condition. The Hand of Sabazios was returned to its place in the courtyard. The beer vat out back had disappeared.

The Phrygians treated me like an honored guest. They installed me on a fine couch—I decided not to ask where it had come from—and they brought me wine and food of the highest quality. Petros sat beside me and we talked as we ate.

I said to Petros, "After that performance you'll be able to win more roles."

"I'm not sure I'll be able to fit it into my schedule," he said. "We have more work than we can cope with."

"You do?" I said, confused.

"After the funeral of Romanos we attracted much attention," said Petros. "We put on a show that was tasteful and elegant, much better than the usual hysterics that our customers demand. We showed Athens how a funeral should be done. Next day, we had a couple of men at our door—your door, rather, Diotima's house—"

"I understand."

"It seems people liked what they saw. They wanted advice on how to stage funerals for their own relatives. Of course, we charged them for our expertise."

"Of course."

"We're very good at burying people. Every day we have more customers lined up outside your house. They want us to manage the funerals of their parents, aunts, uncles, brothers, sisters."

Which meant Diotima's house was being filled every day with people in a state of ritual pollution. The neighbors were going to love me for this.

"We've upgraded from being mere professional mourners," Petros went on. "We think of it as burial consultancy. People come to us for all their funerary needs. We arrange the jars for the ashes—I've done a deal with some potters in Ceramicus—we can get some excellent alabaster. We supply the mourners and build the pyre and sweep up the mess afterward. All you have to do is sit back and enjoy the show."

"I'll keep your services in mind. Are your rates affordable?"

"Oh, we'd bury you for free!"

"You're very kind."

"I can't thank you enough for what you've done for us," Petros said. "If it hadn't been for you, we might already be on our way back to Phrygia. I can't help but feel, now that we're making money, that we should be paying you rent. Would the going rate suit you?"

"I accept," I said at once.

There's a bright side to everything.

# Author Note

GREETINGS TO YOU, cherished reader. Here I'll talk about the real history behind the story. If you haven't finished the book yet, this would be a good time to turn back to the front, because this section is full of spoilers.

If you *have* finished the story, welcome!

THE GREAT DIONYSIA was the premier arts festival of the ancient world. Every great play which has come down to us from ancient times was first shown at a Dionysia.

The three masters of tragedy were Aeschylus, Sophocles, and Euripides. They belonged to successive generations, and they were very different playwrights. If they were alive today, Aeschylus would be writing military adventure and techno-thrillers, Sophocles would be writing courtroom dramas and family sagas, and Euripides would be writing mainstream literary.

I had to set this story in 458BC because it was my only chance to get all three men into the same book. It's the final year for Aeschylus, Sophocles is in his prime, and Euripides is three years away from his first outing.

Aeschylus retired to Sicily, where he was promptly killed in unusual circumstances. History tells us that a passing eagle, seeking to crack open a turtle it had captured, mistook the famous writer's bald head for a rock, and let go. Aeschylus was struck down by the plummeting turtle. Aeschylus was not only the world's first playwright whose works survive, but he also set the standard for tragic author deaths.

Nico mentions in passing the one event that we know for sure did happen at the Great Dionysia of 458BC. Aeschylus's contribution was the famous *Oresteia* trilogy. The chorus was made up of Furies, and they really did rush on stage with live snakes writhing in their hair. Young boys fainted of fright and a pregnant woman immediately went into labor.

This anecdote proves, in passing, that women and children attended the theater, and that the great plays of the ancient world were watched by all the family.

THE STYLIZED MASKS of Comedy and Tragedy that we see on modern theater playbills are wrong. There is a surviving vase illustration that shows an actor holding a mask. It's called the Pronomos Vase and is held at the National Archaeological Museum of Naples. Though there are other vases that depict actors, this vase is one of the oldest, dating to perhaps 400BC, and has greater wealth of detail than any other. The Pronomos Vase is close to being the entire textbook on early acting.

The real Athenian actor mask was more realistic than we imagine, with hair and paint for a lifelike expression. The masks probably were rigid with a fixed face. The mask for comedy had a comic expression, and the masks for tragedy looked serious and grave. The mouth must have been open. The eyeholes were good enough to see forward but with very limited peripheral vision.

The entire staging of *Sisyphus* in this story is my invention. It's known for sure that Sophocles wrote a play by this name, but the play is lost. We don't even know in what year it was placed.

WE KNOW THAT the official cult statue of Dionysos was placed on stage to watch every play. The ancient Greeks believed that the Gods could inhabit the statues created for them.

This is why it is such a big deal that Romanos was murdered in the way that he was. The crime has been committed *in the presence of the God*. It would be hard to conceive anything more likely to bring down a curse on the city.

THESPIS WAS THE world's first actor. We've been calling actors thespians ever since.

Before Thespis, tragedy was a choral performance where the chorus sang the action, and that was it. After Thespis, an actor acted out the story while the chorus sang the action. With only one actor on stage, masks were necessary to denote the different characters.

In the next generation, Aeschylus added a second actor. Dialogue became possible.

In the generation after that, Sophocles added a third actor.

By the time of the Great Dionysia of 458BC, tragedy is a story told between three actors, with a chorus singing to open the play and in between scenes.

THIS ISN'T THE place for literary criticism, but I want to mention briefly the Athenian concept of what made a play a tragedy. It was, simply, the story of a great man who makes a mistake and suffers the consequences. In so doing there's supposed to be some form of catharsis (a very Greek word).

If you're interested in this subject, I encourage you to read *Poetics*, by none other than Aristotle. Aristotle is often translated as saying that tragedy is the tale of a great man with a fatal flaw. But that isn't what he says, strictly speaking. The tragic hero simply makes a big mistake.

In the same context, it's worth mentioning the famous saying, "Those whom the Gods would destroy, they first make mad."

In its usual wording as above, it comes from Henry Wadsworth Longfellow. But he was rephrasing a saying that goes back more than 2,500 years. The earliest use is the play

*Antigone*, by Sophocles. I've stolen this translation from the Perseus version:

> *For with wisdom did someone once reveal the maxim,*
> *now famous,*
> *that evil at one time or another seems good,*
> *to him whose mind a god leads to ruin.*

Sophocles then adds:

> *But for the briefest moment such a man fares free of*
> *destruction.*

Which is a variant of, "Well, it seemed like a good idea at the time!"

THE CLASSICAL TRAGEDIANS riffed on common myths that everyone already knew, very similar to how jazz musicians play standards that they then alter to their own taste. What kept the audience enthralled was how the writer varied the plot and the characters.

That meant if you were sitting in the Theater of Dionysos in 458BC, then the audience about you *already knew how the story ended.*

THE GOD MACHINE on which Romanos dies was very real. It was used as Sophocles explains in the story. No tragedy was complete without the god machine delivering a deity into the thick of the action.

We usually think of the Greeks as being a non-mechanical people, but it would have been impossible for Athens to maintain the world's largest fleet without a thorough practical knowledge of machinery. Greek machines were wooden, which is why none survive.

The very word machine is Greek. In their language it is *mekhane.*

What they didn't know were the laws of mechanics. The rule of the lever and the physics behind the pulley were discovered by Archimedes, two hundred years after the time of this story. The machines in Nico's time were designed with a complete lack of theoretical knowledge but a great deal of practical know-how.

The healing machine used by Doctor Melpon is only partly a figment of my imagination. Most of it was real. Forty years after this story, Hippocrates wrote a treatise called *On Joints*, in which he described a machine much like Melpon's, for the purpose of fixing hips and spines. It's known as the Hippocratic Bench, and it was every bit as horrible an experience as Phellis goes through in this book.

For this reason some people credit Hippocrates, the Father of Medicine, as also being the inventor of that well-known instrument of torture: the rack.

DEUS EX MACHINA means literally "God from the machine," and it's a curiously Latin term for what is very much a Greek concept. *Deus ex machina* means any abrupt, arbitrary action that closes down a story too quickly.

There was a problem with the way the classical playwrights used their divine characters. The Gods tended to appear suddenly right at the end, and close down the story before it could reach a climax. It's like the writers included too much plot and when time ran out simply chopped the story off using divine intervention.

Euripides was a serial offender when it came to deus ex machina.

*Ion* is a good example of his perfidy. In that story an orphan called Ion seeks his true identity. The plot becomes a trifle convoluted. There's a false prophecy which totally confuses everyone. Ion meets his mother, all unknown to them both. She tries to kill him a couple of times (these things happen). He takes a shot at her too. Then Athena turns up for the first time in the story, and in a single speech reconciles everyone and explains away the early false prophecy with a very dodgy throwaway line. Mother and son for some reason think it's cool that they're related, despite recent homicidal attacks, and everyone lives happily ever after. No natural resolution.

Many years ago my wife, Helen, and I saw *Ion* played by the excellent Royal Shakespearean Company. Even knowing what was coming, it was still a huge letdown when Athena stopped the play dead.

That experience was the inspiration for the climax of this book. You may have noticed that Athena appears right at the end, to accuse Theokritos and prove his crime. It is in fact a deus ex machina.

For Athena's speech at the end I shamelessly ripped off Euripides. In fact I ripped off *Ion*. Then I modified the dialogue for Nico's circumstances. I'm fairly sure Euripides would not be the forgiving sort, so it's lucky he's not around to sue me.

WHETHER THERE WERE professional actors in the sense we know them is a moot question. Certainly there were a hundred years later, because a rather interesting man named Thessalus is recorded as having been both a professional actor who won at the Great Dionysia, and also an agent who worked for Alexander the Great. The combination of spying and acting has a venerable history.

By the time of this story, professional bards had been traveling from town to town for centuries. I take it for granted that actors would have done the same from the moment Thespis invented the idea.

Because actors worked behind masks, very few of them are

known to us. The writers were the stars of the show. Hollywood, please take note.

Unfortunately the world of Nico and Diotima isn't quite ready for Euterpe's acting skills. Acting was an all-male affair, as it was in mediaeval times, through the Renaissance, and throughout the life of William Shakespeare, whose female roles were played by boys and men, exactly as was done in the Theater of Dionysos. The first serious actresses would not appear on stage until almost 2,200 years after the time of this story.

PROFESSIONAL MOURNING WAS a for-real occupation of the classical world. It might seem odd to outsource your grieving, but it was because extravagant displays were a status symbol.

This rapidly turned into something akin to an arms race, in which the women of competing families upped the ante with every funeral.

The displays reached such levels that something had to be done. The world's first democratic constitution, written by Solon the Wise, includes an entire section limiting what was permitted during funerals. Women were specifically banned from extravagant displays, and the dead were permitted only three changes of clothing to go with them into the underworld.

Outside working hours, professional mourners must have been instantly recognizable by their shorn, ragged hair. Almost nothing is known about the men and women who mourned for a living. I take it for granted that it was a low status job. As Petros says, it was also a job that called for a great deal of histrionic talent. Possibly then it was something that out-of-work actors did.

WHEN NICO BRINGS in Captain Kordax and the crew of *Salaminia* to stage his spectacular climax, he is anticipating by two thousand years the system used by Shakespeare and his fellows. In Elizabethan England, the stage crews were mostly sailors! If you want to move around heavy stuff with only ropes and pulleys to do it, then it makes sense to hire the experts; that means the men who sail wooden ships.

*Salaminia* and her sister ship *Paralos* were the glory of the Athenian Navy. They were reserved for only the most sensitive diplomatic missions and for religious duties, such as shipping dedications and offerings to the sacred isle of Delos. *Salaminia*'s fittings really were made of gold. Both ships were forbidden to take part in naval actions unless circumstances absolutely required it. Which is hardly surprising since it would be kind of embarrassing to watch all that gold sink.

Captain Kordax is my invention, but of course there must have been a captain of *Salaminia*. Whoever he was, it's very likely that the captain of *Salaminia* really was the fastest man on earth. It's also likely that he kept his record well into mediaeval times, when the Viking longships would have given him a run for his money. (In passing, a longship versus trireme race would be one awesome spectacle.)

*Salaminia* first appears in Nico's earlier adventure, *The Ionia Sanction*.

MY FICTITIOUS CHARACTER Lakon appears to have invented identity theft. In fact, he's late to the party.

The first recorded identity theft that I know of occurred about sixty-five years before this story. When King Cambyses of Persia died, his younger brother Smerdis stepped forward to claim the throne. This came as a surprise because everyone thought Smerdis was long dead.

Which indeed he was. This Smerdis was an imposter. He ruled for a few months before the scheme went horribly wrong, with consequences you can imagine.

Mystery writers spend a lot of time thinking up interesting new ways to commit crimes. The more I thought about it, the more I was convinced that Lakon's identity theft from the grave was close to foolproof. Athenian record keeping was appalling. If anything, the Polemarch's chaotic paper warehouse is being generous.

It's known that a decade or two after this story, the Athenians cleansed their lists of anyone who was faking citizenship. So they must have known that they had some imposters among them.

But I very much suspect that anyone using Lakon's scheme would have gotten away with it.

THANATOS GETS SLIGHTLY bad press in this book, but it's not my fault. Thanatos was the god of gentle death. His brother was Hypnos, god of sleep. Their sisters were the Keres, evil spirits who supported death by violence and pestilence. You might think Zeus would send the Keres to collect irritating mortals, but it's always Thanatos who gets the job.

The story about Thanatos being tricked into chaining himself really is part of the legend of Sisyphus, which I'm afraid makes the god of death look like a total idiot.

THE PREJUDICE AGAINST metics appears to have been generally held. Metics couldn't own real estate, couldn't vote, and were second class citizens in the eyes of the law. But in day-to-day life there was little or no discrimination. Metics in Athens were well situated compared to immigrants in many countries across many locales and times.

There is a documented case where a citizen of Athens wanted to prosecute the men who had murdered his aged nanny. The nanny was a metic and the known killers were citizens. The man was advised by the archons not to pursue the case, because there was no hope of success before a jury, and it would damage his reputation if he even tried. The man was clearly very honorable—to start with, he was looking after his old nanny—but when the city's senior judges told him there was no hope, he had to give up. This case is the inspiration for the difficulty Nico encounters in getting justice for Romanos.

Conversely, metics could do very well for themselves financially. Almost by definition, they were people prepared to go to great lengths to improve their lot in life.

It became something of a trope for wealthy metics to marry their daughters to the sons of citizens. The metic family guaranteed their descendants would be citizens of Athens; the citizen family saw a massive dowry arrive with the daughter, who came from a good and successful family.

Nico and Diotima's marriage is just such a match. He's a citizen. She was born a metic.

IT WAS POSSIBLE but not easy for a metic to become a citizen. Diotima's stepfather is the example in the book, but he's fictitious. It really happened eighty years later to a highly talented man named Pasion. He began his career as a slave, was freed to become a metic, made enormous amounts of money as a banker, and was declared a citizen.

The *only* way for a man to win citizenship was by act of parliament. Since the quorum was six thousand people, that meant there had to be at least three thousand citizens who thought you were worthy to join them. This is why Romanos desperately needs to be seen by the entire city to have done something of the highest merit. Whence his devious scheme.

THAT LAKON IS willing to go to his death rather than admit he's not really a citizen of Athens might seem extreme, but in fact that's how the people of Athens felt about it. In those days, to be a citizen of Athens was the highest honor to which any man could aspire. There are multiple instances of condemned men choosing to die in Athens rather than live in permanent exile outside the city. Not least among these is Socrates.

THE SCYTHIAN GUARD was a for-real force of three hundred slaves whose job was to keep the peace in the streets of Athens. They were so named because the original force was made up of slaves bought from Scythia, a barbarian land to the north of Greece.

It's an odd fact that these slaves were allowed to beat up their owners. Misdemeanors that would get you fined these days were dealt with somewhat more directly in Athens. A drunk and disorderly citizen or a troublemaker could expect to be beaten on the spot by the Scythians, which would not only encourage the troublemaker not to do it again, but deliver a fairly clear, visible reminder to anyone passing by.

The system worked. Ancient writers remarked that Athens had one of the lowest rates of street crime in the world.

Nor did the Scythians themselves ever become a source of trouble. That's a remarkable thing, when you consider that hundreds of years later their equivalent in Rome, the Praetorian Guard, was the source of much of Rome's woes. It speaks well of the men who led the Scythians. Pythax is my invention, but there must certainly have been someone like him: a hard man who kept these guardian slaves in line, yet a man of impeccable morals who never sought to use the power of his position for himself. We don't even know his name.

The standard weapon of the Scythians was a short bow. They unstrung this when on patrol to use as a cudgel.

The idea of using a long rope to herd unruly citizens is thoroughly well documented. Another of the jobs of the Scythians was to force the citizens to turn up to their own parliament. The *ecclesia* of Athens was the world's first parliamentary democracy. Every citizen was automatically a member of the parliament, but on slow days not enough people turned up to vote, so the Scythian slaves would work their way through the agora using the ropes to force their owners to go to parliament to run the city.

THE IDEA OF halting the calendar looks too ridiculous to be true, a kind of ancient Groundhog Day. In fact it really happened on at least one occasion. In 271 BC, almost two centuries after this story, everyone was running late for the Great Dionysia. It was a choice between holding the world's greatest arts festival with everyone under-rehearsed, or else delaying the opening. But this was a sacred festival that *had* to start on the right sacred date. The archons solved the problem by adding four extra days between the 9th and 10th of Elaphebolion. That year the calendar went . . . 8th, 9th, 9th, 9th, 9th, 9th, 10th. At which point the show was ready, and everyone must have breathed a sigh of relief.

One can only imagine with what desperate pleas the city leaders must have urged the artists to get their act together, while they held the calendar in check. There are probably some modern editors in publishing who wish they could pull the same trick. Not that any modern author would be slow delivering his manuscript.

SORRY ABOUT THE month being called Elaphebolion. I know it looks weird, but that's the real name of the month in which the Great Dionysia was held. For the record, the months in the classical calendar were: Hekatombaion, Metageitnion, Boedromion, Pyanepsion, Maimakterion, Poseideon, Gamelion, Anthesterion, Elaphebolion, Munychion, Thargelion, and Skirophorion.

No, I can't remember them either. Every time I need a calendar date, I have to look them up all over again.

THE DESCRIPTION NICO gives of an ancient Greek wine cup that shows a man throwing up is all too accurate. The cup exists and can be found on display at the magnificent Getty Villa in Los Angeles. In fact the Getty Villa has an entire case of classical Greek cups and bowls decorated with themes that you are most unlikely to come across on modern partyware.

ALL RELIGIOUS CEREMONIES of even the slightest importance included a sacrifice. The goat that Theokritos sacrifices at the altar within the theater is a typical example. It was important to the Greeks that the animal seem to agree to the sacrifice. Hence when the goat is shown the knife and appears to nod its head, that's very good news for the people present (though the goat might feel otherwise). Sacrificed meat was barbecued and eaten in almost every instance. It's not much different to having a barbecue after a modern church service. The Greeks also used these events as a charity system to get some quality food to poor families.

I'VE USED THE word ghost to describe the haunting of the theater—the Ghost of Thespis—but that's because ghost is the closest modern word. The Greeks didn't believe in ghosts as we know them. I'd bet there are more people in the western world today per capita who believe in ghosts than there were in classical Athens.

The Greeks did, however, have a total belief in the psyche, which was the spiritual part of a person that survives death. We would call it a soul. Your psyche descends to Hades when you die, where it remains for eternity.

The important thing to a Greek was to make sure the spirits of the dead made it into Hades, after which they weren't coming back. This was largely arranged via the funeral ritual, including the famous placing of a coin under the tongue.

If a burial hadn't been performed properly, then it was possible for a psyche to hang around on earth where it would disturb the living. That's their equivalent of our ghosts. Indeed this happens in several famous classical stories. But it was extremely rare because the Greeks had enormous respect for the dead, even of their enemies, and made sure everyone got a decent burial.

The story of Thespis as a ghost haunting the theater in

Athens is therefore obvious nonsense to Nico. Thespis received a proper burial. Therefore his psyche *must* be safely in Hades.

You might be surprised to learn though that the Ghost of Thespis remains a theatrical superstition to this day. It's well known that actors never refer to *Macbeth* by name, nor will they whistle in a theater. Another of these quaint theater superstitions is that the Ghost of Thespis remains on earth to haunt theaters everywhere, so that whenever something odd happens, the ghost did it. This weird idea must have had its origin somewhere, so I decided it was at the Great Dionysia of 458BC.

THAT EURIPIDES'S MOTHER was a vegetable seller in the agora is the stuff of legend. The great genius of Athenian comedy, Aristophanes, used this little factoid in his plays to skewer Euripides mercilessly. Aristophanes clearly expected everyone in the audience to know all about Euripides's mother, which probably means this formidable lady qualified for the title of Most Embarrassing Mother Ever.

I should add that Aristophanes makes Euripides the butt of many of his most cruel jokes. One assumes the two men were either the best of friends or the worst of enemies.

THE THEATER OF Dionysos that Nico describes is not the one you see when you visit Athens. The Theater was rebuilt in the fourth century, and I have no doubt it was refurbished many times in the Roman period. The Romans venerated Greek culture; they restored or added to many famous Greek sites, just as British, US and now EU funding has restored many Greek sites over the last couple of centuries.

The theater you see today is what survives of the deluxe Roman version. In Nico's time the seating was almost certainly wooden benches. All Greek amphitheaters were placed on the sides of steep slopes, suitably sculpted, so that everyone in the audience could see the action. The amphitheater model also provides superb acoustics as the sound bounces upward, a very important consideration in a world without PA systems. A good example of this is the ancient amphitheater at Ephesus, a vast construction that seats *twenty-five thousand people*. That amphitheater still exists and is in excellent condition. I have stood at the topmost row of seats at Ephesus and could hear with adequate clarity what was being spoken from the orchestra far below.

The Athenian theater was not nearly so grand. It seated at most fifteen thousand people, and that would have been very crowded.

The marble backing wall of later times was certainly a wooden wall when Nico and Diotima saw it. There's a long history to that back stage wall.

When Thespis, the world's first known professional actor, went on tour, he traveled from city to city, taking with him a cart to carry all his stuff. Chief amongst the stuff on the cart was a big tent. The tent wasn't the theater, it was the change room.

Thespis played every role in his plays, while a chorus sang much of the action. Since Thespis was the only actor, he frequently had to duck into the tent to change masks and clothes, and emerge as a different character. The side of the tent thus formed the back wall of his stage.

In classical Greek, the word for tent is *skene*. When they started to build permanent theaters, the Greeks retained the name skene for the wall at the back of the stage. They knew perfectly well they were calling a back wall a tent. It's a testimony to the massive impact Thespis had that they copied the names for everything he did, even when the word no longer applied.

It wasn't until Thespis was long gone, and Aeschylus was the top man in theater, that anyone thought to paint the skene to match the action on stage. It was probably Aeschylus himself who thought of that.

The idea of painting the skene was such a huge success that people began to associate the word *skene* not with the wall (which used to be a tent), but with the images painted on it. Thus was born *scenery*. Later on, directors started to change the scenery as the play progressed, thus creating visible *scenes*.

That is why in modern theaters we see actors in plays broken into scenes, in front of scenery. It's all because 2,600 years ago, Thespis decided to use a tent to make his quick changes.

I WANT TO publicly thank the very excellent illustrator who has provided a cover for every book in Nico's adventures, and long may he continue to do so.

His name is Stefano Vitale. He lives in Venice with his wife and two children, while I am in Sydney, Australia, and the amazing editor, Juliet Grames, is in New York. This has been a truly international effort.

It is no accident that the name of the painter who paints the skene in *Death ex Machina* is Stephanos of Vitale.

THE PAINTING METHOD that Stephanos uses is called encaustic. It's an ancient Greek word that means "in heat" and really did involve pigments embedded in beeswax. The other major painting method for murals was egg tempura, for which you had to work even faster. But encaustic painting came first, and it's almost certain encaustic murals were the standard in Nico's time.

The most famous examples of encaustic painting are not Greek, but Egyptian. You might already know of the incredibly beautiful and poignant portrait paintings found on Egyptian mummies from the Hellenistic Period. The faces seem so fresh and realistic that you might think you're looking at people who you saw only yesterday. Those amazing portraits are all encaustic.

The formula Stephanos gives to make white pigment is

accurate, and in fact it was the Greeks who first discovered how to make white. Their formula of lead, vinegar, and poo remained the standard almost into modern times.

There must have been a world's first scene painter. We don't know his name, but we do know he must have been alive in the time of Nico and Diotima, because it was Aeschylus who first thought to decorate the back wall.

PHRYGIA WAS, AND still is, a province of Anatolia.

Anatolia is the name the Greeks gave to what we now call Turkey. In classical Greek it means "the place where the sun rises," which is rather accurate if you happen to be west of it.

SABAZIOS APPEARS TO have been the most hated god in Athens. This is quite remarkable, considering the Athenians were notably tolerant of other religions.

The followers of Sabazios may have done something to earn such enmity, but if so, it's lost in the mists of time. I decided to supply a reason with the beer versus wine riot.

About a 130 years after the time of this story, one Athenian politician named Demosthenes decided to attack an opponent by claiming he had assisted his mother in the rites of Sabazios. The attack was clearly intended as slander, as if anyone who worships Sabazios is not fit to be a citizen. Demosthenes also implied without saying so that assisting one's mother in the rites of Sabazios went somewhat beyond the normal bounds of filial duty. This is what Demosthenes had to say:

> *"On attaining manhood you abetted your mother in her initiations and the other rituals, and read aloud from the cultic writings . . . You rubbed the fat-cheeked snakes and swung them above your head, crying Euoi saboi and hues attes, attes hues."*

The comic playwright Aristophanes wrote a play, now lost, in which Sabazios and a bunch of other gods are thrown out of the city. Sabazios never was thrown out of Athens. There's a surviving inscription written about 250 years after this story which lists fifty one devotees of Sabazios. It's not many, but 36 of those are citizen names.

Aristophanes uses the term "the sleep of Sabazios" a couple of times to refer to guards who've been drinking on the job and fallen asleep. By implication they were drinking beer. When in my story the Scythians fall asleep while guarding the theater, I stole that wholesale from a play written 2,400 years ago. There's a good chance that beer back then was stronger than the wine. Greeks always drank wine watered down, three parts water to one of wine. Without experience of beer, they probably drank it neat.

Things have obviously changed since classical times, because I've drunk enough modern Greek beer to know it's excellent, but the classical Greeks absolutely loathed the stuff. Watered wine was their tipple of choice and nothing else would do.

Phrygians on the other hand loved their beer. There are plenty of surviving archaeological beer artifacts from Phrygia, mostly pottery beer jars, but also, interestingly, some of the straws through which they drank. The idea of drinking beer through straws from a communal vat may seem odd, but that's how they did it. This seems to have been the standard system across the Middle East for hundreds of years. There are surviving reliefs from Mesopotamia that show the same thing: partygoers dancing in a circle as they drink from a large vat of beer, with everyone holding their own drinking straws.

The Greeks were aware of this odd party trick. There's a fragment of a poem from the poet Archilochos that includes the line, "as a Thracian or a Phrygian sucks his barley beer through a tube . . ."

---

IN EVERY BOOK I include a character list at the front, with my suggestions on how to say those odd-looking Greek names. How I choose the sounding is really quite simple. I look for a similar Greek word that's already been turned into common English, and then I follow the same conventions. Let me give as an example Euterpe, who is Nico's mother-in-law.

At first glance Euterpe and Euripides look tricky to render into English. But in fact, they're easy, because you've probably heard of a place called Europe. Europe is named for the Greek mythological character Europa. In the original, the EU would have been pronounced OY, as in oyster. Europa was probably pronounced OY-ROPE-AY. We moderns have turned it into YOU-RUP. So I follow the same line to render Euterpe as YOU-TERP-E.

THIS HAS BEEN Nico and Diotima's first assignment since their marriage. Their last two jobs have been domestic commissions.

But international events have been continuing apace while our heroes tarried at home. There's a war on far to the south, and political intrigue that demands their attention.

In the next book they are off overseas, to the land called Aegypt.

# GLOSSARY

**Aeschylus** — First of the three great tragic playwrights of the ancient world. The other two were **Sophocles** and **Euripides**. Aeschylus wrote the oldest known play to survive to this day, *The Persians*. For that reason he's considered the founder of modern theater.

**Agora** — The marketplace. Every city and town in Athens has an agora.

**Amphitheater** — The meaning hasn't changed in three thousand years.

**Archon** — A city official, elected for the term of a year. The three most senior archons appear in this story: the **Eponymous Archon**, the **Polemarch**, and the **Basileus**.

**Artemis Agroptera, Artemision** — Artemis is one of the major goddesses of the Greek pantheon. She's usually pictured as a young lady with a bow and arrow and called The Huntress. That's exactly what

**(cont.) Artemis Agroptera, Artemision**

the Agroptera part means in ancient Greek. Artemis Agroptera is Artemis the Huntress.

The Temple of Artemis Agroptera is the name of her temple in Athens. The Artemision is her temple in Ephesus, over on the Asian mainland. There, the goddess Artemis was worshipped not as a huntress, but as a mother goddess. Artemision simply means "place of Artemis." The Artemision was one of the Seven Wonders of the Ancient World.

Diotima has served (across two previous adventures) at both the Temple of Artemis Agroptera in Athens, and the Artemision in Ephesus. This gives her serious credentials as a priestess, as Nico remarks in the book.

**Attica**

The region controlled by Athens. The relative power of each city-state determined how much land it controlled. Attica was very large indeed, comprising what we'd call southeastern Greece. Many villages, towns, and minor cities existed within Attica, one of which was **Rhamnus**.

**Basileus** The **archon** in charge of religious affairs for Athens.

The Romans copied much from Athens, and the role of Basileus is a good example. To do the same job the Romans built an administration center that in Latin they called a Basilica. There are no prizes for guessing what happened next. Thus a Basilica in the Christian Church is a direct descendant of the Basileus of classical and very pagan Athens.

**Choregos** We'd call him the producer. The man who provides the **chorus** and funds the play. The choregos of the oldest known play, *The Persians*, was none other than Pericles.

**Chorus** The small group of boys and men who sing the narration of a play. The first plays were nothing but a chorus. They were musicals! Then Thespis added an actor. Then Aeschylus added a second actor. Then Sophocles added a third. That arrangement proved stable for a thousand or so years. Throughout it all, the chorus sang the action.

**Deme**

Like a modern suburb, with the added rule that to live in a deme you had to belong to the tribe that owned it. Every citizen belonged to one of the ten tribes. By classical times the tribes were purely administrative units for running the city.

**Deuteragonist**

The second actor in a play. All plays had only three actors. They covered every role between them.

**Dionysos**

Greek God of wine and serious partying. A rather rustic fellow, since most parties happen at harvest time, the **Great Dionysia** was held in his honor. The statue of Dionysos was taken from its temple and placed on stage for the duration of the plays, so that the God could watch the action.

**Eponymous Archon**

The closest thing Athens had to a mayor. The Eponymous Archon was responsible for all civic affairs to do with citizens.

Most importantly for our story, he was also in charge of the calendar. The Eponymous Archon had the power to add or subtract days, or even declare an extra month in the year. This was no idle power, since the Athenians had to make their lunar months fit into their solar

**(cont.) Eponymous Archon** years. He's called the *Eponymous* Archon because the year is named after him (they didn't number their years). This story takes place in the Year of Habron.

**Euripides** The third of the three great tragic playwrights. At the time of this story, he's three years away from putting on his first play.

**Great Dionysia** Also known as the City Dionysia, because it was born from a country version. The Great Dionysia was *the* arts festival of the classical world. There were three parts to it: the choral competition, the comedies, and lastly, the three tragedies. In *Death ex Machina* I've concentrated on just one event, because if I tried to cover everything that went on during a Dionysia you'd be reading this book in twelve volumes.

**Mekhane** Machine! Specifically, the god machine used in the Theater of Dionysos. Our English word machine comes directly from classical Greek.

**Metics** Resident aliens with permission to live and work in Athens.

**Phallus**

Yes, we all know what a phallus is. What you probably don't know is that to the Greeks, they were symbols of good fortune. Lots of amulets of erect phalluses have been recovered from the ancient world, but for some reason you don't tend to see them on open display in modern museums. If, however, you go to the **Great Dionysia** in 458BC you'll find boys walking around with large wooden ones that they use to hit people. It's a way of wishing good fortune.

On the sacred isle of Delos there is a marble statue of a huge phallus, raised by a proud man to commemorate his victory in the **Great Dionysia**.

**Polemarch**

The **archon** in charge of everything to do with **metics**.

**Protagonist**

The lead actor in a play. Our word protagonist comes directly from ancient Greek.

**Orchestra**

The stage! This one's confusing. To us the orchestra is the people who play the music. The original orchestra was the place where the chorus stood. In other words, the stage. The orchestra was a semi-circular space that was the lowest point of the theater. The seats rose

| | |
|---|---|
| **(cont.) Orchestra** | up so everyone could look down to see the action. |
| **Rhamnus** | A minor city in the top right hand corner of **Attica**. The ruins of Rhamnus remain to this day. |
| **Sabazios** | The Phrygian god of the harvest and of beer. His opposite number in the Greek pantheon is **Dionysos**. It's known for sure that there were a small number of followers of Sabazios in Athens. |
| **Scythian Guard** | The peacekeeping force of classical Athens. Don't mess with these guys. They might be slaves, but they're slaves with permission to beat you senseless if you're a troublemaker. Classical Athens had a reputation for relatively little street crime. The Scythians are the reason why. |
| **Skene** | In ancient Greek it means tent. Early plays used a regular army tent for a background. The actor ducked into the tent for his quick changes. Later the tent became a back wall, but they still called it a skene. |

**Sophocles** Second of the three great tragic playwrights. Of the three he's probably the best known to modern readers, because Sophocles wrote *Oedipus Rex*.

**Thanatos** The god of death. His brother Hypnos is the god of sleep.

**Theologeion** A balcony at the back of the stage. Gods and goddesses play their parts while standing on the theologeion, so that deities stand above ordinary mortals. This means the stage crew who control the god machine need to be pretty accurate about where they deposit their actor.

**Thespis** The world's first professional actor. We call actors thespians in his honor. Many of the decisions that Thespis made about how to run a play remain with us to this day. Thespis lived right on the cusp between history and prehistory, which is a pity because he was obviously an amazing man, yet we know so little about him.

**Tragedy** Goat Song. No, I'm not making this up. Tragos is goat, ode is song. Tragode is goat song: a song about goats, which totally gives away the farm life origins of our plays. This is the tradition that 2,000 years later

**(cont.) Tragedy** would lead to *Hamlet*. It's amazing what a few talented writers and actors can do with such an inauspicious beginning.

**Trierarch** The commander of a naval vessel. Every year, wealthy men volunteered to pay the upkeep of a **trireme**. In return they got to call themselves trierarch for the year. Men like Kordax loved it so much that they made it their career. They and their opposite numbers among the Phoenicians were probably the first professional naval officers.

**Trireme** The standard navy ship of the Greek world. Triremes are long, low, sleek, incredibly fast machines with a battering ram at the front. Triremes are the first ships in the world designed to sink other ships. In modern terms they would be classed as destroyers. Athens had overwhelmingly the largest fleet around, with 300 triremes. Naval technology has improved a lot in two 2,500 years, but it's worth noting that Athens had as many ships of the line as the modern US Navy.

**Tritagonist** The third actor in a play. The other two are the **protagonist** and the **deuteragonist**.

# Acknowledgments

THANKS OVERWHELMINGLY TO my family. My daughters, Megan and Catriona, were five and eight when I started writing these books. Now they're thirteen and sixteen. They've grown up with Nico and Diotima. (And they know far more ancient history than your average teenager.)

My wife, Helen, is not only my first and best reader, but also your first line of defense against my errors. These books are as much hers as mine.

You're reading this book because the lovely people at Soho Press made it. It's incredibly hard to name names without doing injustice to some poor soul, but I want to thank my editor and Soho's Associate Publisher Juliet Grames; Director of Marketing and beer guru Paul Oliver; publicist Abby Koski who does a terrific job; managing editor Rachel Kowal; art director Janine Agro; Meredith Barnes, who read the manuscript when she was working for my agent, and then read it again when she was working for my publisher; and Bronwen Hruska for leading such a great company.

Janet Reid is the world's best literary agent. I suspected as much when I signed with her as a new writer, eight years ago, and now I know it for sure.